LOST BEFORE YOU

THE LOST AND FOUND SERIES BOOK 1

EA JOY

For my husband and girls. My biggest cheerleaders and greatest motivators.

"Everything starts as somebody's daydream."
Larry Niven

AUTHOR'S NOTE

This book contains scenes not fit for readers under 18 years of age due to their mature nature. 18+ only.

This book comes with a guaranteed happily ever after however there may be scenes that some readers may be sensitive to or triggered by. Included is the content warning list. Verbal abuse and descriptions of physical abuse and threatening violence. Reader discretion is advised.

PROLOGUE

Charlotte

I wince when I hear the remote shatter into pieces as it hits the wall.

"Where the fuck have you been? You said you were coming straight from practice, and that ended an hour ago," Gregory yells after I turn the corner, walking into the finished basement of his parents' house. They are rarely ever home, so there is no one to hear him yelling and throwing things.

I shouldn't have to justify myself, although making him angrier is something I've learned not to engage in, so I attempt to explain.

"I'm sorry. Coach asked if I could stay to go over the program," I reply quietly. I've been helping with the girl's swim team during summer practice. I thought it would be fun to help create a conditioning program for the team after being a part of it all four years of high school; however, it has become a constant source of arguments and something for Gregory to hold against me.

"Don't give me that bullshit, Lottie. I know you're lying. If I find out you were talking to anyone else, so help me God," he spits back, anger in his voice and his hand rising as he stands over me. I hold my breath waiting for what's next, bracing myself for the impact that usually follows.

Gregory and I have been dating for three years, but in the last eighteen months, things have changed, getting more out of control, the past eight months being the worst.

When I met Gregory my sophomore year, he was the guy every girl dreamed about, and every guy envied. Heads turned as he walked down the hall, his sandy blonde hair with a wave in it that fell just right no matter what time of day it was or what he was doing. His emerald-green eyes with a hint of yellow in them when he was in the light were hypnotizing, and the boy had abs you could wash sheets on. As the star quarterback of our high school, he already had scouts looking at him at sixteen.

We had biology together and were teamed up for a partner project. I thought he'd dump it all on me and brush it off, but he didn't. He pulled his weight and put in as much work as I did. Spending time working on the project led to phone calls after getting home, watching movies after Thursday practice or games on Friday, and stealing time and kisses on the weekends behind closed doors. After a month, he asked me to be his girlfriend officially, and for those first eighteen months, I lived in a state of blinded bliss.

I thought I was the luckiest girl at Cedar Ridge High. I always considered myself average looking, with nothing special to offer. My blonde hair always up in a ponytail, and my outfits usually consisting of leggings or jeans and a sweatshirt. Nothing compared to my friends who had new cars and fashionable clothes. They came from two-parent households where, instead of worrying about how to pay the mortgage, they worried about which new destination they were going to visit on their next vacation. Not me; it has always been just my mom, Kelly, and I, along with my grandparents, Charlie and June, who are probably the only reason my mom finished school at all.

I was the product of a college romance. My mom was a sophomore, he was a senior. After finding out she was pregnant, my mom told me my sperm donor, John, said he wanted to make it work, but a few weeks later, he transferred schools, and that was the last she heard from him. She never brings him up, and I don't ask. The curiosity to ask her more about him was always halted by my guilt over wanting to know someone who didn't want us. She worked hard to give me a good life, and if he didn't want to be part of it, that was on him.

Although my grandparents weren't happy when my mom told them about her unplanned pregnancy, they made a pact with her that as long as she finished school and worked a part-time job, they would help her take care of me. They even let my mom move back into her old room so she could save on rent since the campus was only a bus ride away.

Despite the challenges of working part-time and being a single mom, she finished her degree only a year late and has been a paralegal at the same law firm ever since. It's always paid the bills, but we didn't have many luxuries that the kids I grew up with had, and our vacations consisted of camping out in the backyard. We live in a small two-bedroom cape cod on the outside of Cedar Ridge, Tennessee. It's slate gray exterior has white shutters, with five steps that go up to a small porch surrounded by a white railing. It isn't anything fancy, but it has heat, water, and through the years, has housed a million memories I wouldn't trade.

After saving every penny from babysitting and with the help of my mom's three hundred dollars she'd put aside, I bought a 1996 Honda Civic with 186,000 miles on it for nine-hundred dollars as soon as I turned sixteen. So, having the most popular guy in school, who came from a wealthy family, want me, an ordinary girl with no money, most days I thought I'd wake up and realize I was dreaming.

Admittedly, that is part of the reason I didn't walk away when things started to change. They were subtle things at first, a change in the tone of his voice or a slightly firmer grip on my arm when leading me down the hallway. If you weren't paying attention, you would never even notice.

I mentioned something about it to my friend Allie in the spring of our junior year, to which she responded, "Maybe you just aren't giving him enough attention. You are so lucky that he even wants to be with you." She shrugged like she didn't know why I would be upset. "If you ask me, I say if you want to complain, step aside. There is a line of girls behind you that would be happy to give him anything he needs. Count your lucky stars, and don't do things to piss him off."

That was the one and only time I spoke up. After that, I kept my mouth shut, my head down and tried to not make him mad. Only it seemed no matter what I did, it was never enough. The littlest things could set him off, and no one ever spoke up. Teammates would look the other way when he would grab my arm after being a minute late to meet him by his locker, and my so-called friends would chalk it up to him being stressed from the pressure that he was under or something I must have done to upset him when they would hear him yell at me in the parking lot after school.

I kept telling myself if I did more, he would stop. I wore what he bought for me, did my hair just the way he liked, and never talked to any guys unless he was standing right next to me... and only then when I was asked a direct question. I learned that lesson after asking a classmate for a pencil in my algebra class, and Gregory took it as me flirting, resulting in a bright red handprint on my cheek. From that day on, I attempted to make myself invisible, did my schoolwork, and tried to not be noticed by anyone but him.

In the fall of our senior year, I was supposed to meet him at a bonfire to celebrate after a game against our rival school. Although it took an argument and a few bruises on my leg, I had gotten Gregory to agree to let me have dinner with my grandparents first, with the promise of meeting him promptly by nine p.m. As luck would have it, I got a flat tire on the way to the bonfire, and the flip phone that I had for emergencies didn't have a signal, of course.

Everyone at my school had the latest and greatest phones, and yet I still had the phone you paid to put minutes on. My mom had a smartphone, but she could only afford one, so I was grateful to have a phone at all.

Standing on the side of the road, I figured I'd at least see someone going to the bonfire, and they'd stop, yet several cars filled with people I recognized passed me, including the black Lexus SUV I knew was Gregory's, without so much as even slowing down. I was left standing there alone and scared in the dark. After waiting for almost an hour, a car finally pulled over, a husband and wife who were coming home from dinner. He put my spare on while I thanked him profusely. I offered them the seven dollars I had in my wallet, which they declined, and we were both on our way.

When I got to the bonfire, ninety minutes after I said I would be there, the glare in Gregory's green eyes was pure rage. He had been drinking, and as I drew closer, I knew I needed to try to stop it before it began. I walked up slowly with an apology ready. Before I could even speak, he grabbed my arm and dragged me from the group. No one said a word while they watched him haul me away toward our cars.

No explanation was going to get me out of this, and the next day I had the bruises to prove it. I stayed in my room the whole weekend, crying, avoiding my mom, and desperately trying to cover up the marks with make-up for school on Monday.

That's when I knew there was never going to be a way out unless I took control myself. I never told my mom what was going on, hiding bruises and using make-up to cover my eyes, which were often red and swollen from crying myself to sleep. She had enough on her plate, and I didn't want her to have one more reason to worry.

Looking down at the broken remote, I tell him, "I swear I'm not lying. I got here as soon as I could." I keep my voice calm and even, trying not to piss him off further.

Lowering his hand to reach for my arm, he pulls me toward him, grabbing my chin roughly, and says in his condescending voice, "You know I hate having to get angry. Why do you do things to upset me? I'm leaving in a week for Dayton, and we don't have much time."

Dayton University, a Division 1 school known for its football program, was only an hour away from our hometown. It being an hour away and giving him a chance to explore his options weren't acceptable reasons for us to consider a break when I brought it up after he signed a full-ride scholarship. Never mind the fact that the weekend he went for his final tour and met the entire team, Allie showed me videos of him making out with a few different girls at a frat party. She only wanted to throw it in my face that I obviously wasn't satisfying him like other girls could. It wasn't his first indiscretion, and deep down, I knew it wouldn't be his last. None of that mattered anyway because the discussion about us taking a break led to fingerprints on my neck that had me wearing a scarf for a week and a warning to never talk about leaving again.

He was expecting me to go to the community college in Cedar Ridge and then transfer after my first year to be with him, waiting right here where his crony spies could keep an eye on me while he went away doing God knows what with God knows who.

"I know. I'm sorry. I really am. I don't want to upset you. I love you." Wrapping my arms around him, swallowing the bile in my throat from those three words, I waited for what was next. The saddest part was at one time I truly loved him, but somewhere along the way that love had turned to fear.

"I love you too; you know I do. I get so crazy not knowing what you are doing and worrying about who you are with that it makes me do things I don't want to. You are mine, forever, and the only one allowed to touch you is me." His next words would have been romantic if they hadn't been spoken in that low, ominous tone that I had come to fear. "I know you inside and out, and that's how it will always be. No one knows you like I do. No one ever will."

I close my eyes and try to go to my happy place as he reaches down to touch his lips to mine. This was something I had become accustomed to doing so that I didn't cry or throw up when he kissed me.

His hands slide down my back and into the backside of my jeans. I lost my virginity to him my junior year when he was still swoony and attentive. At the time, although it hurt like hell, I thought it was magical and something that changed me forever. When we had sex again the morning after, he was so loving and sweet. I loved him and thought we would spend forever together.

However, shortly after that night, it went from him being gentle and sweet to demanding and painful. He wanted it when he wanted it, and *I'm not in the mood* wasn't an answer he wanted to hear. If I asked him to be gentle or slow down, my request was met with rougher thrusts and harder grasps. There were so many times I cried after leaving his house. What I started out thinking of as making love became aggressive and something I dreaded. This was no different. I close my eyes, and he starts to strip off my clothes as tears fight to escape from my eyes.

After it is over, I lay with my head on his chest on the floor of his parents' fully decked out basement, listening to his version of *I'm sorry* and promises of forever, even as bruises bloom dark on my skin. Shortly after midnight, I hug him, kiss his lips, and with the promise to call him tomorrow, walk to my car, never looking over my shoulder.

My mom's car isn't there when I get home; she must have fallen asleep on my grandparent's couch again, which wasn't unusual when she went there for dinner. Not that she would have woken up anyway, as she is usually so exhausted once her head hits the pillow, she's out until her alarm blasts on her phone.

I numbly walk up to my childhood bedroom, reach

under my bed where I'd hidden three duffle bags, and quickly pack my belongings. Clothes, pictures of my mom and grandparents, and a few small gifts I've kept. My plan started formulating the night after the bonfire. I knew the only way to get away from Gregory would be to start over.

Tears stream from my eyes as the weight of my plan comes down on my mind. To everyone else, including my mom, I was starting community college in a week. What no one knew was that I'd created a P.O. box in the next town where my college application responses and scholarships were sent to. I babysat for a family in that town, so it made a good reason to head that way so I could check my mail.

I had been accepted and received a full academic scholarship to Hampton University, a Division 2 school just outside of Augusta, Georgia. I chose a Division 2 school on purpose so there was no chance of our paths crossing. After getting all my paperwork set, I closed the P.O. box so there was no trail.

Everyone believed I was staying in Cedar Ridge, attending community college, and playing the doting girlfriend to the football star while he lived out his dream. My heart was breaking as the weight of what this meant came crashing down. I hadn't told my mom or my grandparents anything. I knew that they would try to stop me and would go to Gregory's parents. Then Gregory would find a way to get to me. So my only chance of being free was a clean break from everyone and everything. Guilt rips at me for leaving my mom and grandparents, but with tears streaming down my face, I hold on to the hope that this won't last forever. After things settle down and I know I am safe, I could reach out, and pray they would understand and forgive me.

I leave a short note for my mom and grandparents with the words, "I love you and I'm sorry," on the kitchen table and walk out of the only home I've ever known. I put my duffle bags in my car, say a prayer the old Honda makes it, climb into the driver's side, and drive off into the blackness, leaving behind my entire life, including the three people I love most, and the one person I fear most behind.

Charlotte - 6 years later

"Shit," I curse as the hot coffee spills from my cup, hitting the back of my hand. I try hard not to think about the past, but there are times when memories invade my thoughts like ants do a picnic. I must be locked in my own head because I jump when I feel something touch my shoulder. Turning around, I realize where I am as my best friend Grace stares at me like I have three heads.

"Lottie, earth to Lottie. I've been calling your name for, like, two minutes. Well, maybe more like thirty seconds, but still. Where did you go, girl?" Grace asks as if she can see into my head like always. We met at freshman orientation and have been inseparable since. She's the only person who knows the truth about my past and was nothing short of my savior when the guilt and fear that felt like chains on my legs, clung to me my first year of school.

I didn't mean for her to find out, or anyone to for that matter; swearing to myself no one needed or cared to know the truth. Fate intervened when I was supposed to meet Grace at the library for a study session. After coming out of my pre-law class second semester, I swore I saw Gregory walking toward me across the lawn. Fight or flight kicked in, I turned without glancing back, and ran all the way to my dorm, my chest heaving rapidly from exertion and fear. Grace found me curled up in the corner of my room, my hands wrapped around my knees, shaking, after I didn't show up at the library. She approached me slowly and put her hands out in an attempt to calm me without seeming threatening, as I was clearly breaking down.

My walls broke, and I sobbed into her shoulder and told her the whole story, the mental and physical abuse, hiding the bruises, the lies I told my mom, and how after the beating my senior year, I created the plan to get away. She stroked my hair gently while I told her about the guilt of leaving my family, the fear of him finding me, and how I had built walls and told myself I'd never let someone else in so they could do more damage than had already been done. I was exhausted by the time I finished letting it all out. She listened with subtle nods and signs of empathy, not saying a word until I was finished. After the tears started to subside, she told me she was there for me, helped me to my bed, and stayed until I fell asleep.

"Sorry, I was thinking of all the shit I have to get done this week," I say lamely in an attempt to change the subject.

"Hmm," she says before sitting down across from me at the small table I found. Her voice says she doesn't believe one ounce of my bullshit answer, but she lets me off the hook. "Okay, so what's on the docket this week?" she asks, grabbing the caramel latte she always has to have.

"Too much. I have an exam and two papers due. I start

my internship next week, which I'm nowhere near prepared for, and it's only the second week of classes." I rest my chin in my palms, feeling overwhelmed, and the week hasn't even started.

I'm used to grueling schedules. I started my third year of law school at Clayton University two weeks ago, one of the top law schools in the country, located just outside of Phoenix. Between school and working part-time at Cliff's to make ends meet and not drown in loans, I was accustomed to work, school, repeat.

My freshman year of college, I had no idea what I wanted to study. I left everything I knew and everyone I loved to start over without the cloud of Gregory that had left a larger impact on me than I cared to admit. I missed my mom and grandparents terribly, however, I let my fear that somehow Gregory would find me stop me from calling them. Maybe it was irrational to think that he was even looking for me, but nonetheless, I was not willing to test it.

I guess in a weird way, it's what led me to law. I decided to take an intro law class my second semester as a way to keep my mom with me, and I fell in love. Reading cases, trials, and the thought of helping people had me hooked. Family law intrigued me the most, a field where I felt I could make a difference. I wanted to help women who were trying to get out of abusive relationships that couldn't afford a good attorney. I wanted them to feel like they had a voice, a chance, and a safe place to turn to, instead of running away and hiding like I had done.

I applied to several law schools including Clayton, but when Grace got offered a job in Phoenix, it made my choice easy. We made the move together and have shared a two-bedroom apartment ten minutes from campus for the past two years. Grace works for Mercer Advertising Agency and kicks ass at coming up with campaigns that have landed Mercer some of their biggest accounts in the short two years she has been there. She's already worked her way up to junior marketing associate, which is almost unheard of at the young age of twenty-five.

"Well then, we need to celebrate this weekend, before you start your internship and I barely get to see you," she says with a waggle of her eyebrows that only means one thing: mischief.

"Lady, you see me every day, maybe not all day but at some point." I shake my head, trying to shut down the train of naughty thoughts going on in her head.

"No, I don't. And if I do, it's usually while you are drooling over a law book or passed out on the couch after working a shift at Cliff's. We are going out this weekend. I won't take no for an answer. You know what you need?" I don't even respond as I know exactly what she thinks I need. "To get laid, Lottie. You're always studying or working, and a great O will loosen you up and get you ready to kick some internship ass on Monday," she says casually, like she's just told me I need ice cream. Grace has never been shy about her sexuality. She loves sex, anyway, anytime, but doesn't do relationships. Not saying she's easy, but if she is interested, she doesn't hide it and goes after what she wants and needs. A trait I both envy and don't understand at the same time.

I haven't had sex in six years, something else only Grace knows. Not that I haven't gotten a release when I need one. They have battery operated toys for that. I still tense whenever a guy touches me or raises his voice, which makes developing relationships difficult, to say the least. Not to mention, my trust issues with men were substantial. After a while, it became the norm for me to stay away and not engage. I never let my inhibitions down where something could happen I wasn't fully prepared for or in control of, which didn't leave much room for spontaneity or living for the moment.

Since Gregory, control was something I had to have in my life for me to feel safe. For three years my life felt so out of my control... like I was a ventriloquist dummy doing and saying whatever Gregory wanted me to. After freeing myself from those strings and the sacrifices that came with that decision, I vowed that never again would I let a man tell me what to do, control my actions or my body, or touch me without my permission. Wherever I went, I always tried to position myself facing outward so I couldn't be surprised by someone grabbing my arm or shoulder, and if I could, I sat close to an exit. And I never left the house without pepper spray.

"I don't need to get laid. I need to finish my papers and read up on the cases they gave me before I start Monday. I'm so close to finishing, I refuse to get side-tracked now." I give her my most serious *drop it* face and look down to avoid her gaze.

"Nope, not happening. You can spend all week writing papers and preparing. I know Joe gave you this weekend off before starting Monday, so you are coming out with me, even if I have to drag your ass out the damn door." I wasn't getting out of this, and I knew it. I cursed myself for telling her that Joe had given me the weekend off. I was cutting back my hours starting next week due the internship starting, and he had told me I deserved two whole days off before becoming someone else's retriever.

Joe is the owner of Cliff's, a man in his late fifties with

salt and pepper hair and a short beard. He could knock down a bull and has become like a surrogate parent these past two years. He's been running the bar with his wife, Maria, since he was twenty-six, when he inherited it from his uncle. It's a big hangout for college kids and draws big crowds on the weekends.

When we moved, I needed a job, like, yesterday. Grace's mom passed when she was young and her dad had more than enough money, and although her relationship with him was less than ideal, it left her with no college debt and a monthly allowance, which she always put away, using her own money to pay the bills. We had just finished unpacking boxes in our new apartment and decided to walk around and find a bite to eat. Cliff's was down a few blocks from our apartment and had a sign outside advertising five-dollar burgers. We walked in and sat at the bar. Joe was bartending and took our order.

After eating our burgers, we were slowly nursing our beers when I overheard Joe talking to the cook. "We need to find more help, Maria is going to kill me if I keep spending every night till close here. We've been married thirty years, and that woman still scares the shit out of me when she gives me that look. And she'll hold out on me, if you know what I mean." He shivered at the thought as he walked toward us. "Can I get you ladies anything else?"

"Nothing to eat or drink, but if you're looking for someone to work, I can do it."

"Do you do drugs?" he asked with his eyebrows raised.

"Absolutely not, sir," I answered immediately. Never touched drugs, never will. He told me to come back the next day to sign paperwork. I've been working there ever since.

Joe and Maria have become the closest thing I have to a family, besides Grace. Though I technically still have a family, not talking to them for six years left me yearning for somewhere to belong. When Maria found out I wasn't from around here, she invited me to their house for tamales, and the rest is history. They don't know details about my past, only that I left home and haven't spoken to my family in years for reasons I wasn't ready to explain. They continue to encourage me to reach out, except after a certain point, the guilt and shame of leaving without more than an "I'm sorry" became something I couldn't face, so I avoided it all together. Every time they bring it up, I tell them I'll think about it and then change the subject. They usually let it go, but sometimes Maria gently chides, "Life's too short to live with guilt and regrets. You'll feel better if you put the past to rest so you can all heal."

I'm not completely in the dark about my mom. I started checking in on her via social media the year after I left. I couldn't bear doing it before then, or the guilt I already carried would have drown me. I made a fake account, and since my mom has no idea how to make anything private, I can see if and when she posts anything. It isn't often, but occasionally she posts a motivational quote or a picture of her and my grandma at the farmer's market on Sundays. She's always smiling, yet there is always something missing in her eyes. A hole most likely put there by me leaving. It makes it hard to look at for more than a few seconds. I usually take a quick glance to make sure she's ok before quickly shutting it down and busying myself with school to take my mind off of it.

"Fine, I'll go but only for an hour, two, tops. Just so you are aware, this isn't a mission for me to get laid, as you put it. I don't need anyone to be happy, and I certainly don't have time to try," I say, knowing she won't drop it until I relent and give in.

"Yay, I knew you'd see it my way. Gotta go, we have a team meeting at nine, and I want to get there before all the bagels are gone." She winks before standing up, wearing a black pencil skirt that hugs her curves just the right way, a fuchsia blouse with the top two buttons open, accentuating what she calls her greatest assets, and heels that I wouldn't make it five feet in before landing on my face. Grace is stunning. Her chestnut hair with golden highlights is tied back in a neat bun, and her black framed glasses make her green eyes that are the color of an evergreen, pop, giving her the "sexy librarian look," as she calls it. As she sashays away, her hips doing that swivel that you see the runway models do, every guy turns to watch her pass, appreciating the view as she walks by.

I sigh to myself as I return to the case I was reviewing. It isn't that I'm not confident in myself, but I have always seen myself as plain. Wearing jeans and a Clayton sweatshirt that hangs off one shoulder, my honey colored hair a mess on the top of my head, and a pair of Nikes I've owned for three years, I'm not anything special.

With my internship coming up, I knew I would need some semblance of business attire. I went last week to the secondhand store close to campus and bought a few skirts, pants, tops, and a pair of low black heels with the tip money I had been saving over the summer. I loved places like that. Designer clothes for less than half the price. All you needed was patience to look through the racks. I figured I could rotate and mix and match them each week to make it seem like more. It wasn't anywhere close to Grace's closet, which she always offers to let me raid since we were semi-close in size, but after doing it on my own, my stubborn pride kicks in. Even if it isn't the latest fashion, I now had a few outfits that made me look businesslike. One day, after paying off my loans, I'd be able to buy new things, only today was not that day, and I had to be okay with that. After finishing my notes on the case I had out, I packed up my laptop, papers, and grabbed a new coffee that wasn't all over my hand and headed to class for another long week.

One more year.

I can do this.

2

GAVIN

Gavin

"Goood morning, fuckers," Logan yells to James and me in his best Robin Williams voice as he strides into my office with a look on his face like he's the cat that got the cream. Logan is obsessed with *Good Morning, Vietnam,* and it takes everything in me not to chuck my stapler at his big head. The man is entirely too enthusiastic for a Monday morning. He used to watch the film every time he came home drunk in college, and he still carries the same tradition even at the age of twenty-eight, making that movie the bane of my existence.

"What has you so chipper today, dickhead? Wait, let me guess, the redhead you sent us a picture of last night? Do you even remember her name, or are we making one up this time?" James accuses as he sits in the leather chair across from my desk. James has always been on Logan's case about taking girls he meets home. He's been with Lexi since our sophomore year in college, and after proposing at Christmas last year, is getting married next summer.

We'd all met freshman year of college, went through law school together, and now all work at Davis and Jones Law, one of the most sought-after corporate law firms in the country. James has always been a relationship guy, while Logan played the field and was happy being a one-and-done. So, their views on relationships and commitment couldn't be more opposite. I was somewhere in between, I guess. I was the one who did the relationship thing and got burned worse than a third-degree flame, so now I immersed myself in my job, with no plans to ever let someone in the way I had before. Women were beautiful, and I liked getting laid, but that was all it ever was. I never brought women back to my place because I didn't like them in my space. It made it too personal. Maybe that made me an asshole, but at least I was honest. I could deliver multiple mind-blowing orgasms that could make them forget their names, knowing I would never commit to anything more than that.

"Ha-ha-ha, I can't help it if my dick is magic and everyone wants to see it disappear... right into their sweet little holes," he says with a shit-eating grin on his face. Confidence is something Logan has never lacked and probably never will.

"Gross, man, I just ate breakfast, and we are at a place of business, so if you could leave your dick at the door so we could get to work, we'd appreciate it," I say, shaking my head while handing out files to review for the briefing we have later this morning. "By the way, do you have the list of evidence for Judge Matthews? That needs to be in before we go to court on Friday."

"I sent them to him this morning, thank you very much," Logan says as he sits down and puts his feet on my desk.

"Excellent, now get your nasty feet off my desk." I scoff at him. I want to ensure this is an open and shut case before it even starts. Before we sent the settlement proposal to Timothy's lawyers. If he doesn't want this to go to trial and face jail time, he'll take it and pay back the money he stole under the guise of investments to fund his own island getaway." I hated nothing more than people trying to ruin other people's lives with lies for their benefit. I had been on the receiving end of what lies could do, and although not on a monetary or corporate level, it still knocked me over like a linebacker on a rookie quarterback. I took pride in representing those who were being taken advantage of and helping people who had been screwed by corrupt bastards who didn't give a shit about anything but their own bank accounts.

Growing up, my dad being a lawyer and running the family firm with his best friend, going to law school was expected—not suggested—with no room for negotiation. Being a lawyer was in Davis's blood; my grandpa and great-grandfather were both lawyers, so the legacy would continue. Although I come from a loving family, being a lawyer was never not an option for me, although I really can't complain. My little sister Olivia and I had loving parents and a great childhood. My mom founded and ran HAACE, Helping Abused and Abandoned Children Everywhere, which kept her busy fundraising and setting up events. My maternal grandparents both came from old money, and my mom wanted to do more with her trust fund than waste it on frivolous things. She always said growing up, she dreamed of being a mom and helping kids. So after meeting my dad in college and getting married when she was twenty and he was twenty-one, she decided to use her business degree and her money to start a foundation to help children who had been abandoned or abused so they would have a fighting chance at a good life. We did all the normal kid stuff when she wasn't planning or attending events. Zoos, museums, picnics; we never lacked for anything, but with a privileged life also came sacrifices. My mom was amazing, but all her obligations kept her schedule very busy, which meant we also had a nanny, Linda, for when they had events or business dinners for my dad. She was like another grandma to us, kind and always let us have warm chocolate chip cookies before bed when my parents were out.

My dad worked tirelessly like his dad did before him at the firm. Even though it was expected as a Davis that I would continue the line, nepotism wasn't something they supported, firmly believing in earning your place through hard work, not your last name. Dad's hours consisted of being gone before we got up and, most nights, getting home after we had dinner. Every once in a while, he would come home early, and we would do a family movie night with popcorn and candy. Those were some of my favorite memories. On nights they had events, my dad would send his driver to bring my mom to his office so they could go together. On nights when they didn't have social obligations, I'd hear him come in around nine. My mom would reheat his dinner, and they'd talk before heading to bed. It worked for them, and they have been married for twenty-nine years. Sure, they had arguments, as all couples do, but they always tried to keep us out of it. He was busy and worked a lot, but my dad never failed to show my mom how much he appreciated all she did and how much he loved us. I don't think my dad knew how not to work, a trait instilled in him by my grandfather, and one that he made clear to me was how you make it in this world.

After realizing it had been almost two weeks since I'd talked to my sister, I jotted down a note to call her later today and check-in. Olivia is twenty-four, and after finishing fashion school in Los Angeles, she got a once-in-a-lifetime apprenticeship opportunity with Travis Dane, the creator of MAWB, Making All Women Beautiful, and is now co-creating her first fashion line. Her first show is over Halloween weekend. I'm heading to L.A. for it; I wouldn't miss her first show for anything. She's doing fantastic, and I couldn't be prouder of my baby sister kicking ass in the fashion industry.

"Nope, that asshole is going down, and then we're going out to celebrate this weekend. This case has been a bitch; it's only right to reward our hard work." Logan jabs his finger into my desk, emphasizing his point.

"How is that different from any other night, Logan? You seem to reward yourself for making it through the day," James teases.

"Just because you decided to chain yourself down and be a homebody doesn't mean I have to be. And no excuses, lame-o, because you're coming on Friday. Don't make me call Lexi. You know she loves talking to me, and if you aren't satisfying her..." Logan winks as he says it, knowing he's joking but loving pushing James's buttons.

"Stay the hell away from my fiancé, dick," James said, his face turning red. Buttons successfully pushed.

With his hands in the air, Logan retreats, knowing he went a step too far. "Dude, you know I'm only playing. I love

Lexi." Knowing that wasn't enough, he adds, "Sorry man, didn't mean to piss you off. Drinks on me Friday."

"Damn right they are," James shoots back before lifting his arm to give him a handshake, an offer of peace letting Logan know he's calm. They've been playing this game since the beginning, Logan seeing how far he can push James, James going on the defensive in a flash, but just as quickly forgiving him. I guess that's why we became best friends; we all love to give each other shit but trust each other with our lives, brothers, just not by blood.

"I'm in, too, as long as we aren't out too late. I want to come in and get some work done on the Pickett case before we brief on Monday, and don't forget we have three interns starting next week." My usual routine consists of spending more time at the office than at my condo on the weekends. I should get a bed put in here, and I wouldn't even need another place.

"Sweet, new meat. Let's wrap this week up fast and get to it." Logan says, standing and heading for the door.

"It's only Monday," I remind him, knowing we have a long week of work ahead of us before any relaxation can be considered, and even then, said relaxing will be short-lived, as there is always more work to be done.

"Don't be such a killjoy, Gav. Look at it with the glass-half-full mentality. That means boy's night out is only four days away, and you know me, always ready to meet new interns." He smirks before leaving my office and heading to his own. After making sure we're caught up on everything we need to go over, James stands and heads out too. Alone in my office, I finally get to work on what promises to be another long week, like all the rest.

The next few days are a blur of meetings, briefings, and sneaking in workouts, sleeping only a few hours a night. Walking out of the courtroom on Friday feels like walking out of your last exam before winter break. Months of preparation paid off with the sound of a gavel and the promise that rat bastard has to pay back eleven million in restitution to investors. Before we left the courtroom, the representative team for the investors that we have been working with shook our hands, thanked us, and said the investors were happy with the settlement we sent to them earlier this week.

"Are you heading back to the office or home?" James asks as we walk down the courthouse steps.

"I'm going back to the office for a few hours. It's still early, and I have some things I want to finish up. You should go home and surprise Lexi since she won't be expecting it. Only if you promise not to go into the bedroom and not come out though because I'm not getting stuck going out with Logan by myself again." James tends to play the vanishing card with Lexi and not resurface until he has to be back to work. It's gotten worse since they got engaged. Not that I blame him. He and Lexi are perfect for each other. I'm just not in the mood for an all-nighter like Logan is always up for. "He's been texting non-stop about the VIP access he got for the new club, Lit, that just opened downtown."

"I know. He told me he'd put snakes in my office if I didn't show up. I wouldn't put it past that asshole to actually do it. I'll be there. Gotta go if I'm going to have enough time with my sexy wife-to-be." He winks as he starts walking away. "See you tonight." He is a romantic at heart and loves Lexi with everything he has, showing her how much she means to him every chance he gets.

As I walk to my car, my phone rings. Looking down, my

dad's name flashes, and I know he's calling for an update on the case. Hitting accept, "Hey, Dad, walking out of the courthouse, ruled in our favor, paying eleven million in restitution, and he has three months to pay out or a warrant will be issued. He's lucky his ass didn't get jail time, but we avoided trial and saved us man hours. His lawyers didn't say much, which means they knew the bastard was guilty and won't be filing an appeal." I stop to take a breath, waiting for his response.

"Good to hear. I looked over the documents, and with twelve million lost, recovering over ninety percent is above the benchmark. We've got some bigger cases coming up that will require our attention, so having this one settled quickly makes room to switch our focus faster." This was my dad's way of saying that just because one case closed didn't mean we could sit back and relax. There was always more work, the next case, and new clients to focus on. Daniel Davis slept, ate, and shit work. I easily put in sixty to eighty hours a week at work, and it still didn't feel like enough sometimes.

"Understood, sir. I plan on reviewing the Pickett case this weekend, so we'll be fully prepared when the team meets on Monday."

"I know you will. You're a Davis. Being unprepared isn't an option. It's how we got to be the leading law firm in the country for corporate fraud cases." My dad has always been supportive, but a hard ass at the same time. Constantly pushing me to do my best and then some because nothing worth it in life comes without hard work. "Thanks for the update, son. I have to go. I'm meeting your mother for an event this evening, and she will have my hide if I am late. She said you declined and sounded disappointed. You know how hard she works on these events and how much this foundation means to her. It would be nice if you showed your support more often." *Pack your bags, folks, we're going on a guilt trip.*

I could list all the reasons I don't go to all the events. It's a split between work and the fact that my mother has been taking the opportunity to turn events into glorified matchmaking auctions doesn't help. Yet, the thought of disappointing my mom or dad makes my gut churn. I attend the two big galas she throws each year, one around the Fourth of July and the other right before Christmas. Those are torturous enough to sit through, except instead of saying that, I simply reply, "Got it, sir, I'll be sure to accept the next one, and I already told Mom I'd be attending the gala in December."

"Good to hear. Love you, son."

"Love you too, Dad. Give Mom a hug from me."

"Will do."

Feeling bad for making my mom upset, knowing it's too late to go now, I head back to the office to get some work done before meeting the boys. I need a drink.

3

Charlotte

"Nope, not happening. I am not wearing that. I am not about to show my ass to an entire club just by walking, thank you very much," I warn as Grace walks into my room with the shortest skirt I've ever seen. She's dressed in a black cocktail dress that makes her ass look fantastic and leaves nothing to the imagination in the cleavage department. She's paired it with four-inch hot pink stilettos, her chestnut hair in soft waves around her shoulders, and subtle makeup accentuating her eyes and lips.

This week has been hell, but my papers are in, and my exam was completed and passed, so yay me. With some prep time this weekend, I *might* feel ready to start Monday. I had just gotten out of the shower, dried my hair, and started milling through my clothes to find something comfortable but cute when she walked in.

"Come on, live a little; you have such a banging body

hiding under all those sweatshirts. Show it off a little," she chastises me.

"Showing off my ass to every person in the greater Phoenix area is not something I plan on doing tonight," I say, not looking at her because Grace has voodoo magic and with one look into her eyes, you're hypnotized to doing her will. It sounds crazy, but admittedly, it works every time.

"Okay, fine," she relents as she holds out another outfit from behind her back, "What about this one, V-neck but not too deep, *Miss I Love Being Totally Covered*, and stops right above the knee so your ass won't even be close to being on display. I got it for a business dinner a couple of weeks ago, and it will fit you perfectly." I don't miss how she throws in business dinner, insinuating if she can wear it for work, I can definitely wear it out. Relenting and looking up, the dress, I admit, is sexy. With spaghetti straps that cross in the back, it isn't going to fall off, although the open back has me a little leery.

"I was just going to wear my skinny jeans and purple tank with black sandals." I offer my best *work with me* smile.

"Hell no. Sandals scream, *Hi, my name is Lottie, I own twelve cats and use their fur to knit scarves.* Sandals are not sexy, and this club demands sexy. At least try it on, please," she begs, her hands in front of her face like she's praying.

Rolling my eyes, I relent, "Fine, I'll try it on, but when it doesn't fit, jeans and purple top it is." I grab the dress that I'll admit is a beautiful blue, like the deep color of the ocean with a hint of sheen to it. I walk to the bathroom, take off my towel, and slide the dress on. Because of the V-neck and open back, I can't wear a bra, which makes me uncomfortable, but as the soft fabric slides over my breasts and down my body, hugging my hips and fitting like a glove, I feel sexy. Glancing in the mirror, I see the tone of blue matches my eye color and compliments my slightly tanned skin and light hair. I straighten my blond locks, apply light makeup, using only mascara and a red gloss, and boom, I'm done. I add a gold bracelet and hoop earrings to complete the outfit.

As I walk back out of the bathroom to grab my sandals, Grace whistles, "Holy shit, girl, you look hot. Men aren't going to be able to take their eyes off of you. And don't you *dare* reach for those damn sandals; I have the perfect heels to go with it."

"Heels? Do you want me to fall on my face in front of everyone?" The highest heels I've worn since my junior prom have been two-inches maximum. My eyes widen as Grace walks back in, carrying blue heels that match the dress perfectly, only looking like I'll be walking on stilts. At five-foot-seven, I'm not short, but these shoes will give me at least three more inches. Grace can wear four-inch heels without even thinking, being only five-foot-four, and she wears them every day. These have disaster written all over them for me.

"Stop being such a whiny bitch and put the damn things on. We're going to be late. One of my clients knows the club's owner and got us into VIP for tonight. You won't even have to stand except for walking in, but we need to get there before it's too packed." Reluctantly, I put on the death heels, grab my favorite clutch that'll hold my phone, wallet, lip gloss, and keys, and head out the door.

We order a cab, and even with Friday night traffic, we make it downtown in less than twenty minutes. After paying the driver, I carefully step out onto the sidewalk, seeing a line of people waiting to get in. "It's going to take forever to get to the door, Grace. My feet are hurting already," I whine, looking at the line that is down the block and around the corner.

"That's what VIP access is for, girl," she calls over her shoulder at me as she struts up to the bouncer who is guarding a door that has a black rail across it. She leans over, practically putting her breasts on his clipboard, and gives him our names. Within a minute, we have fluorescent orange wristbands and are being escorted through the club to a set of stairs leading to an area above the rest of the club.

I stay close to Grace and hold the railing for dear life as I walk up the five stairs to the VIP area, thanking everything holy I didn't fall flat on my face. Taking in the area, there are black couches along the wall set around low coffee tables that are underlit, making it seem as though they are glowing from the floor, and bar tables with black metal chairs that line the railing looking out over the dance floor. The vibe is modern, and the use of lighting is done well; it's bold but not tacky.

We opt for a bar table, and the waitress takes our drink order, a Cosmo for Grace and a vodka cranberry for me. Looking around, I see the club is packed. The bar on the main floor is three rows deep, and four bartenders are moving quickly back and forth behind the bar making drinks and shots. The glass bar top is underlit, which makes the bar glow. Against the far wall, there is a DJ on an elevated metal platform above the dancefloor, which lights up as if the people dancing there are causing the effect as they step to the beat of the music. The bar is trendy and, judging by the number of people here, is a huge success. Beyoncé's *Break my Soul* blares through the club, packing the dancefloor with women, reveling in its powerful words. People are having fun, drinking, dancing, and relaxing, but I still feel uneasy when I am not close to an exit. However, I can see down the stairs and out onto the floor and position myself so my back is toward the railing so no one can come up behind me without me knowing. I wish the anxiety of being around people would ease, only every time I go into a new place, the same fear creeps back in, having me searching for exits and escape plans if something goes awry.

The waitress delivers our drinks, and I slowly lift mine to take a sip. Sensing my unease, Grace says, "I know it's new, but you're here, and it's okay. Let's enjoy ourselves. Drink up. I have a feeling tonight's going to be a great night. Cheers." Raising her glass to mine, I tap it while putting on my best *I'm good* smile.

Thirty minutes later, only half my drink is gone while Grace is on her second and has already talked to and dismissed a few guys who have come to our table. I feel antsy, ready to go home, put on my pajamas, and call it a night. I lean over the table to break the news to Grace, who is thoroughly enjoying herself and dancing in her seat, when I look up and see three guys walking past where we are perched. Normally, I wouldn't think anything of it, but something about the way these men carry themselves demands attention. It's hard to make out definitive features in the low lighting, however you can tell all of them are tall and built, causing every woman in the VIP area to take notice.

The man leading the group is wearing dark jeans and a sport coat, his lighter hair wavy on top, giving him that just-fucked look that works on him. The way he walks oozes confidence, like a man who knows what and who he wants and how to get it. The guy behind him is wearing dark jeans and a sweater, and he has dark hair and a look on his face that I can't quite place. If I had to guess, it would be something close to annoyance. I glance at the third man, who is wearing dark jeans and a black button-up with the sleeves rolled up. His shirt fits tight around his biceps and hugs his chest perfectly. It's too dark to tell the color of his eyes, but his defined jaw and relaxed face draws me in. He has dark hair that is shorter and more styled, and I can't stop myself from staring, a feeling that I haven't experienced since Gregory and I started dating.

As they pass us, I try to look away, but not before our eyes meet, causing a jolt of shivers down my spine... and not in a bad way. Feeling like a lightning bolt just woke me up, I quickly look down and grab my drink. *What was that?*

"Oh my God, did you see the guys that just walked by?" Grace whisper-yells over the music with her drink up to her mouth, trying to hide what she's saying and failing miserably.

Acting naive, I reply, "I must have missed them. Are you ready to head out? I'm getting tired and have a ton of shit I need to do tomorrow." *Knowing I'll go home and analyze what just happened.*

"We are not leaving," Her voice is stern; she's not kidding. "This is VIP access, we've only been here for forty-five minutes. You don't have to work tomorrow, and you promised a night out to enjoy and let loose before starting your internship Monday. So, drink up, bitch. I want to dance."

"I never promised an all-nighter, and dancing is a hard pass. First, I suck at dancing. Second, I haven't even had one full drink, so my liquid courage level is minimal. And third, and most importantly, me making it up those stairs and to this table without falling on my face in these heels is a miracle in and of itself. I'm not chancing it, but you go right ahead, shake what your momma gave you."

Her tone clipped and annoyed, she stares at me, "Fine, go home then." Her glare is intense as she leans back, crossing her arms over her chest. We've had a few disagreements centered around my inability to let go. I hate that I allow fear dictate my life, and seeing how it affects my best friend when I can't even relax and enjoy time with her, has tears threatening, stinging the back of my eyes.

Sensing my emotional state, she speaks up, protecting me like always. "Look, I'm sorry. I love you. I just want you to have a good time. You've focused so much on studying and being cautious that you're missing out on life. It's been six years, Lottie. He's not coming after you. After his football career went to shit and he moved back, he probably married one of the girls who was pining over him from high school. You need to forgive yourself and move forward. Punishing yourself and hiding out forever isn't any way to live. And sorry for getting deep, and a bar probably isn't the best place to bring it up, but maybe it's time to reach out to your mom, forgive yourself for waiting so long, and let her know you're okay. She loves you, and I'm not going to sugarcoat it. She's probably going to be pissed at you for waiting so long, but she's your mom. She'll get over it and be happy to have you back."

Part of me knows she's right, even if I was getting a therapy moment in the middle of a club on a Friday night. I hadn't had any contact with Gregory since the night I left Cedar Ridge. I started over, and he went to Dayton to start as the new star quarterback. Social media and the news kept me updated, and after he completely shattered his tibial plateau his senior year, requiring surgery and extensive rehab, his dream of being drafted into the NFL was just that... a dream. ESPN interviewed with him, and he looked like a completely different person. Defeated and solemn, the man that was talking to the reporter was the complete opposite of the cocky and arrogant boy I dated in high school who would hit me when we got in his car for what he thought was me looking the wrong way at someone. He told the reporter, after rehab he was going to work for his dad's company, Cole Inc., which created security systems for businesses and hotels. Looking at him during the interview was like looking at a stranger, yet it still gave me the worst feeling in the pit of my stomach. Appearance alone would suggest he'd changed; however, something inside me didn't believe it, and I'm not sure I could ever be convinced otherwise.

Snapping myself back to reality, I shake my head to will away the tears that are fighting to get past. Grace is right. I need to stop living in the past. I need to let go a little and try new things. As for calling my mom, I push that shit down just like everything else I don't want to face, storing it away for another day.

After my internal pep talk, I turn to Grace. No way in hell I'm dancing, but I'll stay for her because that's what she's always done for me. "You're right, and I'm the one who's sorry. I know I need to start moving forward instead of constantly looking over my shoulder. I'm not dancing, but you go shake that ass on the dance floor. I won't ghost you."

"Come on. Just one dance?" She gives me puppy dog eyes and a pouty lip...*I know her game.*

"Sorry. Letting go, I can work on, spending the night in the emergency room... yeah, not something I want to chance. Besides, when I dance, I look like a giraffe that got stung by a bee, not attractive and done only when in my room with the door shut."

"Alright, you staying is enough. I've been waiting to shake my ass all week. Sure you're ok?"

"I'll be fine. I'm going to order another drink and people-watch," Nodding my head toward the dance floor, urging her to go.

"If the waitress comes back, I'll take another Cosmo, please," Grace says as she stands and leaves the table. She walks down the stairs just as the song changes to Rhianna's *Pon de Replay*, which always draws a crowd. She fits right in, walking to the center and starting to move with the rhythm. I swear that girl was born with the innate ability to do anything and make it look easy. The waitress comes by, and I order another round of drinks and sit back to take it all in, trying my best to relax and not feel anxious. Looking out to the dance floor again, I see a guy behind Grace, holding her hips and moving to the music. Her hips mold perfectly to his; her head leans back on his shoulder as she grinds into him. That's Grace, the life of the party, able to put herself out there, and she uses her beauty and brains to her advantage to get what she wants, both in business and her personal life. They start to turn, and I realize it's one of the guys that walked past us earlier. Grace's back is pressed against his chest with her arms around his neck and head back, exposing her neck and making him bend over due to the height difference. His head is by her ear as if he's whispering a secret, and I can make out it's the guy with the lighter hair as he works his arms down her body while she grinds against him. A weird sense of relief washes over me as I realize who she's dancing with.

"What the fuck is that, and why do you even care?" I say

to myself because if it's not enough to be sitting alone at a bar, talking to yourself is even better. Feeling stupid, I turn my head from the dance floor to distract myself from my own ridiculousness when I see the guy in the black button-down standing at my table looking at me, the light above us showing his ice blue eyes that are so bright, they look as though they could see into your soul.

He cocks his head to the side before saying with his lip curled up on one side. "What the fuck is what? And maybe there's a reason you care." His voice is deep and sultry. He's not even that close to me, but his cologne invades my senses. He smells like sin and spice, and for the first time in six years, the sound of a man's voice has made my panties instantly wet, something that is both intriguing and terrifying.

Well shit.

4

Gavin

*A*fter hanging up with my dad, I headed back to the office to start prepping for the Pickett briefing next week. I was re-reading the statement for the third time to make sure I had it committed to memory when my phone vibrated on my desk. Glancing at it, my sister's name lighting up the screen had me realizing that the note I wrote myself Monday to call her must have gotten covered up because four days have passed and I never reached out.

"Hey, little sis. How's life in the big city?" I asked before she could chastise me for not calling her sooner.

"Oh my God, Gavin, is that you? Did you really pick up the phone? I thought I was going to have to call your assistant and schedule a meeting just to talk to my own brother. Weird how the little sister has to check in because her big brother is too busy," she says sarcastically into the phone. Busted. I've always made it a point to check in after she moved for school and to pursue her fashion career. We have always been close, and even though we live in different cities, I am the protective big brother... which recently I have been failing at due to working so much.

"Worst brother of the year award goes to me. I'm sorry I'm an asshole."

"Apology accepted, and you will be forgiven when you take me for my favorite cheesecake at Wren's Bakery when I visit next weekend."

"What? You're coming home? I thought you weren't coming home until Thanksgiving with the show coming up?"

"It's been hell, and yes, I'm coming home, only for two days though. Travis and I have been putting in hours only the devil himself would mandate and have all the pieces designed and the fabric picked. Unfortunately, with shipping taking forever to get the specialty fabric in for a few dresses, we are in a bit of a holding pattern. We can't pick models and create the vision until everything is ready, and I feel like I'm going to have a nervous breakdown. It's my first big show, and if I don't deliver, I'll be dead on arrival before I even get started. Travis said I needed to take a couple days to clear my head and reset. I think I'm annoying the shit out of him, pacing around the studio and tracking the status of the orders every day. We have meetings with the people from the venue early next week, so I fly in on Friday night and leave Sunday late afternoon." She's rambling like she always does when she's stressed, and it's not that I'm not sympathetic to her situation, but if shipping hold-ups mean I get to see my sister for a day or two, I'll take it without letting her know I'm happy about it. "That sucks, Liv, but maybe Travis is right. Take a couple days without stressing about something you have no control over. You can stay at my condo if you want."

"Thanks, but no thanks. I don't need to hear walls knocking on my two-day respite. God only knows what goes on in that condo of yours on the weekends." She makes a gagging noise over the phone. "I already talked to Mom. I'm staying with them, and she wanted me to tell you since I'm home, plan to come to dinner Saturday night. She mentioned something about not seeing you for a few weeks and that you declined the event she is hosting tonight. She said I might have a better chance of talking to you than she would. Turning into Dad, are we?"

I ignore her comment about bringing women home since I haven't had a woman at my place since Rachel. Ugh, even her name pisses me off. I always go to the woman's place and leave before the morning, a fact my baby sister does not need to know.

"I'm not turning into Dad, I just have been focused, and you know Dad's expectations, putting everything and more into the job at all times. I'm not like you, who skidded past joining the family business and got to live your dream in LA." I'm just giving her shit. In reality, somewhere deep down, I am a little envious that she got to choose her own path.

"Hmmm," she hums back, giving me some slack. "Law would've drowned me, and you kill it. Just don't let work run your life. I know since your break-up with *she who shall not be mentioned*, you've forgotten how to have fun and leave work at the office. Before you know it, you'll wake up a sixty-year-old man with nothing but money and a court record of wins to show for it."

"Thank you for the therapy session," I say, letting the sarcasm seep into my voice. "I appreciate your concern. I'm fine and get out plenty, and I'm your big brother who should be worried about you, not the other way around. I'm meeting Logan and James at a new club downtown tonight to celebrate our settlement. Speaking of which, if I don't get through this depo, I'm never going to make it. Call and let me know when your flight comes in. I'll pick you up from the airport."

"Alright, love you, asshole, see you next week," she says sweetly before we hang up.

I make a mental note to call my mom tomorrow, so she stops siccing my sister on me.

Glancing at the clock after getting lost in paperwork, I notice it's already close to eight. I brought clothes with me, knowing this would probably happen. Shutting down my computer, I use my office bathroom to freshen up. One perk of being the son of the head of the firm is that you get one of the nicest offices. Changing quickly into dark jeans and a black button-up, I make it out at a little after eight, and the ten-minute drive to the club goes fast, even with Friday night traffic. That's a nice thing about having the office downtown. It's close to everything. After valet parking and giving my name to the bouncer, I quickly texted Logan and James, letting them know I was walking in, and they told me they were already inside.

After getting through the door and taking a look around, I think the bar is nice but already too busy for my liking. I prefer more of a laid-back scene without all the added fuss. The dimly lit bar and the dark colors go well, but the dance floor, with its lights beating in time to the music, makes me feel like I'm going to have a seizure. Spotting my two asshole best friends by the bar, I head over.

"Well, look who finally decided to grace us with his presence. I thought I would have to put snakes in your office for ditching out. James even beat you here. He actually made it out of the house without having to promise to do the dishes or some shit for the next few weeks." Logan jabs at James as I walk up, handing me a whiskey neat, my drink of choice.

"Fuck off, dude. Lexi had a book club meeting tonight with her friends. I don't have to ask permission, and sure as shit would rather be at home with my fiancée than out with your ugly mug," James jabs back.

"Are you done with your lover's quarrel? I feel bad for Lexi having to put up with your bickering when she's around you. I thought we had VIP. I'd rather not stand around all these people if I could go home and sit on my couch."

"We were waiting for you, Your Highness." Logan bends over as though he's addressing royalty, *dick*. "Let's go grab a table upstairs."

"Lead the way, oh wise one," James tuts back, looking like being here is torture for him. Since meeting Lexi, James is not a fan of being out without her. That man lives and breathes for that woman. Being around other women might as well be like he's around a herd of goats; he doesn't even notice them. Sure, Lexi has a good group of friends she's hung out with since college, and James is not the jealous or possessive type at all, but you would think it's physically painful for them to be apart sometimes. Sounds painful to me just thinking about it, and I've told James such.

He always says, "*I can't wait for the day you meet your match in a woman, one that knocks you on your ass, and you don't know which way is up. I never thought it would happen to me until I met Lexi. It was terrifying, but fuck, is it worth it. It's like you were missing something you didn't even know you needed, the one who makes your soul whole, and I'm going to sit back and enjoy every minute of it after all the shit you and Logan give me."*

My response is always that he needs to get his head checked because that will never happen to me, but he simply shakes his head and laughs as though I've said the funniest joke he's ever heard. I loved once, and it knocked me on my ass, and not in a good way. No thanks. Not going down that road again.

Logan leads us through the path of people up a set of stairs to an area with couches and tables. Everyone in VIP is wearing an orange wristband that matches the one I got when coming in and makes me feel like I'm wearing a ride pass to a carnival like I did as a kid. Some couches line the walls, and bar tables that are along the glass railing look over the dance floor. At the top of the small steps, I glance at the first table to the left of me and catch the eyes of one of the sexiest women I've ever seen.

The recessed lighting above shines down on her like an angelic spotlight. Although I can't tell the color, her eyes have a mystery to them, and her red lips make me want to bite them. Her honey-colored hair is straight and lays over one shoulder, and she is wearing a blue dress that comes to a low V in the front, showing just the top swell of her breasts. The tempting sight causes my dick to twitch in my pants. I force myself to turn and keep walking, discreetly adjusting myself as I go by. I've seen plenty of beautiful women before, but never has my dick immediately tried to stand at attention after less than five seconds. Must be that it's been a few weeks since I've had sex. That's the only explanation. Pushing those thoughts to the back of my mind, I continue moving towards a set of couches where we sit down with our drinks.

"Damn, dude, did you see that girl in the black dress with the ass that looked like an apple I want to take a bite out of?" Logan leans back against the couch, enjoying the view with his arms stretched along the back.

I take the chair to his right that just so happens to face the mystery woman's table. "Do you always have to objectify women based on their bodies? Stop being an asshole," I say aloud to Logan, meaning it more to myself since I just thought about biting a woman's lip and staring at her cleavage. Maybe I'm the asshole.

"I'm not objectifying. I'm simply making an astute observation that her ass is shaped like an apple, and I fucking love apples."

James is in the chair on the other side of Logan and just laughs and shakes his head. "Dude, you are going to be single your whole life."

"That's my plan. Why settle when you can keep rotating? If you always have the same kind, it gets boring, mundane. I like to spice it up and try different kinds. Sex is like cake testing. If you always have vanilla, you'll never know the deliciousness of chocolate, red velvet, or carrot cake, and I never want to stop tasting the flavors."

"Gross, I'm going to pretend you didn't just compare women to flavors of cake," James says as his phone vibrates in his pocket. He reaches for it, reading something before looking up, "I need to go. Lexi got a flat tire and said roadside assistance won't be there for an hour. I don't want her waiting by herself."

"Fuck off. Is this one of those fake calls you have your friends do when you're on a date so you can pretend there's an emergency and leave?" Logan retorts.

"Ha, don't you wish you were that special, dickhead,"

James says as he shows Logan the picture of Lexi's selfie pouting next to her car, where her tire is flat on the pavement.

"Fine, you're lucky you have proof, although I still think this was planned. Next time we go out, Lexi needs to make plans at your condo so she can't have any 'emergencies' calling you away. Tell her we said hi," Logan jokes. In reality, we all love Lexi and know she's not the needy type. None of us would want her to be alone, waiting for roadside assistance in the dark.

As they talk, I can't help stealing glances at the woman at the table. Her friend is wearing a black dress—probably who Logan was talking about. She's beautiful in her own way, but my dick says she does nothing for me. Her face looks almost angry as she says something that looks serious to her friend. I can tell whatever she is saying is affecting the beauty in the blue dress girl because her posture is now slouched, with her arms on the table and head slightly bent forward.

Something makes me want to pull her into me and make sure she's ok. *What is wrong with you?* Damn, maybe I am working too much. I'm starting to lose it. I force myself to look away, shaking my head to clear it of my ridiculous thoughts.

A few minutes later, with James gone, Logan and I are enjoying another round when I look up to see her friend walking down to the dancefloor.

"She's up; that's my cue," Logan says emphatically, putting his scotch down on the glass table. "That siren is calling to me to show her the way home. Get it? She's the siren, but I'll be the one to show her the way home." He chuckles. The man is really a six-year-old trapped in a twenty-eight-year-old's body.

"Just don't use that as your pickup line. You'll be dancing by yourself faster than you can blink. She doesn't look like a woman who will take your shit."

"We'll see. I'm the master, and women melt to my manly charm." Logan waggles his eyebrows like he just can't help himself.

"Whatever dickhead, I'm going to love seeing you fall flat on your ass someday when you meet your match, but sure, go show me how it's done, ye old Yoda Master," I say, shaking my head.

"Watch and learn, son. Watch and learn," he chants as he takes off his sport coat, putting it on the couch before walking down the stairs.

Black dress girl can move, I'll give it to her. I look up and see the woman still sitting at the table, alone now since her friend has gone to the dancefloor. Glancing again, I see Logan attached to her like a magnet. Maybe it's the whiskey, or what my sister said earlier, but before I know it, I'm out of my chair, walking toward the woman in the blue dress, drawn to her like a moth to an open flame.

As I approach her table, I hear her say to herself, "What the fuck is that, and why do you even care?"

With no one else she could possibly be talking to, I wait for her to turn, so she notices me standing there replying, "What the fuck is what, and maybe there's a reason you care."

She stares back at me like a deer caught in the headlights for the briefest second before shaking her head slightly, "Excuse me?"

There's a little bit of bite to her tone, showing I may have overstepped. Being right in front of her and seeing her face up close, her blue eyes are the color of sapphires that match her dress. Her small nose fits her face perfectly, and her full lips look like they yearn to be kissed. She is, in fact, the most beautiful woman I have ever seen. My dick twitches again at the sound of her voice, something I'm going to have to remedy as it clearly wants attention if it's responding to voices now.

"Sorry, I was walking by and heard you, and since no one else was at your table, I thought I'd make sure everything was alright," I said, internally slapping myself in the face for the lame response. I never get tripped up talking to women, and here I am, fumbling over my words like a horny teenager.

"No, I'm fine. I was just thinking out loud about something from work earlier," she clearly tries to cover for herself, sitting up straighter as I stand not even two feet from her. Her scent is intoxicating. Floral with a hint of citrus, making me want to inch closer.

"Ok." I let her off the hook, not wanting to scare her since I can't seem to walk away either. "Can I get you another drink? It's a shame someone as beautiful as you would ever be drinking alone."

She bows her head slightly, as though she's nervous about being called beautiful, before picking her head back up and putting on what looks like a smile she has practiced a million times. "Thank you, but no, I won't be staying too much longer. My friend is on the dance floor, and we are probably heading out soon." She responds with less bite than before, yet there is still hesitation in her voice.

"Your friend that was sitting here earlier? I saw her dancing with my friend Logan; by the looks of it, they aren't going anywhere anytime soon." I pull out the chair her friend vacated and sit down. I am pushing into her space and haven't been invited, but she hasn't told me to fuck off yet either, so I test my luck. Usually, within the first thirty seconds of being around a woman, I can tell where the night will lead, but not with her. She's a puzzle I can't figure out, which intrigues me. I don't like complicated or mysterious, and there are plenty of other choices here tonight, except for some reason I can't figure out, she's the only woman I can see right now. That's something I haven't come close to feeling, *maybe ever.*

She relaxes a bit and chuckles, looking down at where Logan and her friend are dancing. "You're probably right. If Grace has any say in it, she'll be on that dance floor 'til closing, either feeling the music by herself or with your friend since they seem to be glued together." Her lips turn up when she chuckles, and hot damn, if that isn't the cutest grin I've ever seen. *Seriously, what is going on with me? The cutest grin? I need to get my damn head checked.*

Before I completely embarrass myself, "So Grace, she likes to keep you out all night too, huh? Sounds like she and Logan are a match made in heaven," leaning my forearms on the table. "No offense," waving my hands around the bar, "this isn't really my style. I prefer to be at home in sweatpants watching the game on my couch," I'm already questioning myself for throwing the sweatpants and being a homebody out there, yet something tells me this really isn't her scene either.

"Honestly, mine either. I prefer a glass of wine with a movie and pizza over heels, lights, and loud music, but I promised Grace I'd go out tonight, so here I am," she replies as she shrugs her shoulders. "If you don't want to be here, why don't you leave? Weren't there three of you anyway?"

"Oh, so you did notice us come in?" I tease. I'm testing her and secretly high-fiving myself that we at least caught her attention, something that I don't think is easily done, judging by her cool demeanor.

She backpedals, trying to correct her slip-up. "No, Grace did when you came up. I'm merely a good listener when people talk."

Giving her a look that tells her I don't believe one bit of the bullshit she's telling me, I call her bluff, "Oh, makes total sense, Grace noticed us and mentioned it, and you just so happen to commit how many of us there were to memory. Thank goodness you are such a good listener. There were three of us, but our buddy James had to leave. His fiancée got a flat tire, and he didn't want her waiting for roadside assistance by herself."

She looks at me, raising her eyebrows like she did not appreciate my teasing one bit. "Well, that was nice of him. At least there are a few gentlemen left in this world... so Logan is out there grinding on the dancefloor with Grace, and James left to help his fiancée, which leaves you..." Leaving the sentence open-ended, I realize she's fishing for information without directly coming out and saying it.

"Gavin, alone to fend for myself. Whatever shall I do?" I smirk and bat my eyes dramatically at her.

Seemingly unamused by my bullshit, she starts to stand, "Well, Gavin, I guess that's for you to figure out."

Kicking myself for pissing her off and not wanting to let her go—I don't even know her name—I reach out and grab her hand. When our hands touch, a bolt of electricity shoots up my arm and all the way through my body, igniting something in me I've never felt. I know she feels it too when I look in her eyes, but after a millisecond, her gaze becomes wary as her body tenses. Not wanting to make her uncomfortable, I pull my hand away gently and place it on the table, offering an apology, "I'm sorry. I didn't mean to be an asshole. It's been a long week, and not that that's an excuse. I mean, I'm sorry." I'm rambling again. For fucks sake, I'm a lawyer who talks in court for a living, yet I can't have a normal conversation with a woman tonight. What is wrong with me?

Thanking my lucky stars, she sits back down and seems to relax a little. "And your name is..."

"Charlotte, but everyone calls me Lottie." She says softly.

"Charlotte, that is a beautiful name." I like her nickname, but Charlotte seems to fit her perfectly. And I like the way it rolls off my tongue.

She gives me a soft smile. "Thank you."

"What do you do, Charlotte?"

"I'm a graduate student."

Realizing by her short answers and no-return questions, she keeps things pretty close to her chest, and not wanting to push her, I don't dig deeper. But damn, I want to, and that rattles me. The waitress comes by and asks if we want another drink, which Charlotte declines, and so do I since I'm driving. Logan and Grace are still on the dancefloor and, by the looks of it, have no intentions of stopping anytime soon. I want to ask her to go somewhere quieter so we can talk, and before I know it, words are spilling out of my mouth that I never thought I'd say.

"Do you want to get out of here and go somewhere we can relax a little more? We could head back to my condo if you want. It doesn't seem like Grace and Logan are going anywhere." *We could go back to my condo? I never take anyone to my condo, yet here I am asking a stranger to come over... I don't know what is happening, but I have this need to be close to her.* Before I can continue my inner monologue, I realize she's up and out of her chair.

Charlotte looks around a few times before saying in haste, "I'm sorry, I have an early morning and really should get going."

Way to go, dumbass. You freaked her out. She has a look on her face that seems to be a mix of desire and fear, and I want to pull her closer to me and not let her go, a feeling I can analyze the shit out of later, but not right now.

"Ok, let me walk you out." I go to leave some money for the waitress, intending to ask for her number outside, but as I turn around, she's walking through the exit already. Shit, who the hell is she, Batman? I left for five seconds to pull money out of my wallet, and she made it across the bar. I drop the bills on the table and rush down the stairs toward the door. Making my way outside, I look left and right and across the street, not seeing her anywhere. Running my hand through my hair in frustration, I drop my head before relenting and handing my ticket to the valet. *Fucking great.*

5

Charlotte

For the first time in six years, I felt something other than tense when a man touched me. The electricity that jolted up my arm when Gavin took my hand was something I had never felt, and for some reason, it made me feel calm, not nervous. The way he said Charlotte was a pure aphrodisiac. I preferred being called Lottie until I heard Gavin say my full name. I don't think it would sound right coming from anyone else, but from him, it was perfect. And though it probably would've been a horrible idea to leave with him, I considered it for a minute before I looked up and swore I saw Gregory standing by the bar looking around. Instant fear took the place of what, seconds ago, was sexual tension. I didn't want to be a bitch, but in an instant, the need to flee was stronger than anything, and I couldn't wait even a few more seconds to let Gavin walk me out. Thanking my lucky stars that I didn't fall after practically running out of the club, I see a couple getting out of a cab, so I ask the driver if he'll drive me and climb in when he nods.

Getting in and sending an *I'm sorry, but I'm not feeling well* text to Grace, I throw my phone back in my purse. I don't want to worry her because I was sure I'd freaked myself out for no reason. I rub my hand over the spot where Gavin had touched me. I must be losing my mind because I swear I can still feel the warmth of his touch. I can still hear his low sultry voice in my head and smell the faint scent of something uniquely him in my nostrils. I haven't been this affected by a guy in... well, ever, and that both excites me and scares the crap out of me at the same time if I'm pulling the honesty card.

After paying the driver and getting out of the car, I look around to make sure no one is following me before heading inside. I walk up the stairs to our second-floor apartment, put the key in, and throw my purse on the small table right inside the door, feeling eighty percent better once I switch the lock. I immediately feel like an idiot. It's been six years without any sign of Gregory. He has no clue where I am or what I am doing, and he lives and works in Tennessee. Grace was right. I am letting my fear of the past interfere with my present and probably my future. Gavin was hot, I mean, more than hot. He was the definition of panty-melting, and for the first time in forever, I felt something when a man touched me. I felt alive, and I fucking blew it because I'm seeing things. Annoyed at myself, I walk past our living room and kitchen down the hall to the last door on the right, my bedroom, and change into sweats and a Hampton University t-shirt. Realizing I haven't checked my phone, I walk back to the living room, grab my purse, and find a couple of waiting texts from Grace.

GRACE:

Are you really sick or pulling another ghosting act?

GRACE:

Lottie?

GRACE:

Text me, so I know you got home safe.

GRACE:

I might not make it home tonight ;)

Not wanting her to worry, I text back:

ME:

I'm home and safe. Sorry for skipping out, my stomach started feeling off. Be safe, text me if you need me.

Not even a minute later, she responds.

GRACE:

I always am, love you, girl.

ME:

Love you too.

Too amped to go to bed, I grab a bottle of water from the fridge and climb onto our charcoal gray suede couch, tucking my legs underneath me and throwing my favorite purple and gray blanket over my lap. Turning on Netflix and wanting to keep my mind off Gavin, I watch an episode of *Squid Games*, which I find is basically the *Hunger Games* on crack. It's almost eleven thirty when I get off the couch and head to the bathroom to wash up. Pulling my hair into a messy bun on top of my head, I wash my face and apply my night cream because if my grandma taught me anything, it's that it is never too early to start preventing wrinkles, and head to bed. Crawling under the lilac covers of my queen-sized bed, I roll onto my side. After tossing and turning, I can't sleep. I reach into my nightstand and pull out my little purple friend who has helped me through my sex hiatus like a champion. With the lights off, I lay on my back, close my eyes, and let out a relaxing breath.

I feel his weight hovering over me, his spicy scent invading my space, wanting to bathe in it. He leans down onto one elbow and bends towards me, leaving a trail of kisses on my ear, down my neck, and over my collarbone. Whispering in my ear, "What do you need, Charlotte?" Before I can even whisper back, his hand explores my body, gently caressing my breast and giving my nipple a gentle tug that goes straight to my core. His mouth continues its descent downward, placing light kisses over each breast and across my stomach before traveling lower, to right above my pelvic bone. I lift my hips in response, urging him to continue where I so desperately need him to be. Sensing my need, he smirks and dips his head, placing a kiss at the apex of my sex before diving his tongue between my folds and inserting one finger, crooking it upward, hitting a spot I didn't even know existed. He moves his finger in and out a few times, letting me adjust before adding another, applying more pressure with his tongue as my hips lift in reflex, demanding more. I can feel my climax building from my toes, and embarrassingly quick, I am falling over the edge, crying out after having the most intense orgasm I've ever had. Coming down from my high while my breathing returns to normal, I open my eyes and realize the man that got me off in my mind was Gavin, a man I spent no more than ten minutes with yet already have his face memorized.

Great, I just had the best orgasm ever while thinking of the first guy who has done anything for me in six years, and I ran away because of something I "thought" I saw without an explanation or even giving him my number. *Did he ask for my number? He probably didn't even want it. But he did ask if we could go somewhere quieter, even mentioned his condo. God, I'm a mess.*

Grace is right, I internally scold myself. I've been letting Gregory control my life with nothing but self-induced orgasms to show for it. I make a mental promise to myself that I am going to stop living in fear and let life happen, which isn't too hard to do since starting Monday, I will be triple busy with classes, work, and my new internship. *Hey, it's the thought that counts, right?* Internal battle, scolding, and motivational speech over, I roll onto my side, grab my pillow, and at some point, drift off into a restless sleep.

Warm arms hold me tight as I snuggle back into a bare chest and legs that I mold into like a cookie cutter. I could stay like this forever when I hear a distant noise getting louder before I'm hit with something. Dragging my eyes open, I realize I was dreaming of Gavin again, which is something I'll analyze later, to see Grace standing there and the pillow she just threw at me half on my face.

"Lottie, seriously, wake up, I need to vent, and I need to do it now." I glance at the clock, which reads eight seventeen a.m., way too early to be awake on the weekend, but Grace is clearly on a rampage. I doubt telling her to get out will go over well.

Scooting myself up my black padded headboard to sit, I stretch my arms over my head and yawn, "What is so urgent that you barge in my room this early on a Saturday... wait, it's Saturday and you're up, and you texted me that you weren't coming home last night." As the pieces start to fall into place in my head, I ask, "What happened?"

"What happened? What happened, you ask? Logan happened, that's what." Staring at me as my still foggy brain attempts to catch up from the warm and cozy dream I was having, she practically shouts, "Hello?! Are you listening? After practically humping on the dance floor for who knows how long, Logan asked me to go back to his place, so we left. After being all over me on the car ride to his condo, we stumble into his place and onto his couch. Side note, his place is noooicce, but that shit doesn't matter. So, making out on his couch, fully expecting the night to have a happy ending for both of us, I give that asshole the best blow job he's ever had. I mean, moaning my name, fisting his hands in my hair while he can't hold back. And do you know what he does?" I don't dare interrupt her while she's on a roll. "He sits up and buttons his pants, kisses me, and then says, 'Thank you. I'm sorry, but I've got an early morning, so can you see yourself out?' Umm, excuse me, see myself out? Shocked, I mean literally *shook*, I stood there like an idiot for what felt like forever, which was probably only a few seconds thinking he was kidding and I was in some alternate reality until he stood and opened the front door, dismissing me. Grace Hastings does not get dismissed. I fucking picked up my shit and had to call a cab to do the damn ride of shame at three a.m. No one, and I mean no one, has ever done that to me. I couldn't even sleep. I want to go back to his condo and burn it down, but I won't because that's illegal, and I'm just kidding, ha-ha, you know, in case anyone's listening," she said a bit louder, glancing around the room. Grace always has been a little bit of a conspiracy theorist about the government listening in. "I have never met a bigger asshole in my entire life."

She finally takes an exasperated breath, and I take that as my chance to chime in, giving her the validation she needs. "Forget him. He is an asshole. There are so few nice guys left, and you deserve nothing less than the best, babe. If that's how he is, who knows what he's been up to." Deciding definitely not to tell her about Gavin since he came with Logan. If that's the kind of company he keeps, he probably isn't far off that track. At least I tell myself that so I can stop my regret from running and dismiss the fantasy orgasm and dream.

"How about we veg out, watch movies, order in, and spend a day just the two of us? You're right. We haven't gotten real quality time together being so busy. I will prep for the week and brief on my internship tomorrow." I should be doing that today, but sometimes your best friend needs you, and for the countless times she's pulled me through, I can do this for her. "We can even walk down to the store and get some ice cream and toppings to make sundaes, your favorite." Talking about ice cream earns me the slightest smile from Grace, who sits on the edge of my bed.

"Yes, to all of the above. I'm not ruling out my option to burn his place down though. See? This is why I never even pretend that I would or could create something with someone. This very reason. If you can't even get through one night without him being a jerk, it's fucking pointless." Grace does not get bothered by guys. Logan must have gotten to her if she's this worked up. Not downplaying his shitty behavior at all, but it isn't like Grace to get this involved. Usually, she brushes any bullshit off, holds her head high, and keeps walking. She seems actually wounded by his actions, a look I am unfamiliar with on Grace that makes me feel like my friend may have seen the potential and got knocked down. Leaning over, I hug my bestie. After our hug, I turn and stand to slide on some sweatpants over the underwear I slept in and pull a sweatshirt over my t-shirt. Fixing my hair that half fell out, we walk down the hallway to the kitchen, and I turn on some coffee.

"Do you want me to order some donuts to be delivered?" Not that I have the extra cash floating around to have donuts delivered, but if it makes my best friend happy, I'll gladly squeeze in an extra shift at Cliff's to cover the difference.

"I'm fine, thanks, but hell yes to the ice cream. Thank you, Lottie. I love you."

Handing her coffee and sitting next to her on our couch, I say, "I love you too." Starting up Netflix for a day of binge-watching, eating, and not thinking about Logan or Gavin, we settle in for a much-needed bestie day.

I'll spend all day tomorrow at the coffee shop or library getting ready for Monday, and as nervous and stressed as I feel about that, I promise myself I won't let it show. Because today is about hanging out with Grace, my constant for the past six years.

6

Gavin

*G*lancing at the clock reading just after five a.m., I relent and get up to work out. I need to get rid of some of this pent-up energy. I haven't slept much since Friday. After getting home, frustrated, I changed into sweats and a t-shirt and sat down with a beer to watch TV, which was useless, because my mind kept seeing full lips and sapphire blue eyes instead of the screen. My dick was getting uncomfortably hard sitting there, so I decided to shower and release the tension. Letting the water cascade down me, I grabbed the base and started stroking myself, visions of Charlotte's honey hair and that blue dress hugging her body, showing just enough cleavage to leave you wanting more, flooding my mind. As I envisioned fisting my hands in her hair and working my way down her open throat, my hand gripped harder up and down my length with desperation, exploding, more intense and faster than I ever had. Not to mention while dreaming of a woman I had a fifteen-minute interaction with. Fuck, it had been almost four years since a girl had gotten under my skin like this, and that ended in a dumpster fire.

I washed the evidence down the drain before dropping onto my bed and falling into a restless sleep, haunted by royal blue eyes and lips meant for sin. *I know her first name and that she's a graduate student, which isn't much to go off of, but it's a start. I truly am losing it.*

"Get a fucking grip, you lunatic," I yell in the mirror Sunday morning after another night of tossing and turning. I spent Saturday working out, jerking off more times than I care to admit, and reviewing all the documents for the Pickett briefing. Ignoring texts from Logan asking where the fuck I disappeared to, I'm fully expecting a show from him when I get to the office tomorrow.

Steeling myself to stop this ridiculousness, I throw on black sweats and a gray t-shirt and head to the kitchen. After eating a bagel and grabbing my black coffee, I retreat to my home office, which is pretty minimally decorated with a black metal bookshelf that lines the back wall and a black wood desk that sits in the middle of the room with two charcoal leather chairs opposite my desk. And I can't forget my favorite thing, my desk chair. If I'm going to put late nights in at home, I wanted a chair that didn't make my ass fall asleep or feel like I was sitting on cardboard. At least, that was my internal reasoning behind the chair that cost me over five grand. Sitting down, I mold into the soft black leather, making it worth every penny.

Finally, I get my head together enough to focus on the files in front of me just after ten. I'm reading through financial reports when I hear pounding at my front door. It stops for a second and then starts up again. "What the fuck is that...hold on, I'm coming," shouting as I stand and head toward the door. Swinging it open with irritation, I am met with Logan's ugly mug.

"What the fuck, dude? I've been texting you all weekend, and crickets. James hasn't even heard from you. I was about to fill out a missing person's report. Where the hell have you been?"

"Wow, a little early for the dramatics, don't you think? I've been working this weekend, like I told you, and since I didn't want to deal with your dumbass stories of your latest and greatest, I silenced your texts so I could, you know, actually get shit done."

"What if I needed something, huh? What if I got arrested or was in the hospital, and they were trying to reach you? Wouldn't you feel like the asshole?"

"I'm pretty sure you wouldn't be texting me if you were in the hospital or jail. You're a lawyer, for Christ sake. Your argument blows."

"Fine, I didn't go to jail or the hospital, but I did need you. I think I fucked up a little, ok, maybe a lot, and I'm in uncharted territory, man, and you ghost me when I need you."

Logan actually looks flustered. I mean, this man can jump out of bed and make it to court in thirty minutes and still look presentable, but damn, something is off. He strides into my living room while running his hands through his hair before plopping down on the black leather couch and kicking his feet on my coffee table that has a thick wood top and metal legs.

"Sorry, man. I got a headache Friday, so I left to get some sleep, and I've been working on shit for this week until you barged into my condo. So please, pray tell, oh needy one.

How can I help you?" Knowing I'm being a dick, it dawns on me that he was with Grace, maybe he got her number, and he can use it for me to talk to Charlotte again. *Hell Yes.*

"First of all... fuck you. I do not need sarcasm right now. This is an actual situation here, so the theatrics can take a fucking hike." Looking up at the ceiling like he's actually embarrassed to tell me, he takes a breath before going on. "So, you know Friday, right? Of course you know Friday, you were there. Well, until you wussed out and left, but anyways, you know I went to check out the merchandise on the dance floor and found a total gem. Seriously, best ass that I've ever seen with the body and moves to go with it. Like my dick stood at attention just watching her move on the dance floor, so you can imagine how it felt when our bodies connected. Anyway, of course she's into me because, well, it's me, so we have a few more drinks, and Grace, that's her name, Grace, whispers in my ear all seductive siren-like about getting out of there. Of course I want to leave. My dick was so tight in my pants I thought I was going to rip them. Anyway, we go to my condo and stumble in, making it to the couch, and she goes to her knees and starts blowing me. And I don't mean an average blowie, like, she could teach a class on how to get it done. Tilting my head back, cuz damn, it felt amazing, I close my eyes, and I see a flash of her and me sitting on the porch of a house with a huge yard, watching kids running around. I thought I was having a stroke or something and right then, I explode like I never have before while she swallows every bit down like a beer bong champ, and I freaked. I told her I had an early morning and she needed to go. I don't know what happened. I feel like I may have blacked out, but she looked like she was going to murder me and grabbed her shit and left." Logan finally takes a breath after that disturbing recollection of his night.

"So, you dismissed her, and she got pissed and left? How is that different from any other night?" I'm not sure where this is all headed.

"Did you not hear what I said? I had a flash of her and me sitting on the porch, watching kids play in the yard. Like all domestic and shit. And fuck you very much for asking how that's different. I never leave a woman unsatisfied, asshole. I may not do relationships, but the women I spend time with are always sat-is-fied."

"Except one, I guess," I said, chuckling at his ridiculousness.

He whips a coaster at my head. Lucky that shit didn't break the window behind me, or his tantrum would be costing him a few grand.

Running a hand through his hair, he leans his head back. I've actually never seen him seriously worked up about anything, so this is uncharted territory. He's the easygoing one, never worried about exams or papers in college, and now walks into each court case like he's meeting someone for coffee.

"This girl has me all messed up. I never think twice about someone, and I haven't stopped thinking about her since she left. And in the mix of all of it, I never even got her number."

"Damn, I think someone finally got under your skin," I muttered, thinking of my own situation with Charlotte, who seems to have taken up a permanent residence in my head since Friday night.

"I think I need to find another girl to get her out of my head. I stayed in last night. *Stayed in.* And you didn't even return my texts. Yep, that's it. I need to fuck this girl out of my system. Ok yeah, great, thanks for the talk." He stands and walks out of my condo. I don't even know what just happened. I'm not sure he realizes it's only ten-thirty, but he's on a mission, and I doubt anything is going to stop him. Although the conversation with Logan has me a little disappointed, if I'm being honest, since he was with Grace, I thought it would at least be a way to get to Charlotte. Shaking my crazy thoughts off, I stand and walk back to my office, committed to burying my head in these files for the rest of the day.

Walking into my office Monday morning, I'm exhausted after not sleeping all weekend. Logan was on one last night, sending ridiculous texts about his "mission," distracting me from focusing. I tried to get a few hours of work done with my mind wandering to Charlotte every few minutes, proving my efforts useless. Visions of wrapping my fists in her hair while shes on her knees, bending her over my desk, taking her in my bed and on every surface of my condo, all of which led me nowhere but needing to release the built-up tension. I jacked off in the shower last night and again this morning to the visions of a woman I probably won't ever see again, thanks in part to my dickhead friend.

After Elaine, my fifty-four-year-old assistant, goes over my schedule for the morning, I lean back in my chair to regroup, knowing I have an hour before we meet in the conference room with the new interns. Logan walks in looking like shit. He doesn't say anything, just sits down in the chair across from me.

"You look like hell. Did you even sleep last night?" His hair looks like he's been running his hands through it constantly.

"I could ask you the same thing, asshole. You know they have cream for the dark circles under your eyes."

"Fuck off," I offer, throwing a pen at his head. "How was your night? Find someone to get Grace out of your head?"

"Found someone, found several actually, went back to this brunette's place, started fooling around, but every time I closed my eyes, I kept seeing *her* face from Friday night. I made an excuse and left. This shit is messin' with my head."

"Both of your heads, it seems," I say, chuckling at him. Seeing Logan serious freaks me out, so I'm trying to lighten the mood. "Anyway, we have a full day and new interns starting, so get your hormonal head out of your ass and let's get to work."

James walks in and smacks Logan on the back of the head, and it's like hitting a reset button for him. Logan's head pops up. "Let's do it. I love fresh meat."

James rolls his eyes, obviously not privy to Logan's weekend. "Here we go. You are not sleeping with any interns this year, Logan."

"You're just jealous because your dick has been benched to the outside world."

"Yes, I'm jealous that I get the best pussy to myself whenever and however I want for the rest of my life while you're out there waiting to catch some disease that'll make your dick fall off."

"One pussy for the rest of your life sounds like a death sentence, not a trophy, and I poncho my guy up every time. My health teacher would be proud."

"Can we please focus instead of talking about pussy and

your dick falling off?" God, my two best friends can be annoying as shit this early in the morning. I pull out the files of the three new interns starting today. Two females and a male, all in their last year of law school. Two are focused on corporate law and one on family law. Unusual to have a focus outside of corporate law since this is a very sought-after internship, but I don't make the decisions.

Interns are assigned by my father and John, my dad's partner, who's been more of an uncle to me. He's known me my whole life. They pick the interns, however; their management and success lie on the three of us. Being the son of the firm's co-CEO does not afford me any breaks. If anything, it puts more pressure on me to be the best. I hand the files to James and Logan to look over, wishing their pictures were attached. I like to put a face to a name before meeting them whenever possible.

We spend the next hour going over the week, updating cases, and listening to James and Logan exchange jabs. It's close to nine when we walk into the conference room through the private door so we don't walk through the office. I like being there early so we show a united front, and that promptness is important at this firm. I won't waste their time and sure as shit don't want them to waste mine. I sit at the head of the long table with James to my left and Logan to my right. I can hear Elaine talking in the hallway as I flip through some emails on my phone. I hear the door open and look up. There are three people standing in front of me. Well, I think there are three, but I can't be sure because I can only focus on sapphire blue eyes staring back at me. Blinking to make sure I'm not losing it, I refocus. Nope, still there. Standing in the conference room is Charlotte, wearing a black fitted skirt that ends just above her knee showing off the curve of her hips and a sleeveless cream-colored blouse that is unbuttoned at the top in a conservative sexy manner, if that even exists. All I want to do is undo a few more buttons so I can get a better view of her chest. Her hair is in a neat low bun, and with it pulled back, I can see the curve of her neck, the neck I spent hours dreaming of devouring this weekend.

My Monday just got a lot more interesting and complicated at the same time.

7

Charlotte

Oh shit, I think to myself as I walk into the conference room and find Gavin sitting in front of me at the table, looking hotter than he did Friday if that's possible. He's not even standing, but his navy suit, white dress shirt, and gray tie fit perfectly over his shoulders and arms. I squeeze my thighs together while trying to stop the dirty thoughts from running through my head. Glancing to my left, I see the asshole that Grace was with on Friday, and it takes me a few seconds to realize I'm shaking my head. What are the freaking chances that of all the jobs and places to work, I'm interning at a firm that employs a man I can't stop dreaming about and an asshole who hurt my best friend? And I'm assuming, since they are sitting here, they will have some part in my work life for the next few months.

It only takes a second before he looks up and locks eyes with me. His gaze is intense, those ice blue eyes fixated on mine, bringing back memories of his body over mine. *Pull yourself together, Lottie. You are standing in a conference room with your probable boss, and you are thinking of masturbating to him, pervert.* It's only a second before Gavin looks away from me, bringing us both back to reality, as the man on his right looks at his friend before speaking up.

"Welcome to Davis and Jones Law. I'm James, and this is Gavin and Logan." Pointing to each of the men at the table. "We will be your team going forward."

Seeming to snap out of his stupor, Gavin chimes in. "Uhh, yes, welcome to Davis and Jones. We are your leadership team. As you probably know from the information you were sent, you each will be assigned to work with one of us directly; however, we team up on most cases, so expect there to be a lot of crossover and collaboration. We work long hours, which doesn't leave much time for a social life, and we expect nothing less than your best. You are also here to learn from us, so feel free to ask any questions. We have a briefing at one that you will all need to familiarize yourself with. The files you were given contain all the information you will need. IT is still working on getting your access and emails set up, so for the morning, this conference room will be for your use. There usually isn't much time to go out during the day, so plan to bring lunch with you if you want to eat. Any questions?"

He is all business. His voice has my mind wandering, but if he keeps company with people like Logan, he might be really good at putting on a show. I think that bothers me even more, people who pretend to be decent only when they need to.

"Do we run errands for you too, sir?" It's out of my mouth before I even realize I said it. Nothing he said warranted a snide comment from me. I just couldn't help myself. The other two interns I met this morning, Justin and Beth, stare at me like I have two heads while the two other men at the table smirk.

"Excuse me?" Gavin says with his head tilted and a smug grin, like he's both turned on and confused by my comment simultaneously.

I try to rephrase what I'm saying before I get myself fired on the first day, "I'm just wondering if running errands is part of our duties. I want to make sure I have our list of responsibilities committed to memory."

"As an intern, there may be times that we need you to run errands outside of the office that are pertinent to this firm, but we don't ask interns to run personal errands. Is that a problem, Charlotte?" His voice is husky, my name rolling off his tongue seductively.

His voice makes my entire body quiver. "No, it's not a problem."

While the two men give Gavin side glances, he keeps his gaze on me while replying, "Good to hear. Make yourselves at home because you have a lot to go through, and we have our first meeting in a few hours." They all stand and walk out through a different door than the one we walked through. *My new boss is also the hot guy I can't get out of my head.* Not the best-case scenario, but I have three hours to commit this to memory, and I'll be damned if I let someone get in the way of me succeeding, even if my lady parts think otherwise.

Gavin

"What the hell was that? You never stumble in a meeting." James jabs as we walk from the conference room back into my office.

Trying to keep my face even so I don't give anything away to my friends to use as ammo, I simply reply, "Nothing, didn't get much sleep this weekend." Knowing damn well Charlotte is the reason I didn't sleep good only messes with my head more. Her sarcastic mouth and how she said sir almost made me blow right there. She's a damn intern. What are the odds? I knew I was in trouble when I looked up and saw those beautiful baby blues. She said she was a graduate student. Never in a million years would I have guessed she was a law student and our new intern. I never falter in a meeting, but damn if it didn't take me a second to pull it together in there.

My dick didn't get the message, immediately becoming too tight in my pants when I saw her, trying to pry itself out from behind my zipper like a lion in a cage, which is why I needed to exit ASAP. My dick is appreciative he gets to see her sexy ass every day. Keeping my hands off of her is going to be a problem.

"You're acting weird today." James eyes me conspicuously.

"I call dibs on the blonde," Logan speaks up like he hasn't heard any of the conversation.

"Fuck off, Logan. You are the worst, and for all our sanity, you're taking Justin. We are not dealing with you sleeping with another intern." I know it's not my decision, and technically I don't think we have a policy, but I'm not letting him anywhere near her.

"I call bullshit. James should get Justin since he's the one that's already tied down. I don't think Lexi will appreciate a female intern being on his team." Logan makes a sorry-ass attempt at a defense.

"Ha, you're so full of shit. You're the one who slept with two interns who worked here simultaneously, causing a catfight in the lounge and your office being trashed, leaving us short. Not happening again. Lexi has never had a problem with females working on my team because, you see, my friend, I am not an asshole. I only have eyes for my woman, and she knows it." James throws back in his face.

This back and forth was getting us nowhere, and we had shit we needed to do. If I let them continue to bicker, it would be lunch before anyone came up for air.

"Enough. Jesus, you two sound like screeching cats. Logan, I agree with James on this one. Since we have had problems with past interns and your inability to keep it in your pants while they are here. Justin is all yours, James, you take Beth, and Charlotte will be on my team." Did I realize I was punishing myself by pairing her with me? *Yep.* Did I trust her with Logan? *Abso-fucking-lutely not.* Should she be teamed with James? *Definitely*, but I was a greedy fucker and apparently a glutton for punishment, and I wanted to torture myself working closely with her for the next few months.

"Selfish fucker, I see what you did there, keeping the hottest one for yourself...tsk tsk, what would Daniel have to say about it?" Logan shoots back at me.

"What would I have to say about what, Logan?" my dad asks as he walks into my office. His face showing disapproval of the three of us standing around wasting time. "If I'm not mistaken, the interns start today, correct? So why are the three of you jerking off in your office while they are in the conference room?" James and Logan stand up immediately. My dad is a great guy but not someone you want to mess with in the office. When he is at work, he's a shark and takes no excuses for shit not getting done, and my friends know it. I find it amusing that after years of college and working here, my dad still makes them jump.

"We were just going over assignments, sir. The interns have packets they are getting themselves acquainted with before we meet to go over cases. IT is getting their computers organized in the intern office, which is why they are using the conference room. Why don't we go check and see if they have their computers set up and ready?" Logan speaks so fast that it's like he's reciting an apology for putting gum in someone's hair. Before my father can respond, both my best friends are out the door, shutting it behind them.

My father comes in and takes a seat in my chair. He always does this when he comes to my office, and although, at first, I thought it was a dick move, I understand where I stand in line. He is the CEO, and I am busting my ass to prove that when he retires, he will leave the firm in the best hands since John never had any children. Taking a seat across from him, I wait. He only comes in here when he needs to tell me something.

"I wanted to touch base about our quarterly meeting. John and I are flying out tomorrow to meet with a client and won't be back until Thursday, so we'll have to push it back until next week."

"Okay, I'll ask Elaine to touch base with Rose for your schedule next week."

"I am leaving you in charge this week. With both of us being gone, I think this gives you an opportunity to take on more responsibility in this firm. I will be available by phone and email, of course. Still, I'm putting my confidence in you that you can handle anything that comes through, even though it will only be two days."

I didn't know how to respond. He and/or John had been gone in the past. He's never come into my office to "officially" put me in charge. Everything was always routed through Rose or John's assistant Gina or put on hold until they were back. My dad and I have a great relationship outside of work, but inside the office, he expects, and I deliver. He expects more, and I continue to push, never wanting to disappoint him.

"Yes, sir, I'll make sure everything is handled here."

"Good, don't let me down. I'll expect a full report on the Pickett briefing. By the way, your mom wanted me to make sure you were still coming to dinner on Saturday when Olivia is in town."

"I'll be there. I'm picking Olivia up on Friday from the airport. I'll be back on Saturday for dinner."

"I'll pass along the message. I'll see you in the office Friday." He says before standing and striding out of the office.

Moving to sit back in my chair, I lean back and run my hand through my hair, glancing at my desk when visions of Charlotte bent over it with me slamming into her from behind invade my thoughts. Lost in my own perverted mind, I didn't realize Elaine walked in to go through my schedule for the week. I'm not sure how long she was here until she snaps me out of my thoughts, "So should I put myself down for a bonus this month?"

"Bonus?"

"There you are, glad to have you back. Just seeing if you heard anything I said in the past five minutes, but a bonus would be nice. I'll send you another copy of your schedule for the rest of the week as several things have been added. You are expected to meet with the interns in fifteen minutes, the Pickett meeting is at one, and you are booked back to back for the rest of the day. Trish from Jonathon's office called to see if you could meet tomorrow at ten. What would you like me to tell her?"

"Yeah, sorry, that'll be fine. Thanks, Elaine. And you do truly deserve a bonus. I'll discuss it with Dad and John at the next budget meeting."

"I was only half serious, but hey, who am I to turn down a raise? Let me know when you want lunch or dinner, and don't even think about sleeping here." She tells me over her shoulder as she turns to leave.

She does deserve a raise or a bonus. She's been my assistant for three years, and without her, I'd be a mess...not that I'd ever admit that. As soon as she leaves, closing the door behind her, the phone rings, James's name flashing. Telling him I'll be there in a few, I stand and button my suit. Time to get work done, preferably without dirty thoughts of a certain blonde running through my mind. If only my dick would get the message.

8

Charlotte

I sit in the conference room going through the files Gavin, James, and Logan had given us. I had done my research on this firm; however, I didn't think to look at other staff besides Daniel Davis and John Jones, the Co-CEOs. Mentally kicking myself for not going through all the staff, I take my phone out, seeing a text from Grace.

GRACE:

How's the morning going? Any hot guys at the office?

We had a good weekend relaxing and hanging out, and although she didn't say much more about Logan and her encounter Friday night, I could tell she was affected. A little worried this might upset her, but I don't keep shit from my best friend. I give the dirt.

ME:

You aren't going to believe this, but those guys from Friday night are all lawyers here.

GRACE:

Are you fucking kidding me?

ME:

I wish I was. When I walked into the conference room, I saw Logan and wanted to nut-punch him for you.

GRACE:

Do it. Just kidding, don't get fired your first day. But I wouldn't mind if you put some

Miralax in his coffee. Lol. Are they all assholes in the office too?

ME:

Too early to tell. It's going to be long days on top of everything else.

GRACE:

Don't let them mess with you. Be the kick-ass Lottie I know! I might not be home when you get home. I am going for a drink after work with a guy I met at the coffee shop this morning.

This was her way of getting her confidence back. Not letting a guy bring her down by going out and having a good time. Grace could get a different date every night of the week if she wanted. She was that gorgeous.

ME:

Ordering up one fierce Lottie. Be safe, text me if you need me. I'll be home late too. I am heading to the library after work to start on a paper since I work at the bar Thursday and Saturday nights.

GRACE:

You work too hard. How late are you working Saturday?

ME:

I'm scheduled till midnight.

GRACE:

I have dinner with a client Saturday, but it should be fast. I'll come have a drink and wait for you to get off.

ME:

You are too good to me. I just have to make it through this year. I love you.

GRACE:

You got this...I love you too

Slipping my phone back into my bag, I dig back in. Looking up, I see Beth side-eyeing me like a teacher who disapproves of my actions while Justin has his head buried. I'm not sure what I did to piss her off, but I can already feel she doesn't like me. She's going to be a treat to work with. I dive back into the information in front of me. The Davis and Jones firm is known for winning. They have brought some of the biggest fraud cases to light and recovered billions of dollars. There is no question that this firm is the best in the country, which is why it is such a sought-after company to intern with, another reason I'm still baffled I got this internship. I'm a great student, I study hard. When my advisor suggested I apply for this internship, I figured it was a long shot. Wanting to work in family law, I thought they would never look twice at my application, but after making it through the written, phone, and zoom interviews, I was shocked when I received the email saying I was accepted. I had applied and been accepted to other internships that were more in my interest of law but having an internship from Davis and Jones would guarantee you a placement at practically any law firm in the country. Now, I was questioning my decision after the meeting this morning.

Lost in my own thoughts, I didn't realize James, Logan, and Gavin had walked back into the room. By the time I look up, everyone is standing, staring at me. Gavin smirks before saying. "Miss Swanson, will you join us, or should we leave you here?"

Mad at myself that I looked like a fool, I gather my things as quickly as possible and stand up. "I'm sorry. I wanted to finish the last paragraph. I'm ready." It was bullshit, and by his facial expression, he knew it. I was grateful he didn't say anything back, simply turning and walking out of the conference room.

We walk down a long hallway, James pointing out another conference room with a copy machine and supplies and a staff lounge. Modern art lines the walls, and the entire office has a sophisticated yet simplistic feel. The gray walls with the black and white furniture work well with small pops of color here and there. The conference room we had been in had modern chairs and a long black table; the second conference room we passed was the same. There were windows everywhere, which let in a lot of natural light, making the space seem airier. Being five floors up, you also have a good view of the city. The lounge has a fancy coffee maker that I don't think I'll know how to use, a gray leather couch, and a black table with oak wood chairs surrounding it, similar to the conference room, just on a much smaller scale. I wonder if anyone even uses the lounge after Gavin stated most meals were eaten in their offices. We come to the end of a hallway and stop in front of a large office with three desks, one on each wall.

Gavin turns, crossing his arms over his chest. He looked good sitting in his suit, but damn, standing so I can appreciate how well his pants fit his ass is something entirely different. I wipe my hand over my mouth, where I'm sure drool might be coming out. At this moment, all I want to do is unbutton his white dress shirt and feel his bare chest. I must look like an idiot daydreaming as James leans against the wall with his lip curled up on one side, and Logan keeps looking at me like he knows me from somewhere. I doubt he remembered my face from last Friday. I wonder if Gavin had told him I knew Grace while we were in the conference room.

"This will be your office. You each have your own desk, but frequently we will convene in the conference room if we are working together or in one of our offices, based on what is needed. Beth, you will team with James. Justin will team with Logan, and Charlotte, you will team with me." My lady parts do a little celebration at his words, *calm down, you hussy,* while my head says, *that is a terrible idea.* Based on my ability to keep my dirty thoughts at bay since seeing Gavin, at this rate, I'll have to buy a whole new collection of underwear from being around him all the time. I need this internship and am so close to the end; I don't have time to let anyone interfere with that. I lean over, whispering quietly,

"Beth, would you like to switch and work with Gavin, and I'll work with James?"

"Is there a problem, Charlotte?" Gavin's eyes filled with teasing curiosity.

"I was just thinking I would be a better team with James since he has some experience in family law, and that is my interest. Beth would be a better match for you since she is interested in corporate law."

James blatantly smiles at him, and Logan just about chokes on his spit, raising his eyebrows at Gavin. Holding my gaze, he adds, "Teams are not up for discussion. We believe cross training in all areas makes the best lawyer, but if you would like to find a family law internship, I'm sure there are others out there." He had me. Internships had started, and would be difficult to switch. I worked so hard to get where I was, I wasn't going to fail now. I could handle being around this man that screamed sex just standing there. *Ha-ha, keep telling yourself that.*

"Understood. I look forward to it, sir."

James gives Gavin a knowing look, taking over and leading us into the room. Beth takes the desk that faces downtown, and Justin takes the other window wall leaving me the desk facing the wall. Great, I get to stare at a gray wall every day. Instead of dwelling on it, I figure I'll be too busy to look outside and could go to a conference room if I need a change of scenery. As we put our stuff down, Beth asked where their offices were, and Logan explained they were on the other side of the floor and that the CEO's offices were a floor up. Glancing at the clock, I see it is already eleven. The IT department had set up our laptops, and James hands us each a folder containing our login information to their system, email, phone, and the software for all their documents. He says to make ourselves comfortable and to meet in the conference room at one to go over our first case. I put my things away, feeling the burn of Gavin's eyes on me, making me hot in more ways than one. Not giving in to looking, I open my computer and start to get to work. He lingers for a few seconds before turning his head and striding out of the office.

I spent the next two hours learning everything I could in the Pickett file, a complicated case in which they were asking for over twenty million in retribution. Two friends that had known each other since college went into business together. For the past few years, things weren't adding up, and they were losing revenue to what appeared to be a profitable software company. Having a team come in without telling his partner of over twenty years, David Pickett found that his thought-to-be best friend and co-founder had been skimming money for years, hiding it in various accounts, and taking other things from him that were on a personal level, his wife included. I memorized all the information I could, and it seemed to impress the team during the meeting when I interject with details when questions were asked. James was professional during the meeting, but Logan's wandering eyes over Beth only made me hate him more after knowing how he treated Grace.

The meeting lasted until after four, and as I stood up with all my things to go back to my desk, someone knocked my elbow, causing me to drop my entire pile of files and papers on the ground, scattering everywhere. I turned just in time to see Beth smirking at me before waltzing out of the conference room. Bitch. My cheeks red from embarrassment and anger, I go to kneel down on the floor to start picking up the papers, not easy in a pencil skirt, but I'll manage, when a hand on my shoulder stops me.

"Let me get that for you," Gavin's eyes bore into mine as he kneels in front of me, picking up my mess of papers.

When I try to kneel to help him, "Don't, Charlotte," the way he says my name makes me pause, "I don't think I can handle seeing you on your knees right now." His lips curl just a tiny bit at the corner as butterflies swirl in my stomach from his words. I stand there like a gaping fish as he collects the rest of my papers, stands up, looking right into my eyes, and places the stack of files in my hands. As his hand brushes mine, my skin ignites, sending tingles up my arm, and my hand instantly warms from the brief contact.

"Thank you," is all I can manage to get out before sliding around him and walking straight to the bathroom to splash water on my reddened cheeks. Looking in the mirror, I can't help but shake my head. This is going to be a lot harder than I thought.

After cooling down in the bathroom, I went back to my desk and organized the files that fell on the floor while I ate a sandwich. I ran out of the conference room so fast that I forgot to ask Gavin if he needed anything else, but since he didn't email or call me, I spent the time familiarizing myself with their system.

It is after six when I finally look at the clock again. I gather my things to head to the library when my email pings with a message from Gavin asking me to stop by his office before leaving.

I finish packing my stuff and walk to where James had said their offices were. I'm not sure what to do since his assistant isn't at her desk, so I go up to the door and knock. I cautiously open the door after hearing Gavin say, "Come in."

Walking in, there is a couch on the left side of the wall with a small black end table to the side and a large dark wood desk that almost looks black sat in the center of the room. Two black leather armchairs sit in front of the desk, and a bookshelf lines the right wall. The doors on both sides of his office make me wonder where they lead, and the back wall has giant windows overlooking Phoenix. Gavin is at his desk with his head down when I walk in, but he must have looked up at some point while I was surveying the room because when I look back at him, those piercing blue eyes are staring right at me.

What would those eyes look like hovering over me? A six-year hiatus is turning you into a monster. For fucks sake, get it together, Charlotte.

"You wanted to see me before I left?" Not knowing what he wants to talk about has me on edge.

"Yeah, I did. I wanted to tell you that I was impressed with how quickly and thoroughly prepared you were with the case we went over today. It's a lot of information to digest." He leans back, looking me up and down, his posture seeming a little apprehensive.

I was not expecting that, but relieved he didn't mention Friday, I reply, "Thank you, I appreciate that." When he doesn't say anything after a few seconds, I add, "If that's all, have a good night."

Praying I'm in the clear, I turn to leave. "I also wanted to clear the air about Friday. I wanted to apologize if I upset you in any way." He thought he upset me and wanted to apologize? Maybe he teased me a little and maybe was a little forward, asking me to go to his place. I was the one who freaked out when I thought I saw Gregory. All he did was wake up my lady bits. I let fear dictate my life again, ruining the first time I felt true attraction to someone in over six years. I feel like a jerk, I'm the one who ran, and he's the one apologizing. I have never been more affected by a simple touch...ever. I didn't know what to do with that information, which messed with my head. Not wanting him to think I'm a lunatic for leaving because I thought I saw someone and definitely not wanting to get into my past, I do the cowardly thing and say, "No need to apologize, I just needed to be up early, I'm sorry I didn't wait for you, we're all good." *Ugh, smooth, idiot.*

"Okay, that's good to know," he smiles as he stands and comes around his desk closer to where I am standing. "It has been bothering me since you left Friday, and I never thought I'd see you again to apologize." He shakes his head slightly like he just gave something away, that he didn't mean to tell me he's been thinking about it since Friday, but he doesn't correct himself. Stunned by his confession and unable to will my feet to move, I stand there until he is inches away from me, his delicious scent invading my space. The air crackles between us as the tension builds, Gavin's eyes dark as he holds my gaze. I can feel my face flush. Gavin reaches out, gently touching my cheek, as hot electricity shoots down my spine to my lady bits, soaking me in an instant as my breath hitches. This feels too intimate, especially after him helping me in the conference room and what he said. So, I take the chickenshit way out, mumbling a "thank you" as I nod and turn and walk out of his touch without saying another word. Thanking the Gods I have my bag, I make my way to the elevator without incident and walk right out the door, heading to the library where I can lose myself in my paper instead of thoughts of Gavin. This will be the longest internship, and I don't know if I will make it out unscathed.

9

Gavin

*I*t's been a long week, and working with Charlotte every day is pure fucking torture. Watching her walk around in pants that shape her ass, skirts that show her tanned, toned legs, and shirts that hint at what's beneath are driving me crazy. Being in the same room with her is sheer agony. When she dropped those papers, I knew if she got on her knees, it would end me, so I rushed to do it for her. Then, getting a touch of her soft skin in my office lit a fire that I can't put out. When she bolted from my office, I wanted to chase her down so I could touch every inch of her skin; my phone ringing was the only thing that stopped me.

I feel unhinged. I need to sleep. Adding my dad's meetings to my packed schedule has had me not getting home until after ten and being back in the office before seven every day. My only reprieve has been working out after work to release some of the tension. I've been jerking off every night to thoughts of Charlotte bent over my desk, on the conference table, in my bed, pretty much every surface just so I can get a few hours of sleep, and even then, she consumes my dreams.

She has come prepared to every meeting, which doesn't surprise me, and stayed late every night except last night when she said she had to leave by seven. When I asked where she was headed, she said she had a study group. She's a shit liar. Her fidgeting with her hands gives her away. I wanted to call her on it and ask where she was going because the thought of her going out with someone else felt like swallowing acid, making me want to punch something, but I held back, forcing myself not to ask questions I wasn't sure I wanted the answer to.

Except it's been gnawing at me since last night, which is part of the reason I'm waiting with breakfast for her to come to my office after sending her an email that I needed to see her. Not only have I noticed she eats for shit in the morning, and I want her to have a good meal, but also, I wanted to gauge her mood. I put the bags of food on my desk as my intercom goes off, Elaine letting me know she's here.

"Send her in, thanks."

A second later, there is a knock on the door, and as she pushes it open, I can't help but stare at her. Her blue sleeveless blouse accentuates her eyes, and her red lips are calling for me to bite down on them to see if she tastes as sweet as she looks. Today, her hair is in a high ponytail, and visions of me wrapping my hand around it for better access to her neck invade my thoughts.

"You wanted to see me?" Her sweet voice snaps me out of my dirty reverie.

"Yeah, come in," using my hand to gesture her to sit in a chair opposite me. "I brought you breakfast."

"Oh, umm, you didn't have to do that." Her face flushes as she stays standing.

"I didn't, but I wanted to. You've been working long hours, and on top of school, I'm sure eating isn't always the first thing on your list. I wasn't sure what you like, so I went with egg, cheese, and avocado. I hope that's okay."

"Oh, Thank you." Her timid voice makes me smile. As she reaches for the bag, I can't help but reach out, my hand lying over hers. The instant I do, her breath hitches: *she feels it too.* I hold my hand there for a second longer than I should, reveling in touching any part of her, and she stays still, her neck pulsating from her increased heart rate.

Pulling the bag toward her, breaking our touch, "I'll just, umm, take this back to my desk. I have a lot to go over before our meeting. Thank you again. You didn't have to do this."

She turns to leave, and before she can get out the door, I call, "Charlotte." She stops, but she doesn't turn around. "You look beautiful today." She takes a quick breath before she walks out of the door. *Yep, pure torture.*

Looking at the clock, it's almost five. I'm trying to finish stuff before I head to the airport to pick up Olivia. If I'm late picking her up, I know there will be hell to pay.

"What's up, asshole?" Logan asks as he walks into my office, making himself at home in the chair opposite my desk.

"Hello to you too, sweetheart. To what do I owe the pleasure of your company?" Honestly, most weeks, we float in and out of each other's offices, going over files. I have barely seen James or Logan this week except in the three meetings we had with shared cases. Besides the stupid ass text chain we have that always seems to end in throwing insults, I haven't caught up with them all week.

"Haven't seen much of your ugly face, and it's Friday, so we're going to change that, dear. We're going out this weekend."

"Can't. I am picking up Olivia from the airport tonight and taking her to my parents, and tomorrow I promised I'd come for dinner while she's in town." Even in my own head, it's a lame excuse, knowing that dinners at my parents' never go late. I would be able to leave even earlier as long as I stop at Wren's Bakery and bring Olivia cheesecake. Still, my sister is rarely around, and I actually miss spending time with her.

"Bullshit, I'm not buying it. Bring Olivia with you. It's been a minute since I've seen that sexy sister of yours," waggling his eyebrows with the sole intent of getting under my skin.

"You aren't going anywhere near my sister, dickhead. Olivia is way out of your league."

"You wound me, friend. First, you take the hottest intern, and now you're cock-blocking me with your sister. The least you can do is meet me out for a few drinks. James is taking Lexi away for the weekend, so you have to come."

Knowing I am not going to get this fool out of my office without giving him something, I relent and say, "James barely comes out anymore. Stop using that sob story. I'll see what time I can leave my parents. Maybe I'll meet you."

"You better, or I'll show up at your parents' and drag you out."

Knowing he's probably not far off, I give him a nod and look at the clock. Shit, it's six. How did I lose track of time? I wanted to see Charlotte before I left, and Logan came in distracting me.

Now it's too late. I won't see her until Monday, which unsettles me, yet probably is for the best. Grabbing my jacket and my briefcase, I shoot an email to Charlotte letting her know I am heading out, and once she finishes up the summaries on the files I gave her before lunch, she is free for the weekend.

"Alright, asshole, get out of my office. I'm heading to get Olivia, and you wasted too much of my time."

Logan laughs and stands. "I'm heading out soon too. Justin is efficient as fuck and is making my job so much easier. Maybe you were right. When you eliminate the desire to sleep with your intern. Hell, you actually get a lot of work done."

Shaking my head at his comment, he walks out in front of me, and I shut my office door. I put my work bag in the back and climb into my black BMW M4. Even though the airport is only four or five miles from downtown, at six o'clock on a Friday night, it will take me at least twenty minutes to get there, and I don't want to be late, or I'll never hear the end of it.

As I pull into the arrival terminal, I can see Olivia walking out with her luggage. Putting my car in park, I get out as she spots me and runs towards me, wrapping her arms around me in a hug I didn't even know I needed.

"Hi, big brother, I missed you," she says into my chest.

"Hey, little sister, I missed you too," kissing the top of her head before wrapping her around my shoulder, guiding her toward the car before airport security starts yelling. I throw her bag in the trunk as she gets in, and we head toward my parents' house as she fills me in on everything LA on the ride there. When we get to our parents', I give her another hug before she heads in, realizing how much I missed our talks. I don't go in with her. I have work to get done, besides I'll be back here tomorrow for dinner.

●

Dinner at my parents' is actually nice. It's been too long since we've all been together, making me feel guilty for being absent from my parents' lives outside of my dad at work. We spent most of dinner catching up on all that Olivia is accomplishing in LA. I couldn't be prouder of my little sister. She is killing it, and I can't wait to see where she goes. I brought Wren's for Olivia today since I pretty much dropped her off last night and left, heading straight home for a workout and crashing. A little peace offering, so my sister didn't hate me for dropping and ditching.

Drinks, dinner, and dessert are done, and we're sitting in the living room. Olivia is on her phone, and my parents are relaxing, which I didn't know my dad knew how to do. I take that as my cue to go home and put a few hours of work in before going to bed.

"Where do you think you're sneaking off to?" My sister's voice perks up as I stand from the red wingback chair I was sitting in.

"I'm going to head out. I told Logan I'd meet him for a drink before heading home." It's not a total lie. I told him maybe, but I plan to bypass that.

"Can you give me a ride?" Olivia asks, climbing off the cream couch she was curled up on. "Gabby and Liza just texted and are out. I thought laying low for two days was what I needed, but after twenty-four hours of lazing, I feel antsy."

"I'm not sure where Logan is, but I don't plan on staying too long, and I don't want to leave you alone."

"I'm twenty-four, not twelve. I'll either grab a cab to your condo or crash at Gabby's. She has a two bedroom and already said I could stay there. My flight isn't until late afternoon, so that gives me plenty of time to come back and get my bag before heading to the airport." She's giving me those puppy dog eyes she knows I can't resist. "Please, big brother, you are going out anyways."

The guilt creeping in for not checking in on her like I should, I relent, "Ok, fine, text them back and see where they're at, and I'll text Logan and have him meet us. I don't like you being out alone, twenty-four or not," grabbing her around her shoulder, tucking her into my side.

Rolling her eyes at my protective big brother bullshit, she pushes off me, kisses my mom on the cheek, and runs up the stairs to get ready. "It's nice to see you taking some time to go out and have fun, Gavin. You work so much at such a young age. I worry about you. We never see you anymore, and when was the last time you went on a date? You're twenty-eight and haven't brought anyone around since Rachel." My mom's kind eyes show her genuine concern. I love my mom, but hearing her say Rachel's name makes my insides cringe. Not that I intend on letting her in on that little fact.

"I'm fine, Mom, don't worry about me. I've been busy. We've got a few big cases coming up, new interns, and meetings with new clients."

"Life isn't all about work, sweetheart. Taking time to enjoy your life with someone makes it all worth it. If you have no one to share it with, what's the point?"

My mom always mentions me not dating. She thought Rachel and I were going to settle down. I haven't told her the details of our breakup, telling my parents I just didn't see it working out versus the ugly, sordid truth of it. I think she knew there was more but never pushed for answers.

Rachel and I met when we were juniors in college, she was studying psychology, and that semester I had decided to take a psychology class, thinking it would help me be able to read clients. The first time I saw her walking out of the building after lecture, I thought she was beautiful, tall with long wavy locks the color of a dark chocolate Hershey's bar that hung down to the middle of her back with green eyes that looked like emeralds. She wore black leggings that showed off her long legs, hugged her hips, and defined her well-rounded ass. Her oversized dark green sweater hanging off of one shoulder made her eyes shine, and the skin peeking out on her shoulder called me. I hadn't seen her before on campus, but something made me walk right up to her and ask if she wanted to get coffee with me that week. I had dated here and there, nothing serious, but after just a few weeks, we fell into an easy routine of spending time at her apartment or the house I shared with my law fraternity brothers. Our relationship was easy and uncomplicated, and the sex was good. Our junior year flew by, and I fell in love for the first time in my life.

The summer between our junior and senior years, she went back home to Palm Springs while I stayed in Arizona, working at my dad's firm. We talked every day, and I took two trips up to see her. Being apart made me realize how much I missed her when we weren't together. We had talked about moving in together our senior year, but she had promised her best friend she would share an apartment, and since I already had a room at the frat house, I decided not to push her on it. The start of our senior year flew by. Before I knew it, I was putting in applications for Law School. She was applying to grad school to get her Master's in Psychology. I flew to California with her for the holidays and spent them with her family and friends. While we were on that trip I asked her dad for permission to propose to her after we graduated. We were still young, but I wanted to start our lives together, even if we waited a few years to actually get married.

We planned to move in together after graduation, and Rachel was going to attend grad school in Phoenix while I attended Law School at Clayton so we could be together, not wanting to spend more time apart. She wanted to become a counselor and said she could start a practice anywhere after graduating, and since Arizona was where I was, this is where she wanted to be. I bought a modest oval ring in a platinum setting, the first big purchase I had ever made, and even got Logan and James in on the plan to help me propose the night after graduation. Everything was going how I envisioned it, and I wanted it to be perfect for my girl. I decided to surprise her at her apartment one night two weeks before graduation when I was supposed to be working late helping at the firm. Things had been so busy between us that we hadn't been able to spend a lot of time together the last few weeks except for a few hours here and there. And that consisted mostly of catching up on sex. I couldn't wait until we could have the summer together and wake up next to each other every morning without the disruption of roommates. I had found the perfect condo for us, and I couldn't wait to show it to her. Someone was coming out of the door as I was walking up, so instead of ringing her apartment, I just went to the door and knocked.

Her roommate Chelsey answered the door. As soon as she saw me, her face turned from a smile to a mixture of surprise and fear. Before I could even say anything, I heard Rachel's voice coming from the hallway, but the noises she was making were the ones she only made for me.

Chelsey tried to stop me. I walked right past her, hearing behind me a mixture of "I'm sorry" and "Gavin, don't." Without thinking it through, I opened her bedroom door, that she didn't even have the decency to lock, to find one of my frat brothers kneeling behind Rachel, who was on all fours on her bed. Her moans filled the room, and my head started to spin as I saw red. They didn't even realize I was there. This was the girl I was going to move in with, propose to, start a life with. I had her dad's blessing. I was so sure about us, and here she was fucking someone I considered a good friend while she thought I was working. I couldn't even find the words. I picked up a picture of us that was on the side table next to the door and threw it against the wall. The sound of the glass smashing had Rachel and Ben looking up. Ben immediately pulled out and scrambled to find his clothes. Rachel's eyes were wide with shock as she tried to cover herself up, which meant shit since I had already seen way too much.

"I'm so sorry, Gav," Ben said as he rushed to pull his sweatpants on. I couldn't even look at the fucker I had called my friend.

"Get the fuck out and pack your shit from the house, Ben. If I see your fucking face back there before graduation, I will end you." I seethed without looking at him, my eyes fixed on Rachel. Ben and I had lived in the same house since Sophomore year. I thought we were friends.

"Gavin..." Rachel pleaded, "Let me explain."

"Yes, please explain to me why I'm here to surprise my girlfriend, and she is sleeping with one of my roommates."

"I just...Gavin, I'm sorry." Her face fell in defeat. "I was going to tell you, honest I was. I just didn't know how. Ben and I started talking a few months ago at one of the mixers at your house on that night you had that conference with your dad. One thing led to another, and... I'm sorry. I didn't mean to fall for him, but I did, and we're moving back to California together this summer before I start grad school in Palm Springs."

I felt like a house had just fallen on me. A few months? Months this has been going on? Moving to California? Grad school...Palm Springs? Everything we had built and planned the last two years was blown apart in a matter of minutes.

"And when were you going to tell me this, Rachel?"

"I've been trying, but we've both been so busy lately."

"Busy, huh yeah, I've been busy working and finding us a place to live, and you've been busy being nailed by my roommate. I'd say our ideas of busy are a little different, Rachel."

"I didn't want you to find out like this, honest I didn't. I wanted to talk to you, but there was never a good time."

"NEVER A GOOD TIME?" I yelled, making her pull back a little. In the almost two years we had been together, I don't think I'd ever even raised my voice at her, but fuck! I couldn't contain my anger right now. "You couldn't find a good time to tell me you are screwing someone else behind my back while still sleeping with me and that you are leaving and moving to another state when we were planning to move in together in three weeks?"

"I'm sorry, Gavin, I didn't mean for Ben to happen. He just did. He's the one for me."

I couldn't help but laugh, which made her confused. "The

one for you? You think someone who is okay fucking you while you are still involved with someone else is the one for you? You are delusional, but you know what? I'm glad. You two deserve each other, thank Jesus I found out before I proposed to you." I didn't mean for that to slip out, but I couldn't take it back now.

"You were going to propose?"

"You know what? Screw this."I couldn't look at her for one second longer. I turned on my heel and walked down the hallway while Chelsey was still standing there with sympathetic eyes. Rachel came running out of her room, but at least Chelsey had the decency to stop her before she could reach me. I kept walking and never looked back, promising myself I would never let another woman in like I had let Rachel. Loving someone was bullshit. It left you vulnerable, and I would never do it again. While I was planning our future, she was banging my friend. I thought she was the one for me, but that night I realized there was no such thing as "the one."

Nope, not going there. Learned my lesson. Suddenly I needed to get out of my parents' house. Now. I need to have a drink and find someone to get this tension out of my body. This is the exact reason I don't think about Rachel. Grabbing my phone out of my pocket, I go to text Logan when Olivia calls out, bounding down the stairs in tight jeans, a pink top, and heels.

"Alright, let's go." She goes to kiss and hug my mom and dad before adding. "I packed my bag and am staying at Gabby's tonight, and she said she'll drop me at the airport tomorrow, so you don't have to come get me and then drive back."

"Have fun and be safe. I'm so glad you came home even

for a day, Livy. We miss you so much and are so proud of you. Your show is going to be a huge success. I know it." My mom stands to hug her properly.

"Love you, Liv." My dad stands, hugging her, before coming over to me and shaking my hand. "Good to see you, son. Glad you could make it for dinner." I shake his hand, itching to get out. My mom's prodding and my walk down memory lane have made me feel uneasy, something I haven't allowed myself to feel since that night.

"Love you guys. Liv, let's head out."

Olivia follows after me with her bag waving to my mom and dad, who stand outside as we head down to my car. She throws her bag in my trunk and gets in the passenger seat. "Can we drop my bag off first before we meet them? Gabby gave me the code to her apartment."

"Sure, that's fine. Where are we headed so I can let Logan know?"

"They're at Cliff's."

I shoot off a text to Logan, telling him where to meet us. I guess it's off to Cliff's we go. I'm ready for a drink and to get thoughts of Rachel out of my head.

10

Charlotte

Saturday nights are always busy, but after this week of interning at the firm, keeping up with work from class, and closing here Thursday night, I'm beyond tired and am not in the mood to deal with people. Spending every day around Gavin is not helping. I haven't slept well since the night I met him, needing my BOB (battery-operated-boyfriend) to get a release so I can get a few hours in. Which seems useless since once I fall asleep, I have dreams of me under him, on top of him, behind me, every which way you can imagine, and it's driving me crazy.

I kept as much distance as possible after the conference room and him touching my cheek in his office because being near him makes me want to wrap my arms around him so I can soak up his scent. When Gavin had breakfast waiting for me on Friday, I wanted to jump him in his chair. Partially because no one has ever brought me breakfast before and partially because a whole week of staring at him in those suits that he fills out perfectly were wearing me down. I have never had such a reaction to a man, and of course, the first guy in six years I want to be around happens to be my "boss." That's why I took the bag back to my office, so I didn't do anything stupid, but not before he told me I was beautiful, and it took everything I had to keep walking. Ever since my talk with Grace, my mind has been reeling about letting go and trying to have some fun, and the first man I even consider doing it with is unavailable.

When he asked me what I was doing on Thursday, I almost gave in and told him I was working here, only I couldn't get the words out, so I told him I had a study group at the library. I think he knew I was lying. If he did, he didn't say anything. *Why do you care? You are not messing up this internship because your vagina wants attention.* Another group of people walk into the bar, and several tickets have come through the register system, alerting me this is going to be a busy night.

"Ugh, my feet are killing me already, and it's only eight o'clock. Wearing wedges was a bad idea." Claire, one of the other bartenders I work most of my shifts with whines, as she grabs a bottle from the shelf next to me. She started working here a few months after I did, and we always get into a good groove when we're both behind the bar. She's a fiery redhead that loves giving guys shit when they come in.

"I told you flats are where it's at on a Saturday night. Especially at the start of the year when everyone is coming out every weekend before classes get intense."

"I know, but my legs look longer in wedges. I'm only five-foot-four Lottie. I need all the help I can get." She smiles and winks at me as she walks away with three drinks in her hand. She may be only five-four, but she can put any man on his back that puts his hands on her without her permission. She is a black belt in Taekwondo, and I wouldn't want to be on the receiving end of her wrath.

"Here you go, guys. Have a great night," I say, handing drinks and shots to a group at the bar before closing out another tab for a couple on their way out.

"How are you doing up here, Lottie? You guys need anything?" Joe says as he comes up with a couple cases of beer and starts restocking.

"No, we're good. I came in early to prep extra since the first few weekends are always busier with students returning to campus."

"Are you coming over for dinner tomorrow? Maria asked earlier this week, and I forgot to mention it on Thursday."

"Yeah, I'll be there. She texted me yesterday since she didn't hear from you. It might be a while before I can come again with school and my internship."

"Sounds good. We know you're busy. I'll be back up later and make sure you and Claire get a break. Shout if you need anything. I'll be in the dungeon cooking," he says as he walks back toward the kitchen. He has been trying to pull back more and let the other staff handle the weekends and late nights, but I know he has a hard time letting go. He treats his staff like family and is always worried about us.

Getting back into a rhythm, the next hour passed quickly. We don't have a DJ, which means staff takes turns making and picking playlists, and tonight is a mix of rock and country that seems to keep the college crowd happy, with a few people up dancing by their tables since we don't have a true dance floor. Morgan Wallen's *You Proof* pours out of the speakers, with people belting out the lyrics as though it was karaoke night. The dart boards and the three pool tables haven't been empty all night. We have two bouncers that card and keep people in line when things get a little crowded or people have had too much.

I am just about to tell Claire to take a break since things are steady when I see Logan walking into the bar, followed by Gavin, who has a woman holding onto his arm. My stomach does a weird flip, and my pulse rate picks up. She is gorgeous, with dark brown hair hanging in thick waves down the middle of her back. It's almost the same color as Gavin's. She's wearing jeans that cling to every curve, a pink one-shoulder top, and heels that would land me in the emergency room. The bombshell must see people she knows because she squeals and runs over, hugging two girls before they wave over a waitress to order drinks. Gavin watches her as he and Logan move toward the table where his date went. The two girls his date hugged stand and hug Gavin, obviously familiar with each other, and stupid me can't take my eyes off them.

Of course, he would be here with someone. *He apologized to you on your first day about his behavior at the club and hasn't spoken to you since unless it was work-related. He's obviously in a relationship, and he didn't want the guilt on his conscience. God, you're such an idiot, lusting after someone who has a girlfriend.*

I need some air. Claire's going to have to wait for her break. Before I can tell her I'm going to step outside, his eyes lock with mine, my breathing instantly becoming shallow, my palms sweaty as I hold them in front of me. He lifts his eyebrow as if he's taunting me. Crap. He leans over and says something to Logan before standing up from his seat and taking a step toward the bar. I walk as fast as I can to the end of the bar towards the door that leads to the kitchen, telling Claire as I pass behind her that I need a minute. I burst through the kitchen doors, ignoring the few kitchen staff, down the hallway past Joe's office door, thank God it's closed, to the back exit. I shove it open as the warm night air hits me, allowing me to take a full breath, filling my lungs with air and slowing my heart rate. Walking a few steps, placing my back against the alley wall, I take a few more deep breaths, steadying myself. I feel like such a fool. *You've been dreaming and fantasizing all week about someone who is taken.* Shame that I didn't see it and disappointment that the first person to make me feel anything is taken churn in my gut. This is why you don't even pretend to want to let people in. I should have known better, after how Logan treated Grace, that Gavin wouldn't be any different.

"Charlotte?" I hear my name, and my head snaps up, seeing a broad male figure standing several feet away from me. It's dark outside, and he's not under a light, so I can't see his face. Instantly, my body switches into high alert, trying to move my hand to the door so I can get back inside. Before I can grab it, the figure steps into the light further, and I realize it is Gavin, stepping toward me with purpose.

Oh no, asshole. Not tonight. I'm exhausted from school and work, and I don't have the physical or mental energy to listen to his excuses. "What are you doing out here? Your girlfriend is probably waiting for her drink." I turn, facing him head-on, my fists clenched at my side, willing him to go back inside so I can finish my shift and go home and sleep.

"Girlfriend?" he questions, lifting his eyebrow and chuckling before continuing. "You mean the woman I came in with?" He paused. "That would be my sister, Olivia, but it's nice to know you were thinking about me."

Wow, Lottie, nothing like showing all your cards right away. Ever heard of keeping things close to your chest?

"Sister...?" I stumble, realizing they looked similar, with the same dark brown hair and sea-blue eyes. Thinking more about it, they even had the same smile. *Crap.*

"Yes, sister. She's in town and wanted to meet some friends, so Logan and I came with her. I don't like her being out by herself. I saw you across the room and came to talk to you, but you turned and bolted. That's the second time you've done that to me. I'm beginning to get a complex." He gives me a small smirk before he takes a step, closing in on the space between us. The smell of his cologne invades my senses, and the ache I've felt between my legs every time I've been in the same room with him starts to pulse.

"I didn't bolt," I mumble. "It was my time for my break, and it's almost over, so I should get back in there." I attempt to turn to go back to the door to my left.

Before I can, Gavin leans into my space, causing me to shift, my back hitting the wall of the building, caging me in, placing his hands on either side of my head. I'm not short by any means, but Gavin has at least five inches on me, dwarfing me in this position. His stance is firm but not threatening, and I can feel my nipples harden from his closeness. Normally any man being this close to me would have me in a panic, because every time Gregory would get this close to me, it was either out of anger or right before he took what he wanted from my body. Being in this position used to make my heart race, having to fight back the fear and nausea that would take over when he got close to me. I wait for that feeling to hit me with Gavin mere inches from my face. My heart is racing, but not from fear, from anticipation. I feel something in my stomach, but it isn't nausea, it's need.

"You look gorgeous, Firecracker. Do you know how many times I've thought of getting you alone this week?" I pause at the nickname he gives me, not sure why he said it, but I love it. He's so close to me I can feel the heat of his breath on my neck as he says the words. Goosebumps pepper my skin, and tingles run up my arms.

Gorgeous? I'm wearing jean shorts and a green tank top with black sneakers since I knew I'd be on my feet all night. My hair is pulled up into a high ponytail, and I only have mascara and lip gloss on. I feel far from gorgeous.

Feeling a little embarrassed, nervous, and a whole lot of tingling between my thighs at the thought of what he would do to me if we were alone, I don't know how to react, so I stand there and shrug my shoulders as if I don't know what he's talking about.

"No? Well, let me enlighten you, Firecracker. I have had very dirty thoughts about you. I shouldn't because you're an intern, but those skirts you've had on this week are driving me wild. All I can think about is running my hands up them to find out if you want me as much as I want you." Hearing his nickname for me only turns me on more.

I am too stunned to say a word. His voice is low and sultry, and hearing him say he's been thinking about me makes me wet. A minute ago, I thought he had a girlfriend, and now he has me pinned to the wall in an alley, telling me that I drive him wild. I'm more turned on than I've ever been.

I might be losing my mind, but something that has been dormant for years awakens, ripping away years of hiding and fear, and letting my past rule me, giving me the courage to be bold, honest, and adventurous. "What if I tell you I've been having some thoughts of my own about you this week?" I don't recognize the voice coming out of my mouth, my tone seductive, and my hand has gone from holding the wall up to being planted firmly on his chest. *I don't know what's happening, but I like it.*

He holds my gaze, his eyes blazing with hunger. "I'd say I want to hear more about these thoughts and make them a reality. Sadly, we don't have that kind of time since you are currently leaning against a wall in an alley, and there is a bar full of people inside wanting drinks." Gavin lifts his head slightly from my neck, his lips ghostly touching the outside of my ear, and I shiver. He whispers with a voice so heavy with lust that I can feel it in my toes, "But I am going to kiss you."

He leans slightly back to look at me, giving me a second to stop this, but when I lift my chin, he takes it as a green light. His lips crash onto mine, in a mix of heat and softness, while one hand strokes my cheek, the other holding me at the base of my neck. He's firm but gentle and glides his tongue along the seam of my lips until I open for him. Once I do, his tongue searches for mine, and the kiss becomes desperate. He pushes off the wall, grabbing my waist as I grab for his shirt with my other hand, fisting the material as he pulls me closer. I have never been kissed like this before. It's dominant and passionate.

He reaches behind me and grabs my ass, giving it a squeeze, and I tighten my thighs together to stave off the ache of desire. He leans against me, and I can feel my erect nipples pressing into his chest while his hard length pushes against my stomach, silently telling me that he is enjoying this as much as I am. I want more, but remembering who he is and where we are—in an alley while I'm supposed to be working—has me gently pulling back, finding his eyes full of pure lust and desire. Touching my hand to my mouth, I can feel my swollen lips from his attention.

"I should...umm...I should probably get back before they start to worry. Shouldn't you get back to your friends?" My breathing is rapid, and my voice is shaky, trying to regain composure.

"My sister is staying with her friends tonight, and Logan won't even notice I'm gone. Leave with me." He grabs my hand and holds it tight, his voice dripping with desire and dominance. He's not asking me a question. It's a command, a wave of electricity runs from where his hand holds mine through my entire body, and I like it.

Trying to keep my breathing under control and my hormones in check, I say, "I can't leave them. It's busy, and I'm here till midnight."

"Then I'll wait for you... I'm not done with you yet." *That voice.* This is a whole different side of Gavin, and I am drawn to it, evidenced by the wetness in my panties and my nipples, so hard they could probably cut glass.

"Okay," I reply quietly, shocked by my own words. It's so out of my character, except I want this for the first time in forever. My head is screaming, *you work with him, this is a bad idea,* but my lady parts are screaming; *yes, it's about damn time!*

I have listened to my head for the past six years, and even though my head knows that getting involved with a co-worker can have negative repercussions, I can't seem to care right now. He gives me a smile that promises all kinds of dirty things, and I shudder at the thought of what's to come. He stands and watches me press in the code and open the door, making sure I get inside safely. I see him turn as I close the door all the way shut, still reeling from our moment.

By the time I get back to the bar to switch with Claire, Gavin is already back with Logan, his sister, and a few others, only his eyes are directed right at me, making my skin tingle, desperate for him to be close to me again, to touch me again. I look at the clock, willing it to speed up. I can still feel his kiss on my lips, and his words ring in my ears... *I'm not done with you yet.*

I should be focusing on work, school, and my internship, not the man undressing me with his eyes from his table. The reasonable me would run, except the reasonable me is a boring chickenshit, who hasn't let go in six years. I don't want to worry about the consequences or what comes next. I just want to feel and live for now, and right now, all I want is *him*.

11

Gavin

*O*kay. One word that had me smiling like a fucking Cheshire cat while my dick was screaming for an escape from my jeans as I walked back to the table where Logan, Olivia, Gabby, and Liza were. The girls didn't seem any the wiser, but Logan had a stupid smirk on his face, proving he knew something. Seeing Charlotte at Cliff's was the last thing I thought would happen when I walked in with Olivia, but damn if it didn't make my night a million times better. That is until she tried to hide from me and slip out. Something snapped inside of me, and I wasn't going to let her get away that easily again. Maybe it had been seeing her in those fitted skirts or the shirts that are just a tease to what lies beneath, or maybe it had been working so closely with her in the office every day, being tortured by her scent. Whatever it was, it had me giving zero fucks about the fact that we work together or the potential consequences as I walked right out the door, desperate to get a minute alone with her.

Lucky for me, the guy at the door worked out at the same gym, and he and I had played pick-up basketball games several times, so when I'd asked him if there was a backdoor, he pointed me to the alley without asking questions. I wasn't even sure she'd be out there, but when I turned the corner of the building and saw her leaning against the wall, my feet stalked toward her without even thinking.

The fact she thought Olivia was my date made me feel like a damn king. Even though she wouldn't admit it, she was jealous. The chemistry between us was palpable. When I gave her a second to refuse before kissing her, I could see the lust in her eyes staring back at me, giving me the go-ahead.

The second our lips touched, a fire lit inside me that I had never felt before. Her lips were like butter that melted at my touch, and when I ran my tongue along the seam, she opened for me like a present on Christmas morning. It took everything I had in me to stop myself from grabbing her ass harder and putting my hand down the front of her shorts just to see how wet she was for me. My guess...she'd be soaked. I wanted her right then, but an alley was not where I wanted anything with Charlotte to happen, and that thought had me reeling.

"Ah-ah-ah, look who's back, you sneaky fucker." Logan gave a dramatic slow clap as I sidled up to the table. I played innocent, though his gaze shifting back and forth between Charlotte and me proved he knew, but I'd hold off as long as I could.

"I went to the bathroom," I say, avoiding eye contact.

"Oh, right, and the bathroom is outside now? Gavin Davis hoarding the hot intern for himself, and lo and behold, we come to the same bar said intern works at, and she and you just happen to go missing at the same time." He waggled a long finger at me. "You can't slip shit past me, Gav. I notice everything. Don't get me wrong, she's hot, but aren't you the one who told me no boinking the interns?"

"What? You and an intern? Damn, Gav, I didn't think you had it in you. Good for you for getting laid." Olivia chimes in as she lifts her hand to give me a high five.

"Fuck off, no one has gotten laid. I didn't even know she worked here. If you remember, we came here to meet Gabby and Liza. It wasn't me who suggested it." I lifted my eyebrows pointedly.

"I say go for it, big bro. You haven't even attempted a relationship since Rachel; yes, I'll say her name, Rachel. You have a lot to offer, and never letting anyone else in would be letting that wench win." I love my sister; however, this is getting a little deep for me.

Logan is about to chime in when his face lights up. I turn to see what he's smiling at and watch who I assume is Charlotte's roommate walk up to the end of the bar and take a seat. Glancing at Logan, his gaze is solely focused on her. Charlotte walks right over to her, and within seconds she is smiling and laughing at something her friend said. *I want to make her laugh like that.*

After a few seconds, I can tell Charlotte mentioned something about me because her cheeks turn a shade of pink, and she lifts her eyes ever so slightly in my direction before her roommate, Grace, turns and looks in our direction. Grace smiles for a second before her eyes scan slightly to my left, and that smile turns to a straight, firm line, her eyes narrowing on her target. She turns back around as if looking over here just burned her, and I put the pieces together. If looks could kill, Logan would be dead, done-zo, finished, toast.

Does that deter Logan? Of course not. He puts his drink down and stalks toward where she is sitting on the stool like a fucking peacock fanning his feathers. Charlotte looks pensive as she sees him coming, gives her friend a nod, and stands back a few feet. If I was a good person, I would feel bad for what happens in the next few minutes, except seeing Logan have his ass handed to him by a woman for the first time in, well, forever, is highly entertaining. I can't hear what she says exactly, but her scowl and his face say it all. Grace finishes her rant and turns, completely ignoring Logan's attempts to talk to her. The poor guy should know when to give up, but he's a persistent fucker until she throws her hands in the air, says something to Charlotte, grabs her things, and leaves. Logan starts to walk after her before thinking better of it. He sulks back to our table like a puppy with his tail between his legs. I can't help but cross my arms over my chest and shake my head at the man.

"Damn, dude, that looked brutal. Not the reunion you thought it would be, hey?" I'm trying to fight my smile, failing miserably. This is just too good.

"Fuck man, she legit hates me. Handed me my ass and told me she hopes I get syphilis and my penis falls off. My balls tried to crawl back into my stomach with her even mentioning that word."

I burst out laughing, not being able to help myself. "Sorry, that shit is funny. The famous panty-dropping Logan finally got his ass handed to him by a woman. One word, my man, Karma."

"Nah, man, I just need some time and more

opportunities to turn it around." He sounds confident and stands taller, although he looks a little wounded.

"Turn what around? She seemed pretty clear she didn't want whatever you were offering, and since when do you go back for seconds?"

"We have unfinished business, and I intend to finish it. She just doesn't know it yet."

"Good luck with that," I say, patting him on the shoulder. He shakes me off like he's unaffected, but Logan's demeanor says differently. His ego took a hit tonight, and his alcohol consumption reflects that.

Four shots and a few drinks later, he is now determined, and I can't say I'm not disappointed when a brunette walks up to him and whispers something in his ear, and he gets that look. Waggling his eyebrows at me leans over, "We're leaving, going to go deep sea diving, if you know what I mean. Enjoy the intern, and don't think you're off the hook. We'll be coming back to that shit tomorrow."

"I'm going to ignore your comment about Charlotte. Are you sure you know what you're doing?" Usually I don't give two shits what Logan does, but I know Grace affected him, and I think he actually feels a pull toward her. So, Charlotte seeing him leave with another woman is not going to bode well for his chances at getting more opportunities with Grace.

Alcohol and a bruised ego—not a good combination for Logan—seem to trump logic. "Yep. I'm out." Logan puts his arm around brunette whoever's neck and heads toward the door. At least I know he won't be driving since he doesn't have his car. I look up and connect with Charlotte's eyes. You can clearly tell she's pissed seeing him as she shakes her head, looks at me, and turns to make a few more drinks. Is she pissed at me? How was I supposed to stop him?

Olivia and her friends decide to go to another bar around eleven-thirty. "You staying here waiting for her says a lot Gav; just saying. One-night stands only get you so far. Don't be a dick." For a younger sibling, she seems to have me pegged. I hug my sister and tell her to text me when they get back to Gabby's so I know she made it safely before watching them all walk out the door in a fit of giggles.

I take the opportunity to go to the bathroom, and when I return, Charlotte is talking to the other bartender at the end of the bar. Watching her while she works and not being able to touch her since she went back inside is torture. I've been thinking about all the ways I want to explore her tonight. It also makes me worry that the moment may have passed for her, which I hope isn't the case. Seeing as it's just after midnight, I walk toward her and see an older guy, maybe in his fifties if I had to guess, come through the kitchen and stop in front of Charlotte. I stay a few feet back while he talks to her.

"I thought Grace was coming in tonight?"

"She did, but she saw someone she didn't want to see, so she left. I'm fine, Joe. My apartment is a few blocks away."

"Let me grab Conner to walk you home. You know I don't let anyone leave alone. You never know what could happen."

Before thinking if she'd want me to, I hear myself saying, "I'll make sure she gets home safe." Reaching out my hand to the man who clearly cares for Charlotte's safety, I say, "I'm Gavin. I work at the law firm where Charlotte interns, and since Grace left early, I told Charlotte I'd give her a ride." He eyes me warily and takes my hand with a handshake so firm it is clearly warning me not to mess with her. I grab just as hard back and keep eye contact, silently saying I got her.

"Are you sure, Lottie? I've never heard you mention this guy's name; not sure he should be driving you home."

"I'm good, really, Joe."

"Fine, but text me when you get home, so I know you are safe. You know we worry about you."

"Deal, see you tomorrow."

"Night, Lottie, I'll be waiting for that text," he says, staring me down like a father watching his daughter go out on a first date.

"She's in good hands. I'll make sure she's taken care of." I know she can handle herself, but I couldn't stop myself.

"You'd better. See you tomorrow, Lottie." He's still eying me, and I'm glad she has someone in her corner looking out for her.

"Night, Joe." She hugs him before walking toward the door with me on her heels. She says goodnight to the bouncers, and I nod at them. She seems tense, and I can't quite read her as we make our way out onto the sidewalk. We walk about fifty feet in the opposite direction of my car before she turns around and looks at me. She's about to tell me she's changed her mind, I can feel it, so before she gets the chance, I cut her off.

"Don't. I see your mind turning. You're going to tell me earlier was a mistake, which would be a lie." She hasn't run yet, so I step closer, cupping her cheek and rubbing my thumb along it. "I know you can feel this energy between us. I felt it the first night I met you and every day this week. I can feel your presence when you are within ten feet of me. Fuck if I know what that means, but don't shut this down, Charlotte." I move into her space, mere inches from her. "Come to my condo and have a drink. Whenever you want to go, I'll make sure you are safe. Don't pretend what happened earlier meant nothing. I meant what I said before. I'm not done with you yet." I really want to throw her over my shoulder and not give her a choice. Instead, I control my inner caveman and wait for her response. After a few pensive seconds, she looks up at me.

"Okay."

That seems to be her go-to response when she's battling between what her body wants and what her mind is telling her. Before her mind wins, I reach out and take her hand in mine. When our skin connects, electricity shoots up my arm all the way to my spine, and my dick instantly stands at attention. *Touching her hand makes you hard? What are you, fifteen?* Turning us both, I head towards my car. I only had one beer and then switched to soda after kissing her in the alley, so I could drive. I open the door for her, and she climbs in. Closing the door, I head to my side of the car and settle into the driver's seat. My condo isn't far from here, and I can't wait to have her all to myself. The fact that I've never brought a woman back to my place is not lost on me, but I'll deal with that thought later. Right now, I need to get her alone and continue where we left off in the alley...if she'll let me.

12

Charlotte

*A*fter Grace's run-in with Logan, I should have gone straight home to check on her, except knowing her, she would have deadbolted the door. She said so herself. After I told her what happened in the alley while she was sitting at the bar, she said, "If you even try to come home tonight, you can cozy up in the hallway cuz I'm deadbolting your ass out." She reminded me to live my life unafraid and for me, which is what has me getting out of Gavin's black BMW after we parked in an underground garage and walking toward the elevator.

We didn't talk much on the way over, but Gavin reached for my hand and held it the entire way. My hand fit perfectly in his, and as he rubbed small circles on my thumb, I could feel his warmth through my entire body. I was afraid if I said something, I would talk myself out of coming here and ask him to take me home. Deep down, I didn't want to, but I still have a long way to go when it comes to living in the moment. This, right here, is as much of living in the moment as I have done in six years, hell, my entire life.

The elevator doors open, and we walk in. Gavin swipes a card and hits "P," which I can only assume means penthouse. *He lives in the penthouse?He is so far out of your league, Charlotte.*

Snapping me out of my stupor, Gavin prods, "Stop thinking."

"I...uh...you live in the penthouse?"

"Yes, I do. Is that a problem, Firecracker?" His eyebrows lift like he's nervous I'm going to bolt.

"No, it's just, I've never been in a penthouse. Why do you call me Firecracker?" I ask, trying to contain my nerves.

"Because you have a fire and a strength in you that I don't even think you realize, and you light up a room whenever you enter. You burn bright, and damn if I don't want to bask in the glow you create," he says as he looks at me with a smile that melts my insides. I've never been one for pet names. *Until now.*

The elevator comes to a stop, and the doors open to a small open area and one door. Gavin waits for me to walk out of the elevator and pulls out a key for the door. He opens it and waits for me to walk through. Stepping into his condo, I notice that the back wall is floor-to-ceiling windows so you can see the Phoenix skyline. The dark wood floors run through the entire open-concept living space. Two couches separated by a coffee table with a thick wood top span the living room with a huge TV over an expansive gas fireplace. Everything feels open and airy, with modern touches that make the space look clean but not cold. A hallway to the right and to the left opens up to a dining area, which I'm guessing is the kitchen.

Before I walk further toward the living room, Gavin grabs my waist and spins me to the door he closed without me noticing. Any other time a man would touch me, I would tense, but Gavin's touch lights my body on fire in ways I've never experienced. His touch is strong but gentle, making me feel both safe and desired.

"I don't think I can wait any longer. Kissing you in the alley and then having to watch you behind that bar for another two hours almost killed me. Watching all those guys smiling and trying to flirt with you made me want to punch something, and I'm not sure what to do with that. I want to be a gentleman, but damn it, Charlotte, I'm hanging by a thread."

I'm nervous. I'm inexperienced, only having sex with one other person. I've relied on a battery-operated stick to give me pleasure since I was eighteen. I have a million things running through my head.

This is a mistake.

This could ruin your internship.

He smells delicious

I want to climb him like a koala.

What if I suck at this?

It's been six years. Live for now, Lottie.

What happens after...

The mental montage could go on for hours if I let it. Gavin senses me overthinking and leans in, capturing my lips before I can talk myself around anymore. His kiss is demanding, sliding his tongue on my lips and pushing them to gain entrance. My nipples harden like icepicks stabbing him in the chest where our bodies connect as his hardened length presses into my stomach. A flush of arousal rushes through me from his touch. *Oh, sweet Jesus, this man knows how to kiss.*

Gavin grabs my thighs and hoists me up, pressing me back into the door as my legs voluntarily wrap around his waist. My hands move down his back, my nails scratching as they go as if I'm trying to rip the wrapping paper off a gift. His hands grasp my hips, squeezing me, letting a guttural moan escape his lips. He squeezes a little harder, causing me to tighten my legs around his waist. My phone chimes from my back pocket. I try to ignore it until I realize I never texted Grace, letting her know I was safe. I pull back slightly, looking up at Gavin, who has a concerned look on his face, "I'm sorry, I should check that. It's probably my roommate, Grace. I told her I'd text her when I got here."

His concerned face relaxes almost instantaneously. Attempting to slow his own panting breaths, he says, "I'll go grab us some water."

He slides me down his chest, so my feet hit the floor before turning and heading toward where I am guessing the kitchen is. Pulling out my phone. I see exactly what I was expecting.

GRACE:

Just making sure you're safe.

I text back quickly.

ME:

I'm safe. We just got to Gavin's. Not sure how long I'll stay, don't deadbolt me out.

GRACE:

I won't, but don't run. For once in your life, Lottie, let go. You need anything, you know what to do.

ME:

I want to...I really do. And yep, never forget, I love you.

GRACE:

Love you too. See you tomorrow ;)

I want to respond with a don't be so sure, but I know she'll keep going back and forth until she's satisfied. Grace and I made a safe word back in undergrad that if anything bad had ever happened, but we couldn't explain, one word would clue us in. Sunshine. We also had our phones linked so I could track her and her me if needed. We've never had to use it, thank God, but it gives us a sense of safety.

I text Joe quickly too, letting him know I'm safe before sliding my phone back into my pocket and heading toward where Gavin went. Further into the condo, the dining room is on the left and opens to the kitchen, where I find Gavin standing, leaning against the counter. The kitchen is big and open with all-white cabinets, gray slate countertops, and top-of-the-line appliances. There is a large breakfast bar that has four black metal stools at it. I am about to pull one out and take a seat when Gavin pushes off the counter and stalks towards me.

"Don't sit down," he says with his eyes so dark blue that he looks transfixed as he takes another step.

"Oh...umm...ok." I stand with the intent of walking toward the door. I only make a quarter turn when he says, "Where are you going? I told you not to sit down. I didn't say anything about walking anywhere." He's about four steps away from me.

"I thought maybe you wanted to take me home." *God, Lottie, get it together.*

Two steps away.

One step.

Gavin is right in front of me, leaning down, brushing against my lips before moving toward my ear. "I told you I wasn't done with you yet, never mentioned wanting you to leave. I told you not to sit because I plan to carry you to my bedroom and find out what's beneath these shorts that mold to your ass so perfectly. Now if you want to leave, I respect that, and I'll take you home. I'm not that guy. But if you want to do this, see what this is, jump up and hold on, Firecracker."

Hearing him call me that and knowing why he does has me squeezing my thighs together to stave off the ache pulsing in my core.

I want to jump.

I'm scared.

So many thoughts are running through my head, but one sticks out clearer than all the others. *Let go, Lottie.* Letting go is something I haven't done since I left Cedar Ridge. *How much have I missed by holding onto my fears so tightly?* Grace is right. Living in fear and always shutting people out is letting Gregory win. I refuse to let him rule my life anymore. As if a switch flips, lighting my darkened, dull life up for me again, I am ready to take on the world. Or at least for now, jump into Gavin's arms and see where that takes us, but you know, who says you shouldn't reach for the stars.

Not giving myself more time to second guess, I leap up and wrap my legs around him tightly. I look into his eyes, and with confidence I'm not sure I've ever had, I tell him, "I don't want to leave. I want to see what this is. I'm holding on, so take me for a ride." The words sound foreign leaving my mouth, but new Lottie is going with it.

Gavin gives me a wicked smile as he heads toward the hallway with me wrapped around him, "Oh, beautiful girl, I plan on it."

We pass several doors and come to the end of a hallway. He kicks the door open with his foot and carries me into his bedroom. The wall of the door we walked through was gray with a long, black dresser with a TV mounted on the wall. I look to my right, seeing another wall full of windows, the same as in the living room. There are shades on them that are halfway down. Turning to my left, I see a walk-in closet and next to that, an open door I'm assuming is a bathroom. Gavin lowers me down, and my butt comes in contact with the edge of his king-sized bed. I look around, taking the whole room in, before placing my hands down, feeling the soft navy comforter beneath me, and leaning back, pushing myself further onto the bed.

Gavin stands back, undoing his green button-down shirt, and my breath hitches. One button. Two. Three. I can't take my eyes off him, my mouth gaping open in awe. As he slides the shirt off his shoulders, his chest and arms are on full display, and I realize that this man is built. Tight muscular arms, a broad chest with a minimal sprinkling of dark hair at the top, and abs that I swear if I wasn't seeing form myself I'd think were fake. His stomach muscles create the perfect V leading down to his dark jeans sitting low on his hips. I sit up on my knees and reach for the button on his jeans.

"Uh-uh-uh, patience, Charlotte. All good things come to those who wait," he says, smirking at me as I look up at him. He reaches down and grabs the hem of my shirt, and I lift my arms so he can slide it over my head. Slowly, he reaches behind my back and undoes the clasp of my black lace bra, sliding it down each of my arms. Kneeling before him in my jean shorts and bare chest, he gently presses on my stomach so I'm lying on my back. Grabbing my legs, he pulls me down until they dangle off the bed.

"Still too many clothes. Take your shorts off." That voice will be my undoing. I hesitate for a second before sliding my hands to the top of my shorts, undoing the one button, and sliding the small zipper down. I lift my hips slightly and slide the shorts over my hips, revealing a matching pair of black lace underwear. I may not have much money, but I like to feel pretty. You'd be amazed at the deals you can find on the clearance racks at TJ Maxx. I slide my shorts the rest of the way off and let them fall to the floor.

"So. Fucking. Beautiful." Gavin leans over me, placing his hands on either side of my head, caging me in before capturing my lips with his. He starts there before releasing me and leaving a trail of kisses down my neck and over my collarbone. I writhe beneath him, a hunger building inside me that I have never felt. Sensing my need, he takes one of my nipples into his mouth and sucks hard, causing me to gasp.

Releasing my nipple with a pop, he smiles at me. "You like that, Firecracker?" He returns to his glorious assault before I can even respond. Circling his tongue around the bud, he moves to my other breast, not wanting her to feel left out. His tongue is hot on my breasts, and I can feel his touch down to my toes. He releases my nipple and kisses down my stomach before kneeling off the bed, sliding my underwear off, leaving me bare to him. He grabs my leg, putting it over his shoulder.

I have never had a man go down on me. Gregory was

only ever interested in his own needs after the first few times, and he never used his tongue. He'd push a finger inside me once or twice to make sure I was ready for him, and if I winced or whimpered when he entered, he would slam in harder.

Shivering from those memories, Gavin must sense it and lifts his head up, "Are you okay with this?" Genuine concern crossing his face.

"Y-Yes," I stumble, "I've, umm, never done this before." I turn my head to avoid his stare.

Gavin gently puts my leg down, my body immediately missing the heat from his touch, and slides up my body, turning my head to look at him. "Charlotte, we don't have to do anything you don't want to do. I want to make you feel good, but if you aren't ready..."

Finding my backbone, I turn my head and look at him, losing myself in his blue eyes. "I. Want. You."

That's the green light for Gavin, smiling and kissing my lips chastely before returning to his position with my leg over his shoulder. He plants kisses on my inner thigh and licks his way up until he's just below my sex. He lifts his head slightly. "You smell amazing. I can't wait to taste you," he says before dipping his head back down. My breath catches when he licks me from the tip all the way down. *Oh, my God.* He does it again with more pressure, and my body is already climbing. Sensations I have never felt before are going off in my body as I grab the sheet with one hand, my other hand going to his hair and holding on.

"Oh...oh...that feels so good," I pant as he continues worshiping me. Lick, suck, circle. It's only a few more times until I feel it starting in my toes, and I cry out. "Gavin, I'm going to come." I try to push his head away, but he presses in further as I come undone on his tongue, my body writhing and turning with explosions of pleasure I have never felt before. *So this is what it's supposed to feel like.* He licks me clean before sitting back on his heels, smiling. "Sweet and delicious. I knew it. I could feast on you all day." I blush.

I'm still lying there, feeling boneless after my intense orgasm as he stands and undoes his jeans and slides them down, letting them pool at his feet. His boxers are next, and I almost giggle, watching him spring free like an animal trying to escape its cage. My eyes widen at the sight. Gavin stands naked before me, and I can't help but gawk a little. He. Is. Beautiful. Not even sure if you should call a man that, but I did, and I'm not ashamed of it.

There is a little light coming through the windows from the city, and he looks like a dream standing in front of me. He walks around his king-size bed to the nightstand and opens the drawer, pulling out a condom. Walking back around toward me, he leans over, sliding me up the bed until my head is on the pillows as he crawls up, leaning over the top of me, caging me in, hands on either side of my head.

He lifts one arm and reaches down, stroking his length a few times and using his other hand to hold his weight as he stares into my eyes. "I'll ask you again, Charlotte. Are you sure about this? Now that I've tasted you, I want to feel you come undone with me inside you."

"Yes, but...umm...I'm not sure it'll fit," I say quietly, embarrassed by my lack of experience.

"It'll fit. I would never hurt you." Gavin leans forward and kisses me so deeply I feel it in my bones. While still connected to my lips, he tilts himself off me onto his side, sliding his hand over my stomach down to my sex, making slow circles with his thumb. My clit is still sensitive from my orgasm, but when Gavin pinches it gently, I feel a gush of wetness, my pleasure building. "So. Wet." He slowly presses a finger into me, circling it slightly before pulsing in and out a few times, my body responding with jolts of pleasure.

"Ahh, Gavin, don't stop," I plead. He adds another finger, and I can feel the burn of the stretch. Once he's in, he lets me adjust before pulsing in and out, increasing speed and force. Gregory was always rough, and it hurt. This is a totally new experience. The intent to pleasure me, not himself.

"Hmmm, that feels so good." I whimper. *I can't possibly orgasm again.*

Gavin picks up the pace and crooks his finger, hitting that spot inside me no one ever has, and I moan in pleasure. He takes that as his go-ahead and pumps harder as I buck my hips to match his pace, now chasing my own pleasure. A few more times, and I'm coming undone again as another orgasm rips through me, causing me to see stars. *If I die right now, I'd be satisfied.* Before I can come down from my orgasm high, Gavin rips the condom open and sheaths himself, rolling back on top of me and placing himself at my entrance.

"I'll go slow, it might sting a little, but once I'm in, I'll give you time to adjust." The gentleness in his tone has me nodding in understanding. He pushes forward until the tip is in, and I tense slightly. "Relax, baby. Breathe." Taking a deep breath helps me to loosen, and I can feel my body relax. Pushing in slowly, Gavin watches me the entire time. It's tight and a little painful, breathing helps me to relax, and the pain is quickly replaced by a sense of fullness in the best way. He thrusts one more time, looking at me, "I'm in. God, you feel amazing." I nod to let him know I'm good, and he pulls out and pushes back in with a little more force this time. And ahhh, does that feel different in the best way. The pain that was there is replaced by tingles of pleasure as he continues to thrust, increasing his pace with every stroke. "You are so tight. I won't last long." After a few more thrusts, I feel the need to get closer to him, wrapping my legs around his waist to tilt my hips up. Ooh, that feels deeper.

From that angle, he hits a spot inside me that lights me on fire. A few more thrusts and out of nowhere, another orgasm rips through me as I chant his name like a prayer.

"Charlotte. Fuuuckkk...." His words are a jumbled mess with a few more thrusts before he stills inside of me, and I can feel his release as he twitches from his own orgasm. He stays still, riding out his pleasure before leaning down and taking my lips in a soft and gentle kiss.

"That was amazing. You. Were. Amazing." He holds my chin, not letting me look away even as shyness tries to creep in. "I'm going to get rid of this condom, and I'll be right back." Gavin slowly pulls out, and I instantaneously miss the feeling of him inside me. He stands and walks into the bathroom while I lay there in post-orgasmic bliss. When he gets back, I take my turn in the bathroom as well, and when I walk back toward the bed, Gavin is lying on his back with the covers turned down. One arm under his head and the other outstretched, welcoming me back.

"Climb in."

"Are you sure? I don't want you to—I mean, I can get a cab and...," I mutter, feeling extremely awkward now that my euphoric haze has lifted.

"Get your sweet ass in here, Charlotte, before I come

make you," he says jokingly, so I know he's not threatening in a serious way. At least, I don't think he is.

Trying to push my insecurities aside, I walk toward the bed and reach for my underwear. "No clothes allowed," Gavin demands with a grin before I can put them on.

"Okay." I give him a shy smile and climb into bed next to him naked. As soon as I sidle up to him, I feel this overwhelming sense of calmness that makes me instantly want to curl up and stay here forever. I lay my head on his chest, and he wraps his outstretched arm around me, rubbing small circles on my back.

"How are we going to do this? I mean, that is if you want to do this?" I mentally kick myself for opening my big fat mouth.

"Let's figure it out in the morning. I don't know all the specifics, but I know that I want more of you, Fire, and that's saying a lot for me," he responds, placing a kiss on the top of my head.

My breathing evens out as I lay on his chest, and the last thing I hear is him whispering something I couldn't quite make out before losing myself to the best night's sleep I've had in six years.

13

Gavin

Grateful that I closed the shades before climbing back into bed last night, I gently roll over and check the time, nine-thirty a.m. I haven't slept this late or solid since college. Looking over at the sleeping beauty on my pillow, on her side facing me, her blonde hair splayed across the light gray fabric, her face looking like an angel. The sheet has fallen, so her breasts and the top of her stomach are exposed, one hand tucked under her pillow, the other relaxed by her side. I could watch her sleep for hours.

After crawling into bed with me last night, she fit into the crook of my arm like she was made to be there. I could tell she was nervous to talk about what this meant after she came out of the bathroom. When I suggested tabling it for the night, she didn't seem upset by it. She was exhausted after three orgasms, *not that I'm counting or anything*, her breathing evening out after a few minutes with her head on my chest as I rubbed circles on her back. I couldn't help whispering, *mine,* before kissing her head and nodding off.

Visions of last night fly through my head. The way her body responded to me and how she tasted when she came was incredible. Then watching her come undone on my fingers and again underneath me, squeezing my cock like a vice grip, was my undoing. God, the way she looked when she lost control, her body tightening, eyes squeezed close, face cinched up, and chanting my name like a prayer on her lips, is forever imprinted in my brain. She may be inexperienced, but sex with Charlotte was easily the best I've ever had. *Because it was with her.*

I've had a lot of meaningless sex over the past four years. Something to scratch an itch, no feelings, no strings, a means to an end. From the moment I saw Charlotte, something pulled me toward her. I wanted to know her. Touch her. Feel her. The way her body opened to me last night was amazing. Now that I've had a taste, my thirst for her has increased tenfold. I don't think I'll ever get enough. I only hope the light of day doesn't bring regret on her part, 'cuz I sure as shit don't regret it. Our situation isn't ideal since we work together, but damn if I'm not determined to figure it out and see where this goes. *I know, I know, shocking, right?*

Charlotte stirs and slowly opens her eyes. I feel a little like a creeper staring at her while she sleeps, yet I can't tear my eyes away from her beautiful face. She blinks sleepily and looks back at me. Her eyes widen a little for a second before relaxing, a small smile forming on her lips when I whisper, "Good morning, beautiful girl."

Tucking her hand under her chin, she says, "Good

morning," before covering her mouth, "sorry, I probably have morning breath."

Leaning my head forward, I capture her lips with mine, caressing her tongue with mine as she opens for me. I continue my onslaught of kisses before pulling back slightly, "Nope, no morning breath. Absolutely perfect. Are you sore?"

"A little, but in a good way, if that makes sense," she reaches for the covers trying to pull them to cover herself. I grab her wrist gently to stop her.

"Don't cover up. Your naked body happens to be one of my new favorite things to look at."

She pauses before dropping the sheet and moving her hand to my chest, and rubbing her hand down it slowly. "Ditto."

I reach out and pull her close to me and hike her thigh over mine. She doesn't resist as I slide my hand down lower between us and find her warm center, circling her clit slowly. Charlotte closes her eyes and lets out the sexiest moan I've ever heard.

"So wet for me, my sweet Charlotte," I say as I lean close to her ear, increasing my speed and pressure a little. I slip down lower and slide two fingers into her center. She arches into me as I enter her, a soft "mmmm" escaping her lips.

"You like that, baby?" I slowly push in and out before crooking my finger up on the next push in.

"Oh my, yes."

Her eyes are closed, but she is writhing into me, pressing down onto my fingers to find her own rhythm. I can tell she's close as she tightens around my fingers, her moans increasing and her hand going from my chest to my shoulder and pulling me toward her.

Three more pumps, and I can feel her coming on my fingers. The look on her face—mouth slightly agape, eyes closed, head back—as her back arches into me when she comes is so fucking sexy. My fingers ride out her orgasm before slowly sliding out of her.

"Open your eyes, Charlotte."

As she slowly does, I slide the two fingers that were just in her into my mouth, licking her essence off them, tasting her sweet nectar. Her eyes show a shy side of her, but how her body responds to me is completely different. I can feel the shivers down her body, her hard nipples peaking, while her toes gently dig into the back of my calf. Charlotte's body is dying to be worshiped. Explored. Cared for.

I slide her leg off of me and pull her under me, reaching over and pulling another condom from the top drawer. I lift up slightly, rip the package, and roll it on. Grabbing my length and giving a few strong strokes, I guide it to her entrance, rubbing it up and down through her slickness.

"Does that feel good, Charlotte?" I ask as her legs fall open wider, allowing me to push in slightly.

"God, yes, I need to feel you inside of me," she groans, arching her hips to encourage me further.

Grabbing the side of her hip, I thrust in all the way in one strong stroke, and she gasps, a soft, feminine little sound that goes straight to my groin. Feeling her tense, I stop, making small circles to let her adjust, "Are you ok?"

"Yes, just needed a second. You can move." Her eyes are locked on mine. I can tell by the way she looks at me she's ready.

I start to move with more force and speed than I did last night. I didn't want to hurt her, but it took everything I had in me to hold back from taking her the way I wanted to. Charlotte digs her heels into the bed and lifts her hips, creating a new angle and allowing me to get deeper.

"You are perfect. It's like you were made to fit around me," I confess as I push harder into her. She responds with a moan as I feel her body start to tense again. I lower one hand and flick my finger over her clit. Balancing on one hand while slamming into her isn't easy—thank you pushups and triceps dips—but seeing her fall over the edge again, chanting my name, makes it totally worth it.

Two more thrusts, and I follow her into my own release, my entire body buzzing. I couldn't hold back anymore, watching her come undone, her muscles squeezing me so tight I shot off like a rocket inside the condom. Seeing starts from the orgasm that rips through me. I wait until my body comes down from its high before sliding out and rolling onto my back, waiting for my breathing to even out.

"You are the definition of perfection." I turn my head to look at her. I've never been a sweet talker, but she brings out a side of me I didn't even know existed. I want her to know how she makes me feel and what her body does to mine.

Smirking, she responds cheekily, "You aren't so bad yourself." The smile that follows her response makes my heart beat faster again.

"Do you want a shower before breakfast?" I pray she isn't going to jump out of this bed and run.

"That would be great. I usually take a shower when I get home from working a shift. That obviously didn't happen. On top of our own extracurricular activities, I could definitely use one." I'm getting more than two- and three-word responses, so I'll take that as a good sign.

"I'll get you a towel and grab some girl stuff for the shower. I keep it in the other bathroom for when my sister stays here. I'll be right back." She gifts me a shy nod as I throw back the covers and slide out of bed. I pull on a pair of black athletic shorts that were lying on the floor from the other night.

My heart skips a beat when I find her still lying in bed when I quickly stride back into the room. I'm desperate to be beside her again. *A feeling I've never had before.* Even popping into the next room was too long to be away from her. *I'm so screwed.*

With my arms full of my sister's many beauty products, I fan them out on the bed to allow her to choose what scent she prefers. I turn and walk into the bathroom, the urge to look after her needs driving me, and turn on the shower to warm it up before grabbing a towel from the rack and carefully placing it on the side, so it's waiting for her when she's finished.

Heading back into my bedroom, I stop in my tracks and my mouth turns dry as Charlotte stands before me in all her naked beauty. Flawless skin. Toned. And every inch of her begging to be worshiped. Memories of last night fill my head, making my cock twitch in my shorts.

"Are you going to join me? Or am I showering alone?" Gone is the shy Charlotte of last night. Before me stands a woman confident in her body and what she wants.

I don't even get a response out before she beats me to it. "I'd say the answer is yes if we go off what he thinks," she says, looking down at my full erection trying to escape my shorts.

"Hell yes, I will," I manage to get out as she walks towards me, grabbing my hand and leading me into the shower. *This girl is unexpected in all the best ways.*

Twenty minutes and two orgasms later, we are standing

in the bathroom as I help her dry her back and blonde locks off.

"No one has ever dried my back or hair for me," she smiles as she turns over her shoulder to look at me, "Unless you count my mom when I was a kid."

The minute she mentions her mom, her face falls, sadness instantly filling her eyes, as if she regrets saying that. She turns back around and her demeanor changes. Shoulders tensing and standing stiff.

"Are you close with your mom?" I can't help asking, feeling the need to know everything about her.

She doesn't look at me, "We used to be."

Letting the towel drop, I grab her shoulders, pulling her back to my chest, "I'm so sorry, Charlotte. I can't imagine losing a parent."

She doesn't pull away, but she's still tense. "She isn't dead. It's just been a while since I've talked to her. It's a long story." I can see her profile in the mirror, and the drop in her face makes my heart ache for her.

I want to know her story.

I want to make it so her face never looks like that.

It's only been one night, Gav. Slow down, my conscience chastises me. I should be freaking out at my internal confession. *What has this girl done to me?* One night, and I want more. One night, and I'll take as much as she'll give me. For as long as she'll give it to me. One night and everything has changed.

14

Charlotte

Standing in the bathroom, Gavin holds me until my shoulders start to relax. I hadn't meant to mention my mom. The second I did, the hurt of missing her hit me instantly. It made me even sadder that Gavin had thought I had lost her. Well, I guess I kind of did, only not in the sense he had assumed. Gavin whispers in my ear, "Are you ok?"

Am I ok? If you'd asked me two minutes ago, I would've said I was perfect. Last night was more than I could've imagined. Gavin seems to know my body better than I do, and it's been mine for the past twenty-five years. I had never had more than one orgasm, and that was only when I had self-induced it with my vibrator. After my third orgasm, *yes, you heard right, my third orgasm,* my body felt like Jell-O, and I wasn't sure my legs still worked. Waking up this morning, I was afraid it would be awkward. It had been six years since I had sex. Six years since I stayed overnight with a man, and staying with Gregory always had me waking up on edge, so I wasn't sure what to expect.

When my lids finally opened, I was met with Gavin looking at me with those crystal blue eyes that I swear see right through me. His gentle hands when I went to cover up made me feel sexy. His eyes and body language proved he enjoyed looking at me—well, that and his substantial erection —giving me confidence I didn't know I had. I was deliciously sore between my legs, reminding me where Gavin had been and how good it had felt.

The feel of him inside me again this morning was different than last night. His thrusts were harder, faster, stronger, and I was there for it. The forcefulness with which he took me should have scared me, but somehow, I innately knew that Gavin wouldn't overlook my own needs. That his hard, eager thrusts were the result of passion rather than him not caring if he hurt me. After the initial sting faded into pleasure, I couldn't get enough. The tension in my body built like a volcano, ready to erupt, and when I fell over the edge with him inside me, it was like an out-of-body experience.

The second Gavin left to grab the shower stuff, my mind warred with itself.

What happens next?

Stop worrying and soak this in.

You work together.

Let go and live, Lottie.

Should I ask him to shower with me?

Nope...too far.

No, it's not, be the badass you are.

Holding onto that last statement, I stood up after he walked into the bathroom and turned the shower on for me. My old self would have worried he would reject me, but my in-the-moment badass self didn't care. Only, Gavin didn't reject me, and the feel of his hands on my back as the water cascaded down my body felt amazing. I didn't think we had any more orgasms left in us but Gavin proved me wrong when he grabbed my wrists and held them above my head on the wall as he used his other hand to push two fingers inside and pleasured me until my knees buckled. I would have fallen if Gavin hadn't been there to hold me steady.

I wanted to see him come undone. Turning in his embrace, I lowered myself to my knees and turned my gaze upward to Gavin's. The lust in his eyes was all the encouragement I needed. Using my hand to stroke his erection, I wrapped my mouth around his tip and sucked slightly. The moan that escaped his lips was low and sultry. I had very little experience, but that moan urged me on. I licked him from base to tip, sucking the tip hard between my lips while one hand twisted his shaft. As I got into a rhythm, Gavin's moans became louder, and words left his mouth in a jumbled mess until he tried to pull back as I sucked him harder. A second later, Gavin's body tensed, as he groaned my name while hot ribbons shot down my throat, and I swallowed every drop of his release.

After coming down from his high, Gavin lifted me by the shoulders until I was standing and devoured my mouth in the hottest kiss that had me feeling like I might fall again. Gregory never wanted to kiss me after I gave him a blow job. He would always make me brush my teeth, and then he would still only give me closed-mouth kisses. Gavin wanting to kiss me after made me feel appreciated. Sexy. Wanted.

After we got out of the shower, I relished Gavin drying

my hair until I stupidly mentioned my mom. *Blissful bubble effectively popped.*

Coming back to the present, I reply, "I'm fine," my tone more clipped than I mean it to be, surprised I even remember the question he asked. I don't mean to be rude, but my mom and my past always puts me in a defensive mode, and the last thing I want is for Gavin to have to deal with my baggage.

Rubbing his hands over my arms that I protectively have crossed over my chest, he says, "I don't want to push, but I'm here to listen if you ever want to talk about it."

Did I want to talk about it? With anyone else besides Grace, the answer would have been an emphatic *no*. Even when Joe and Maria, people I felt completely comfortable with and considered family, tried to breach the subject, I'd avoid the topic. With Gavin though, I can't explain it. He makes me feel safe in a way I had never felt before. We've only spent one night together, but it feels different. Being with him feels different.

Leaning my head back into his chest, I soak in his scent. Breathing him in fills me with a sense of calm. "Thank you. Maybe, but not today."

Kissing the top of my head, "No problem. Let's get you dressed, and I'll make some coffee."

"Sounds perfect." I put on a smile, not wanting to ruin the morning we're having with my internal meltdown. He wraps me in a towel before wrapping his own around his waist, and we walk back into his bedroom.

"I can grab you some clean clothes if you want. My sister left some of her clothes here a few times, and she's about your height."

"Oh, that'd be great."

I can't help but stare at his muscular back and shoulders,

leading down to where the towel lays low on his hips as he walks down the hallway. I can't see his ass, but the outline it makes in the towel makes me want to grab on. *Down, girl.*

Gavin's back a minute later, catching me in a trance, fangirling about his ass. Reaching out and handing me leggings and a T-shirt, he asks, "Like what you see? Looking is free of charge, but touching, that will cost you." The cocky bastard raises his eyebrow at me and grins.

I swat him with the pile of clothes he handed me. "As a matter of fact, I do, but my lady bits tell me they need a break, so can you kindly cover yourself up?"

Chuckling at my confession, Gavin turns and makes his way into his walk-in closet. I dress quickly and pick up my clothes. Strutting, yes strutting, out of the closet in a pair of faded jeans that sit low on his hips and a tight white T-shirt, Gavin grabs my hand. And together we walk down the hallway towards the kitchen.

Pulling out the breakfast bar stool for me, I sit, and he maneuvers around the island and goes to work making coffee and pulling food out of the stainless-steel French door refrigerator. He grabs a pan from the sliding shelf in the cabinet next to the stove and cracks a few eggs into a bowl.

With my elbows on the counter and my chin in my hands, I take in the sight before me. I've never had a man cook me anything. *Ever.* Much less my sexy boss making me food after a night of the most pleasurable sex I've ever experienced. He hums lightly while he scrambles the eggs, pouring them into the pan he heated up. He seems at ease, and no conversation is needed as I watch him move around the kitchen. A few minutes later, he places the plates and forks in front of me, along with two cups of coffee and a container of creamer, before coming around the island and sitting on the stool next to me.

Looking down at my plate, my stomach growls in appreciation. The plate is filled with scrambled eggs, watermelon, pineapple, and a croissant. My breakfasts usually consist of a protein bar or a bagel on my way to the law firm or class. This is a treat.

"This looks amazing. Thank you," I say before picking up my fork and taking a bite of the eggs. They are soft and buttery, melting in my mouth, and I moan in appreciation.

"I love that sound, but I'd rather it be me making you moan." He places his hand on my thigh, running up toward where the ache is starting again.

Playfully swatting his arm away, "Well, it kind of is. You made the eggs."

"I'll make you eggs every day if they make you sound like that. He might get a little jealous though," he said, looking down at the bulge in his pants and putting his left hand back on my thigh and squeezing before grabbing his fork and diving into his plate as well.

We eat without much conversation, both of us needing sustenance after the night and morning we had. I pick up my plate when I finish and grab his as well. Reaching to stop me, "You don't need to do that. You're my guest."

"I don't mind. You cooked, so I'll clean up." Walking through the kitchen with plates and cups in hand, I rinse them and put them into the stainless-steel dishwasher.

Glancing at the stove, I see it's already almost eleven. I should go. I have assignments to work on before heading to Joe and Maria's this afternoon. The confidence I had just hours ago slips away, and I can feel myself questioning what happens next. I don't know how he does it, but Gavin seems to be able to read me before I can even work out what I'm thinking myself. Making his way toward me and pulling me into his arms, he leans his head down and takes a deep breath. "I don't like this shampoo. It doesn't smell like you." How he can get me to instantly relax is beyond me, but with one sentence, I'm laughing at his comment.

"And what do I smell like?" Wrapping my arms tightly around his waist.

"You smell like the perfect mix of flowers and citrus, and it drives me insane. You. Charlotte. Drive me fucking insane." He grabs my chin with his finger and thumb, gently tilting my head to look him in those beautiful blues. "I'm going to talk to my Dad and John tomorrow and tell them about us. It's not against the rules, but I don't like hiding things either. Unless you tell me otherwise, I want this. I can see you questioning where my head is at, and I know it sounds crazy but, fuck..." he runs his fingers through his hair with his free hand as if trying to pull the words he wants to say from his follicles, "I can't explain it, but this isn't a one-night thing for me."

With his arms bound tightly around me, he looks down at me, waiting for me to respond.

"I don't want this to be a one-night thing either. Honestly, I'm scared of what this means with my internship, but I'd be lying if I said I could walk away and not want more." I don't know how he gets me to tell him my feelings so easily. He must practice some sort of magic. Grace tells me getting me to talk about my feelings is like pulling teeth.

"Don't be scared, Fire. We'll figure it out. Together. I promise you your internship is safe. No matter what." Lowering himself to take my lips, I willingly open to him. Twenty-four hours ago, I was perfectly fine, living my life the way it was. Work, internship, school, repeat. I was a robot with no desire to start any kind of relationship.

One Kiss.

One question.

One night.

Everything has changed.

I've had the best sex of my life and told my "boss" that I want to see where this takes us.

Knowing if we keep this up, I'll never get anything done today. I reluctantly pull back, planting a few short kisses before opening my eyes and looking at him. "As much as I'd love to keep this up, I promised Joe I'd be there for dinner today, and I have some papers I need to work on. I'll call for a cab."

"The fuck you will. I don't want you to go, but if you're going home, I'll take you. No way are you leaving my house in a cab. For the record, from now on, papers will not be an excuse to leave so fast. The only reason I'm letting you go is that Joe will probably hunt me down if you don't show up this afternoon," he says as he plants a kiss on my nose. "I'm going to need your number before I let you go home. Don't make me look it up in your HR file."

"Ok, stalker, let me grab my things, and I'll be right back." He swats my ass as I scurry away. I'm all smiles as I head into his room to grab my clothes, finding my phone on the ground. It must have fallen out of my pocket when he took off my shorts last night. I see I have four texts from Grace. Figuring I'm on my way home, I leave them be and head back to the entryway where Gavin is waiting for me, leaning on the wall with his tennis shoe-clad feet crossed. *How do you make tennis shoes sexy? Put them on Gavin, that's how.*

He's holding his phone in his hand. He wasn't kidding about not letting me leave before exchanging numbers. Reading my mind, he says with a smirk, "You think I'm kidding. We aren't leaving this building without your number in my phone."

Laughing before reciting my number, I hear my phone beep a few seconds later, and I can't help but look at it.

UNKNOWN:

You look so beautiful today, Firecracker

Unable to stop myself from blushing, I save his contact before sliding my phone into my purse and reaching forward to plant a kiss on his lips. "Thank you."

"Don't thank me. I speak the truth. I'm a lawyer after all." He winks, weaving his hand through mine as we leave the condo, and he locks up. Riding down the elevator and walking to his car, his hand never lets go. *And I don't think I ever want him to.*

15

Charlotte

Thank God I only let Gavin walk me to the elevator of my apartment building instead of all the way to the door like he wanted to. He was adamant about parking and walking me in. Luckily, he found a spot a few buildings away from ours. Grace and I each have a reserved parking spot that we pay for monthly. Other than that, it's the luck of the draw on parking on the street.

When I got out of the car, I barely got the door shut before Gavin pressed me up against it, grabbing the back of my neck with one hand, holding my lower back with the other, and crashing his lips to mine like he had been lost in the desert and I was his only source of water. Every kiss with Gavin is intense, lighting my entire body on fire, yet somehow each one is better than the last. I had to make myself push him away before I ended up with a public indecency ticket for stripping his clothes off. We walked into my apartment building, his hand weaving through mine like a key fitting perfectly into a lock, and he stood and waited until the elevator closed before he left.

We didn't make any plans of when we were going to see each other again outside of work tomorrow. I shouldn't care. I have so much on my plate. That didn't stop me from feeling slightly disappointed when he didn't mention anything.

Tomorrow, we have a three-hour meeting scheduled to go through all the updated information on the Pickett case. Three hours of sitting in the same conference room, him in one of his perfectly fitted suits, smelling like my own personal drug. Three hours of keeping my mind out of the gutter. *Good luck with that.*

Gavin said he would talk to his dad and Mr. Davis about us. After trying to talk him out of it because I wanted to keep whatever this is completely separate, I gave up because he declared that he wanted everyone to know I was off limits. After Gregory, I never wanted to feel like someone's possession, so him saying that should have made me feel uneasy with the uncertainty of navigating this. Since leaving home, I haven't done well with the unknown. What this was with Gavin was unknown. However, instead of feeling uneasy and scared, I wanted him to make me his, possess me. After only twenty-four hours with him, possession with Gavin meant something completely different than it did with Gregory.

I did though, make it clear that we will be keeping things professional inside work walls. I worked my ass off these past six years and want to be taken seriously. Not the office gossip.

"Damn, girl. The thoroughly fucked look suits you," Grace catcalls from the couch as I walk into our apartment.

"Who says I've been thoroughly fucked?" I ask as I plop

down on the couch beside her. I have so much to do, but *ahhh* this feels nice.

"Ha-ha, you aren't fooling anyone, Chica. The glow in your cheeks, the smile on your damn face. Not to mention the slight waddle you have going on." I swat her arm, and she burst out laughing.

"You bitch!"

Straightening up, still laughing, she leans her head back for a second before looking at me again, "Seriously, I couldn't be happier for you. Now, I need specifics. I've waited six years for some sexy spillage from you, so I'm cashing in!"

"My lips are sealed," I say as I mimic zipping my lips from left to right with my fingers.

"Hell no. I always fill you in. Don't leave a girl hanging. I came home and watched *Bridgerton* before using my vibrator and going to bed. I'm now living vicariously through you."

"I never asked you to fill me in; you give me all the details whether I want them or not." She knows I'm stalling. I couldn't keep this from Grace if I tried. She'll wait me out as long as she needs to, and I have shit to do. Relenting. I fill her in on most of the night and this morning. I leave out the bit about my mom, not wanting to go down that rabbit hole again. Since this morning, I can't seem to get her off my mind. Pushing it down again, *I'll deal with that later.*

"Oh, my God. How are you upright right now? Don't get me wrong, I'm so happy for you, but damn...six? The most I've ever had was four. I'm jealous." She shakes her head at me.

"Ha-ha, well, I am sore, but in the best way," I chuckle, "God, Grace, it was soo good. Like, better than anything I could conjure up in my fantasies." My phone buzzes when I am leaning back and swooning, thinking about last night. Sitting up, I pick it up off the arm of the couch.

GAVIN:

Stay with me tomorrow.

No question mark. A statement, as if he has already determined the outcome of my answer. *Stay with me tomorrow.*

"Is that Gavin? What did he say?" Grace asks, attempting to peek over my shoulder.

"Yeah, he asked me to stay with him tomorrow."

"OMG, girl, what kind of magic vajayjay do you have? He wants you so bad he can't wait more than an hour to ask to see you again?" She nudges my shoulder.

"He didn't put a question mark, just a period. Maybe it was a mistake?" Although I already knew it wasn't. I should hate the fact he's telling me instead of asking me, but I don't. I like him taking control, something that makes absolutely zero sense to me, as for the past six years, I've tolerated nothing but having one hundred percent control of my life and decisions. *He's not Gregory. He doesn't want to control you, only be in control of giving you pleasure.*

"Damn, my guess would not be a mistake. He's making his wants known. And what he wants is you, lady." She looks at me, wiggling her eyebrows before sobering a little. "In all seriousness though, this is your decision. Take it at your pace. I'm so proud of you for letting go and taking a chance, but don't do anything you aren't comfortable with. If he's worth it, he'll understand that you need more time." Another reason I love Grace, she pushes me to live and let go but also knows how much of a change this is for me.

The thought of more time with Gavin sends shivers

down my spine. Is this too fast? *Probably*. Do I want more now that I've had a taste of what good sex is? *Hell yes*.

I hug Grace because who could ask for a better ride or die? And then I lean back again, staring at the ceiling, "This is fast. And a lot. And I work with him. This could all turn out so bad. At least that's what my head says." I take a deep breath, still staring upward. "The other parts of me...last night you told me to let go and live. You've been so right. I've been living under this umbrella of fear, not letting anyone close or even giving life a chance, always waiting for the other shoe to drop." I shake my head and sit up, looking at her.

"About damn time you listened to me," she says with a grin.

"I'm serious, Grace. I'm fucking sick of it. It's like last night, when I decided to go for it, a switch flipped. I'm tired of letting my past dictate my life. I want to experience life. I left Tennessee to start a new life, but I got lost along the way and ended up stuck in a cycle of avoidance led by fear," I say, shaking my head before continuing my epiphany. "Maybe this thing with Gavin is a mistake. It's probably only so good because it's been so long, and my limited experience was horrible so I don't have much to go off of. But I don't care. Being with Gavin last night made me feel alive, like a me I didn't even know. It felt fucking amazing. I want amazing, Grace." Blowing out a breath and evening my racing heart after the admission, Grace looks at me, eyes glistening.

"God, Lottie," she says, reaching over and hugging me, then pulling back to look at me, wiping under her eye. "I want you to have amazing too. You deserve amazing. It's all I've wanted for you since I found you in your dorm room shaking. That fucker took so much from you, and then he held that power over you for so long. He still had control of your decisions. Last night you finally took your power back. I am so fucking proud of you, Lottie."

Tears now glistening in my eyes too, I say, "I don't think I would have ever done it without you being there for me, pushing me. You're the best." I hug her again because I couldn't imagine life without Grace.

I look back at her, still feeling guilty about leaving her after Logan last night. "Hey, I'm sorry about Logan showing up. I didn't know any of them would be there, or I would've texted you."

"Don't worry about it, Lottie. I'm a big girl and can handle jackwagons when I need to. Besides, if you and Gavin work out, I'm sure we'll run into each other again. Better to get it over with sooner rather than later." She shrugs like she doesn't care, but her eyes tell a different story.

Now it's her turn to change the subject, "I need to get off my lazy ass and get some shit done. I have a huge week this week and want to make sure I'm ready to kiss ass." She switches back into confident take no shit Grace, putting the blanket on the couch and standing up.

"I should get some stuff done too," I say, pushing off the couch and standing. "I have a paper to finish and I'm going to Joe and Maria's for dinner tonight. I'm guessing you're not coming?"

"Yeah, sorry, I want to make sure everything is perfect for my two pitches, and meetings start at eight, but tell Joe and Maria next time."

"I will. I'll check on you before I go." I start walking down the hallway but not before Grace gets one more shot in, "That waddle you got though...." I can hear her cackling as she closes the door to her room. I pick up my phone and type out a text.

ME:

Okay.

Within seconds, a response appears.

GAVIN:

Never thought the word Okay would make me hard. Proven wrong. I now have to try to work like this. You'll pay for that.

ME:

Pay how?

GAVIN:

Fuck, Firecracker, I'm about to come over there and show you. Pack a bag and bring it with you to the office. We're going straight to my condo. Sleep tonight. Tomorrow you won't be getting much.

ME:

Sir, yes sir.

GAVIN:

I like when you call me sir.

ME:

Go back to work. I'm very busy. I'll see you tomorrow, sir.

GAVIN:

Fuck. Me. Enjoy your day, baby *winking emoji*

The rest of Sunday flew by. I spent a few hours after texting Gavin, putting the finishing touches on my paper, and reviewing my case studies before sending them in, check and check. This year, my classes are geared toward family law, my area of focus. My assignments consist mostly of case studies and papers, along with tracking my internship hours. It is much better than all the exams and long study hours my first two years entailed, but I was still ready to be done.

After I finished, I took a quick shower, dressed in a pair of navy leggings and a gray T-shirt from when my mom and I got grass seats and saw Kenny Chesney, and went to Joe and Maria's. Maria made tamales, one of my favorites. The whole time I was there though, I couldn't get my mom off my mind. Of all the shirts, I subconsciously picked one we bought together. It was like mentioning her to Gavin, and having him ask about her, opened the safe that I kept her in. She never stayed in my head this long when Grace or Maria would bring it up. This time, I couldn't shake it. I left earlier than usual, blaming homework. I hugged them both goodbye and told Joe I'd see him on Thursday for my shift.

When I got home, there was a takeout box in the kitchen, and Grace was locked in her room, presumably preparing for tomorrow. After letting it air dry from my shower, I pulled my blonde hair in a messy bun, slid out of my leggings and t-shirt, replaced them with my favorite blue sleep shorts and white tank top, and crawled into bed. I tried to sleep, unable to shut my mind off, thoughts running back to my mom. *Should I call her? Would she even want to talk to me? What would I say?* These questions ran on repeat until, at some point, I finally fell into a restless sleep with dreams of my past.

16

Gavin

I got a couple hours of work done yesterday with several distractions involving visual images of a sexy blonde. Those and an annoying friend who kept incessantly calling and texting me, wanting to know all the details of what happened. Logan is worse than small-town old ladies when it comes to gossip and being nosey. I ended up turning off my phone to make it stop. I'm surprised he didn't show up at my condo, actually.

When I got into bed last night, my sheets still smelled like her, which made my other head ready for action. *Horny bastard.* I wanted to text her, forcing myself to not do it. To be honest, I was hoping she would text me. No such luck. In a span of forty-eight hours, I went from a man who swore off relationships to a man wanting more from a woman I had known for a week. I don't know what is happening, but Saturday night changed everything for me. Saturday night is why I called my dad yesterday asking for a meeting this morning to tell him and John about Charlotte. Maybe I was jumping the gun, but in my gut, I knew she was something special, and I didn't want to start with secrets.

I picked up coffee on my way in for the three of us, black for my dad and me and one sugar and cream for John, from their favorite coffee shop around the corner from our office. I came in early so I could go through what I wanted to say before I met with them at seven-thirty. Most of our office staff come in around eight, and I wanted to keep this private, meeting before people filtered in.

After being with my parents on Saturday, just hours before seeing Charlotte, my dad had heard me say I wasn't looking for anything. Now here I am, ready to tell him I am pursuing a relationship with someone, and that someone just happens to be an intern at our firm.

Squaring my shoulders, I take the coffee holder and walk to my dad's office.

"Good morning, Rose. Hope you had a good weekend with Craig and the boys," I greet my Dad's assistant.

"We did, thanks for asking. How was your weekend?" she asks, looking up at me from her computer, pushing her black-rimmed glasses up her nose. Rose is in her mid-forties, married to a police officer, and has two teenage sons. She has worked for my dad since he became a lawyer and feels like family.

"It was great, thanks. Can I head in?"

"Yeah, Mr. Jones walked in just a minute ago."

"Thanks, Rose. Have a great day." I should've bought her a coffee too.

"You too, don't work too hard." She winks at me as I walk past.

Knocking lightly, I hear my dad say, "Come in."

Walking into his office, I see my dad sitting at his desk on the right side of the room while John is sitting on the couch that lines the left wall, his foot across his knee reading something on his phone. I set my dad's coffee down, and he grabs it as he stands and sits in the chair facing the door. I hand John his coffee and sit in the chair that faces the windows looking out into Phoenix.

"So, Gavin, you called and asked to meet with John and me, which you've never done, and since you wouldn't give me any details yesterday, I'm curious what this is about." My dad says, looking at me with his brows raised, concern laced in his eyes.

"I wanted to talk to you both to let you know I am seeing Charlotte Swanson, one of the interns, and I didn't want to hide anything."

John's eyes snap up and look at me with something I can't quite decipher.

"You were at our house on Saturday and told your mother you were too busy to date. Were you seeing her then?" My dad asks, like he's more upset thinking I might have lied to my mom.

Sucking in a breath, I tell them the story. "No. I wasn't. We met a few days before her internship started when I was out with James and Logan. We talked for a bit, but she had to leave, and we didn't exchange information. When I saw her in the office on Monday, to say I was surprised would be an understatement." I shake my head, remembering looking into her eyes in the conference room. John is still staring at me with his eyebrow raised as if asking *did you fool around in the office?* "Nothing happened last week. Saturday, after leaving you and mom, Olivia and I met up with a few of her friends, and surprisingly,

Charlotte was working at the bar we went to. We started talking, and I gave her a ride home. We spent time together yesterday and want to see where this goes. I know we don't have a policy against inter-office relationships, but I wanted to let you both know out of respect." I take a breath after rambling that all off and wait.

"She works in a bar? Which one?" John asks with his arms crossed over his chest.

"She bartends a few nights a week at Cliffs. Why?" Confused by his inquisitions about where she works.

Shaking his head as if shaking himself out of his own thoughts, he says, "No reason, we just know we work interns a lot here on top of their school work. It seems a little excessive to hold a job outside of all of that."

"She works there to pay for her rent and tuition. Is there a policy against working outside of the internship?" I ask, wondering why he cares so much. I look at my dad, who is looking at John with questioning eyes as well.

"No, there isn't. As long as she's able to keep up with the requirements of her internship here, it's none of our concern. On that note, relationships in the office should hold up to the same standards. They should not interfere with your ability to get your work done." His tone is a little clipped, which is unusual for John. I thought that of the two of them, my dad would have more of a problem with this, not John.

"I think what John means is that we have a reputation to uphold. There is no policy against it, but this is a professional workplace, and we want it to stay that way. After the shitshow with Logan last year, it makes us a little leery that something could go wrong, and this all seems very new." My dad's voice is softer but still firm as concrete.

"I understand that. I wouldn't be considering this or

telling you if I wasn't serious," I say adamantly, defending myself.

"How can you be serious, son? You said yourself, it's been, what? Two days?" My dad eyes me questioningly.

"I know, Dad. I do. And I can't explain how or why, but I am serious." I shake my head, exasperated at my own feelings.

After what feels like an hour, which, in reality, is only a few seconds, my dad responds, "I believe you. I know that feeling. I felt the same way about your mom; don't tell her I said that." He chuckles before continuing, "If you want to pursue this, I support you, and thank you for coming to us. If she's special, hold onto that. You don't find it often. I warn you though, don't expect me to keep this from your mom for long. She can sniff out news like a drug dog. She'll sense I know something."

Having my dad's blessing means a lot. I wouldn't mention anything to them if I wasn't sure as if asking, Charlotte was what I wanted. I look toward John, who is still staring at me. I raise my silently asking, *and you?*

His face gives nothing away, though he says, "If you're serious, and it won't affect your work or hers, I'm okay with it. Don't mess around with her, Gavin...we don't want another situation like we had last year."

"I won't, John. She's special." *She is. She really is.*

"You're a good man, Gavin. She's lucky to have you." His voice has softened a bit. John stands, "Sorry, I have to head out. I have a client coming in and have some things to attend to before that. Daniel, see you for our lunch meeting?"

"Yeah, Rose made the reservation at one. Do you need anything else, Gavin?" My dad asks.

Standing, I say, "No, we have the Pickett meeting

scheduled for one o'clock today. I'll update you after. Thank you both for meeting with me." John nods before walking out the door.

My dad stands, walks over, and puts his hand on my shoulder, "I want you to be happy, son, and if she makes you happy, I'm on board." He gives me a pat before walking back to his desk and sliding back into business mode. "I expect a full update before the end of day. I know this is taking a lot of time from our team, but we want this settled. This case is huge for our company."

"Yes, sir. Understood." I nod to him and walk back to my office. *I need to see her.*

I can hear my two best friends before I even get into my office. As I walk in, I see Logan and James sitting on my couch, razzing each other as usual, and they both look up at me as I come in. Trying to ignore them, I head straight to my desk and start going through emails.

Logan is the first to chime in, "So...that's how it's gonna be? You're just going to ignore us?"

"I'm not ignoring you. I have work to do. Don't you?" I ask as I lift my head to meet his eyes, raising my eyebrows at him.

"Oh, I have work to do. That work includes finding out just what the fuck happened Saturday between you and hottie intern, since you have decided to ghost me and turn your damn phone off instead of answering it like a man." Logan raises his eyebrows right back at me. *Fucker.*

"First, her name is Lottie, not hottie intern." Fuck if I want him calling her Charlotte. That's reserved for me. "Second, it's none of your business, you nosey ass. Third, I'm sure you told James all about my Saturday night, but did you inform him of your little run-in?" I point at him accusingly while James' eyes light up with a *damn, you got called out* look.

"Tsk, tsk, Logan, did you get yourself into trouble again?" James gives him a disappointed mom look.

"No, I didn't. I merely had a small, insignificant roadblock placed in the route that is Grace Hastings." Logan puffs out his chest.

"Small roadblock? She all but macheted off your balls and handed them to you on a shiny, silver platter." I point out. "And how did you find out her last name? Stalker much?"

Shaking me off, Logan points his finger right back at me. "It's not stalking. It's called social media. However, this isn't about me, Gavin. We are talking about you and a certain intern. Stop avoiding. Spill."

I'm not getting rid of these knobs until I give them something, and we have shit to do. I also want to see Charlotte before I start my meetings. Relenting, I say, "I'm not giving you details, but yes, Charlotte and I are seeing each other. I talked to my dad and John this morning."

James looks surprised at my confession, and Logan just smirks that asshole smirk he always has. "I knew it. I knew it. Damn, Gav, way to get it in."

"Fuck off, Logan." I spit at him, annoyed he thinks of her as a game.

James leans back, smiling, crossing his arms over his chest, while Logan throws his hands up and says, "I'm just saying, why are you telling your dad and John already? It's been two days."

"I don't want to hide anything from them. This isn't a one-night thing." I shake my head, feeling like I went from giving away nothing about Charlotte to spilling my damn guts to everyone in the building.

"I knew this would happen," James chimes in with a slow clap. "Honestly, I didn't think it would happen this soon, but I knew there would come a day when a woman would change your way of thinking. Seems like Lottie is that woman." He's got the biggest smile on his face. "Seriously, man. I'm happy for you. You deserve it, especially after the whole Rachel thing. Lexi is going to want to meet her, you know? She knows Logan is a lost cause."

Chuckling, I say, "Tell Lexi she'll have to wait. I want her all to myself for a while before I'm ready to share our time with others." I know that sounds possessive, and it is, because I am. I want my time with her to be ours.

James laughs at me. "I remember those days with Lexi. I get it."

"Okay, okay, you twitterpated love birds." Logan chimes in, his shoulders stiff and his posture rigid. "Don't we have shit to do?"

"You are the one who started this whole conversation," James chides.

"Yeah, and I'm ending it. Let's get ready for this week," he clips.

I'm not sure what made his attitude shift, but he is right. We have shit to do. I'm also fine with not discussing Charlotte in detail with them.

"Alright, boys. Let's get it done," I say. We get through what we need to, and Logan and James are out of my office before nine. By now, Charlotte will be in, so I type out a quick email.

To: *Charlotte Swanson*

From: *Gavin Davis*
Subject: *Urgent request*
Charlotte, your presence is required in my office at 9:15.
There is an urgent matter to discuss.
Sincerely,
Gavin Davis, Esq., M.B.A
Senior Associate
Davis and Jones Law

Hitting send, I lean back in my chair and take a breath. I have so much shit to do. Instead, I'll watch the clock until it hits nine-fifteen.

17

Charlotte

*A*fter a night of tossing in turning, I relented and got out of bed before six, worked on a paper due this week, and was in the office before eight. Failing to put my mom back in the box I've kept her in the past six years, she flooded my thoughts with guilt and an immense sense of missing her. Mentioning her to Gavin, and his concerned response and caring, was like lighting a detonator to a whole crap-ton of feelings I've been holding back, and last night they seem to have exploded.

I took an extra-long shower, shaving all my lady bits in anticipation of this evening. I spent extra time on my hair, drying it and curling it in soft waves, and left my makeup minimal applying mascara, blush, and a bright pink lip gloss. I decided to wear my black pencil skirt, and a pink sleeveless blouse, leaving the top two buttons undone, hiding the sexiest lace pink bra and matching lace panties I own underneath. I put on my highest heels, towering at just over an inch, and packed an overnight bag before grabbing a bagel and coffee on my way out. Grace was already gone when I left, which I expected since her meetings started early. That woman would've been in her power suit and at the office by six a.m., ready to kill it.

I was going through the notes on the Pickett case when my email pinged. *Urgent matter?* Gavin hadn't texted me since yesterday—something I was a little disappointed in, to be honest, but would never admit it—and now he wanted me in his office? He said he was going to talk to his dad. *Maybe he changed his mind? Maybe it didn't go well. Stop this, Lottie. Grow up.*

Looking at my clock reading nine-thirteen a.m., I run my hands down my skirt after standing and walk toward Gavin's office with my head held high. *Whatever he wants to talk to me about will be fine. I'm a grown-ass woman who has made it through leaving home and a bad situation, and I have taken care of myself for the past six years. I've got this.*

I finish my mental pep talk as I walk up to Elaine's desk, "Good morning, Elaine. Gavin said he needed to see me in his office. Is he available?"

"Good morning, Lottie. Yes, he's in there. I'll send him a message telling him you're here, but you can head right in." She gives me a kind smile.

"Thank you," I say as I walk past her desk toward Gavin's slightly ajar door.

Knocking softly before walking in, I take a second to take in the sight that is Gavin. Sitting behind his desk, his navy-blue suit jacket hung over the back of his chair. He's wearing a light gray dress shirt that fits his chest and arms like a glove with a lighter blue tie with a soft wavy pattern. His hair is perfect, and he looks so in control with his eyes set on his computer. He truly is a sight to take in, my insides igniting a fire of need just by looking at him.

Finding my voice, I say, "You wanted to see me?"

Gavin pops up, and a bright smile crosses his lips. "Good morning, beautiful. Yes. I did. Please close the door." I turn to close the door, and before I can even digest what he said, I feel him behind me, the warmth of his arm around my waist while the other arm reaches forward, hitting the lock on the door.

My breath hitches at his closeness. Taking the hand he used to lock the door, he moves the curls from my shoulder, placing my hair over the other shoulder, and leans down, running his lips up my neck and over my ear before he whispers, "I've been dreaming of the curve of this neck since you left yesterday." He plants a kiss below my ear, his lips sending shivers down my spine as goosebumps line my arms. He presses my back so it's against his chest, and I can feel him hard against my ass as I involuntarily lean my head back into him.

"Gavin, we're at work. This can't happen," I moan, my breathing erratic, pulse racing in my neck, and my heart fluttering with him being this close.

Turning me around and using his thumb and finger to lift my chin to look at him. "We are at work. And I promise to keep it professional. After I do this." He crashes his lips to mine, and I melt into him. Opening willingly to let him in, my tongue dances with his, forgetting that on the other side of that door are a whole office of people.

Tilting his head to change the angle, a moan escapes my mouth, bringing me back to the present and where we are. Reluctantly, I put my hand on his chest, giving us some much-needed distance, although only a few inches, my body misses him. Catching my breath and shaking myself out of my lust-filled stupor, "We have to stop. God, I don't want to, but we need to."

Taking a side step and coming around him, so I am not pinned close to the door, I give us some much-needed breathing room.

"You're right. I'd say I'm sorry, but I'm not. I suggest you stop wearing skirts and shirts like that if you want me to get any work done. You're a vision, Fire."

I give him a shy smile but mentally give myself a high five for picking the right outfit, "Thank you. You don't look half bad yourself in that suit. I was admiring you in it when I came in."

"Were you? Want to come over here and show me how much?" He eyes me like a hungry tiger, ready to pounce.

"See. That. We can't do that." I shake my head at the evil, sexy man in front of me.

"You're right, you just..." he says, raking his hands through his perfect hair, "I can't think straight when I'm alone with you."

Trying to change the subject and pause the sexual tension building, I ask again, "You said you wanted to discuss something with me?"

"Yeah, I did. Come sit with me," he says, motioning to the couch. He sits, and I walk and sit down too, giving us more than a foot of space and turning my legs towards him.

"I talked to my dad and John this morning. I told them about us, and they are on board with it. As long as it doesn't interfere with our work." He shakes his head at himself. "Ha, well, I guess I need to work on that part; the minute I saw you, all I could think about was devouring you. It's going to be harder than I thought keeping my hands off of you here."

"You talked to them already? I wasn't expecting you to do that so soon." I feel a sense of unease about what they think about this.

"I didn't want to wait. I told them this was serious. And to me, Charlotte, it is. I want a relationship with you, and I don't want to start it off with secrets." He reaches out, grabbing one of my hands. "I'll be professional at work. Fuck, it might kill me to not touch you, but I'll try. Outside of work, all bets are off. I'll need to make up for all the hours I have to spend not having my hands on your gorgeous body."

This man is going to be the death of me with his words. "It won't be easy for me either, but the build-up will make it even better." Gavin squeezes my hand at my confession.

"You're coming home with me tonight," he says, holding my gaze. Again, he doesn't ask. Just states a fact, but in a way that melts my insides and makes me crave him like an animal starved.

"I have my bag in my car." I smile at him.

"Wow, a whole seven words. I was expecting an okay, but shit, I'll take it. We'll drop off your car at your place after work, and you can drive in with me tomorrow." His smile could melt the panties off any woman, I swear.

"Okay," I say with a smile.

"And there it is. He leans in and kisses me again. It's quick yet not any less soul-stealing than his other kisses. "That's the last one, promise."

I stand up. "I should go. Is there anything else you need me to get done before the meeting today? I sent you all of the updated notes when I got in."

"I got them. They look great. Your ability to find the hidden details is amazing. Hopefully, we can get this case done sooner than anticipated with all of us on it. The information we gathered last week alone might be able to keep us from going to trial once that asshat sees what we have on him," he says as he walks towards me.

"Just doing my job. I'll see you at the meeting. If you need anything else, let me know."

"I will, but I don't think you are willing to help me with what I need at work." He gave me a sly smile. "Tonight, though, Charlotte, is a different story. Tonight, I'm going to worship every inch of your body, making sure when you walk around, you'll still feel me tomorrow."

My face flush and panties thoroughly soaked, I bite my bottom lip and look at him. "Okay," I respond quickly, opening the door and walking out before he can catch me. The growl he makes as I leave echoes in my ears the whole way back to my desk.

Surprisingly, I'm able to get back to work, even with visions of Gavin swirling through my head. I eat the sandwich I brought from home at my desk before heading into the conference room. Needing some space from Gavin so I could concentrate, I sit next to Beth at the end of the table. Gavin eyes me suspiciously. I give him a small smile and nod, letting him know I needed the distance to concentrate. Reluctantly, he takes a seat at the head between James and Logan, and we dive in.

There was a lot to unpack, but after three hours, the team feels we have a strong portfolio to present to their lawyers, proving we have more on them than they think we do. James explained this is what we aim for. First, create an evidence portfolio and give the other side a chance to back down without getting a judge involved. If that doesn't do it, file it formally, in which a date with a judge is set to hear the case. The hope of this is to come to a settlement instead of going to trial with the judge's decision.

Trial takes a lot more time and man hours, not to mention money; therefore, trying to cut out the nonsense and recover a higher amount is beneficial to our clients. This equates to more money saved as outlined in the contract when a client retains Davis and Jones. I guess either way, the firm wins because they are getting paid, but it is Daniel and John's belief that the sooner they close up cases, the sooner they can move onto the next one, in the end, creating a bigger revenue return.

After the meeting ends, I head back to my office and check my phone, seeing an email from my law advisor asking if I can come to her office today or tomorrow as a matter of urgency. She never needs to see me outside our yearly scheduled meetings, making sure everything is in order financially and class-wise. I had my meeting at the end of August, so her asking to see me just three weeks later makes me nervous. I don't want to ditch Gavin, but I can't let this wait until tomorrow, or I won't be able to relax. Responding to my advisor that I can come now, I pack up my things and open up my messages.

ME:

Something came up, and I need to leave. I don't know what time I'll be done. I'll text and maybe can come over after. I'm sorry.

Gavin responds immediately.

GAVIN:

Are you okay? I can take you, whatever it is.

ME:

Thank you, but I can take myself.

GAVIN:

Text me when you're done. I still want you to come to my place, no matter what time. Please.

ME:

I'll try.

I shut my messages and grab my bag. Feeling bad I'm leaving early; even though I stayed until late every night last week, I'm putting in enough hours. I walk out, get in my car, and head toward campus. I don't want Gavin to worry, I wanted to tell him, but my self-preservation stopped me. Whatever she tells me, I can face on my own; I've been doing it on my own for a long time. I only wish I knew what it was I was walking into.

18

Gavin

CHARLOTTE:

I'll try.

I kept reading and re-reading her text. I should've run out and stopped her. I have this sick feeling she's running. I pushed her too far this morning. *Stupid.* After attempting to focus and get some work done, which proved fruitless, I gave up and headed home just after five. Something I haven't done in, well, probably ever. I wanted to be home if she came. Keeping my phone by me and looking at it every couple minutes like a pathetic teenager, I put in five miles on the treadmill and then take a shower.

With no text from Charlotte, I throw some black athletic shorts and a white t-shirt on, make a sandwich, and sit on the couch to watch TV when I hear a knock on the door. Figuring it was Logan or maybe James, I swung it open, not expecting Charlotte to be standing on the other side.

"Can I come in?" she asks shyly.

"Of course," I say, opening the door wider so she can come through. Not forgetting to realize she was carrying a small bag with her. *Phew.*

I close the door behind her, resisting my urge to grab her waist and kiss her like I've been wanting to since she left my office this morning. Charlotte slips off her shoes, puts her bag down on the side of the couch, and takes a seat, folding her legs underneath her gently as she's still in her skirt from work.

Wanting to be close to her but not wanting to push, I sit next to her on the couch, making sure to give her some space even though it's killing me not to touch her.

Testing the waters, I ask, "Is everything okay?"

After several seconds of her staring straight out into the Phoenix sky, "Yes and no, I don't know. Did you talk to anyone at Clayton?" She still won't look at me.

"No, was I supposed to?" I'm confused about where this is going.

"I needed to ask." She shakes her head like she is trying to work something out in her head. I hold my breath and wait for her to continue. She takes a deep breath and turns towards me.

"My advisor emailed me when we left the meeting today asking to see me. She said it was important and asked that I come in either today or tomorrow." She's looking down, fidgeting with her hands in her lap. "I had a meeting with her a few weeks ago, like I do every year, so I wasn't sure what she wanted to talk about since she never contacts me except at check-in times. Anyway, I didn't want to wait because I thought it might be something bad." I can see her pulse racing in her neck.

She stops talking, her hands writhing in her lap. With a soft voice, I push her to continue, "Was it bad?"

Shaking her head slightly, she continues, "I got to her office, and she told me I've been selected for a scholarship that I didn't even know I applied for. I mean, every year, you can fill out paperwork for financial aid and scholarships, but you usually find out before school starts."

"That's good news, isn't it? Maybe the scholarship committee decided late. Any money helps with school, right?" I keep my voice soft and even, trying to keep her talking. From our earlier conversations, opening up about things isn't something Charlotte does easily or often, so I'm trying to tread lightly.

"Gavin, the scholarship is for two-hundred thousand dollars. It's not just a small amount. That pays for my school this year, a part of my loans, apartment, food, everything. Please tell me you didn't have anything to do with this." She's looking at me like a detective looks at a criminal trying to get a confession.

"You think I did this? Don't get me wrong, I would give you the money in a heartbeat if you needed it and asked. But in the short time I've known you, I can tell you like to do things your way, and me offering you money seems like a one-way street for you to run." My tone is as gentle as it can be after being accused of going behind her back to get her to take money.

Her face falls, and a tear drops onto her cheek. *Shit, I made her cry.*

"I'm sorry, I just didn't. I don't know. It's a lot of money, and it seemed to come at a weird time after meeting you. I've been on my own for six years, working and taking out loans to finish school and live, and this...it's too much."

Tears are steadily streaming down her face. *Six years? What the hell happened?* She seems like a dam is breaking that she's been holding in for a long time, and I want to hold her up. I scoot closer so our knees are touching, and reach over, grabbing her hand gently squeezing it.

"Don't be sorry. I can see where the timing seems strange, but I swear I had nothing to do with it." She's squeezing my hand like a lifeline, so I dive in for the deep. "What happened six years ago?"

Her eyes widened at my question, like she didn't mean for me to catch that little tidbit, then again...maybe subconsciously she did. I use my thumb to wipe away the tears on her cheek and wait for her to answer. I can tell there is a war waging inside her head, one that she seems to have been fighting for a long time now.

I don't move for fear of scaring her, and for what feels like forever, we sit there with my thumb on her cheek and her looking down. Slowly she inhales a deep breath, tilting her head to look at me.

"I left everything I knew six years ago...." Charlotte fills me in on all the details about her abusive relationship with some douchebag, Gregory, *who I'd like to kill if I ever get my hands on him,* and how she tried to tell her friends but pretty much got slapped in the face when she did. Through tears, she explained about getting a PO Box and how she never told anyone, afraid they would think she was overreacting or try to talk her out of it. She explains that the night she ran away, leaving only a note, she was filled with guilt over leaving her family behind that way. She told me how she met Grace and how/why she told her about everything that had happened. How they ended up here, and Grace has been pushing her to let go and live, to call her mom, and not be controlled by her past. Her confession is like a vault being opened, spilling years of shit she's held in. She takes short breaks to breathe but doesn't move a muscle or stop. I'm guessing she's afraid she won't be able to continue if she pauses. She finishes by confessing how, last night, she realized how much she misses her mom, and all the guilt she's been carrying around all this time.

"...so yeah, that's it." She blinks through the tears that have kept a steady stream down her face, regardless of my thumb rubbing them away.

Moving my hand down, I grab her chin gently with my thumb and finger, forcing her to tilt her head and look at me. "Thank you for telling me. You, Charlotte, are the strongest woman I have ever met. You don't have to be alone. You have Grace. You have Joe and Maria. You have me." Holding her chin while a sob escapes her throat, I grab her and pull her into my lap, letting years of emotions run their course. I hold her against me, her head resting against my chest, pressing kisses to her hair until her crying slows and finally stops, and her breathing regulates.

She lifts her head and looks at me, a look that shows me right into her soul, before leaning in and kissing me. *God, what this woman does to me that I never thought I'd do or want ever again, and it's only been a few days.* I hold her to me, our kiss filled with desperation and lust. I'll be whatever she needs. Charlotte pulls back and turns, lifting her skirt to allow her to straddle me, wrapping her hands around my neck and grabbing my hair.

After her confession, I don't want to continue this in my living room. I want to savor her, care for her, take away her pain, and I plan on taking my time. Pushing up to stand with her securely wrapped around my waist while internally high-fiving myself, I actually could accomplish that—thank you squats and box jumps—I hold her under her perfect ass, her skirt now up at her hips, and walk with her toward my bedroom, never letting our lips separate. Thankfully, I know my condo well.

Kicking open my bedroom door, I walk to the edge of the bed, sliding her down my body as she unlocks her legs from my waist. Her eyes are a little red and puffy from crying, but she's also aroused, noticeable by the way her back arches at the separation of our bodies, her nipples piercing, attempting to get out of her blouse. Running my arms up her thighs and back down, her eyes close, a soft *hmmm* escaping her lips.

Reaching to her left hip, I grab the zipper on her skirt—yes, I know where the zipper is. I've paid damn close attention to all things Charlotte, for moments like this—pulling it down as she lifts her hips to assist me. Letting her skirt drop to the ground, I go back and undo the third button of her blouse, those two buttons she left undone taunted me the whole meeting, her breasts being held by a sexy pink lace bra peeking out. When I grab the hem of her blouse and pull upward, Charlotte lifts her arms until it is over her head, and I toss it over my shoulder, leaving her in a pink matching bra and thong set. I climb on the bed and guide her, gently laying her down before leaning back on my knees to admire her.

"You are so sexy. Everything about you." I say, taking in the breathtaking view. She hasn't said anything other than moans since her tell-all in the living room. "Let me take care of you, Firecracker."

Her eyes are so blue and full of something I can't quite decipher. "Okay."

That. Word. Will. End. Me.

Smiling at me as I descend on her mouth, I take her lips

between mine, fusing us together as my hands roam from her thigh to her waist, dipping into her panties and finding her soaking wet center. I grab hold of the tiny garment and pull hard, tearing them off her without much protest.

She breaks the kiss, "Those were my favorite."

"I'll buy you new ones; hell, I'll buy you an endless supply of them if I can do that more often," I respond before capturing her lips and returning my hand to her wet heat. "Ahh, mmm." She cries as I push two fingers in, circling slowly to loosen her up. She's already writhing beneath me, and the way her body responds to me makes me feel like a king. I use my thumb to press on her swollen bundle of nerves as she bucks her hips into me, seeking her own release. "Please, Gavin, please." She needs this. A release. I wanted to go slow, savor and worship every inch of her, and I will. But not right now. Right now, her body craves a release, and I oblige. Picking up speed, I add another finger as she cries out before curling them up to find the spot that will make her come undone and varying my circles on her clit. Her orgasm takes over her body, exploding on my fingers. Her eyes squeeze shut, legs shaking, and her entire torso goes rigid. Charlotte's orgasms are a beautiful thing to watch. A sight seared into my brain, listed as Gavin's favorite thing to see.

Lifting myself up, I reach over to the nightstand, taking out a condom to roll it on my erection that is begging to be inside her. I grip myself, lining up at her center and slowly pushing in, feeling her muscles grab me as she continues to come down from her high, pulling me in. This is pure heaven. She wraps her legs around my waist, hands grabbing my shoulders, digging her nails into me as they run down my back.

"Yes, Gavin, I need this. I need you."

Control. Obliterated. I pump a few more times slowly before picking up the pace, grabbing a pillow and pushing it under Charlotte's ass, angling her hips so I can go deeper as I close my eyes and pray that I don't finish in the next few seconds. *Hold. On.*

"Oh, oh...I'm...again..." Charlotte's words are my undoing. Her muscles tense as her walls spasm, clamping down on me like a wrench on a bolt, and I can't hold back. My balls draw up, tingles shooting up my spine, "Fire..," I growl out as my own release takes hold, and in one more thrust, I'm filling her. My vision goes black briefly. I've never felt that before. I open my eyes, lean down and roll us to the side, holding her close as we both continue the descent from our high, our breaths ragged, my heart racing like it's trying to escape my chest. Instantly missing her heat as I slide out, I reluctantly get up, take care of the condom and climb back into bed, pulling her head to my chest, realizing I never even took her bra off.

"I'm sorry, I wanted to go slow." I apologize as I stroke her hair. "You make me lose all cohesive thoughts."

"Don't be sorry, I needed that. I'm sorry I questioned you about the money. It's been a lot in the last few days." She never moves her head. I continue to stroke her hair. I don't want to patronize her by saying I understand because I don't. I've never had to leave home, and I've never been without my parents and on my own. Sure, my girlfriend cheated, and that sucked, but it doesn't hold a candle to being physically and mentally abused. I can't begin to imagine everything she has overcome and the demons she might still be fighting.

As we lay there in a comfortable silence, I thought maybe

Charlotte had fallen asleep as her breathing regulated until she whispered, "I think I want to call my mom."

"Then I think you should." When she doesn't respond, I take a step further. "Do you want me there with you when you do? Or maybe Grace?"

"You.... Please." The words are barely audible, but I hear them.

"Okay," I whisper to her before kissing the top of her head and pulling her closer. She looks at me with her beautiful smile before laying her head back on my chest. Within a few minutes, her breathing evens out, and I can tell she's asleep. Holding her close, I lay there, except my mind won't shut off.

She's been living without her family for six years because Gregory scared her enough to leave it behind. Anger pumps through my veins, making me concentrate on my breathing, so I don't wake her. There is never a reason to abuse someone mentally or physically in a relationship. The fact that her so-called friends made excuses kills me. Charlotte needs her family back. I know she's afraid they won't understand, but I'd put money on it that they are feeling just as lost as she is.

Squeezing her to me once more, I stroke her hair and whisper, "I've got you. I promise. You aren't alone anymore, and if I have my way, you will never be again." I kiss the top of her head once more before drifting off.

19

Charlotte

*a*fter spilling my guts, I fell asleep in Gavin's arms and slept solid, even with so much on my mind. Grace is the only one who knows the truth, never opening up to anyone else, yet with Gavin, I didn't want to keep it in. This man makes me feel a sense of comfort that I'm still trying to wrap my head around. My eyes flutter open as I feel Gavin's lips spreading kisses from my neck to my shoulder. *Hmmm.* My body instantly peppers in goosebumps from his touch. I can feel his length pressing into my back, and I want more. Pressing my ass into him and moving my hips a little, I feel the growl in his chest at my movement. Gavin twists his torso, my body instantly missing the connection of our skin touching. A second later, he's back, and my body hums as his skin molds to mine. He lifts my leg over his, opening me to him, lines himself up at my entrance, and slowly slides all the way home. *Wow, this position feels different.* His hand wraps around and pinches my hard nipple, which causes me to cry out.

Gavin bends his leg and uses that as leverage as he thrusts harder into me. His hand moves from my nipple to my nerve bundle, and when he pinches it between his thumb and finger, my orgasm hits with full force. My body tenses as tingles of pleasure run through every part of me. My orgasm spurs him on each time he enters me, demanding and with purpose until his body tightens, and I feel him spasm inside of me, his own release taking hold.

"Fire, a guy could get used to waking up like that every day."

"He could, could he?"

He peppers kisses on my bare shoulder and says, "Definitely, baby. Shower?"

"Sounds perfect."

After showering and getting ready, we ate breakfast together before going to work separately since I had my car. We had been "dating" for less than a week, and this morning felt so easy. *Honeymoon phase.* He didn't bring up my mom, and I was grateful for that. I wasn't lying, I do want to call her, and for some reason, I have yet to figure out myself; I want him to be there when I do; but I need some time to muster up the courage to do so, which includes talking to Grace, my reality checker, pep talker, and the only person I've had consistent in my life since I left home.

Unfortunately, I haven't seen her since Sunday, and it's lunchtime on Friday already. She's been swamped at work. I haven't even told her about the scholarship money. It didn't feel like something I could explain in a text, especially when I still didn't understand how it happened.

I haven't seen Gavin outside of the office. I had study

groups Tuesday and Wednesday and then worked at the bar last night. He pouted like a petulant toddler when I told him I wasn't going to come over at midnight during the week and wake him up. As much as I have been craving him, if I went over there, my five hours of sleep would have dwindled to two or three, and I would be a walking zombie.

I could only take so much though, breaking my own rules and making out in his office under the guise of going over files several times in the past two days. As much as it killed me not to take things further at work, I promised myself that I would keep my professional and personal life separate, and I intended to do so. Gavin has been so patient, even though I can tell it's taking all his restraint. I've tried to wear my most conservative outfits, cutting out the skirts this week, but he says it's teasing him more since he knows what's underneath.

His dirty texts are relentless making it harder to stay away.

I accepted the scholarship, signed the paperwork before my study group Tuesday, and the money was deposited into my bank yesterday. I almost threw up when I saw the amount in my bank account. I already budgeted how much I'll need for rent, food, gas, etc., with a buffer to spare and went online and made a payment for my student loans.

Last night I told Joe about the scholarship money. After a few *holy shits,* he told me it was fate smiling on me, giving me a chance to enjoy my last year a little instead of killing myself. He also told me he's taking my telling him as my notice. I tried to talk him out of it, but he was relentless.

"If you don't quit, I'm firing you. Do you know how many college kids beg me for a job every weekend?"

"You want me to leave?"

"Of course, I don't. You are the closest thing to a daughter

I have, and people love you here. However...I know you've been killing yourself the past two years between school and this job to make ends meet."

"I don't want to leave you shorthanded. You and Maria are family to me."

"And we always will be, which is why we'll still expect you for Sunday dinners. Lottie, you need to stop worrying about everyone else and put yourself first for once. This scholarship lets you do that. Saturday is your last shift. I won't take no for an answer."

Before I could even respond, he hugged me tightly, and a grateful tear slipped down my cheek. Joe and Maria were my saving grace when I moved here. My job at Cliff's has been my sole income source, and the *bonus* checks that I know not all employees get have helped me in more ways than I can count. I will forever be grateful for their support. Joe squeezed me tighter before straightening himself up and turning to walk away; my guess was to hide his emotions. It'll be weird not working at Cliff's every weekend; however, leaving last night knowing I would have two free nights felt like a small weight lifted off my shoulders. I texted Gavin to tell him, and his response consisted of *Hell Yes, those days are mine. Make sure you stretch since it's been a week. I have plans to make up for lost time.* He's insatiable, and I'm not mad about it. I told him I'd come over after work Saturday since I'm only working until eleven.

I pull my phone out and text Grace.

ME:

Dinner tonight?

GRACE:

Lottie? Is that you? Are you real?

ME:

This week has been crazy, sorry.

GRACE:

No sweat. This week has been bananas for me as well. Landed my two accounts and got three more proposals to work on. I don't even remember hitting my pillow between business dinners and working late since last weekend. I should be done by six.

ME:

Perfect. Meet at Blue at 6:30.

GRACE:

Hell yes. I deserve at least four margaritas after this week.

ME:

I've been craving nachos.

GRACE:

Cue my mouth salivating.

ME:

See you at 6:30

GRACE:

Gotcha babe

I put my phone on my lap, hiding it from Beth, the phone police, who gives me the death glare whenever she sees me even look at it. I've accepted she hates me, and honestly, I don't have the energy to care. I start to open another file when my phone vibrates on my lap. I push my chair back slightly, look down, expecting another text from Grace, and find myself smiling like a fool when I see Gavin's name on my notifications.

GAVIN:

I need to see you tonight. And by need, I mean it's necessary for my survival. You don't want to be responsible for my death.

ME:

I'm meeting Grace at Blue for dinner at 6:30. I haven't seen her all week. I said I'd stay with you tomorrow. I think you can survive one more night.

GAVIN:

No, Fire, I don't think I can. I'm dying over here seeing you every day and unable to do anything about it. Our make out sessions are creating one hell of a case of blue balls.

ME:

Ha-ha, they say absence makes the heart grow fonder.

GAVIN:

Whoever said that is a sadist. Absence makes the dick ache harder; that's all absence does.

ME:

Why don't you meet us there at 8:00. I need to talk to Grace.

GAVIN:

I guess I can wait another seven hours to touch you, but I make no promises that once I start, I'll be able to stop no matter who is there.

ME:

I'm sure you'll survive. I'll make it up to you.

GAVIN:

I like the sound of that.

ME:

I need to get back to work before my boss fires me. I'll see you tonight, sir.

GAVIN:

(dead emoji)

Laughing to myself, I tuck my phone into my purse, not expecting any more texts from the peanut gallery, and get back to work so I can leave by five and go home, shower, and change before meeting Grace.

"What the what?" Grace stares at me with wide eyes after I tell her about the scholarship, leaving Cliff's, and wanting to reach out to my mom. We're seated in a corner booth at Blue, the best Mexican restaurant in Phoenix, in my opinion, while Latin music plays softly through the overhead speakers. She takes a huge gulp of her margarita before continuing. "Holy shit Lottie, I can't even wrap my head around all this...in a good way."

"I know. I'm still in shock about it. I talked to my advisor again Tuesday, and she said the applications we fill out are sent to all available scholarships, and this was a new one that was added this year, which is why I wasn't aware of it." I grab a chip and shove the warm salty goodness into my mouth, moaning when it hits my lips. *God, I love chips.*

"It's a miracle; that's what it is. Girl, this is huge. You deserve this." She says just as our food arrives. Nachos for me and a chicken chimichanga for her. The waiter asks if we need anything else. Even after saying we're good, he lingers with his eyes glued to Grace's chest and the cleavage peeking out of her periwinkle sleeveless top. "Need a closer look?" she asks, pushing her chest out, snapping him out of his stupor. He apologizes, shakes his head, and stumbles back, almost knocking over another waiter carrying a tray. Both of us bend over, laughing.

We dig into our food. My nachos are piled high with steak, pico de gallo, cheese, sour cream, guacamole, and cilantro, with every bite a foodgasm in my mouth.

"What are you going to tell her?" Grace asks, taking a break from stuffing her face.

"I don't know. The truth? God, Grace, I'm terrified." I feel the sting behind my eyes and look up, refusing to let my emotions take over in the middle of this restaurant.

She reaches over and grabs my hand. "I know you are; you've been living with this guilt since our freshman year of college. You've held yourself back from living, blaming yourself, and letting fear rule your life. You've been stuck, not able to move forward." I shake my head, trying to defend myself, but she squeezes my hand tighter. "Don't try to say you haven't because you know it's true. I love you. It's killed me to watch you shut yourself off from life for years, Lottie. You know I don't believe in fate and all that everything happens for a reason bullshit, but it's like your meeting Gavin is the push you needed to want to live again. Truly live again. Whatever happens from calling your mom, I'll be there. I promise. I don't think you can find peace and move forward until you've talked to her. She's the last piece of your unfinished business." She doesn't let go of my hand as we sit there, and her words sink in. After a minute or so, she lets go.

I lean back into the booth we are sitting in and let out a deep breath.

"I hate that you're right. I love you, you know that, right?" Grabbing my drink to give myself the liquid courage not to hide behind my past anymore.

"Damn right you do. And you need to do it before you talk yourself out of it again. I'm not letting you hold back anymore. Lottie 2.0 is in full swing." She signals the waiter and orders two more margaritas to replace our almost empty glasses.

"I've decided to call her Sunday, so I don't lose my nerve. She's always home Sunday afternoons. Well, she used to be." I shake my head, realizing her routines may have changed, and I'd have no clue.

"I've got some work to do this weekend, but if you need me, I'll be there." This is why I needed to talk to Grace. She's real and honest and always has my back. I'm honestly not sure I would've made it without her.

"You're the best," I say as the waiter comes to drop off our drinks. I'm just about to tell her Gavin is going to meet us for a drink when I see the man of the hour walking toward our table. I'm all smiles until I see who's walking behind him. Gavin gives me a sympathetic look, mouthing *I'm sorry* before he reaches our table.

As I open my mouth to warn Grace, the perpetrator behind Gavin beats me to it, "Good evening, ladies. Mind if we join you?" Grace snaps her head up, her smile immediately turning into a tight-lipped line.

Gavin is giving me his best *please don't kill me look* as Grace shoots daggers toward the uninvited guest.

"Didn't know we were expecting guests tonight, Lottie," Grace says sarcastically.

"I expected one, which I was just about to mention but wasn't expecting multiple." I offer apologetically. Gavin sits down next to me. Logan slides in next to Grace as she scoots her plate, drink, and self as far away from him as possible.

"I'm sorry, I told him he wasn't invited, but he followed me here anyway," Gavin says to Grace.

"True story," Logan offers.

"So, you just stalk people now?" Grace quips.

Gavin chuckles as Logan crosses his arms over his chest. "No, Gavin and I were supposed to go out tonight, and then he changed plans to meet you guys. Since I wasn't doing anything else, I thought this way you wouldn't be the third wheel, so in reality, I came to do you a favor."

Gavin is staring at him like he's lost his mind. The waiter stops by, not allowing Grace to comment. Gavin and Logan order a drink. I guess this means they're both staying.

The waiter walks away with a dejected look after seeing Logan sitting next to Grace. The poor guy still wanted to stare at her. "If you want to do me a favor, choke on your drink."

"You wound me, Jade." Logan puts his hand over his heart like he's been stabbed.

Grace scoffs, "Asshole, my name is Grace, not Jade." She looks like she could kill him.

"I know your name is Grace, but Jade reminds me of the color of your eyes, so you're my Jade."

Grace stills for a second, taking in his comment. I feel like I'm watching a soap opera, and I can't turn away. "I'm not your Jade," she says, but her cheeks have turned a shade of rosy pink, and her lips have ever so slightly curled up. She quickly grabs her drink to hide her blush and smile.

You can feel the tension between these two. I swear they

will either end up screwing or killing each other, both of which are dangerous for their health.

Gavin leans into me as he grabs my thigh and drags his hands up and down my leg. "One drink, Firecracker, then we're going to my place."

The waiter delivers the boys' drinks. Grace and Logan continue to swap jabs at each other. However, her posture has relaxed, and her tone is more teasing than menacing. Gavin keeps his promise, and when our glasses are empty, the waiter informs us our tab has been taken care of. I glance at Gavin, and he gives me a shit-eating grin, grabs my hand, and pulls me out of the booth.

"We're leaving. I'd say I'm sorry for ditching out, but I've waited all week to be with my girl, and nothing is stopping me from taking her home," Gavin says, not sorry at all. "Don't kill him, Grace."

"She won't kill me, will you Jade? Let's grab another drink. Just because these party poopers are leaving doesn't mean we have to." Logan nudges Grace's shoulder with his.

"Call me Jade one more time, and I might." She nudges his shoulder back. "One drink. And you're buying."

I give her a look, and she nods slightly. Silently telling me, she's truly okay with having a drink with him. If she wasn't, I would make Gavin stay, or we'd make sure she left with us.

Gavin grabs my hand to lead us out when Grace says, "Sunday, Lottie."

I look back and nod, knowing she's holding me accountable, "Sunday. Be safe. Love you."

"Be safe. Love you."

Gavin practically runs out of Blue, dragging me behind him. He gives his ticket to the valet, and while we wait his hands never leave my body, wrapping them around me, cocooning me in his embrace. When the valet brings his car, we drive to my apartment to get a weekend bag before going back to his house and not sleeping most of the night. All I can say is, *Thank God I stretched before I went to dinner, cuz damn, he wasn't kidding.*

20

Charlotte

*W*armth. My backside pressed against his frontside. Our bodies fit together like a puzzle that has finally found its missing piece. I slowly open my eyes as Gavin's hand runs lazily along the underside of my breast, across my ribs, repeating its slow path. I don't want to move because laying here in bed with Gavin is the most at ease I've felt since before I met Gregory.

As soon as we got in the car, Gavin said there was no other option besides me staying with him this weekend after spending zero time together the whole week outside work. I couldn't argue because I wanted nothing more than to be wrapped up in his arms.

Which is crazy right? I've gone years not being able to get past a first date, and within a couple of weeks, I crave this man's touch. I don't shy away. I don't flinch. I want more. I want to explore things with Gavin I only fantasized about but never thought I would actually want. It's more than the sexual craving, though. Talking to him and being in the same space gives me a sense of peace I didn't think I'd ever feel with a man.

Friday night, we spent hours worshiping each other before falling into an exhausted sleep, tangled up in each other. Saturday, I woke up to an empty bed. To say I was disappointed would be an understatement until Gavin walked in and handed me a cup of coffee, just the way I like it, equal amounts of cream and coffee. We laid in bed awhile before getting up and making French toast together. It was easy, moving seamlessly around the kitchen and working together as if we had done it a hundred times.

We spent most of Saturday on the couch and in bed. Talking, laughing, and exploring each other's bodies. We talked about anything and everything. When I talk, Gavin listens. He hears me. When I opened up more about my past, he didn't judge or give his opinion. He didn't tell me he would kill Gregory, although his face and body language suggested otherwise. Gavin told me about his ex, Rachel. He told me what happened and how after their breakup, he never saw himself getting serious again. *Until me.* Those words slayed me. Hearing Gavin say that feels right in a way that scares the shit out of me.

At four o'clock, I had to force myself to get up and shower to get ready for work. I had texted Grace earlier to check in and make sure she didn't kill Logan. It took her two hours to respond, and when she did, she replied, *I didn't kill him...yet.* I instantly replied, asking for more, but that's all I got. A follow-up conversation is much needed on that topic.

Gavin insisted on dropping me off at work. He went back home and got a few hours of work done before coming back at eleven to pick me up so I didn't have to take a cab back to his house. It felt surreal clocking out for the last time. Maria was there, which I'm sure wasn't a coincidence. She hugged me close and made me promise to come over for Sunday dinner when I could, and Joe made me swear I'd stop by and visit.

I held it together until I got into Gavin's car before tears slid down my cheeks. Gavin held my hand, not saying a word. He let me have my moment; his presence was all the support I needed. When we got back to his condo, we showered together, slid into bed, and I wrapped myself around him. I think I was asleep before my head hit his chest.

"Mm-hmm, that feels good," I hum as Gavin's warm hand rubs the underside of my breast in a slow, repeated path.

"You feel good. How did you sleep?" Gavin whispers before kissing the spot behind my ear, leaving a runway of kisses down my neck that sets my body on fire.

"Like a rock," I manage while trying to stay focused as he continues his descent, kissing my shoulder, down my ribs, toward my hip.

"Speaking of rocks...I'm hard as one," he says through a smile before biting into my bare cheek, not hard, just enough to make me squirm.

"Ahh," I shudder in anticipation from his touch. *This man.* "Let me see if I can help you with that." I roll over, push him from his side onto his back, and straddle him.

"Be my guest," Gavin says, placing his hands on my backside and squeezing it. I reach over to the nightstand and grab a condom. I've never put one on someone before, but there is a first time for everything. I open it up, and Gavin watches with rapt attention as I roll it over his hardened length, his eyes turning to deep blue as want and need overtake him.

After I make sure it's all the way down, I lift my legs so my feet are on the bed and I'm hovering over him. Slowly lowering myself onto him, inch by inch, I let him stretch me as I go. I have never been this bold or open, ever. Gavin makes me feel brave. Sexy. Wanted. I feel confident and want to pleasure him as much as he has pleasured me.

"God, Charlotte, you feel like heaven." Gavin's hands never leave my ass while I swivel and move up and down until he's seated all the way inside of me. Shit, I need to work out more; less than a minute of this, and my quads are burning. The things we do for pleasure are totally worth it.

I continue doing mini squats finding a rhythm. Lifting up until he almost slides out and then pushing back down, swiveling my hips in a circular motion as I go. My legs are burning, and so is the ache inside me. Gavin hisses as I come down again. I can tell he's close, and so am I. I come up again, and before I come back down, Gavin releases one of his hands and brings it around, pinching my clit, and I can't hold it anymore. "Oh, Ahh...Yes..." I cry as my vision goes black, and I see spots. Gavin holds my hips and slams up inside me a few more pulses until I feel him stiffen beneath me and curses out his release.

Coming down from my high, I literally fall over to the side, my legs no longer able to hold me. It's not graceful or sexy by any means, and I can't hold back my giggle at my unceremonious dismount. I place my hand over my face to hide my embarrassment. Gavin gets up and goes to the bathroom to dispose of the condom and crawls right back into bed, leaning over me.

He grabs my hand and pulls it away from my eyes,

"Don't hide from me, beautiful. Ever."

How can he read me so well? It's as if he has a telescope into my brain.

"I wasn't hiding; I was recovering from that... Plop," I scoff, trying to keep it light.

Gavin leans down and kisses me deeply, grabbing the back of my head and holding me in place. I should feel trapped; instead, I feel protected. I wrap my hands around his back and hold him in place, wishing we could stay like this, right here, in this bubble, forever.

After several minutes he pulls back slightly, placing a few light kisses on my lips, nose, and forehead. "I love waking up next to you, Fire."

"Me too," I confess.

"Come with me to my sister's show in LA? It's at the end of October, and I know it's only mid-September, but I want you to come. I want her and my parents to meet you." Gavin is now leaning on his elbow, hand on his head, still naked, laying on his side.

"Are you sure? We've only been seeing each other officially for a week. Don't you think it's too soon for me to be meeting your family?" Part of me is excited he's making plans for us. Her show is six weeks away. The other part of me is scared shitless to take this outside of us.

"I couldn't be more sure. It sounds crazy, but it's true. I never thought I'd want to date anyone again. Never bring someone home again. After Rachel, I was fine with working and meeting women to satisfy a need. That might make me an asshole, but it was how I felt. I didn't spend more than one night with anyone. Until I met you. I want to make plans. Spending time with you, Charlotte, makes me crave you more. Not just your body but your mind. Your soul. I want to cherish you and know you down to your very core. I want to support you. Prove to you that you don't have to do this alone. I want everyone to know you're mine." That word. *Mine.* Gregory always used to say that. *You are Mine, no one else's, and you never will be.* It made me feel like a possession. Property. A tangible thing that could be pushed around and played with instead of a human that could make her own choices.

I wait for those same feelings to come when Gavin says it, but they don't. I don't feel like property. I don't feel like a possession. I feel wanted. Worshiped. Adored. He wants me to meet his sister and his family. This. Us. It's happening at warp speed. I'm afraid if I don't slow down, I might end up heartbroken. Afraid if I do slow down, I might miss out on the best thing.

My face must show the war in my brain because Gavin follows that with, "I don't want to scare you. Please don't shut me out." He offers gently.

I don't want to shut him out. I want to let him in. I've already shown him more of me than anyone besides Grace, and I've known him for two weeks. So much about how I approach life has changed in the past two weeks compared to how I've lived the past six years. I feel happier than I have since I don't know when. Though I know life is not a fairy tale, and happiness can be ripped away from you in a blink of an eye. *Let go, Lottie. Live.* Grace's words swirl in my head. Words she's been trying to drill into me for years. I never listened. Until now.

"Okay," I whisper. He leans over and captures my lips, and I melt. Leap of faith meet ledge. Ledge meet leap of faith. I'm jumping off the ledge into the unknown with Gavin. Praying that I don't end up lost again. "I'm going to start the coffee," Gavin says before rolling over and sliding out of bed. I can't help but stare as he puts on a pair of gray sweatpants and pulls a black t-shirt over his head.

After he leaves the bedroom, I grab my phone off the nightstand and see a text from Grace.

GRACE:

It's Sunday. You know what that means.
Will you be home today?

Always holding me accountable.

ME:

I know. I'll be back later. I told Joe and Maria I couldn't do dinner tonight. Are you home?

GRACE:

I'm going to the office to get some work done, but I'll be available if you need me. See you tonight?

ME:

Yes

GRACE:

Love you

ME:

Love you too

I grab a pair of navy leggings and a Clayton shirt from the bag on the chair in the corner. My insides feel warm as I stand, taking in his room. The bed is a mess of sheets and comforter, the wrinkles holding memories of us together the past two nights. Thinking about it has me smiling like a lovesick fool. *I am a total cliché right now.*

After making the bed, I walk toward the kitchen quietly

in hopes Gavin doesn't hear me. Country music plays through his Bluetooth speaker as he moves around the kitchen, grabbing mugs and putting bagels into the toaster. I lean against the wall, admiring the sight before me. I am fangirling hard for this man. His dark hair is disheveled in the best way possible. His sweatpants sit low on his hips, the outline of his perfect ass on full display with his back to me. And he's singing. Not loud, but enough that I can hear him, and holy shit, I'm wet again. I've never heard him sing; his voice could bring any woman to their knees.

"Hey, handsome. Got any coffee for me?" I say, pushing off the wall and strutting toward him. Yes, strutting, swaying my hips, and all that jazz trying to seem as sexy as he was a second ago, lost in his own world.

He turns with a mug in his hands, "As a matter of fact, gorgeous, I do." He gives me his content smile as he hands me another perfect cup of coffee. In the couple weeks I've known him, I am already starting to learn his different smiles. And this one, the one he's giving me right now, is the one he gives me every time he turns and sees me. It could be a minute, an hour, or the whole day. And damn, if that doesn't make me feel like the luckiest girl in the world.

"Thank you. Do you have work you need to do today?" I ask as I sit at the breakfast bar, holding my coffee with both hands.

"I have some files I should go over. I want to spend the day with you." He comes around and sits next to me, placing a plate for me and one for himself on the counter that consists of a bagel with cream cheese, strawberries, and blueberries.

"I don't want to be in your way. I was actually thinking of calling my mom today." I say, waiting for his response.

"First, you're never in my way. Second, I'm really proud of you." He grabs my chin and lifts it up, so our eyes meet, effectively blocking me from dipping my head down. His blue eyes are warm, the emotion behind them seeping into my bones.

"Don't be so proud yet. I still have to actually do it." I say, not losing eye contact with him.

"You will. You've made your decision, and you aren't the type of person to allow yourself to go back on it. If you want to do it in private, I understand, and I'll either give you space or take you home. I promised I'd be there for you. And I will, whatever that looks like." His gaze is intense, filled with pride and compassion. It makes me feel that with him next to me, I could slay a freaking dragon, let alone call my own mom.

"Thank you. Let's eat and take a shower. Then, I'll see. She used to go to church and be home around lunchtime, so I don't want to call until then anyways."

"Sounds good, beautiful girl." He lets go of my chin but kisses my nose before returning to his plate to take a bite of his bagel. He's leaving it up to me. My choice. When. Where. How. Pushing me to take the step to call her, yet letting it be on my terms. My terms. Something Gregory never allowed. I feel myself falling for Gavin Davis a little more with every conversation we have. *I could love this man.*

Our conversation turns lighter as we finish breakfast. When we're done cleaning up, we take a shower, where Gavin takes me against the wall, legs wrapped around him like a koala, as he drives deep into me, my back thrusting upward with each pulse until we come together, moans of our release filling the bathroom. Afterward, we wash each other and lazily get dressed.

I worked on a case study while Gavin checked in with Logan and James. They're coming to his house for the game tonight. We went over some files together, and I made ham, cheese, and cucumber sandwiches with apples and chips for lunch.

Gavin is laying on the couch watching football, and I'm pacing the floors with my phone in my hand, willing myself the courage to put in the numbers.

Gavin hasn't said anything. He's giving me the space to do this while silently supporting me. I do two more laps before sitting at the dining room table, staring at the phone. He looks up and gives me a smile as if he's silently saying, *you can do this. I'm here if you need me.* His faith in me has me pressing the numbers into the phone, my hands shaking as I do.

I hear the ring of the call going through, and I press the phone to my ear and hold my breath. *Holy shit, this is it.*

It rings twice before I hear a sound that instantly has tears welling in my eyes. A sound I haven't heard in six years.

"Hello?"

I freeze. Gavin looks up, smiles, and nods his head. Such a simple gesture, the impact and meaning are enormous. He's telling me I can do this. Giving me the courage to take the step.

"Hello?" Her voice is the exact same. I'm trying not to lose my courage.

"Mom?" I say almost a whisper in a voice I don't even recognize. Then I wait. What seems like forever.

"Lottie? Is that you?" Her voice now shaky and choked with emotion.

The shake in her voice breaks my heart. I did that.

"Yes, Mom. It's me. I'm sorry." That's all I can manage.

Her sobs fill the phone. I want to hang up, the sadness in her sobs breaking me into a million pieces I didn't know I was holding together so loosely all this time. Tears slide down my face as I sit there like a statue, the weight of holding all this in for so long crashing down on me like a ton of bricks. I feel a hand grab mine and squeeze. I didn't even realize Gavin got up and moved to a chair next to me. He's holding my hand, silently holding me up, when I feel like I'm falling.

"Oh, Lottie. Are you okay?" Her voice is hoarse already.

"I'm okay mom. I promise." I whisper back.

"I've been waiting for your call. I can't tell you the number of times I've tried your old number, praying one time it would stop saying this number is no longer in service. I went to the police, and they wouldn't file a missing person's report. They said you left a note and were eighteen." She sighs, not an angry sigh, a sigh as if she's taking a deep breath for the first time.

"I am so, so sorry." I wish I had better words for her than that. I owe that to her. Instead, I tell her everything. I spew it all out, along with everything I've wanted to tell her since I was seventeen. I tell her about Gregory. Everything about Gregory. That crashing feeling I felt when she answered the phone is lifting as I spill my truths, even though she hasn't said anything back yet. "I didn't know what else to do, and I didn't want you to get hurt, so I left. I should've told you. I should've called you, and I don't know if I'll ever be able to show you how sorry I am, but I didn't think I had any other choice." My breathing is short and ragged. Gavin's hand still holds mine tightly.

"Oh, Charlotte, I'm sorry too. If I was home more or asked more questions...." Her feeling guilty about me leaving breaks me more. This wasn't on her. It was me. My decision. My choice.

"No, mom, don't be sorry...." There is so much to unpack between the two of us, but hearing her voice is like music to my ears. Even her crying. I didn't realize how much I needed my mom until I heard her voice.

We talk for over two hours. It's not all amazing. It's fucking hard actually, and therapeutic in ways I could never imagine. Going through things I never told her. Her being upset, and rightfully so, that I stayed away and didn't confide in her. I let fear lead my way and hid behind that fear and guilt for so long. I could go back and forth about the what-ifs, only that won't change the past. All I can do is move forward and not let fear dictate my life again. I tell her about my internship and law school. And last but not in the slightest least, I tell her I've met an amazing man who makes me happy. Gavin, who has sat in silent support next to me this entire time, never releasing my hand, smiles before leaning in and planting a kiss on my temple.

She tells me about my grandparents and how much they will want to talk to me. She tells me about work and how she's poured herself into it since I left. We're both exhausted from the conversation. It's been emotionally draining on both ends.

"I love you so much, Charlotte." Those words are words I didn't even realize I needed to hear from her. "I don't ever want to lose you again. You have to promise me. You cannot disappear on me." It's a plea.

"You won't mom. I promise. I'm so sorry it took me so long. I love you." We plan to talk this week via video call, which is scary on a whole other level, to see her on the other end of the phone. Planning a few times that work in both of our schedules. The last thing I want is for her to sit around waiting for me to call.

"I love you too. I'll talk to you on Tuesday?" I can't blame her for repeating it to make sure it's real.

"Yes, Tuesday. Promise." I wait for her to hang up, which takes her a few extra seconds as though she's afraid I'll run again once she does. I won't. Talking to her was terrifying but easy at the same time. Though I already feel lighter, I know my guilt won't go away overnight.

Another kiss to my temple pulls me out of my stupor. "I am so fucking proud of you, Charlotte. You are amazing. I'm getting up because I have to pee like a racehorse. I've been holding it in for at least thirty minutes, not wanting to let go of your hand, but I don't want to embarrass myself."

"Oh my God, Gavin, go," I giggle, realizing I've been squeezing his hand the whole time and that he's been sitting here for two hours while I talked to my mom. What kind of man does that? Gavin. That's the kind.

He literally runs down the hallway to the bathroom, and I can't stop laughing, making me realize how much I have to pee too. I get up, run into the next closest bathroom, and feel a new sense of relief after going to the bathroom myself.

Walking back into the living room, Gavin is on the couch, his arms open, and I climb in beside him, pressing my head to his chest as he wraps me up in a hug.

"Thank you. For being here. For being you." I say, breathing him in.

"Nowhere else I want to be, babe." He kisses the top of my head. And we stay like that. Wrapped in his arms. Wrapped in his strength. I am falling for this man. The man helping me tear down walls I've held so tightly around myself for years, making me feel stronger than I ever have.

21

Gavin

*L*istening to Charlotte talk to her mom on the phone made me so damn proud of her. This woman has been through so much. Has been on her own for so long. It took a lot of courage to finally call her mom. And I'll be damned if I wasn't going to be there for her the whole time she was doing it. I told her I would, and I meant every word.

Even though that meant my hand went numb from her squeezing it when she talked about tough things. Even though, as a twenty-eight-year-old man, I wasn't sure if I was going to piss myself from holding it in, I was afraid to let go of her. I was in awe of her today. And when we sat together on the couch, I felt it down to my bones that I could love this woman; hell, maybe I already did. A thought that should scare the ever-loving shit out of me as I had sworn off relationships and the idea of love after Rachel, *yet it doesn't.*

I dropped Charlotte off at her house so she and Grace

could have time. As much as I wanted to hog her, I knew she needed Grace tonight. They have a lot to catch up on from both ends, so I invited Logan and James over to watch the Sunday night game at my house to keep me occupied.

When I got home, I booked another plane ticket to my sister's show online. I wanted to make sure I could get Charlotte on the same flight in first class with me. No way we were flying separately or not sitting together. I texted Olivia and told her to make sure she got another ticket. I know there will be a phone call from her soon demanding an explanation. I ordered wings to be delivered, and Logan is bringing beer.

If I can't spend the night with Charlotte, hanging out with my two best friends is a fairly close second best.

The door to my condo opens, and Logan walks in wearing his Cardinals jersey singing the Sunday night theme song like he's Carrie Underwood. The Cardinals are playing the Rams tonight. We probably don't stand a chance against the Rams, but when you're a fan, you cannot be a fair-weather fan; it's all or nothing.

He takes the six packs he's carrying to the fridge, pulls out and opens two bottles before placing the others inside, and brings them out for us. "When is James getting here?" he says, handing me a beer and plopping on the other end of the couch.

"He said he'd be here by kick-off. They went to see Lexi's parents to do some wedding stuff. He needed to drop Lexi off before heading over." I say as the doorbell rings. Wings are here. I grab the food and put it on the breakfast bar.

I throw some wings on my plate and make my ass

comfortable on the couch again. Logan does the same, and when I look at him, he's staring at me.

"Can I help you, or are you just going to stare at me?" I ask with a wing in my mouth.

"You're totally screwed." He says.

"What the hell are you talking about?"

"Dude, you have the look James did when he met Lexi. You're screwed. Toast. Done for. I'm losing another friend to the love fairy." He retorts, popping a wing into his mouth.

"I'm not screwed. I'm not going to fuck around and lie to you. She's different." I tell him honestly.

"You've been screwing. Several times if I had to guess." He smirks.

"You are such an asshole." I'd throw something at him if I didn't have wing sauce on my hands.

"Sorry, not sorry. I calls them as I sees them." He sing songs before popping a wing in his mouth.

"And what about you? What happened with Grace Friday?" Putting the heat back on him.

"She's the devil in disguise, is what she is."

"Who's the devil in disguise?" James asks as he walks into the living room. I didn't hear him come in.

"Grace fucking Hastings. That's who. Grab me another beer before you sit down."

"Yes, your highness...demanding bastard. Could at least say please." James argues but gets Logan his beer anyways.

"She is the ultimate cock tease. Never, and I mean never, have I chased a woman. But fuck, she's got me twisted." He takes a long sip of his new beer.

"Friday didn't go well?" I ask.

Logan puts his plate down on the coffee table. "Oh, it was. It was going fan-fucking-tastic, until it wasn't. We stayed at Blue, had a drink and talked. Actually talked. She invited me back to her place, so I followed her there. Everything was going to plan, and since you know what happened last time, I wanted to make sure she came first. And she did. Twice." Logan runs his hands through his hair.

"I don't get it. How is that not going well?" James asks from the chair across from us.

"I'll tell you how. She fucking sits up, says thank you, and that she has an early morning so I could see myself out."

I laugh and spew beer on my coffee table. *Karma. Is. A. Bitch.*

"Holy shit. She pulled a you. Damn, man, I give her credit. She held onto that one." I cannot hold in my laughter.

"Wait a minute. I'm missing something?" James says.

I fill him in on their first encounter. The night that he left the club early. I forgot James wasn't there when Logan told me about it.

"That's priceless. The mighty Logan, brought down a peg or two by Grace Hastings. I mean, you did deserve it. Payback's a bitch." James states matter of factly.

"So, did you leave?" I ask.

"I thought she was joking, but she got up and left her room. I found her by the front door holding it open. I wasn't undressed yet, you know, taking care of the lady, and all, so yeah. I left. Went home with the hardest dick I've ever had and jerked off three times before I could even fall asleep." He looks distressed.

"And you don't have a way to get a hold of her, I'm guessing," James adds in.

"Oh, I have her number. She left her phone out when she went to the bathroom, so I put my name in her phone and sent myself a message. I texted her last night, but she never responded. Did Charlotte say anything? Guys. Fuck. I think there is something wrong with me." Logan leans back into the couch; his face actually looks pained.

"I don't think I'm the one that's screwed, my friend. That would be you. Charlotte talked to Grace Saturday and today, but she didn't say anything about you to me." I feel bad for the guy.

"At least now you're even." James laughs.

"Fuck off, dude. She cracked a little Friday. I could tell in her eyes she was into me. She just needs to realize it." He sits up, shaking off his defeat.

"Are you sure that's what you want? No offense, but Grace doesn't seem like the type of girl you fuck around with. Especially with Charlotte and me, if you just want to bang her and move on, I'd rather you not. I don't want things to be perpetually awkward." I'm serious. I see a future with Charlotte, and if he just wants to get his dick wet, I'd rather him not go there with Grace. She's important to Charlotte and would always take her side.

"I don't know man. Seriously. It's like I can't shake her."

"Well, figure your shit out. Because if you're just trying to fuck her out of your system, that's not going to fly with Grace, I can tell. And she's Charlotte's best friend, so I don't want her pissed at me because I'm guilty by association knowing your horny ass."

"Truth, Logan. All joking aside. Don't mess with a friend's girlfriend's friend. It won't end well." James looks Logan in the eyes, not being a dick but being genuine.

"I know. I know. I get it. Can we move on? We're missing the game?"

And we do. We watch football. James fills us in on wedding stuff, none of which we really care about, but it's

James, so we listen. We have a few beers and don't bring up Grace the rest of the night. After the game ends, the boys leave. So I clean up and get ready for bed. Sliding into my bed that still smells like her, I wish she was here. I grab my phone and send a text before holding her pillow like a fool, so I can fall asleep to her smell.

ME:

> I hope you had a good time with Grace. My bed is missing you. Goodnight, beautiful.

22

Charlotte

I stare at the file on my laptop, willing my eyes to stay open. The entire team has been working tirelessly on the Pickett case and keeping up with other clients, and the influx of new clients hasn't slowed since I started my internship. The long hours and late nights have me feeling ever more grateful for the scholarship I received, or else I don't know when I would sleep.

The past few weeks have flown by. It's been four weeks since my first conversation with my mom. Since then, we've talked at least three times a week, most now via video chat. I'll admit we both cried through most of it the first time we did. It was as if I was seeing a ghost. Keeping tabs on her on social media has nothing on seeing her over video. It wasn't until I watched her face, and heard her voice while looking into her eyes, that it truly hit me how much I had missed her.

We've talked about everything. Gregory, her job, school, moving to Phoenix, Grace, my internship, the scholarship,

Gavin, and so much more. She's met Gavin a few times on video chat. Of course, my mom asked if he was taking good care of me, which both he and I assured her he was. I also know he gave her his number, and they have also texted. I swear she likes him more than me already.

I talked with my grandparents too. My grandpa, a man of few words, simply said, "It's good to have you back, kiddo, don't do that to us again." My grandma wasn't as easily forgiving. Our first conversation was hard to swallow. She wanted me to know and feel the hurt and worry they and my mom felt all this time. Trust me when I say I did. I know I hurt them. I know now, at twenty-five, running and protecting myself also sacrificed their happiness. At eighteen, I was scared and thought I was doing the right thing. A mistake I promised my grandma I wouldn't make again. We're making progress, and every conversation gets easier.

My mom wanted me to come home immediately. I couldn't. I don't know if I'll ever be ready to return to Cedar Ridge as long as Gregory still lives there. In our conversations, my mom told me Gregory is, in fact, working with his father, being groomed to take over as CEO of Cole Inc. when his dad retires. I didn't want more information about him; my mom respected that. Gavin didn't push me to go either. He simply said he would go with me if I wanted, but even with him by my side, I still was not ready to take that step.

We fly to LA for Olivia's show next weekend, which is crazy. I am not sure where the rest of September and most of October went. I'm so nervous to meet his family. I mean, I've met his Dad in a professional sense. This will be different. Meeting his dad, mom, and sister as his girlfriend. I haven't been anyone's girlfriend since high school. *What if they don't like me? What if I say something stupid.* Ugh, I need to get out of my own head. If they are anything like Gavin, it'll be fine, and I need to stop being a baby about it.

But before I meet his parents, Gavin is meeting my mom. She is coming to Phoenix this weekend. Talk about a couple of weeks of a lot. I am both excited to see her and freaking out simultaneously. Talking to her on the phone and even seeing her on video chat is different from in person. I haven't seen her in six years, and that terrifies me.

Her flight arrives at seven, and I am picking her up from the airport. I planned to get a hotel since Grace and I share a two-bedroom that is small, but Gavin insisted she stay at his place. Truth be told, it's where I spend most of my time anyways. Being the lawyer he is, he brought a good argument to the table, and I didn't have a proper defense against it.

"There is plenty of space here. You spend most nights here. I have three bedrooms, Charlotte. Your mom can stay in one, and although it would kill me, you could stay in the other if you don't feel comfortable with your mom knowing we share a room, although don't expect me not to sneak in after she goes to bed." I do spend most nights there. I have some work clothes in the closet, a drawer he cleared out for me in his dresser, and some of my make-up/toiletries in the bathroom. I thought I would freak out being in a man's space after years of needing my own, but being with Gavin feels right in a way I can't explain, so instead, I relish the feeling.

Gavin has hinted at me moving in since I'm there so often; I'm just not sure I'm ready to take that step. Grace and I have a lease until May, and although she's already assured me she wouldn't mind taking it over if that is what I truly wanted, I can't do that to her. Grace has been my other half since my Freshman year of undergrad. She's my safety net, and as dependent as that sounds, I don't know if I'm ready to give that up.

She's been swamped at work, the same as me with my internship and school, so sometimes, even keeping up via text is difficult. Logan has been relentlessly texting her since their night at Blue; although she won't admit it, I think she likes it and has been texting back. I want to push for more details but I know Grace, if you push when she's not ready, she'll shut down. Her family life isn't sunshine and rainbows, *a story that's for her to tell*, which is a big reason she doesn't do relationships. So, whatever she and Logan have going on is between them. She'll tell me when she's ready or if she needs me, and I'll be there every step of the way in whatever capacity.

Gavin wanted to go with me to pick up my mom from the airport but understood that this was something I needed to do on my own. Instead, we compromised on him picking up dinner and meeting at the condo. I didn't feel like going out on her first night here. We're going to lunch tomorrow with Grace, and I can't wait for them to meet.

My desk phone ringing snaps me out of my trance, and I fumble with the receiver, not even bothering to look at the name.

"Hello."

"Hey, Fire, I knew you wouldn't check the time or your phone, so this is your alarm to pack up and head to the airport. It's six already, and you don't want to be late." Gavin's deep voice purrs through the other end. *Fire.* He often shortens his nickname for me, Firecracker, to Fire, and I can't even pretend to be upset about it. I used to hate pet names, but coming out of his mouth, it's a turn-on.

Mostly everyone in the office knows we are together. Daniel and John told Gavin as long as it didn't affect the production of the office or cause drama, there was no policy against it. Beth has been the only drama. When she found out, that solidified her hate for me, mumbling under her breath whenever she walks past me with words like *slut, gold-digger, whore.* I would be upset or offended, except I learned a long time ago that women using shaming words to bring other women down without reason reflects their own insecurities, jealousy, and lack of confidence. If anything, it makes me feel bad for her. I simply kill her with kindness, which pisses her off more. Justin and I aren't close, but he is easy to work with and even has opened up a little during the long days.

"Ahh, shit, oh sorry, I mean shoot, yes, thank you. I need to go." I ramble into the phone while simultaneously closing my computer and gathering my stuff.

"Breathe, Charlotte. Relax, I didn't mean to freak you out. I just didn't want you to be late." His voice immediately calming my racing heart. *God, I can't believe I'm so nervous.*

"Breathe, yeah, you're right. Thank you. I'm going to head out. I'll meet you at the condo. I lo- I mean, see you soon." I hang up and slap my hand on my head. Shit, I almost said I love you on the phone while sitting in my shared office, something we've danced around but most definitely haven't said to each other. I don't even know where that came from. *Am I falling in love with Gavin? Or have I already fallen?* Fuck, I don't have time to analyze all that right now.

I sling my bag over my shoulder and grab my phone off my desk. Saying my goodnight's to Beth and Justin, Justin tells me to have a good weekend; Beth grunts, and I walk out of the office. My phone pings as I'm reaching my car.

GAVIN:

> It's going to be fine. Drive careful.

ME:

> I will. xo

I turn on the car radio and head toward the airport, trying not to let my nerves get the better of me. Vance Joy's *Missing Piece* plays through my speakers, and the words hit me like a semi. Tears fill my eyes as the full weight of my realization washes over me. Gavin has been my missing piece. I am not just falling in love with him but am truly, irrevocably, and unconditionally in love with him. I am stronger because of him. He lets me be me. He lifts me up and supports me. Not with huge things, but with little gestures. Snacks while I'm studying, rubbing my feet while we sit on the couch. When we are ass deep in cases, bringing me a coffee or sending me a text to let me know he's thinking of me when I'm at a study group. And the way he commands my body in the bedroom is beyond hot. His dirty words, the way he takes charge, possesses me, worships me, pulling things from me that I never thought possible. *Great, now my panties are soaking, and I'm horny right before I pick up my mom.*

I get off 143 onto Sky Harbour Blvd toward the cell phone lot while I wait for my mom to let me know she's here. After parking, I take a few deep breaths, make sure my makeup isn't smeared and re-apply my lip gloss. It's six thirty-five, and her flight is set to arrive at seven, I can't park and wait at the terminal; Gavin told me airport security will ticket you if you are there more than a minute or two and aren't actively putting someone's luggage in your trunk. While I wait, I pull up VH Nicolson's latest book *Jacob* on my phone and get so pulled into their story I almost accidentally dismiss the text from my mom, telling me she's walking out and will meet me at Terminal 4.

Forcing myself to close the app, I take a deep breath. *This is it.* I pull out of the lot and head toward the Terminal 4 arrival gate. I see her before she sees me, and I feel my lungs seize up, my eyes misting over as I pull to the curb and put my hazard flashers on. *Here goes nothing.* Willing myself to move, I step out of the car and come around, her eyes catching mine and instantly filling with tears.

She drops her carry-on bag she was pulling and walks straight up to me, wrapping me in a hug that I didn't realize I desperately needed.

She pulls back, putting her hands on either side of my face, "Oh, my, Lottie, you are so beautiful. I have missed you so much." Tears are now streaming down my face, mascara be damned, because I couldn't stop this if I tried. She pulls me back into a tight hug, her hand on my hair, "God, I can't believe this is real."

"Me, either. I'm so sorry, mom. I never meant to hurt you or wait so long. I just..." I can't find the words, and she shhhh's me, a simple thing backed with so much meaning.

Our moment is interrupted by the security cop telling us we need to move or get ticketed. I want to flip him off and tell him to go fuck himself, but I don't feel like spending the night in airport jail, so we release each other, my mom grabbing her bag as I open the back seat. We both get in and head to Gavin's.

I was worried the car ride would be awkward, but it wasn't. She filled me in on her flight, and I told her about work and lunch tomorrow. I've talked to her about Grace, but I'm so excited for her to finally meet her in person. I put in the code and pull into the parking garage of Gavin's condo. Another new thing, he added another spot for parking so I wouldn't have to park on the street, especially if I came over after a study group which can go late.

"Penthouse, huh? I'm impressed," my mom muses after getting into the elevator. I haven't talked to my mom about Gavin's money. Mostly because it isn't a factor to me. I couldn't care less about his bank account, and I don't ever want him to think otherwise.

"He works hard, mom," I reply flatly.

"I didn't mean anything by it, Lottie. I know I couldn't give you everything you deserved growing up." That's not where I expected that to go. The door opens to the foyer leading to Gavin's door. This is something I don't want looming over us this weekend.

I turn to her and stop us before coming to the door. "Mom, you gave me everything I needed. I never cared about money. Did it bother me in high school? Yes, maybe; I don't know? But I am not with Gavin for his money and never will be. I've worked hard to get where I am and know that once I graduate, things will be easier for me. My scholarship helped move up that timeline, but that doesn't change how I feel. You raised me on your own, and I am so proud to call you my mom. You taught me the value of hard work, and yes, money can make things easier, but it doesn't buy happiness."

"When did you get so wise?" My mom says, hugging me again.

"We should probably go inside. Gavin was ordering dinner, and I'm sure it's here already." I turn and open the door to the condo. Gavin walks through the door and comes to me, wrapping me in a big hug, breathing me in, and whispering in my ear, "I missed you."

"It's been two hours. I missed you too." God, I can't get enough of this man.

A throat clearing behind me jolts us back, returning us to reality. Gavin lets go of me and turns, tucking me into his side and reaching out his hand.

"I'm sorry, Kelly. I didn't mean to be rude. I missed my girl." *Kelly, he's on a first-name basis with her? How much have they been texting?*

My face must say it all because my mom interjects in a laugh, "I told Gavin he better not even think of calling me Ms. Swanson when he called to tell me he upgraded my flight to first class."

Lifting my chin to look at him, he simply smiles and shrugs. Smug bastard, *we'll talk about that later,* I say with my eyes.

"Let me show you your room," I say, grabbing my mom's bag.

"Thank you. It's been a long day traveling, and I'd like to freshen up."

I walk down the hallway and show her to the guest room, making sure she has what she needs before meeting Gavin back in the kitchen.

He instantly wraps me in his arms, my head against his chest. "Not stripping you naked right here is taking all my willpower."

Running my hand down his chest, grabbing the bulge over his jeans, I laugh, "I can tell, you sex-crazed maniac, my mom is right down the hall."

"I know. I'm seriously rethinking her staying in a hotel; I'm used to us having privacy." He grabs my ass and squeezes hard.

"I wanted to do that, and you wouldn't let me. Besides,

it's only two nights. You'll survive." I say that for myself as much as him. Every time I see him, I want to climb him like a tree. My need for him never satisfied.

"Oh, but my sweet Charlotte, I don't think I will. Which is why I'm glad her room is three doors away from ours. No way in hell I'm waiting to have you until Sunday." *Ours.*

Gavin leans back slightly, grabbing my chin with his thumb and finger, tilting it up until our eyes meet. They are full of heat and lust; *damn, maybe we should've done the hotel.* He kisses me, sweeping his tongue into my mouth, a kiss full of promises of things to come later. *I can't wait.* I put my hands on his chest and force myself to break our kiss, just in time to hear my mom's door close, and seconds later, she's walking towards us. *Here we go.*

23

Charlotte

Gavin grabs my hand, lacing our fingers together and pulling my hand into his lap to stop me from fidgeting in my seat. We're sitting in first class on our way to LA to see Olivia's fashion show tomorrow night.

I've never flown first class. I've never flown at all. I feel underdressed in my leggings and off-the-shoulder shirt, my hair in a bun, and no make-up. I thought you should dress comfortably for traveling and we aren't seeing his family until dinner. When Gavin picked me up wearing dark jeans and black Henley, looking good enough to eat, I wanted to change. He said I looked perfect, and we didn't have time since I insisted on staying at my apartment so Grace could help me pack.

I thought I'd be fine flying. I wasn't. I freaked out on the tarmac before the plane took off. Shaking and hyperventilating isn't exactly how I wanted to start our trip. I should've had a drink before we got on the plane. Or a Xanax.

Gavin held my hand and rubbed my leg through the whole take-off, and as soon as we were in the air, the flight attendant brought me a glass of champagne. It's not only the flight that has me on edge. I'm terrified to meet his family. I haven't said anything, but my insides are tied in nervous knots, and I feel nauseous. Gavin wanted us to do dinner this week, so I could meet them before we left. However, my school schedule was packed, and they flew out a few days earlier, leaving us no choice but to meet once we were there. *I hope they don't see me looking like this.*

I want them to like me. He told his mom about us a week after telling his dad. She's been hounding him to bring me over since. Still, Gavin told her he wanted time for us to get to know each other before adding in families. His mom, although reluctant, understood that, but we can't avoid it any longer.

Last weekend with my mom went better than I ever could have expected, and I want this weekend to be the same. Spending time with my mom was amazing; she loved Gavin and Grace. All my insecurities about her coming and how it would go were unfounded. I felt a weight lifted off my chest and could breathe when it felt like we picked up right where we left off. We left the past in the past and focused on going forward, and it couldn't have been more perfect. We stayed in, had dinner Friday, and talked until my mom was too tired to keep her eyes open. Saturday, we had lunch with Grace, and my mom said after meeting her how grateful she was that I had Grace as a best friend.

After lunch, Gavin and I showed her around Phoenix, including the University and the office, before heading out for a late dinner. She was quiet after showing her the office. I'm sure she was tired since I had her going non-stop since she woke up. Her flight left mid-morning on Sunday, so it was hard to say goodbye.

We booked her a flight for Thanksgiving, and I promised her I'd think about coming back after the Christmas Gala that Gavin has already asked me to attend with him. Gavin said he could take some time and come with me, knowing how hard it would be going back the first time. I'm still not sure I can do it. Last weekend solidified two things in my mind: one, that my mom and I were going to be okay, feeling a lot of guilt leave my body, and two, that I am undeniably and completely in love with Gavin Davis.

I couldn't have gotten through it without him. His support when I word vomited about her in his condo, sitting with me through our first phone call and not letting me get in my head before her visit. Spending time with Gavin has made me realize how lost I was before him. Having my mom back was a piece of that, but I feel whole when I am with Gavin. I was living a life afraid of everything, even though I wouldn't admit it. I was going through the motions working to achieve the next task without ever experiencing anything. Grace had brought it up a few times over the years, but I wasn't ready to listen. It's like Gavin took the blindfold off my eyes, and I see life in a new light. Not to mention our sexual chemistry, I will never tire of getting my fill of that man.

I haven't said anything, mostly because I'm a chickenshit. I have never felt more cared for or worshiped than with Gavin. It's as if he knows what I need before I do and can read my mind with a simple look. The damaged part of me always worries that he'll realize I'm not enough or that he won't feel the same way. That I'll never be enough. Something I've learned I never ever fully worked through after Gregory. And that scared part of me worries if I lay it out there and he doesn't feel the same way, I will break.

Gregory made me feel like I wasn't enough. I used to think maybe if I was more, he wouldn't hit me. If I was better, then he wouldn't be so rough. It never mattered what I did, and deep down, I know that all the things that happened were not my fault and that his actions are not a reflection of me, but I haven't truly let go of that mindset. I'm working on it; however, old habits die hard.

"Want to join the mile-high club, Fire?" Gavin snaps me from my negative thoughts as he leans over his oversized seat, nudging my shoulder with that sexy smirk of his.

"Getting kicked off a plane is not on my bucket list, you deviant," I muse, shoving him back toward his seat.

Undeterred, he puts his hand on my inner thigh, sliding up my leggings slowly, "You have a bucket list? I'm happy to help you check things off said list."

Grabbing his hand in an attempt to stop him before he reaches where I always ache for him. This is not the place. I look around to make sure no one is listening, "Not a sexual bucket list. Is sex all you think about?"

He leans in, placing a kiss below my ear as a shiver runs through me from his touch, whispering, "Only with you, babe, only with you. Shame about the bucket list, but no worries, I have one, and I can't wait to start crossing things off the list with you, starting when we get to our hotel."

"We're meeting your parents for dinner, and I need to shower and change before we go." I try to play it cool even though I know my resolve is already waning. If we weren't so close to landing, I might even take him up on the mile-high offer. He swipes his hand over me, pinching my center and even through my leggings; the jolt of pleasure causes my breath to hitch. Placing one more kiss on my neck, he smiles at me, eyes full of promises of things to come, and goes back to going through emails on his phone. *Bastard.*

Walking hand in hand, we head outside to meet the car that Gavin ordered. He thought renting a car would be a waste of time since we are only here for two nights. I have no experience with traveling, so I'm just going with it as we slide into the sleek black leather seats.

We only brought carry-ons as it is only for a weekend. I packed as much as I could into that tiny suitcase. Grace saved my ass and let me borrow outfits for this weekend. My closet consists of bargain buys and clearance racks and is, in no way, shape, or form, up to LA standards. I hated to admit it, but I needed Grace's fashion sense to make it through this trip.

Gavin told me I'd look good in anything, which we all know is guy talk, for *I want to get in your pants.* So that was no help. Silently trying to not freak out, I feel Gavin's mouth on the side of my neck, and I involuntarily moan.

Lifting his lips from my neck, he whispers in my ear while pressing a button, a screen dividing the front from the back raising up, "You have to be quiet, Fire, there's a privacy screen, but this car isn't soundproof," before returning his mouth to my skin, placing kisses up and down my neck while his hand slides over my thigh traveling upward.

"Gavin..." The word comes out with a moan as he continues his onslaught of kisses while rubbing me over my leggings. "Shouldn't we...umm...wait?"

Pulling back slightly and pinching me over my clothes, making me squirm, he says, "No. We shouldn't. It's a thirty-minute drive to the hotel, Charlotte, and I can't wait that long. You already made me wait on the plane."

"The flight was only ninety minutes." My breathing becoming rapid as he continues to pinch and slide, repeating his rhythm. He's not even touching my skin, and I'm about to combust.

"Ninety minutes is a long time when I can't get anything but tasting you out of my head. No. More. Talking." He says before biting down slightly on my neck and gliding his hand up to pull on my leggings, his fingers sliding into my panties, finding me soaked. A loud "Mmm" slips from my mouth as he circles my clit, setting my nerves on high alert.

"I told you, you have to be quiet, baby. I guess I will have to keep your mouth occupied as well." He whispers before covering my mouth in a deep kiss. At the same time, two of his fingers impale me, my back arching off the seat as he swallows my cries. He sets a relentless pace, scissoring his fingers inside of me, my body doing everything it can to stay on the seat as Gavin uses his mouth to silence mine. His thumb rubs my clit, sending me higher and higher, and once his fingers press against my G-spot, I fall, shaking and writhing, as Gavin pulls every last jolt from my body. I swear Gavin has a treasure map to all my pleasure spots. And let me tell you, he hits the Xs every time. A limp noodle in the seat, Gavin releases our kiss. Removing his hand from my leggings, he closes his mouth around his fingers, sucking the juices from my release.

"You taste like the sweetest honey. I could feast on your nectar every damn day." He says, adjusting himself in his pants as the car slows down.

Pulling up outside our hotel, I do my best to put myself back together, putting my hair back into a messy bun and fanning my face. I would probably be embarrassed about what just happened as a stranger drove us through the streets of Los Angeles if I wasn't so sated from my otherworldly orgasm.

The driver opens the trunk for the staff to grab our luggage before getting out and coming to open the door for us. Gavin steps out, thanking the driver and speaking to him about our plans for the weekend before reaching in and grabbing my hand, helping me to my feet.

Walking into The Ritz Carlton, I can't help but stop and gawk. The marble floors with a circular pattern tiled into them in black, white, and gray is stunning. Modern metal lighting fixtures hang throughout the entryway, giving off soft lighting that makes you feel warm and welcome. White leather lounge chairs sit off to the side, where a few people occupy them, and to the left, you can see a walkway that leads to a bar area. The nicest hotel I ever stayed at had free continental breakfast and a pool, and I thought that was living large. I feel out of my league.

"Don't be nervous ," Gavin says, placing his hand on the small of my back, under my shirt, urging me forward. My skin buzzes from the simple contact.

"This place is beautiful. I feel so underdressed." Looking down at my clothes.

"You are beautiful. It doesn't matter what you're wearing. Once I get you upstairs, it's all coming off anyways," he says above a whisper so only I can hear before releasing his touch on my back and grabbing my hand heading toward the reception desk.

Goosebumps line my skin, and where his hand touched my skin feels on fire. How can I be so desperate for him right after our car quickie?

We stand at the welcome desk as Gavin checks us in. I can't help seeing the receptionist lean forward, pushing her breasts as close to his face as she can over the counter while she bats her eyelashes. I find it amusing how hard she's trying. Gavin doesn't pay her any attention at all, and my inner bitch does a little happy dance.

Taking the elevator to the eighteenth floor, we walk down the hallway. Gavin uses the keycard to open the executive suite we are staying in. He opens the door, and I walk in. The main room is all creams, grays, and whites, with a long dining table in the center, while windows line the entire back wall overlooking downtown LA. There is a white leather couch and two chairs with an espresso-colored coffee table on the other side. Beyond that is a hallway that leads to double doors. Gavin stays in the main room as I wander around this suite that is right out of a magazine. I push open the double doors into the bedroom. A king-sized bed sits in the middle with a down-white comforter. An ottoman sits at the end of the bed, with a black chair in the corner. Windows line the west wall, which gives us a spectacular view of the sunset. There is a bathroom attached with a shower that is the size of my kitchen, lined with gray tile, a bench on one side, and multiple shower heads. There is a massive white bathtub as well that is calling my name. Being up at six for our flight after getting little sleep from nerves last night is catching up with me.

I walk back into the main room, finding Gavin sitting on the couch with his feet on the coffee table. He opens his arms up, willing me to his side. It's just after one o'clock in the afternoon, giving us time to relax and get ready before meeting his parents for drinks and dinner at seven.

I sit on the couch, tucking my legs underneath me and

curling into him as his arm comes around my shoulder. "I ordered room service, a chicken wrap for you. It'll be here in fifteen minutes. I figured you'd be hungry, seeing as the protein bar on the way to the airport was the only thing I saw you eat today."

"Thank you. I am hungry. I'm glad I didn't eat anything else this morning. I probably would've gotten sick on the plane otherwise." I close my eyes and simply breathe him in.

"Thank you for coming with me." Squeezing me to his side and kissing the top of my head.

"Thank you for inviting me," I say with as much courage behind my statement as I can muster. Truly, I am glad I'm here, but I'm still so nervous about meeting his parents and being around all those people tomorrow. I don't want to embarrass him, and I've kept myself limited to very controlled environments for a long time. I'm not sure how this is going to go.

Reading me as always, he pulls me away from him, using his hand to grab my chin and lift my head up so he can look me in the eyes, his go-to when he knows I'm hiding something. "Hey, beautiful, what's going on in that head of yours?"

"It's nothing...silly, really. I want everything to go well this weekend. My mom can't stop talking about you. What if your parents don't like me? What if I embarrass you? What if I freak out?" All my fears and insecurities come sliding out. He's like my own version of truth serum.

Tilting my head and placing a searing kiss that I feel to my soul, he leans back and says, "My parents and my sister are going to love you, and do you know how I know this?"

"How?"

He stills for a second before taking a deep breath.

"Because I love you, Charlotte. I have been waiting for the right time to tell you, but I don't know if there ever is a perfect time. I love your strength, your smile, and the way your eyes light up when you talk about someone you care about. I love that you set a goal and stick to it, as well as your loyalty to Grace, Joe, and Maria. I love that you took a chance with me. Before you, I didn't want anything from a woman besides getting laid. I know that makes me sound like a douche, and I probably was, but after Rachel, fuck, I told myself I never was going to let myself get involved again. And that worked for me until one night when I walked into a bar and saw the most beautiful woman I'd ever seen in a blue dress, talking to herself. Maybe I didn't want to admit it then, but that night I think I already knew you would be different. And from the moment you said *Okay*, you have been weaving yourself through this dead heart of mine, bringing it back to life. So, we'll do this together. Nothing you do could embarrass me, and if you freak out, I'll be there to help you because you, Fire, are worth everything." He sighs as I feel tears of happiness slip down my cheek. Holding my emotions back is not an option. He wipes my tears with the pad of his thumb.

"I love you too ," I whisper.

"Say it again." His face lighting up with the biggest grin reaching all the way to his gorgeous baby blues.

"I love you, Gavin." There is so much more I want to say, but my brain and mouth are not working together.

"Damn right." He leans in, capturing my mouth again as I wrap my arms around him, untangling my legs from underneath me and climbing over to straddle him. I love this man, and he loves me. He helps me chase my demons and melt my fears, and with him by my side, I feel like I can fly.

Our mouths are fused as I shamelessly rub myself over his already hardened length as he moans into my mouth and moves his hands to grab both of my ass cheeks, squeezing hard. I go to lift my shirt off when there is a knock at the door.

Reluctantly, Gavin pulls back, lifting me off his lap, "Fuck, it's our food. To be continued." He stands and adjusts the very hard bulge in his jeans before opening the door and taking the cart, handing over a tip to the employee who delivered it.

The food smells amazing, and as much as I want him right now, my stomach growls loudly, demanding food.

"I guess we better feed you. I don't want my girl to get hangry." Gavin laughs, bringing the food to the dining table as I stand to meet him.

"Guess so. Who knew flying, orgasms in the backseat of a car, and I love you could make a girl so hungry." I joke, taking a seat at the table and lifting the covers while Gavin grabs the water from the lower cart.

Sitting down next to me, Gavin opens my bottle of water before his and then looks at me with heated eyes, "I'm going to down this burger, and then I'm going to take you into that bedroom and eat you for dessert." *Yes, please!*

24

Gavin

*R*eady for the night, I walk out of the bathroom, freezing at the sight in front of me. I can't help but stare at my beautiful girl. Charlotte is staring out the windows, lost in her own head. Standing there with her reflection bouncing off the mirrored windows, the look of contentment on her face my undoing. The emerald green cocktail dress she has on has an open back, not allowing her to wear a bra, giving me a full view of her smooth as silk back. The dress sits right above her ass, hugging her sexy hips that no doubt have my fingerprints on them from holding on so tight to her earlier, landing just below her knee. Gold strappy heels weave up her ankles, making my dick twitch at the thought of taking her later with nothing but those on. Her golden locks are in beachy waves down her back, the light shining in through the windows, creating a halo around her. Never in a million years would I have thought I'd want a woman back in my life, let alone fall in love with one again. *Until her.*

She is strong and independent and has guarded herself for so long after everything she went through with her dickhead of an ex. The day she opened up to me about him, and her past was the day that cemented for me that I didn't want to ever let her go. *Crazy right?* It hadn't even been two weeks, and my life's perspective on relationships changed. I know it was because it was her. No one else would've ever made me think differently about it. She made me want to think differently. Which is why I couldn't wait any longer to tell her I loved her.

I knew she was nervous about coming to LA to meet my parents and Olivia. She keeps things close to her chest, but she has her tells, and her various smiles give away where her head is at. She has so many of them, and I love every one. Her genuinely happy smile, post-orgasm smile, polite professional smile, I'm smiling but, on the inside, I'm freaking out smile, to name only a few. For the entire plane ride, she gave me her nervous, but I'm acting strong smile whenever I asked her anything.

She needed to relax. I knew getting her out of her own head by focusing on her pleasure would help. Still, after hearing what she said about meeting my parents, I desperately needed her to know that my feelings for her were not based on what my parents thought. However, I know my mom and dad will love her too. Granted, she has already met my dad professionally. Honestly, I don't think they've seen each other more than in passing at the office since I talked with him and John about us dating. Hell, I haven't even seen him. Things at the office have been crazy, in a good way, business is going well, and new clients are seeking us out every day. It's great for the bottom line; however, it doesn't bode well for our personal lives. I worked fourteen to sixteen-hour days the past three weeks straight so I could be around when Kelly came to visit and be able to take the weekend for Olivia's show.

Long days make having uninterrupted hours with her worth it. After throwing Charlotte over my shoulder and carrying her to the bedroom, where I feasted on her for dessert, she rode me reverse cowgirl, a new favorite position, before we both took a much-needed nap. Gratefully, she set an alarm for us to get up so we could get ready to meet my parents for dinner.

I offered to shower with her to save water, but she gave me a *don't even think about it* look, jumped out of bed, and locked the bathroom door behind her. I know she's sore, but I can't get enough of her. I've never had this insane need to be close to someone, in someone, as often as possible. And it isn't just about the outcome. The connection I feel when I'm buried deep inside her is indescribable. That might make me sound sappy, and maybe I am, but damn that woman does things to me.

When Charlotte got out of the shower, I handed her a box wrapped with a yellow ribbon on it. She had tears in her eyes as she unwrapped the tissue paper, the dress, and gold strappy heels to go with it inside. Little does she know there are a few more where that came from. I asked Olivia to pick out a few dresses and shoes for her as a surprise. I wasn't expecting her to send over some of her designs, but when she told me she had the perfect dresses for Charlotte, I trusted my sister. She even dropped them off before we arrived, so I called and had them delivered to our room before our check-in.

If I had told her that I wanted to take her shopping or given her my card, she would have made a million excuses or flat-out refused. Money is not a turn-on for Charlotte, and it's another reason I love her. She sees people for who they are, not how much they have. All I want to do is spoil my girl, and since she won't let me do it openly, I have to be a little sneaky about it.

"Hey beautiful," I say, coming up behind her and wrapping my arms around her as she turns to look over her shoulder, those ocean baby blues staring up at me.

"Hey, yourself. Have a good shower?"

"I did. Would have been better if you were in there with me." I say, giving her a kiss on her forehead as she leans back into my chest.

"We'd never leave this hotel room if I did that. This view is amazing." She says, turning her eyes back from me, overlooking the city.

Grabbing her chin to bring her attention back to me, "Yes, it is."

"Thank you for bringing me. And thank you for this." She motions down to her dress. "I can't believe your sister wants me to wear an original design of hers."

"Of course she does; your perfect body was made for it." Holding her chin and kissing her perfectly red-colored lips, forcing myself to keep it quick. "We should get going before I rip this dress off you and take you in nothing but those shoes."

"Hmmm, can't wait," she says cheekily. She's a fucking tease, and she knows it.

"You'll pay for that later." She jumps as I slap her ass when she shimmies away from me. Adjusting myself in my now-too-tight pants, I follow behind her so we aren't late to meet my parents.

I am rethinking dinner with my parents on the ride down to the lobby. Charlotte is fucking stunning. Her makeup is heavier than normal but not overdone, and the green of the dress compliments her eyes, making them shine even brighter. This is going to be torture, keeping my hands to myself for the next few hours.

Charlotte must read my thoughts because she looks up at me at that exact moment, her eyes full of dirty promises. "I can't wait to be on my knees for you in nothing but these heels," she whispers as the elevator doors open, taking a step out in front of me, leaving me to adjust myself before stepping out. *Yep, definitely trying to kill me.*

I quicken my step to catch up, intertwining her hand with mine, as she looks up at me, giving me a cheeky smile with her eyebrow hitched, and together we head toward the lounge where we are meeting my parents. Before we even get to the entry, I spot my mother coming toward us. Charlotte must too, because the grip on my hand tightens, her smile falling instantly into a nervous smile that doesn't reach her eyes.

My mother comes straight at us, wrapping her arms around Charlotte, forcing me to let go.

"Charlotte." She leans back, looking at Charlotte before pulling her back into a hug again. "It's so good to finally meet you. You are even more beautiful in person." She gushes over her.

"Mom, let go. We're in the lobby. For God's sake, let her breathe." I chime in.

She pulls back slightly, "Oh, gosh, I'm so sorry, I got

carried away. I just couldn't wait to meet you." She's still holding onto her shoulders though.

Charlotte smiles at her. "It's so nice to meet you too Mrs. Davis. Thank you for letting me tag along to support Olivia this weekend."

"Please, call me Kristina. Mrs. Davis is my mother-in-law and makes me feel old." She chuckles but still hasn't let go of Charlotte. My mom finally releases her shoulders after my dad clears his throat behind her after shaking my hand, snapping her from fangirling over Charlotte. She finally remembers I'm standing here too and gives me a hug.

"Hello, Charlotte. It's so nice to meet you outside of the office. I've heard nothing but great things about you." My dad says with a smile, showing he already has a soft spot for her.

Charlotte reaches out her hand, "You as well, Mr. Davis. I'm honored to have the opportunity to intern at your company."

"Call me Daniel, please, and not only are we lucky to have you in a professional capacity, but also for my son, pulling the stick out of his ass." My dad chuckles.

"Thanks, Dad. Nothing like talking me up to my girlfriend."

Charlotte laughs, "Glad to be of service. He was walking quite stiffly."

My mom and dad start laughing as well. Interrupting their roast fest, I chime in. "Sorry to stop this make fun of Gavin session, but we need to go. We'll be late for our reservation."

Charlotte approaches me and pats my cheek, "Aww, I'm sorry, we didn't mean to hurt your feelings." Her sarcastic tone only makes my parents laugh more.

Leaning into her ear, I whisper, "Keep it up, Firecracker, and you will be the one walking stiffly tomorrow."

Her eyes light up with mischief, "Sir, yes sir." She winks, fucking winks, before my mom grabs her hand, effectively cutting off our conversation and leading her toward the restaurant. My dad and I follow behind.

She is going to be the death of me.

"Your parents are so sweet. It's so strange to see your dad outside of the office. He's like a different person." Charlotte says, placing her clutch on the table after walking back into our suite.

To say Charlotte was a hit with my parents would be an understatement. My mom gushed over her the entire dinner, and my dad couldn't stop telling me how lucky I was. As the night went on, I could tell Charlotte was more comfortable as her posture relaxed, her smile becoming more genuine, and her entire face lighting up. Which also meant she was more at ease giving me shit right along with them. Now I get what Charlotte meant when she worried her mom loved me more. My parents definitely love her more than me already. My mom insisted on us bringing Charlotte's mom, Kelly, for Thanksgiving and practically jumped out of her seat when we told her Charlotte would be coming to the Christmas Gala.

"I told you they'd love you. They love you more than me already." I say with a fake pout.

Charlotte saunters over to me, "Oh baby, let me make you feel better." She backs away from me and turns, so her back is facing me. Reaching for the zipper on the side of her one-shoulder dress, she lets it slide off her body. Revealing her black lace thong and those damn heels that have been killing me, picturing her naked in them all night.

Taking a step, she slides her panties down, leaving her standing in nothing but those fucking heels. She turns so she's facing me. Glued to my spot, I'm taking in the show. "I'm ready for you sir."

"Hell yes you are. I've been waiting all night for this." Kicking off my shoes, I unbutton my shirt and strip it off as she stands there in nothing but those heels, eyes heated over her shoulder, watching me. She's rooted to her spot, waiting for me. I unbuckle my pants and in one swift move, pull them and my boxers down my legs and step out. My cock springs free and is already dripping with pre-cum at the sight of her.

She takes two steps to get to me before lowering herself to her knees, taking me in her hand as she looks up at me through hooded lashes.

"You look perfect like this, Fire," I growl.

She leans forward, sucking me into her hot mouth, taking me all the way to the back in one go, "Holy shit that feels amazing."

Charlotte sucks me in deep again, causing my eyes to roll back and my knees to buckle, taking all of my focus to not blow in the next ten seconds.

"You take me so good, baby. I'm not going to last."

She hums around my shaft, the vibration of her lips setting me off as I feel my release build in my spine. Charlotte, on her knees, in nothing but those sexy heels, and the feeling of her hot mouth on me sets me off, starting in my toes and shooting up my spine as my body tenses, not even giving me a chance to warn her, as I explode into her perfect mouth. "Uuuuggh..." being the only noise I can get out as I try not to pass out, feeling dizzy, reaching for the couch nearby to steady myself.

Looking down at her as she pulls back, licking me dry with the sexiest smile on her face, my breaths uneven as I say in a voice I don't even recognize. "Get your ass in the bedroom, Charlotte." Her eyes lighting up at my command.

"Sir, yes sir." As I help her to stand, she sashays her sexy hips through the double doors, me hot on her heels, still catching my breath as I move.

The city's lights coming in from the windows give off a glow that illuminates the room with a warm sexy glow.

"Put your hands on the windows and spread your legs, Fire." My voice is low and husky. My breathing heavy, lust and my need for this woman taking control.

She does as I ask, placing her hands at shoulder height on the windows spreading her toned, heeled legs apart before looking at me, "Is this how you want me, sir?" She asks, her tone coy but confident. I love this side of her.

"Fuck yes. You are so beautiful, always, but especially like this." My dick stood at attention at her sight, ready for round two. "Can I go bare?" I ask her with heated breath as I bring my hands down her spine, and she shivers. I bring my hand around her waist to find her dripping wet already. We've talked about it before but have always used condoms. She's on the pill, but I never want to assume and want her to be comfortable.

"Yes, please. I want to feel all of you, Gavin." She pants as I continue to rub her clit in circles, making her writhe under my hands as she holds herself up.

"I've never gone bare with anyone before, Fire; I've been

waiting for you." Rachel and I always used protection, but I have wanted to take Charlotte skin-on-skin for weeks.

I place my hand on her back and push her down slightly, effectively bending her over, so her ass is perched right in front of me as I push two fingers inside her to stretch her out, scissoring in and out of her as I move.

"You have all of me, Gavin." She says between gasps, she's already close.

I pull my fingers out and line myself up behind her, using one hand to grab her hips and the other on her back to steady myself before I slam all the way in, my legs almost giving out at the feel of her tight pussy wrapping itself around me.

"Fuck, Charlotte, you feel incredible." I try to control myself, forcing myself to slow down.

She pushes her ass back into me, and I can't hold back. I slam into her hard and fast, the slap of our bodies and our moans filling the room. Grabbing her hips to hold myself steady, I pound into her as she moans, and I can feel her clenching around me.

I bring the hand I had on her back around and pinch her clit. She detonates. Yelling my name as she rides out her orgasms, her muscles clenching my cock. Pushing me over the edge, spilling my load deep inside of her, "Charlotte, fuck, oh...," my words jumbled as I ride out my own euphoria.

My legs wobbly as we come down from our high, I bend down, still connected to her. I placed kisses up her spine as she catches her breath, hands still firmly placed on the windows for support. When my strength returns, I slide out of her warmth, wrap my hand around her stomach, and pull her up and back towards me.

Holding her back to my chest, the LA skyline before us, I tell her, "I love you, Charlotte. You are mine. I am never letting you go."

"I love you, Gavin. I am yours." She sighs happily.

We stay like that for a few minutes before I lead her to the bathroom, where we shower and put some clothes on. One of my t-shirts for her and boxers for me. Climbing into bed, exhausted from a long but amazing day. I open my arm as she snuggles into my side, placing her head on my chest and her arm around my stomach.

I'm almost asleep when I hear, "I felt lost before you. Thank you for making me feel whole again. For loving me." Her confession, a whisper almost too low for me to hear, sinks deeper into my soul with every word. She lets out a content sigh, and within seconds, her breathing evens out, and I know she is asleep. *This beautiful girl is mine, and I will spend my life protecting her and making her feel cherished.* I gently kiss the top of her head and fall into the best sleep I've ever had.

25

Charlotte

Our weekend in LA started out perfectly. I was so nervous to meet Gavin's family and his sister. His mom coming up and pulling me into an instant hug, as awkward as it was, instantly made me feel better. It also probably helped that I was still floating in my post-orgasmic bliss and the promises of dirty things to come after dinner.

Something shifted when Gavin told me he loved me. Our attraction and sexual chemistry weren't lacking in the slightest, however when he kissed me after asking me to say it again, it was something I still find hard to describe. It's as if we hadn't even scratched the surface of our want for each other. I was afraid to tell him how I felt. After hearing him say those three words, knowing he was in this as deep as me, once I said them back, something released in my soul, and I felt like I could fly. Having him inside me after he said those words was so much better than I could've ever imagined. I've never been made love to before, and it was the best thing I've ever felt.

Loving someone, the right someone, and having them love you in return, really love you, makes you feel like you have discovered the world's rarest treasure, giving you a euphoric feeling that makes you feel untouchable. I meant what I told Gavin, even if he was sleeping. I was lost. My heart was afraid to ever let anyone in. My guilt from leaving my mom weighed me down, making it feel like I was struggling to breathe, and my fear of my past dictated my every move.

He found me, pulled, and ripped the chains weighing on me. When he told me he'd be there when I called my mom. He kept his word, letting me take a full breath for the first time in six years. Making me feel loved, showing me what real love from a man is supposed to be, and bringing out my naughty side behind closed doors. I know in my soul I was meant to find Gavin.

His parents made me feel like I belonged. Daniel Davis is surprisingly sarcastic and funny, something I never would've imagined from seeing him at the office, and his mom is the sweetest. The love and pride she has for both Gavin and Olivia is written all over her face when she talks about them.

Olivia's show was an amazing success. Travis Dane, the designer she works with, is well known, so reporters and paparazzi were in there in spades. Their reviews raved about her classic meets edgy style. She's already had several celebrities reach out to her in the few days since the show, asking for specialized, personally designed items. Something as a first-time fashion designer is a dream come true. At least that's what she said when I talked to her last night.

Meeting Olivia was like when I met Grace; I instantly felt a connection to her. She teased me about the night at Cliff's, thinking she was Gavin's girlfriend, causing me to shoot daggers that truthfully weren't backed by much at Gavin. I know they are close, even if they don't talk as often as they used to with busy schedules. As embarrassed as I was, it warmed my insides, knowing he's been talking about me to his family since the beginning. She's coming back for Thanksgiving now that the show is done, and she doesn't have the pressure of a deadline. I'm so looking forward to spending more time with her.

When I said it started out perfect, I meant it. I just wish it ended that way. Everything was amazing until after Olivia's show. Gavin, Daniel, Kristina, and I sat in the front row during the show, but with all of the dim lighting and the focus on the runway, it was hard to see anyone else. The effect of making you feel like you were being sucked into each piece worked.

Once the show was over, we went backstage to congratulate Olivia before coming back out to where we were previously seated for the cocktail after-party. The runway and chairs were cleared, and black covered, high-top cocktail tables with votive candles giving a soft glow were placed in the open area, while black leather couches were placed in groups with metal coffee tables between them to give you a more intimate feel if you wanted to sit. The lighting was switched to dim up lighting in various shades of blue that changed the feel of the room, highlighting white curtains that hung from the ceiling that I didn't even notice when we first arrived. Waiters were walking around with canapes, music played through speakers, and two bars had been set up on either side of the room. The space was transformed into a laid-back lounge as if by magic. I guess for the right price, you can get anything done quickly.

Gavin and I were enjoying a cocktail, chatting at a high-top table while we waited for Olivia to finish up with interviews and photos. Daniel and Kristina had gone to say hello to a couple of people they knew from Kristina's Foundation. Groups of people were sitting on the sofas and mingling around the room with a mix of photographers there to capture the high-profile celebrities that had come since Travis's name was attached to Olivia's line.

Looking over Gavin's shoulder, I saw a woman and a man approaching us. I'd say she was about my height, but her bright green stilettos made her easily taller than me. Her dark brown hair was pulled over one shoulder and clipped back. She was wearing a stunning form-fitting cream dress that showed off her hourglass figure and left little to the imagination in the cleavage department with the low dip in the front. She was beautiful, and the man whose arm she was holding onto wasn't hard to look at either. A little shorter than Gavin, his dark hair was shorter on the sides and longer on top, slicked over to the side. His black suit pants contrasted well with his dark green shirt that rolled up his forearms. He was definitely dressed more laid back than Gavin, but he pulled it off. Gavin's back was toward them as they made their way to where we were standing. I should've said something. Instead, I stood there as the beautiful woman tapped Gavin on the shoulder, surprising him as he turned.

As soon as he turned, his entire body stiffened. Posture rigid, and although I couldn't see his face head on, I could see his jaw clench in his profile.

"Hello, Gavin. It's been a while." Her voice sounded almost suggestive, and something inside me burned.

The man beside her offered his hand to Gavin, "Hey, Gavin. It's good to see you." Gavin stood stoic, his hands clenching at his sides.

Feeling the need to be close to him, I walked around the high top and stood next to Gavin. His hands clenched into fists. I could feel the tension coming off of him without even touching him.

"Rachel, Ben. What are you doing here?" His voice was flat. No emotion. No warmth, and in an instant, it dawned on me. *This is his ex. Great.*

"Ben was in LA for business this week, so I joined him. When I heard about Olivia's show, I pulled some strings to get tickets. I always knew Olivia was going to make it big in fashion. I wanted to support her." She acted as though she and Olivia had been friends for years. Gavin told me that Olivia and Rachel had not spoken since they broke up.

"You shouldn't have come," Gavin replied, lips in a firm line. He stared straight ahead. I felt like an extra as they exchanged in an awkward conversation.

"I didn't think you would mind. After all, Olivia and I were close." She reached out to touch Gavin's arm, and I couldn't help but notice the teardrop-shaped diamond on a platinum band that encased her left hand. My guess was Gavin didn't either because he flinched at her touch. Not seeming to care, *this woman is something else.* She flattened her hand on his arm before she looked at me, giving me the quintessential once-over from head to toe and then turning her attention back to Gavin, actively dismissing me. I hate women who try to make other women feel inferior; even without words, their eyes and body language can make you go from feeling confident and sexy to small and insignificant.

"Who's this?" She tilted her head gently toward me. I

look up to find Ben staring at me with eyes that make my skin crawl. His dilated pupils, dark as he roamed over my body, made me shiver, and not in a good way.

Snapping out of his stupor, he wrapped his arm around my waist and pulled me close to his side, "This is Charlotte, my girlfriend."

His grip on my hip was tight, as if he was holding onto me for dear life, claiming me and needing me to keep him standing. He snapped his gaze to Ben, catching him looking at me, and if eyes could shoot lasers, Ben would have been a goner.

Trying to be polite, I reached out to Rachel, "Hello, it's nice to meet you."

Nothing. Rachel's brow furrowed, but she didn't move her hand, eyeing me as if I were a piece of moldy cheese on her plate that she didn't want to touch. How could he have loved this woman?

Effectively dismissing me, she turned back to Gavin. "We should grab drinks tonight. It would be nice to catch up since we're all here. Wouldn't that be fun? I've missed you." *Excuse me? Did she just say I miss you to her ex in front of who I am guessing is her husband without a care in the world ?*

"There is nothing to catch up on. I wish I could say it was nice to see you, but it wasn't. Now, if you'll excuse us, we need to go find my sister and celebrate with her. Feel free to leave, as I'm sure Olivia could give two shits if she sees you or not." His tone clipped as he used his hand on my waist to guide me away from the table, leaving a gaping Rachel standing there. Looking over my shoulder, Ben stared after us before looking down at Rachel and saying something with an annoyed look on his face.

He walked me down a hallway behind a corner, so we had some privacy. Once we moved out of sight, Gavin turned me into him, "I'm sorry about that. I had no idea they would be here. They shouldn't be here."

"You don't have to apologize. It wasn't your fault. She's beautiful." I wanted to ask how he could have dated a woman like that. I restrained myself, knowing it was my own insecurities from that interaction spurring the thoughts in my head. I wrapped my arms around his back and pulled him in close. I needed his reassurance.

Sensing my unease, he pinched my chin and tilted my head to look him in the eyes, "Charlotte, I want you to get one thing straight. I do not now, nor will I ever want her. She is insignificant. In fact, I'm glad she cheated on me. If she hadn't then, she would've at some point, most likey after I made the mistake of marrying her. In retrospect, she did me a favor by showing her true colors before we took it any further. She may seem attractive on the outside, but what is on the inside makes her ugly. How she treated you proves it. You, Charlotte, are beautiful inside and out. She could never compare to you. You are smart, funny, strong, caring, and compassionate. You are the most beautiful woman I have ever seen, but I want you to know I fell in love with you for a million other reasons, not your looks. I am so damn lucky to have you. So, get out of that head of yours because I can see your mind overthinking. Let's enjoy the rest of the night. I am not going to let Rachel spoil this for us."

"Okay." Is all I could say as a tear fell down my cheek. His love for me is boundless. His confidence in me, in us, and knowing when I need to hear it makes me feel like I could fly. He released my chin, letting me fall back into his chest as I held on for dear life. As I basked in the safety of his arms, the hairs on the back of my neck stood up, and I got the strangest feeling that someone was watching us. I pulled back a little to look around, people were walking through the hallway, but nothing seemed out of the ordinary.

Since meeting Gavin, I hadn't felt that need to know where all the exits were and be as aware of my surroundings. He made me feel safe wherever we were, and that fear I had always had when I was out was waning by the day. Except, for the rest of the evening, I couldn't shake the feeling that something wasn't right. I kept getting this tingle up my spine that made me feel on edge. Something I hadn't felt in weeks. Not wanting to ruin anyone's time, I didn't say anything and brushed it off that if anyone was looking, it was most likely because they recognized Daniel or Kristina. Daniel being one of the biggest lawyers in the country and Kristina's Foundation getting national recognition last year really brought a spotlight to their family, Gavin had told me. We didn't see Rachel or Ben for the rest of the evening, which made me feel better.

I figured I was just being paranoid when everything, of course, was fine. After we visited and had a few drinks with Olivia, we went back to the hotel where, after we made love, we fell into a peaceful sleep before flying back to Phoenix late Sunday morning. It's Friday already, and I still can't seem to shake this feeling, and frankly, it's starting to piss me off.

"Earth to Lottie," Grace says, putting her margarita down on the bar. We decided to come to Cliff's after dinner to have a drink or two and sit at the bar's end so we could catch up with Claire, not being hit on by undergrads.

Shaking myself from my reverie, I blink, returning to planet earth, "I'm sorry, what were you saying?"

"Where did you go? I lost you there for a second. I explained about the new account I landed and the insanely hot team lead I get to work with."

Becoming more present, feeling bad I wasn't fully listening, I praise her, "Congratulations, lady. What is the account?"

"It's an Eco-friendly Children's Sports Company. Their company focuses on creating exercise products out of recycled and sustainable materials for kids at affordable prices. They came to us because they want to launch a new marketing campaign to reach a bigger demographic. Three team members presented pitches for their new products, and they chose mine."

"Holy shit, Grace. That's amazing. Not that I'm surprised. You're kick ass. Grace Hastings, Executive Marketer. I see your office door decal now."

"Someday. Landing this contract brings several million in revenue to Mercer. I've never been so excited about a project. I really believe in what they are creating; I've never cared about what we market before."

"Could it have something to do with the hot team lead you mentioned? Tell me more." I smirk at her.

"Maybe, but it's more than just him. He's the lead designer for their sports division. When we met to go over what they wanted to highlight, listening to him talk about what he creates and how passionate he is about these products and helping get sustainable and eco-friendly equipment to kids captured me. I mean, along with his tight ass, how he fills out pants, and how his biceps beg to be let out of his shirt, Girl, let me tell you. On top of it, he has these gray-blue eyes that made me lose my concentration. I swear

I've had to bring an extra pair of underwear to work the last two days."

"Ha-ha, damn lady. Good luck with all that. And good luck to...? What's his name?" I lean over, tapping my shoulder with hers to razz her a little.

"Matthew Delton. He's thirty and graduated with his MBA from UCLA. He's originally from Denver." She says, quickly shifting her eyes away from my gaze, trying to brush it off.

"So, you pitched it Monday, got the contract, you already know all of this about him, and it's Friday? Who are you, and what have you done with Grace?" I eye her suspiciously. She never mixes business with pleasure, says it gets too messy, and usually loses interest fast.

"I don't know, truthfully. With all my family shit, you know how hard it is for me to trust or let anyone in. After the shit with Logan, it felt like my point was proven more. I was good until seeing you so happy with Gavin, and honestly, it has made me a little jealous, maybe. This week, Matthew and I have spent a lot of time together going over the projects, and talking to him has been surprisingly easy." Her hands are clenched around her drink. Talking about anything deeper than surface level is so hard for her. I can't say I blame her, she's been through a lot and learned to push it all down, which probably hasn't helped her, but it's how she copes, and I'm in no position to judge her for that.

"Has anything happened?" I ask, leaning back to give her time to respond. She has always been my sounding board and rarely opens up about her feelings. Maybe it's time I pushed her just like she's always pushed me.

"No, not in that way. We exchanged numbers for business purposes. He has texted me the last two nights to say goodnight, and just before I met up with you, he texted asking me to dinner tomorrow. I'll probably say no."

"Don't say no. Grace, you never talk to people. Never. And if he makes you feel comfortable and you are attracted to him, you owe it to yourself to at least have a meal with the man. You've told me before that your company doesn't have a policy against dating clients. Maybe it's time for you to open up a little. At least try."

She takes a few breaths, letting what I said sink in. "Ugh, you're right, and if anything, it's just a meal, right? Ok, I'll text him back before I change my mind." Straightening her shoulders, she digs her phone out of her purse and shoots off a reply. Looking back up at me. "God, who are you, and what have you done with Lottie? Dating Gavin has turned you into a therapist. I love you for it. Thank you for listening."

"Ha-ha, it was you who gave me the strength to even attempt things with Gavin, so now it's my turn to push you."

"Okay okay, enough. I'll let you know how it goes. So, fill me in on all things LA."

I filled Grace in on everything that happened over the weekend. Gavin and I saying the "L" word, our sexy escapades, and meeting his parents. The run in with Gavin's ex, how she eyed me down like I was lowly trash, and what Gavin told me afterward. I even told her about the creepy feeling I kept getting, as if we were being watched. If anyone could talk me off that ledge, it's her.

"You naughty bitch. I knew you had kink in you. I love this new side. I'm glad you had a great time. Gavin's ex seems like a real treat. And honestly, you probably felt weird because it was a new place. I'm sure people were watching Gavin's parents and even more so when his sister was with you. You're safe, Lottie." She reaches over and puts her hand over mine, a comfort I didn't even know I needed.

"You're right. This is why I tell you these things: you can straighten me out and reel in my crazy." Relaxing my shoulders that I hadn't realized were at my ears from tension.

"What are besties for? Are you heading to Gavin's tonight?"

"Yeah, I told him I'd text him when we wanted to leave. He's out with James and Logan, so he said he'd pick me up. I'm sure he'll take you too, so you don't have to take a cab home. Are you ready to go?" She tenses at the mention of Logan's name. Honestly, I'm glad she met Matthew. I can tell that Logan gets to her, and although I don't know the whole story, I know she's not over it. Maybe going out with Matthew will help her move on and find her happy.

"Is it okay if I say yes? It's been a long ass week, and I'm ready to fall into my bed and sleep for fourteen hours, but I don't want to bail on you."

I shake my head in relief. I love Grace, but I've wanted to shower and get lost in everything that is Gavin. I pull out my phone and text Gavin to see how long he'll be or if I should order a cab back to his house.

"Totally good. I'm so ready to get in bed," I wiggle my eyebrows, never able to get enough of my man.

GAVIN:

> Don't order a ride. We're just settling up, and I'll head over. Give me ten.

ME:

> Perfect. Can we drop Grace off? We'll be out front.

GAVIN:

No problem, stand by the bouncer. I love you.

ME:

Yes, sir. Love you

"Ugh, stop before I gag with all your sex-crazed shit." She fakes a gag and then smiles a genuine smile at me. I know she is happy for me, and I can see in her eyes a shift. She wants that too, and damn, do I want that for her. Once you find your happiness, you want everyone in your life to be as cared for and loved as you feel.

We finish our drinks and head to the front to wait for Gavin. Grace is right. There is nothing to worry about, I'm safe, and for once, everything in my life is going the way it was meant to be.

26

Charlotte

"Hey, mom, ready for your flight Wednesday?" I ask, after pressing the accept button and putting her on speaker while I get some work done at Gavin's dining room table. We haven't been able to talk as much these past few weeks, missing each other's phone calls and relying more on short texts to keep in touch. Fall is flying by, Thanksgiving being only a few days away.

My internship and school have been hectic, keeping me busy. Gavin and I went to Joe and Maria's for dinner last Sunday and had a pre-Thanksgiving meal. After Joe gave him what felt like the Spanish Inquisition the first time he came with me in early October, they've been close since. When I asked him to stop, he simply shrugged his shoulders, saying I was the closest thing he had to a daughter, so deal with it. Gavin acted like it was no big deal, telling me he was glad I had people who wanted to look out for me. While Joe and Gavin had a beer and sat in the living room yelling at the

TV while they watched football, I filled Maria in on everything that had happened in the past few weeks.

We hadn't been there since I brought Gavin a couple weeks before we went to Olivia's show, and with the holidays and the gala coming in December, we probably won't see them until after Christmas. It makes me feel terrible, seeing as they took me under their wing and treated me like family when I moved to Phoenix. When I almost cried talking to Maria about feeling guilty, she hugged me and told me that this was my time to live life, knowing that even if we don't see each other as often as we used to, they will always be there. *"This is your time to spread your wings and fly, Mija (my daughter). You have let yourself stay caged for so long, and now that you've found love and have settled things with your mom, you need to let the wind take you where you have always meant to go."*

Olivia is coming in for Thanksgiving too, and I can't wait. Her show was a freaking hit, and she has been swamped since we left. We text almost daily. She said Travis told her he had never seen a response like she had after a first show. The press review from the show called her *The Best Thing to Hit Fashion in Decades,* equating her talent to Alexander McQueen and Versace, to name a few. Gavin is so proud of his little sister, as am I. She's staying until Sunday, and I really want to introduce her to Grace while she's in town.

"Hi, sweetie, that's why I called. I'm actually in town already. I just checked into my hotel." Her voice was soft with a slight hesitation in it. Her response surprises me, making me pick up the phone and take it off speaker.

"What? Gavin booked your flight for Wednesday, and today is Monday. Did you have him change it? And why are

you staying in a hotel? I thought you were staying with us."
My questions rapid firing.

Something isn't right. Our conversations were fine, and
we had an awesome weekend when she came to visit.
However, she seems different when I talk to her since
coming here. Almost like she's hiding something. Gavin told
me I was being paranoid, which annoyed the shit out of me.
Actually, it caused our first real argument. He put the mirror
in front of my face and told me I couldn't expect her to go
back to when we used to tell each other everything
overnight. That me leaving her and keeping all the stuff with
Gregory from her caused hurt for her too, and there may be
things that have happened while I was gone she isn't ready to
tell me yet. I knew he was right. Deep down, I knew it, but I
wasn't ready to admit it. I was mostly pissed at myself,
knowing I was the one who put that rift between us in the
first place. That didn't mean I wanted him to be the one to
call me out about it, and I took my anger at myself out on
him. Not my proudest moment. One thing I did learn from
that is.... make up sex is everything they say it is.

"My flight was for Wednesday, but I had it moved up to
today. I decided to stay at a hotel to give you and Gavin your
space." Her voice still quiet.

"Okay," pulling my phone back to glance at the time. It's
almost seven, "Gavin should be back soon, and I'm just
finishing some school work. We can have dinner. What hotel
are you staying at? We can pick you up."

"I can't...I mean, I'm pretty tired. I wouldn't be good
company tonight. I was calling to see if you could meet for
lunch tomorrow, just you and me?" She almost sounds
nervous and didn't answer my question about where she is
staying.

"I have my internship tomorrow. I'll talk to Gavin and see if I can step out for an hour. Is everything okay? Where are you even staying?" Leaving shouldn't be a problem. With it being a holiday week, there isn't a ton going on, and no court dates on the calendar until next week.

"Everything is fine. I just really want to have lunch with you...since I... I'm bailing tonight. I'm staying at The Phoenician." The uneasiness in her voice would suggest otherwise.

"The Phoenician?" Where the hell is that? Tapping it into my phone. Twenty minutes from Phoenix. That's where it is. "Mom, that's twenty minutes outside of Phoenix. I won't have enough time to drive there, have lunch, and drive back." Looking down, this place is a thousand dollars a night. She doesn't have that kind of money.

"Oh...well, I have a rental car. I can come to you. I can pick you up at the office. You showed me where it was last time, and if I get lost, I'll put it into the GPS. I'll pick you up at noon? Okay? Sound good? I love you." Click.

Did she just hang up on me? I pull my phone away from my ear, and yup. Sure as shit, she did. She rented a car? My mind is spinning with a million questions, the number one being, what in the hell is going on? Shaking my head at the clusterfuck that was that call, I start organizing the stuff I had out, knowing full well I am not going to be able to concentrate anymore tonight.

Piling it all into the bag that I keep all my school files in. I look up when I hear the door open, seeing Gavin walking in with flowers in his hand, a bouquet of Alliums, firework flowers, and that panty-melting smile on his face. They actually are a flower in the onion family, *fun fact,* but when they bloom, they look like fireworks exploding in the night sky. I truly am the luckiest girl alive.

"Hey, Firecracker," he says, leaning down and kissing my temple, having walked all the way to me while I stood there and gawked at my sexy man. He bends over the table, placing the flowers in the middle, then pulls me up from my chair into him, hugging me to his chest as I wrap my arms around his midsection, holding on tight. Gavin kisses the top of my head, inhaling a deep breath as he lingers in my hair. "You smell good. I've missed you all day."

"You saw me a few hours ago." Laying my head on his chest, I swoon over how sweet he is.

"Yes, but I haven't been able to touch or kiss you since this morning." Gavin tilts back, releasing my backside, using his hand to grab my chin to tilt my head up until our eyes lock. Shivers run up my spine as his thumb swipes over my bottom lip. Instinctively I lift up onto my toes to meet his lips, unable to wait one more second without his mouth on mine. Our kiss is sweet and sensual, tongues gliding over each slowly, getting reacquainted since we went our separate ways this morning.

Gavin's hands slide slowly down my back as he releases our kiss, moving from my lips to my neck. Instinctively, I tilt my head, allowing him better access. Gavin kisses the spot just below my ear that drives me wild, igniting my entire body and spreading goosebumps up my arms instantly.

"What do you want for dinner?" I ask in panted breaths while he continues his exploration of my neck and collar bone.

Without stopping his glorious assault of kisses, he replies. "You, Fire. I could feast on you every day and never go hungry. Lift your arms." His voice is low and husky, making my insides ache for him.

Within seconds of my arms going over my head, my sweatshirt is gone. Gavin reaches back behind me, and with one expertise pinch, my bra straps fall down my arms, leaving my breasts on display for him.

"You are so beautiful, inside and out." His voice full of love. I know he isn't saying these things just to appease me. He means what he says, and the confidence and esteem he instills in me gets stronger every time.

For so long, I could still hear Gregory's words. *Not enough, stupid, ugly.* Those being the PG-rated version. Grace has mentioned in the past how seeing a counselor might help me work through some of the trauma surrounding the entire Gregory situation. I always shut her down, adamant I didn't need it. That I was strong enough to let my past go. It wasn't until Gavin's constant positive affirmations that I realized that maybe part of the reason I never got close or even attempted to let anyone in was because, deep down, I didn't think I was worth it. It was better to be alone than to chance going through that again. The other reason I waited so long was that my soul somehow knew it was waiting for Gavin.

His loving me for me and me accepting that was like shining a big freaking spotlight on things I have pushed down and kept hidden for a long time. I was good at putting on a show, pretending what happened didn't affect me as much as it did. I don't want to do that anymore. *Who the hell knows?* Maybe I do need counseling. I love Gavin and do not want anything from my past to ruin my future, and if that means working through this shit, so be it.

"Where did you go, Fire?" Gavin's thumb and finger

gently tilt my chin, angling my face upward until my eyes meet his, instantly breaking me from my internal parade of thoughts.

Not wanting to ruin the moment, I smiled back and softly replied, "I'm right here. With you. Always with you," snaking my arms around his neck. Because, in this moment, I couldn't mean it more.

Gavin's hand moves from my chin to cup my face as he leans forward, whispering against my lips, "Exactly where you are meant to be, Fire," before pressing his lips to mine, his tongue demanding entrance that my mouth willingly gives while his hands drop down from my face, sliding around my waist and seamlessly lifting me up while my legs voluntarily wrap around his waist like a ribbon around a gift, without our lips breaking contact. I can feel him hard against my stomach, and my core aches with need. He turns and jogs while holding me in his arms as if I weighed nothing through the living area, down the hall, and into the bedroom.

The shades are still open from this morning, the nighttime lights of downtown Phoenix illuminating the room in a soft glow as Gavin marches toward the king-sized bed. Unwrapping my legs from him as if peeling off the wrapping paper of a box, he deposits me on top of the down navy comforter. I slide off my leggings and panties in one quick motion, letting them land somewhere on the floor without a care in the world, beyond ready to get this show on the road. I scoot myself back on the bed as I watch Gavin take a step back. Ooh, ok, I'm down for this. I lean onto my elbows to appreciate the man in front of me.

His hands reach up to the neck of his charcoal gray shirt, loosening the navy-blue tie that sits in a perfect Windsor knot and lifting it off over his head, tossing it over his shoulder where it lands haphazardly on the floor. He slowly undoes each button, and I have to lean to the side to balance myself as I lift my left hand up to wipe my mouth. Pretty sure I'm literally drooling watching my beautiful man undress for me.

He chuckles lightly at me, swiping my mouth, "Like what you see, Fire?"

"Immensely," I whisper, my breaths hitching as my heart pounds against my chest.

The last button undone, he holds each side, sliding the shirt off his broad shoulders, revealing his muscular chest, defined abs, and a tiny trail of hair that starts below his belly button, following the glorious V that leads down to where his pants are still sitting on his hips. *Holy crap, I think I might come just from watching him take his clothes off.*

Shirt discarded, he unbuckles and pulls on his black leather belt in one swift motion yanking it from his belt loops to hit the ground. The crack when it snaps against the hardwood makes me jump. Gavin's lips turned up on one side into the sexiest smirk at my reaction. He knows exactly what he is doing. Continuing this delicious game of let's drive Charlotte crazy, he pops open the button on his black dress pants, slowly sliding down the zipper, letting the fabric slide down his toned thighs, pooling at his feet, leaving him in nothing but his boxer briefs and dress socks.

With my core aching and heart racing, my hands burn with the need to touch him. I have to force myself to stay rooted to my spot as his hands slip into the waistband of his boxers, sliding them down. As he frees himself, his hard cock springs up, hitting him against his stomach with a small slapping sound, forcing me to hold in my giggle. *Don't ruin this sexy moment.* His eyebrows dip at me as his boxers continue their journey down his legs allowing him to step out of them. I wait in anticipation for him to take off his socks so I can pounce on him, except instead of taking off his socks, he starts stalking toward me.

"Umm, aren't you going to take off your socks?" I ask as he climbs onto the bed, putting his hands on either side of my head as he holds himself up over me. I squeeze my thighs together to suppress the throbbing in my core.

"Nope," he says with a smirk, "I figure they'll give me more traction. You don't think my socks are sexy?" *Is he serious? I mean, maybe they would give him traction. I don't know, but how can he think socks are sexy? After that strip tease, he's going to leave his socks on?*

His laughter effectively makes my eyes snap back to his. "You should see your face right now, Fire. The look you are giving me is priceless. I wanted to see your response, message received. Socks are not sexy."

I fall back onto the bed, freeing my hands so they can slap at his chest. *Ass.* I get one swat in before he catches them with his right hand, balancing his weight on his left arm, pinning my hands above my head.

"Nuh uh uh, baby…no slapping, at least not yet. I'm going to let go, and you are going to keep your hands over your head. Understood." His eyes were now dark and lust filled, the laughter gone, replaced with desire pierce into me, freezing me to my spot. I nod my head.

"I'm going to need your words, Charlotte." He commands.

"Understood." My voice coming out a moan.

"Good girl." Gavin lets go of my arms, and as he asked, I keep them over my head as he contorts his body to reach down, sliding off his socks and tossing them.

I can feel my wetness sliding down my leg, and he hasn't even touched me. Rocking back onto his knees, so his hands are free, he spreads my legs before planting them on either side of my hips and dropping himself down, running his tongue through my slit. Releasing a moan, I arch into his mouth, wanting, no, needing more. His pace stays constant, calculated movements up and down with slight suction, my hips thrusting upwards, desperate. "Please, Gavin."

Pulling back slightly, instantly missing his warmth, he looks up at me. "So impatient, my little Firecracker." He tsks before returning to his slow, torturous movements. I tilt my hips again, only to be met with him using his hand to hold me down.

"I want you to come in my mouth, but I need to be inside you." *Who is impatient now?*

Gavin leans back, stroking himself a few times before leaning over me, lining up, and rubbing the hard tip through my entrance. His head dips, capturing my nipple in his mouth, biting down, sending waves of pleasure straight to my sex as he slides home in one thrust. The unexpected fullness I feel causes me to arch my back in pleasure and the best kind of pain. I can feel myself stretch to accommodate him as he pulls out and pushes back in until he is fully seated. He continues his assault on my nipple, biting and sucking, moving his hand to rub circles on my clit as he slams hard into me, my orgasm building fast and furious. He pinches my clit between his fingers and pumps two more times as I detonate around him; black dots sparkle my already darkened vision as my entire body spasms. My orgasm sets Gavin off as I feel his body tense as he grunts out, "Fire," before I feel him filling me. Neither of us moves as we come down from our high.

His mouth now planting featherlight kisses on my stomach, chest, collarbone, up my neck, and finding my lips. I could stay wrapped up in this man forever.

Gavin releases my lips, still supporting his weight over me. "That was amazing. I love the way you taste and how your body responds to me. I don't want to move from this spot...ever, though I'm afraid I might crush you if my arms give out. I'll be right back, baby." Leaning down, kissing me one more time before slowly pulling out and climbing over me to head toward the bathroom, my body instantly missing the feeling of him inside me.

Walking back in a few minutes later with a warm washcloth, after trying to snatch it away from him unsuccessfully, he gently washes me up, turns, tosses the washcloth toward the bathroom floor, and climbs into bed next to me. He then turns me to my side so our fronts are facing each other.

I wrap my arm around his back and breathe him in. Feeling a sense of complete calmness, the feeling I only have when I'm with him, as he rubs his hand lazily up and down my spine. "I don't want to get up, but we should eat something." Lifting my leg up and over him as he pulls me closer to his chest.

"Five more minutes, Fire, five more minutes." He says into my hair before kissing the top of my head. This man. I never want this feeling to end.

"Okay."

* * *

"What do you mean your mom is already here? I booked her flight for Wednesday." Gavin says with a bite of pizza in his mouth. After we reluctantly got up, we ordered a thin-crust chicken, spinach, and fresh mozzarella pizza, had it delivered, and are currently lounging on the couch with the pizza box between us.

"That's what I asked her. She blew me off, saying she had changed it. When I told her we'd pick her up for dinner tonight, she said she couldn't, then said she was too tired and wanted to meet for lunch tomorrow instead. I told her I would talk to you and offered to pick her up, thinking she was staying close, but she's staying at The Phoenician."

"That's like twenty minutes away. Did she order a ride all that way from the airport? Why didn't she call you?" Grabbing my bottle of water off the coffee table, Gavin looks at me with the same look I probably had when she told me about it on the phone before opening the bottle and downing half of it.

"I don't know. She told me she rented a car, and when I told her I wouldn't be able to make it out there, have lunch, and get back in an hour, she said she'd come pick me up. I looked it up, and rooms there are nearly a thousand dollars a night. She doesn't have that kind of money." I can feel my shoulders tensing. I felt so calm and relaxed laying in Gavin's arms, now talking about my mom's weirdness on the phone is undoing all my post-orgasmic bliss.

"I'm sure it's fine, babe. Maybe she wanted to surprise you and was saving up for a vacation before you reconnected, so instead, she decided to spend her money on a nice place while visiting." Tossing the empty pizza box on the table, Gavin reaches down, pulls my leg in his lap, and starts applying pressure to my foot, instantly relaxing me a little.

"You're right. I'm sorry I'm being a spaz. This is all new

to me, and I know it's my fault it's weird, so I can't blame her for not just opening up and telling me everything." My eyes roll back in my head as he applies more pressure, hitting all the right spots in the arch of my foot.

"It's not your fault. It's just going to take time. Why don't you take the afternoon off tomorrow? Have lunch with your mom, spend the day, that way you don't have to rush. The office is quiet this week, and I plan on spending the day holed up in my office to finish paperwork I need to get done before the weekend, so I can actually enjoy it."

"You? Work free? Your mom would pass out hearing you say that." I chuckle. His mom always tells him he works too hard.

"I guess all it took was finding the right woman to make me realize I want to work hard and do right by my family's firm, but I don't want to spend my life at work. I want to be able to enjoy life outside of the four walls of my office. I've promised myself to work on finding a work-life balance."

"I like the sound of that. You really think everything is good with my mom?" I know I'm being annoying by asking the same thing over and over. I just can't help feeling like something is off.

"I'm sure it is, baby. Stop worrying. Enjoy the time with your mom. Heck, maybe she's going to tell you she's moving to Arizona, and that's what she's nervous about." He shrugs his shoulders like it's no big deal.

Is that what she's hiding? Would she move here? Leave my grandparents?

"Hey, I can hear you thinking over there. Do I need to make your brain shut off?" His eyes have mischief in them.

Two can play that game. "Yes, sir, I think you do."

Tossing my leg off him and jumping up, he reaches down

and lifts me as if I weigh nothing tossing me over his shoulder.

"You know what happens when you call me sir," he says, swatting my ass as he charges toward the bedroom.

Yes. Yes I do.

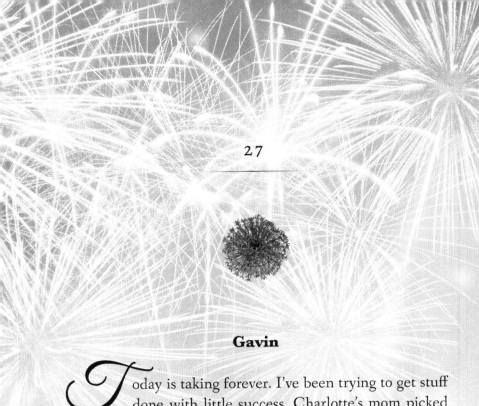

27

Gavin

*T*oday is taking forever. I've been trying to get stuff done with little success. Charlotte's mom picked her up a few hours ago. I haven't heard from her yet, and I'm a little concerned. *Why? I'm not sure.* I texted her an hour ago, and after checking my phone an embarrassing amount of times, I sent her a text saying I'd be at the office until six and would meet her at the condo before shutting my phone off in an attempt to concentrate. I could tell she was worried last night about her mom coming early. Heck, to be honest, I was a little too. Was I going to tell Charlotte that? *Hell no.*

I booked Kelly's flight for Thanksgiving right after she came to Phoenix a month ago. She hadn't mentioned anything to me that she needed or was thinking of changing it, and since the plan was for her to stay with us during the long weekend, I have no clue why she would decide to stay at a hotel. Maybe we were too loud the last time she was here? Or maybe she did want to move to Phoenix and didn't want to say anything to Charlotte until she knew.

I hadn't meant to come home last night and immediately get carried away with her, but when I walked in the door, she took my breath away. She always does. I had just seen her a few hours earlier at the office, yet it felt like days. Charlotte has been spending most of her time at the condo. She even took over a drawer, and a little space in the closet which I'd never tell her, made me feel like a king. I want her to move in with me. I want to be with her all the time. I know only being together for a few months seems fast, especially since before her I was only interested in a one and done, keeping women at a distance, never getting close. I don't give a shit; I want her.

For four years, that's what I did. Kept people at bay and didn't get close. *Until her.* From the minute I saw her, I felt drawn to her. Every moment together after that, the innate need to be close to her consumed me, and I never felt the urge to fight it. That, my friends, is what my mom would call one half of a soul calling to its other half. I thought all of my mom's talk about fate and soulmates growing up was bullshit. *Until now.* I can't explain it, but if my need to be close to Charlotte is my soul seeking its other half, then you're damn right; I believe in it.

It's been easier for Charlotte to stay by me too, with Grace working so much on her new project and spending time with Matthew. We haven't met him yet. But we have plans to have dinner together next week. I have been careful not to mention dinner to Logan. Knowing him, he would show up. Logan does know Grace is seeing someone, though. Charlotte let it out when he made some lewd comment when he was over to watch football last week. He didn't take it well.

"What do you mean she's seeing someone?" His head pops up from his plate.

"Exactly what I said. She is seeing someone she met at work. She's happy. Let her be happy, Logan. Honestly, all you ever cared about was getting in her pants. She deserves more than that. And this guy seems really nice." Charlotte shoots back with a warning in her voice. She is fiercely protective of Grace.

"That's not all I care about. She knows that." His brows furrowed.

"Could've fooled us. Matthew is the opposite of you. He wants a relationship, isn't a player, and most importantly, treats her the way she deserves to be treated, unlike you, who only cares about getting some. Don't ruin this for her with your childish shit."

His entire body deflates with her comment. Charlotte usually is calm and jokes around with Logan, but he's definitely hit a nerve, her tone is anything but joking.

"Charlotte, I...umm should get going. I have some stuff I need to get done that I forgot about."

"Logan, look..."

"I'm good, really. I just have stuff to do." And with that, he grabbed his wallet and keys and left without another word.

Charlotte felt horrible and wanted to call him, which I talked her out of. Honestly, he needed to hear it. I understand why Logan jokes and doesn't get close, but at some point, he needs to decide what he wants and stop letting his past define him. If he wanted to be a bachelor for life, I would fully support that. Deep down though, I think he wants more and is scared. Except I can't be the one to realize that for him.

The knock on my door brings me back to the present.

"Come in." I regret my comment the second I look up.

"Hello. Gavin." Rachel has closed the door behind her and is standing in front of my desk in a navy wrap dress with black heels. Her hair is in a soft bun at the base of her neck, a neck that used to draw me in, except looking at it now only annoys me.

My jaw tics in frustration as I look at her. Standing in front of me is someone I once thought I wanted to spend the rest of my life with. Now, I feel nothing except pissed at the unannounced intrusion into my office.

"What are you doing here?" my tone clipped, not hiding my irritation.

"I came to see you. I tried calling you a few times but couldn't get through, and I've left several messages with your secretary." She says as she walks around my desk and perches her fake ass on the corner as if she does this all the time, making me roll my chair back slightly.

"I blocked your number and told Elaine that if you ever called to take a message and forget to give me said message. What do you want, Rachel?" The only reason she got past today is that Elaine is off this week, the office being sparse of people with not a lot going on. I want her to get to the point. I don't want her here.

"I miss you," Leaning forward to show me her ample cleavage as she reaches for my thigh, I push it away, not deterring her in the slightest. The mere thought of her touching me makes my stomach turn.

"I made a mistake, Gavin. I've spent the past four years regretting what Ben and I did. Seeing you in LA brought back all of those feelings. Ben and I aren't working; we haven't been for a while. He cheated on me and is never around. You and I worked, and we can work again." Tears in her eyes threaten to fall. Tears that I can't tell are real or fake. Either way, I don't give a shit.

"I wish I could say sorry, Rachel. Your relationship with Ben is not my problem. Hasn't been for a long time. I am with Charlotte, and I'm really fucking happy. I don't miss you and never will," folding my arms across my chest, hoping she gets the message.

"We could be happy again. I know we could. I haven't forgotten all the things that make you lose control," she says, her voice seductive, as she drops to her knees in front of me, grabbing my thighs, making me cringe.

I uncross my hands to grab hers and push them from my thigh. Letting go of her wrists, I lean forward, right in her face, not threatening, but just enough, so she knows I mean business. "Listen, and listen good, because I will only say this once more. You and I are *nothing*. Never will be. You need to get that through your thick head and leave Charlotte and me the hell alone. Do you understand me?" A tear slips down her cheek as I lean back to stand up, and I get caught off guard when she leans forward and tries to kiss me. It's as if time has slowed and is moving at a snail's pace as she leans forward. I look up as my door opens, and Charlotte walks in.

She stares at me in disbelief, with Rachel on her knees in front of me. Thankfully, I turned my head enough that her kiss landed on the corner of my mouth, catching mostly my cheek, but in this moment, that doesn't fucking matter because all she sees is my ex on her knees behind my desk.

"Charlotte," I say as she turns and walks right back out the door she was standing in. I want to run after her, but I need to get Rachel out, not trusting what she'd do left to her own devices. I back away, standing up, and only because my mom taught me manners, I help her up. Once she is on her feet, I let go and bend, so we are at eye level, making sure she hears me loud and clear. "Don't you ever come back here again. Do you hear me? Your selfish bullshit has caused me enough problems. Grow up and get the fuck out." Her stunned face stares back at me. She has nothing to say, no remorse. She is evil to the bone, not caring about anyone other than herself and having no thought for what her actions do to others.

"Get Out." I yell, causing her to jump. Finally snapping out of it, she turns and walks out the door. She looks over her shoulder in the frame, shrugging her shoulders, "Sorry," she sarcastically says before walking out.

I power down my computer, not caring if I saved what I was working on, grab my suit coat, phone, wallet, and keys, and run to the elevator. I turn my phone on and shoot a message to James, letting him know I have an emergency and have to go before calling Charlotte, the call going straight to voicemail.

"Fuck." Running my hands through my hair as I wait for the elevator doors to open. She doesn't have a car because we drove together. Getting outside, I look left and right without any sign of her. Knowing she had a few minutes jump on me, she could've walked a few blocks or got into a cab. Not wanting to go the wrong way, I suck it up and call Grace.

"You better have a fucking good explanation," Her voice is venom.

"It wasn't what it looked like, fuck, Grace, you know me. It was my ex. She showed up without warning and got past because Elaine was gone. I told her I wanted nothing to do with her. Charlotte walked in after I told her to get out, and that's when she tried to kiss me. I turned my head, and she missed mostly, but she was on her knees, and I know it looked terrible. Please, Grace, I would never do anything to hurt her. Where is she? Please." I know I'm begging, and I don't care.

After a few agonizing seconds, "She told me about Rachel after your trip to LA, and she sounds like a downright bitch. Not sure how you dated her, real winner that one." Sighing into the phone, "Honestly, Gavin, it wasn't just what she saw that she's got going on. She called me when she couldn't get a hold of you, but I was leaving a meeting thirty minutes away. I told her to go to your office and that you'd take her home because she didn't want to go to the condo without you. Adding Rachel to it just made it worse. I'm on my way back now. She's going to our place. If you tell her I told you, I'll kill you, but she's going to need you." The concern in her voice has me shaking. *What the hell happened?*

"I'm coming. Meet me there in case she won't let me in." I plead.

"I'm on my way."

"Thank you, Grace," I say, hanging up and racing to the parking garage to get my car.

"Charlotte. Open the door, baby, please." I pound on the door again. She hasn't let me in, but I know she's here. I heard her footsteps when I first knocked. I was hoping she'd answer if I didn't say who it was...dumb move.

Knocking again, "Please, it wasn't what you thought, I promise you that. Open the door, Fire, so we can talk. Don't run. Don't shut me out. I called Grace and told her everything. She's the one who told me where you were. If she didn't believe me, you know she wouldn't have let me come here." I lean my forehead against the door and wait.

After what feels like forever, I hear the door unlock, making me back up and rock back on my heels. I am prepared to fight for her. I've done nothing wrong, but I know what it must have looked like. Add that to whatever Grace wouldn't tell me, I know Charlotte will be on the defensive.

The door opens slightly, and her face comes into view, red and blotchy, and my heart instantly sinks. Unable to help myself, I push the door open and wrap her in my arms, not allowing her time to push me away, using my foot to kick the door closed behind me. I hold her tight and close to me, running my hand into her messy bun as I tuck her head into my chest. She's changed from her work clothes and is now in a pair of black leggings and a hoodie, her hair up and out of her face and her makeup smudged from crying. *Fuck, I did this to her, not on purpose, but I'm part of it.*

Before she can say anything, I bend my knees and pull back slightly to be at eye level with her, "I'm so sorry, baby. I was working at my desk, trying to concentrate after texting you. I kept checking my phone, so I shut it off to force myself to get something done. I wasn't expecting anyone with Elaine gone. Rachel knocked and walked in. I thought it was Logan or James, I swear. She told me she missed me and wanted to try again. She tried to grab my leg, and I pushed her away. I got in her face and told her to go away, that you were it for me, and I never wanted to see her again. She tried to kiss me, I turned my head, and that's when you walked in. I know it didn't look good, and I'm so sorry, but I promise you, nothing happened. I would never do that to you, could never do that to you. Please, Fire, talk to me." Finally stopping to breathe, I wait while she stares at me, her expression unreadable, scaring me shitless that I can't tell what she's thinking.

"John is my dad."

Of all the things I thought would come out of her mouth, that was not it.

I don't want to sound like an ass, yet wanting to make sure I understand her, I gently prod, "John as in John Jones?"

Something breaks inside her, and I can see it unleash in her eyes, "Yes. As in John Jones. As in my boss. As in, he's known I was his daughter this entire time, and my mom has known who my dad is my entire life and has never, not once, said anything to me about it. My entire life, she's been hiding this from me, telling me for as long as I can remember he left and never contacted her again, which is total bullshit, and I've been working at his firm for the past three months without a fucking clue." Her voice is laced with hurt and anger.

"Turns out, everyone has been hiding things from me my entire life, but nope doesn't stop there. When I need you, I have the pleasure of finding your bitch of an ex-girlfriend on her knees in your office on a day you knew I'd be gone. How convenient." Her chest heaves, attempting to pull air into her lungs.

Her anger and hurt taking over, she tries to push against my chest. Unwilling to let her go, she turns her hands into fists, pounding into my chest, and I let her. I let her bang on my chest to let all the hurt, anger, frustration, and confusion leak out. I hold her, knowing that if I try to talk, it won't help. Afraid if I let go of her, she'll run, and I'll lose her as this clusterfuck of information weighs heavy on her shoulders.

All the while wanting to hunt Rachel down for her impeccably shitty timing to be a psycho.

Charlotte's fists slow down as emotional fatigue sets in, silence turning into sobs until she literally can't take anymore, sliding down my body as I go with her into a heap on the floor. Her sobs fill the room as I pull her into my lap and turn us, so my back leans against the side of the couch. I didn't notice Grace even came in until she was kneeling in front of us, placing her hand on Charlotte's back and rubbing it in small circles.

I give her an appreciative nod, barely holding back my own emotions. I am so grateful for Grace, not only for her understanding and telling me where Charlotte was and believing me I would never hurt her on purpose, but for always being there for Charlotte, being her family.

"Charlotte, babe, it's Grace," she says softly to her. Charlotte doesn't move.

"I know this is a lot. I'm here. Gavin is here. He called me and told me what had happened. I know it looked bad, I can't imagine, but I believe him, and I know deep down you do too." Her voice is calm and soft. Charlotte still doesn't respond.

"I'll be here. I'm going to go to my room to give you some space, but I'm here." Grace gives her a hug from behind before standing and mouthing *Thank you,* and then walks down the hall to her room to give us some space.

My legs are starting to go numb, but I don't dare attempt to move us from this position. Charlotte is still curled up in my lap. Her sobs have stopped, her breathing slowly returning to a normal rhythm, and the tears she's cried have soaked through my dress shirt. As I sit, running my fingers through her hair, my mind goes through what she said.

John is her dad. Her mom has always known where he was. Has he tried to contact her? And a lightbulb goes off in my head. *He knew.* When I told him and my dad about our relationship, he acted strange and almost protective, and I brushed it off. *What a shitshow.*

As I sit in my own thoughts, Charlotte starts to lift her head. Instinctively I go to hold her cheek, assuring she can't hide from me. She doesn't pull or look away, so I steal the chance to talk. "I am so sorry, Fire. I am sorry your mom hid that from you. I'm sorry for downplaying why she was here last night. I'm sorry that you've been lied to. And I'm sorry for what you saw in my office. God, I'm sorry. I hope you know; I need you to know Rachel is nothing to me. All the other stuff we will figure out together. I promise." Silently praying to anyone who will listen, she won't run.

Wiping her nose with the back of her hand, she stares back at me. Even through her puffy and redness, she has the most beautiful blue eyes I've ever seen. As those eyes that bring me to my knees search my face, I hold my breath.

Finally, she says, just above a whisper, "I believe you." And I feel like I can breathe again.

28

Charlotte

*E*ver heard the saying, *well, that didn't go the way I thought it would?* Today was the epitome of that statement. Lunch with my mom was nothing short of a five-ring circus. *"I'm sorry, Charlotte. I was going to tell you when you graduated, but then you left, and I never could. I was trying to protect you from getting hurt. I don't think I ever stopped loving him."* When my brain couldn't take in anymore, I got up and left the restaurant without saying a word.

Pissed I didn't have my own car to leave in, I turned into an alley around the corner from where we were eating and called Gavin. Getting his voicemail, I texted him that I would come back to the office before trying Grace. She was just leaving a meeting outside of the city in the other direction, so after giving her the thirty-second run down of my shitshow of a lunch, I ordered a cab that was a minute away. Walking to the sidewalk to wait, I couldn't shake this eerie feeling that I was being watched as chills ran up the back of my neck, making my heart race and my hands clammy. I had the same feeling at Olivia's show in LA. However, when I looked around, I didn't see anyone. I chalked it up to being shaken after the shit show of a lunch, causing my mind to get the better of me. My phone beeped, alerting me that my ride was here. I shook my head at my paranoia and got in. I couldn't wait to get to Gavin. My safe space.

What I didn't expect was to walk into his office and his ex on her knees behind his desk. My brain was too jumbled from the sequence of events to comprehend what I was seeing, so I numbly turned, ran out of his office, and left the building. I called Grace, tears streaming down my face as I rushed down the sidewalk, needing to get as far away from there as possible. Mumbling out something along the lines of "Gavin, ex, office, knees," she told me she'd meet me at the apartment, so that's where I went.

I couldn't stop the waterfall of emotions coming from my eyes, not through the car ride to the apartment, not while I mindlessly changed my clothes, and not when I heard the door. As Gavin talked on the other side, anger took over. I had every intention of opening that door and telling him to shove it until he charged in, grabbing me and not letting go.

Thankfully, he let me spew my venom at him while I pounded my fists until Grace came home and repeated Gavin's words. Hearing the story from her allowed my brain to slow its pace for the first time since I rushed out of the restaurant.

Rachel was evil, this much I could tell from our one encounter. Gavin had never hidden anything about their relationship from me, and his text said he would be at the office, telling me where I could find him. And I knew deep down Gavin wouldn't do that to me. *He isn't Gregory.*

"I believe you." I knew, looking into his eyes, he wasn't lying to me. I trusted him. With every ounce I had, I trusted him.

My body was exhausted from the gauntlet that was the last few hours. I knew that if I wasn't so emotionally raw from lunch, I would've reacted differently and probably smacked her when I came into his office. It was a culmination of events, and Rachel in Gavin's office was the proverbial horse that broke the camel's back.

"Thank you. I love you, Fire. I'm sorry. So damn sorry for putting you through that after the day you've had." The sincerity in his eyes told me everything I needed to know. That no matter what was going on, he was my center. Even as mad as I was, his holding me gave me relief from the shit poured down on me today.

His hand still gently on my cheek, his touch calming me in a way only he can, "Do you want to talk about it?"

"Yes...no...I don't know. I don't even know where to start."

"How about from the beginning? First though, can we get off the floor? I can't feel my legs." He gave me a little smirk, lightening the mood a tiny bit.

"Oh, God. I'm crushing you," pushing myself back and up to lift the weight off his legs. After standing up, I use my sleeve to wipe my tears and nose from ugly crying. Gross, but in the moment, you use what you have.

"You'd never crush me, baby," Gavin pulls me back close to him after wobbly standing up like a baby giraffe trying to find his feet. When his legs stabilize, he effortlessly lifts me into his arms. I'm cradled into his chest as he walks us to my room. Placing me on the edge of the bed to climb in, he rests against my headboard before leaning forward and pulling me back, so my back is on his chest. Our legs intertwine with each other, and his hands are wrapped tightly around my waist, as if he's afraid to let me go.

"John was my mom's college boyfriend. She got pregnant during her sophomore year. He said he wanted to make it work, but a few weeks later, he transferred schools. Never hearing from him again. At least that's the story she told me when I was a kid." Saying the words out loud felt like pouring alcohol on an open wound, knowing everything I thought about my dad was a lie.

Gavin stays silent, giving me the time to compose my thoughts and get this out. The conversation with my mom spills out to him.

"So, you lied. You told me he left, and you never heard from him again."

"He did leave, but before he did, he came over, explaining that his parents threatened to cut him off if he didn't transfer schools. They didn't want their precious name tarnished with a baby out of wedlock, and I wasn't the pedigree of woman they wanted marrying their son. He promised to take care of us, but I was so angry and hurt that he wouldn't stand up to his parents for us. For you. It crushed me that he let money and status come before love. I knew his parents would never change their minds. Even if they came to terms with it, at some point, they would hold this over his head. I knew it would leak into your life, and that was something that I wasn't willing to sacrifice. I told him if he left, that was it."

"He wanted to be a part of my life, and you wouldn't let him, so he left and never looked back."

"Not exactly. I loved your father with everything I had,

and it broke me when he bent to his parent's wishes. I was young, angry, and hurt, but I was also going to be a mom and wanted to protect you from what his parents could do. So when he returned when I was six months pregnant, I refused to see him. And again when I was eight months pregnant. He came one last time when you were a few months old. I was so scared that letting him meet you would, in the end, hurt you, so I didn't open the door. After that, he stopped coming, but he wrote letters and sent you a check every month. I knew he lived in Phoenix from the stamp on the envelope. Never allowing myself to look into where or what he was doing. I could never bring myself to read the letters, and my pride wouldn't allow me to use his money. I kept the letters in a box and opened an account for you, promising myself to tell you everything when you were eighteen. I planned on giving you all the money he had sent over the years to pay for college, but then you were gone."

Realization hits me that I could have known this six years ago if I hadn't left. No, fuck that. She had eighteen years to tell me.

"I don't understand how you thought making me think my father didn't care was better?"

"I knew what his parents were like, and I didn't want that life for you. I was trying to protect you growing up. Confident that you would understand when I explained it to you, but I never got the chance. When I came to visit you, and we went to the office, I realized you were working at his firm, and when we were leaving, he walked out and saw us. The next week, he showed up at our house, and for the first time, I let him in. He told me he knew you were his daughter the moment he saw your application, and since I had blocked him at every point, this was his chance to watch over you the only way he knew how. We talked for hours. It was then that I realized I had pushed down my feelings and covered them with pride for years. When I refused to see him, he thought he had ruined his chance to change things, so he stopped coming, thinking that would make me happy. He married to please his parents and lived in a loveless marriage until his parents died. Charlotte, I'm so sorry I kept this from you. I wanted to tell you, but I didn't know how after I got back. We were just finding each other again, and I wasn't ready to bring that up."

"This is why you came early? To tell me."

"Yes and no."

"Yes and no what? I'm confused."

"Lottie, after he came to the house, we've talked every day. I don't think I ever didn't love your father, and he never stopped loving me. He just let a screwed-up sense of loyalty to his parents get in the way. Add to that his fear of rejection from me stopped him from trying harder to be in your life. But he wanted to be Charlotte, and that is on me. I am so sorry. We want to be together, I am thinking about moving here to make it work, but I told him I needed to tell you this on my own first."

"My brain felt like it was going to explode, so I got up and left. The flight, the hotel, and the rental car. It all makes sense," I say in a huff, pissed that she had eighteen years to tell me that I had a father that wanted to be part of my life, she just wouldn't let him, and he knew who I was the whole time.

"That's how I got my internship. I knew it sounded too good to be true. It wasn't because I was good enough; it was because he felt guilty," I say, feeling defeated.

Gavin's hand turns my head to see his face, "Fire, listen to me. I know this is a lot, and you have every right to be mad, but I also know how brilliant you are, and even if you weren't John's daughter, you deserve this internship. You are so valuable to our firm, and I can't say his motive, but I do know that you earned your spot." Gavin says firmly, making sure I hear them as he encases me around him, arms crossing over my body tightly again.

We just sit there, both of us not saying anything, as the gravity of everything sinks in. After a few minutes of silence, it dawns on me, "The scholarship money."

"What about it?" Confusion in his voice.

"It's John's. I never saw a scholarship listed for that much. I know I didn't. I didn't dive deep, but I read over all the available ones, and I swear it wasn't listed. I got the call a couple weeks after I started at your firm. It was guilt money." Tears well in my eyes.

"Ok, so that's possible. Maybe it's not guilt money though. He didn't know you hadn't gotten the money from your...." he trails off. When I turn to look at him, he looks like a deer caught in the headlights.

"What?"

"Shit, the day I told my dad and him about us. He was asking why you worked in a bar. I told him it was to pay your rent and tuition. I didn't think anything of it at the time." Gavin gives me a worried look.

I didn't earn any of this. The job, the scholarship, all of it is a lie. Reading my thoughts, Gavin turns me so I am straddling him, grabbing my chin gently to look me in the eye.

"You listen here, Fire. Stop right now. I can practically hear the doubt in your brain. Honestly, there is a real possibility that money came from him, now that doesn't mean you don't deserve every penny. You lived alone and worked your ass off to get through college without a single dime of help from anyone. You got into college and law school of your own accord and would have paid off every penny of debt after graduation. I know that. We are the lucky bastards that got you. I won't let you second guess why you are here because it brought you to me, and I will be forever grateful for that. If you had been at any other firm, we might not have reconnected after the first night. Fate had other plans, so I will not for one second let you think you aren't exactly where you are meant to be." His voice full of conviction and his eyes soft and loving, I can't help but lean forward, pressing my lips to his, letting him take away all the pain and bullshit of the day, getting lost in him.

"Make me forget, Gavin," I whisper against him.

"Are you sure, baby?" His eyebrows raised in question.

"I've never been more sure, I need you. Just us, nothing else. Please."

"Anything for you, Fire. Just us." He says before taking my mouth in an earth-shattering kiss.

"Next time you are going to have sex in our apartment, let me know so I can leave. Even my noise-canceling headphones didn't block out your screams, Lottie." Grace teases as we walk back to the living room.

Gavin shrugs at her, "Sorry, not sorry."

"I'm only half serious, honestly, babe. You ok?" Grace envelops me in a hug. I grab around her waist and squeeze her back. She has been there for me every step of the way, and I couldn't be more grateful for her.

Stepping back, I reply, "I will be. Thank you for being

here." As I get the words out, Gavin wraps his arms around my waist, holding my back to his chest. Maybe not today, but I will be.

After Gavin read me like a comic book, as if my thoughts were displayed in a bubble over my head, I couldn't do anything else other than kiss him. I won't say the self-doubt is gone, and I'm still not sold that him being my biological father didn't influence me getting my internship. However, I do know I got myself into college on my own and was accepted into law school because I worked and studied hard. I can't explain how he knows exactly what I need when I need it.

My mind is still reeling from this afternoon's lunch with my mom and the events after.

"Today has been a lot," I say with a laugh, trying to lighten the mood.

"Hell yeah it has. I was going to have a drink with Matthew tonight. Why don't I text him, then we can order in and have a glass of wine?" Grace offers, grabbing her phone off the counter.

"No, don't cancel. Go see Matthew, I'm exhausted anyways, and after eating, I just want to sleep." I know she was excited to see him before he flew home for Thanksgiving. No way am I making her miss that because I had a shitty day.

"Charlotte is right. Go have a drink. I'm not going anywhere." Gavin adds, releasing me and pulling us toward the couch.

"Are you sure? I don't want to ditch you after today."

"I'm sure. Spend time with Matthew before he goes home for the weekend. Maybe even spend the night there," I wink at her, knowing they haven't had sex yet, which is a huge deal for Grace and something new she is trying.

"Okay, if you're sure, I'm going to freshen up before I head out. If you need me, text, and I'll leave."

"Go get ready. I'm fine, really," looking over at Gavin, "we probably need to go to your place; you have no clothes here."

"We can do whatever you want, Fire. I'm not letting you out of my sight," he says while pulling my feet up onto his lap and rubbing circles along my arch.

"Alright, lovebirds, I'm going to go change," Grace starts walking down the hallway before stopping and looking at me hesitantly, "Oh, and Lottie, you might want to check your phone. You left it out here, not that I was snooping, but it kept going off. Your mom called several times and sent a few texts." I nod, letting her know I'll check it, and she turns and closes her bedroom door.

Dropping my head back on the pillow, I take a deep breath before leaning forward and grabbing my phone off the coffee table. Nine missed calls and six texts. Taking a deep breath, I open my phone to read the messages.

MOM:

I'm sorry, Lottie. I never meant to hurt you. I thought I was doing what was best for you at the time. When you are a mother, I hope you understand where I was coming from.

MOM:

When you are ready, can you call me?

MOM:

Please let me know you got home okay.

MOM:

I tried Gavin with no response. Please, Lottie, I'm worried.

MOM:

Please don't shut me out. I can't lose you again.

MOM:

I love you. Please call me.

As overwhelming as today has been, I know what I put her through when I disappeared last time, so I text back.

ME:

I'm safe.

Instantly my phone buzzes.

MOM:

Thank you. I am so sorry, Lottie. I love you.

ME:

Love you too.

MOM:

Can you forgive me?

ME:

We can talk tomorrow.

Talk about horrible timing. Thanksgiving is only two days away. We were planning on going to Daniel and Kristina's with my mom and Grace. I don't want to ruin everyone's day with my family drama.

Putting my phone down, I look over at Gavin, "I don't want to bring my drama to your family's Thanksgiving."

Taking both of my hands in his, he makes sure I am

looking at him, "Fire, stop worrying. I know this is a lot, and I'll be here every step of the way. You don't have to talk to her if you aren't ready. We don't even have to go to my parents. We can do something else."

Shaking my head, "No, I just need tonight. Part of me understands, and part of me is angry. I also know I would've known this years ago if I hadn't run, which is on me. Can you come with me tomorrow if I talk to her?" Feeling weak, knowing him being near will give me strength.

"Of course, baby. Why don't you see if she will come to the condo so you can have privacy versus being out in public? I'll be there if you need me."

"Okay, thank you. For everything. I feel like I've been a mess lately."

Pulling me into him, "You are not a mess, baby. I love you. You have faced a lot of hurdles lately. I am so proud of you and so fucking sorry that the shit in my office only made it worse. I will always be there for you through anything. I. Am. Yours. However, and whenever you need me."

"I love you too, so much." I let him hold me, allowing his hands and his warmth to calm me. As shitty as today has felt, being in his arms makes me feel safe and that everything will be okay.

We sit there for who knows how long, wanting to stay in our bubble. Until my stomach growls, letting me know it needs food. I pack a bag for the weekend, deciding to pick up food and go to Gavin's. On the drive over there, I texted my mom, and she agreed to come to the condo tomorrow for brunch so we could talk. I guess we'll see what tomorrow brings.

29

Gavin

*A*fter texting her mom, Charlotte was quiet on the drive back to my condo. She dropped her bag in the bedroom before we ate the tacos we had picked up on the way. When we finished eating, we moved to the couch, and within five minutes, she was curled up and asleep with her head in my lap. She didn't even flinch when I carried her into the bedroom and tucked her in. I knew she was exhausted after today, so I let her sleep while I worked out to run off some of my built-up energy from the fuck up of a day.

She was still sleeping peacefully when I came out of the shower. Too wired to sleep, I put on some black sweatpants and a green t-shirt and snuck out into the living room. Glancing at the clock, I saw it was only after nine. Picking up my phone, I find the name I need and press call.

"Hello, Gavin. To what do I owe the pleasure?" *Smartass.*

"Did you know about John being Charlotte's dad?" My

words are firmer than I mean them to be. For some reason, since Charlotte told me about lunch with her mom, I couldn't help thinking my dad knew about this the whole time.

The line is silent for a few seconds, confirming what I thought was true, "Not until last week."

"Why didn't you tell me? She was blindsided today, Dad. I would've gone with her, talked to her, fuck, I don't know, done something to help this not be such a shock." My voice was stern with the frustration of how this could have been handled so differently, *especially if I had been with her. The whole Rachel situation never would have happened.*

My dad sighs into the phone, "I'm sorry, Gavin. John and I met last week for a drink, and he told me he had found Kelly and that Charlotte was his daughter. You know he was miserable being married to Lisa. He only married and stayed with her because of his parents; once they were gone, he could be free. I had known about Kelly and that she had gotten pregnant. However, I didn't know how Charlotte played into this whole thing until Friday. He went several times to try and make it work, but she wouldn't see him. I never knew the child's name because she never told him. He knew he screwed up, but she had shut him out when he went to make it right. After he lost her, he did what his parents wanted, went to law school, and married Lisa, except I don't think he ever let go of Kelly."

"Wait, so you knew he had a child this whole time? You should have told me, at least, so I could give her a warning. She went there alone, and her mom dropped this bomb on her. Did John donate money to Clayton for a scholarship?" Running my hands through my hair in frustration about how this whole thing went down.

"It wasn't my news to tell. He was a mess back then, Gavin, miserable. Being a father myself, I can't imagine what it was like to know you had a child but couldn't be a part of their life. Once he knew who she was, he wanted to do what he could without her knowing. You can't blame him for wanting to take care of his daughter. He called me Monday and told me Kelly was meeting Charlotte today to tell her. John wanted to go, but Kelly insisted she do this alone, so he respected that."

Pacing my living room floor back and forth, my heart aching for her, "Fuck, I wish I would've gone, been there with her. She thinks the only reason she got the internship is because John is her dad, and she thinks the scholarship money came from him as a handout from guilt."

"You know that's not true. I was there for all the interviews, and she deserved a spot at Davis and Jones. Yes, he may have wanted her there for other reasons, but she earned her spot. As for the money, son, I would've done the same thing. To know she has been on her own and struggling all this time, it's a father's instinct to fix it." His voice is calm and soft as if he can feel John's pain, missing his daughter all this time.

"How do I fix this for her?" My voice sounding defeated; she has been through so much.

"Love her. Support her. Listen to her. This is all a lot to take in, I'm sure. John loves her, Gavin, like any father, and he just wants a chance to get to know his daughter. That was taken away from him, and he blames himself for his choices back then. He wants to make it right and have a shot at having a real family, not a facade." His words hit me hard. He wants a real family. That's all Charlotte wanted, her family back.

"Thanks, Dad. Kelly is coming over tomorrow, so they can talk without distractions. I am not sure how Thursday will go. Tell mom I'm sorry."

"There is nothing to be sorry for. Your mother knows about all of this too. I couldn't keep it from her. She's worried about Charlotte." His voice laced with concern.

"Me too, Dad, me too."

"Call me if you need anything. I love you, son."

"Love you too, Dad."

Leaving my phone on the table, I walk to the bedroom, strip down to my boxers, and crawl into bed. Pulling Charlotte tight to my side, she sighs and wiggles back into me before her breathing evens out again. My dad's words ring in my head. *Love her, support her, listen to her. I would do anything for my family.* He is right. She is going to be my family. I know it, and I will do anything to protect her.

I wake up and reach over, only to find an empty spot. The sheets are cold, alerting me that she has been gone for some time. My clock reads just after seven. I can smell coffee. I use the bathroom and put my sweatpants on, dragging a t-shirt over my head as I walk toward the living area.

Charlotte is standing in one of my t-shirts that hangs just below her gorgeous ass, staring out the windows that overlook downtown, her face lost in thought. She must really be in her own head because she doesn't even notice me coming up behind her until I gently grab her waist and pull her back toward me, breathing in her scent.

I place a kiss on her temple. "Good morning, my beautiful girl. How long have you been up?"

She leans back into me, and I squeeze her tighter, never

wanting to let her go, "A couple hours, I couldn't sleep. I don't even remember going to bed last night."

"I carried you. You fell asleep on the couch. I took off your leggings so you wouldn't get too hot."

"Are you sure it wasn't because you wanted to check me out?" She turns her head, giving me a little smirk.

"Oh, Fire, I'm always checking you out." Wanting to see where her head is at, I take a risk by asking, "How are you feeling?"

She turns in my arms, looking up at me, "Honestly, better. I woke up this morning and had time to think. As angry as I am at my mom for keeping this from me, I kind of get it, you know? She found out she was pregnant, and then he left. If I was her, I'd feel betrayed and would've been protective too. Do I wish she would have told me sooner? Yes, but in her mind, she was scared that if she let him in, he'd leave again. Not to mention by that time, he was probably already married. I also kind of get the pressure he must have felt. I can relate to faking it, the facade I put up for two years pretending to be happy, trying to please everyone. The pressure of trying to be who someone wants you to be was suffocating, and they weren't even my family, so I can't imagine what it would've felt like for him. I also understand her wanting to tell me when I was an adult, to give me the choice of what I wanted to do, and I took that chance away from her, probably adding to her guilt of not telling me sooner. I also take some fault in all of this with my choices. Don't get me wrong, it's going to take time to work through all these emotions. However, I woke up clearer than I was yesterday. And at the end of the day, it all comes down to *you*."

She must see the confusion I feel at her words as she

reaches around and runs her fingers down my cheek. "You, Gavin, are the key to this all." Her smile eases my fear slightly, but I'm still lost.

"I don't understand, Fire." Keeping my hold around her tight, worried about where this is going to go.

"Finding you helped me find my family. If I had never met you, I would have probably, *no*, I definitely would have waited a lot longer to reach out to my mom, if I ever did at all. Without reaching out to my mom, she would never have come here and run into John. Without dating you, John would never have known that I had left and was doing this all alone and that my mom was alone. If my mom hadn't run into John, there is a good chance he never would have gone to see her. Even though I was angry and confused yesterday, I could hear in her voice that she loves him. Growing up, she never dated anyone, never even let anyone close, and now I know why. She gave her heart away a long time ago and never got it back. You see, you were the missing piece. My entire family, including mom, John, and me, were all lost before you."

A single tear runs down her cheek, and I move my arm to wipe it away. "Fire" is all I can manage to get out.

"I love you, Gavin. I know it will take time, but I woke up this morning with a sense of calm, which is crazy after yesterday, right? I know there is a lot to figure out, yet somehow with you, I know it will all work out. Thank you, for finding me, for finding my family." Her arms come around me as she buries her head into my chest. This beautiful, strong woman in my arms is everything to me. Her compassion, perseverance, and love knows no bounds, and I am in awe of her. I hold her close to me, relishing the fact that I have found my other half, and I am never letting her go.

✦

Charlotte

I woke up this morning a little out of it after sleeping better than I expected, given everything that went down yesterday. The last thing I remember was snuggling up to Gavin on the couch. Looking over, Gavin was sleeping soundly on his back with his arm over his head, so I slipped out of bed as quietly as I could, knowing I wasn't going to be able to fall back asleep.

As the sun rose over downtown Phoenix, I made a cup of coffee, and the fog from yesterday lifted, allowing me to rationalize things. I couldn't imagine being my mom, young, pregnant, and finding out the man you thought would stay forever was choosing money over love. Letting fear of what his parents thought or would do define his life. *And didn't I do the same? Let someone else force me to make decisions and let fear dictate my life.*

Her heart had been broken, and she didn't want me to ever feel the pain or rejection she did. A mother's first instinct is to protect her child. Even though it may not have been the right decision forever, she truly believed it was the right decision at the time. Ultimately, I can't say I would have done anything different if it were me.

She kept things from me, and that hurts. But was I any different from her? I kept things from her about Gregory and running, leaving everything I knew behind without a word. I let my fear lead me and paid the price for that, and so did she, in a way. She never let anyone in, living for me and me alone. Finally, after all these years, she is hopefully getting her happy ending.

Knowing that he sent letters, that he wanted to know me, or at the very least support me, made me feel worth it, wanted. Deep down, the feeling of abandonment has always been there, we weren't good enough for him, yet that wasn't the case. It makes my stomach turn thinking of all the years that were wasted because of secrets, fear, and not communicating between my mom, John, and me when I left.

It wasn't until I found Gavin that all the missing pieces started to fall into place. Even with all the hurt and secrets, I truly believe this all happened for a reason. If I had never left, I would never have met Grace, Joe, and Maria, and I probably would have never met Gavin. Finding him was the key to finding my family and myself. And the first thing I wanted to do when he came up and wrapped his arms around me was tell him that. No matter what, I know it will all work out with him, and I never want to let him go.

After an extremely tearful and emotional conversation, my mom and I are sitting on Gavin's couch. I called Grace this morning, telling her everything I told Gavin. She told me she was proud of me and she'd be there if I needed her. She always is. When my mom came to the condo, Gavin went into his office to give us space but kept the door open in case I needed him. We've spent the last three hours talking about everything. The good, the bad, and the ugly. She told me that he was responsible for the money I received. Not a handout or out of guilt. It was, in his mind, the only way of supporting me without telling me who he was, something he didn't want to do without my mom's permission. Also, I read the letters John wrote to me that my mom had kept. Sixteen to be exact, all telling me how much he loved me and was proud of me even though he had never met me. *He loved me even when he didn't know me.* Somehow reading his letters helped me understand his need to help me however he could.

Yesterday I was angry, and I'm not totally over that feeling, but I don't want to waste more time letting fear and miscommunications affect my life.

"He wants to see you. He wanted to come with me yesterday, but I wouldn't let him. Me keeping you from him all these years was my decision, and I needed to tell you myself. He usually goes to Gavin's parents for Thanksgiving. He told them he wouldn't come unless you were okay with it." My mom's voice is hoarse from crying as we face each other.

"I think I'd like that. So," waving my fingers in the air, "you two are for real? Like, really going to give it a shot?"

"Yeah, we are. I pushed my feelings down for a long time, but I have loved your father for over twenty-six years, and I let my fear and pride stand in the way of that for too long. I don't regret a single day of raising you, though. I will always wonder if I had just listened if things could have been different for you."

"Mom, my life was great. Well, until I met Gregory." I give a halfhearted laugh trying to break up the intensity of our conversation. "We can't change the past, and we can't live in what-ifs. All we have is today. We need to let go of our past choices, knowing that the choices we make now will define how we live moving forward."

"You have grown into such a wise and amazing woman, Lottie. When did that happen? It feels like yesterday you were six with pigtails."

"Ha, I'd like to say it's all me, only it's not. Meeting

Gavin has opened my eyes to so much and made me think and look at things in a whole new light. I don't want to let my past rule me. I want to submerge myself in my present and plan for my future. Do you think you'll move here? What will Grandma and Grandpa do?"

Sighing with hope twinkling in her eyes, "Yes, that's our plan; well, it was dependent on you. I've already talked to your grandparents about it, and they have been thinking of moving for some time now, unsure where they want to go. They want a condo where they don't have to do yard work. John sent me some brochures for senior living communities in the greater Phoenix area that they have been looking at. Watch out; before you know it, we'll all be here."

"That wouldn't be bad, all my family together in one place." Taking another leap of faith, I add, "Maybe John could come have dinner here tonight. I don't want him to avoid Thanksgiving on my account." I lean my head onto her shoulder. Today has been emotionally exhausting, but I don't want our family issues to bleed into Gavin's family's holidays.

"Are you sure? I don't want to push you into anything you aren't ready for." She eyes me cautiously.

"I'm sure. I've seen him plenty of times at the office. It's not like I'm meeting him for the first time." I'm nervous yet excited. "Gavin," I yell from the couch, and instantaneously he appears from the hallway.

"Yeah, baby?" He says, trying to act like he wasn't eavesdropping on our conversation.

"Would you mind if John came for dinner tonight? We can order something."

"I'm okay with anything you need, Fire," he says, coming over and grabbing my hand, placing kisses on the back of my knuckles. My mom nods and picks up her phone to text John. Gavin leans in and whispers at the shell of my ear, "I'm so proud of you, baby."

"I love you," I whisper back.

"I love you more."

An hour later, I hear the doorbell ring while I am in the master bathroom freshening up, using concealer to cover up the puffiness under my eyes, a result of all the emotions from the last two days. I can hear voices in the foyer, and suddenly I'm stuck to my spot. *What if he realizes I'm not worth it?* As I stare in the mirror, I hear Gavin call my name again. Refusing to let anxiety and fear win, I straighten my back and force my feet to propel me out of the bathroom and down the hall.

I am grateful that they aren't crowded in the foyer. As I walk into the open living space, I can't help the overwhelming feeling consuming every part of my body. *I was ready a few seconds ago, now I want to run.* Sensing what I need without words, Gavin is next to me, kissing the top of my head, wrapping his arm to tuck me into his side, filling me with his warmth and strength.

I look up, and John is standing next to my mom, tears in his eyes. At twenty-five years old, I never imagined what it would be like to see my dad for the first time. As time seems to stand still, John steps forward after a silent exchange between him and Gavin. Gavin allowed space enough for John to wrap his arms around me as tears roll down my face. *My family.*

My arms limp at my side as he hugs me, leaning down and kissing the top of my head before saying, "Finally. I've waited twenty-five years to hug you. I've never not loved you, Charlotte."

Tension falls away as years of emotions let loose. I wrap my arms around him, burying my head into his chest as tears stream down my face as I hug my dad for the first time in my life. In this moment, no matter what it took us to get here, I feel complete, and nothing can take that away from me.

30

Charlotte

Staring in the mirror in the master bathroom in my robe, I can't stop the smile on my face, feeling utterly content. My hair is in soft waves with one side in a twist pinned back, keeping it off my face. The gold tones of eyeshadow, dramatic mascara, and ruby-red lips make me feel like a princess. After finding out about my dad, things have been a whirlwind since Thanksgiving. Yes, I said it, *Dad*, and although I never thought it was something I needed in my life, the last few weeks of getting to know him and spending time together have been fulfilling in a way I can't explain.

We spent Thanksgiving at Daniel and Kristina's. I was worried it would be awkward given the events of the days previous, but after Daniel made one dad joke, making us all pause for a second before laughing until our stomachs hurt, the tension broke, and everything was great.

After dinner was finished, James, Lexi, and Logan came

over. The boys retreated to the patio to smoke cigars while Kristina and my mom hid in the kitchen chatting. The girls and I filled our wine glasses and sat in the family room. I was excited to finally meet James' fiancé Lexi, and within minutes, we were gossiping like we had been friends for ages.

As we enjoyed the Moscato, Lexi filled us in on all the details about the wedding and how great James has been with planning. Olivia updated us on how crazy life has been since her show and Jeremy, the guy she met at a bar last week. She played it cool, but I could tell there was more to the story, and by the picture she showed us, I was surprised her phone didn't light on fire. Shockingly, Grace opened up a little about Matthew and how they had finally sealed the deal on Tuesday night and were officially seeing each other.

We had dinner with Grace and Matthew last week. He is really nice and Grace was right, he has beautiful gray-blue eyes. He was a gentleman to her, pulling out her chair and being attentive. Gavin and Matthew got along, talking business and sports. Grace seemed happy, except I couldn't help but feel something was missing. She seemed more subdued, not cracking her usual jokes, and actually seemed shy around him. I wanted to ask her, but instead, I decided to let her figure it out. She doesn't do relationships, and if I question the first guy I've seen her try with, I'm afraid she will shut down. She deserves to be happy; damn, does she deserve it.

My mom spent the week after Thanksgiving in Phoenix. We spent as much time as we could together around my school and internship schedules. Seeing my mom and dad together, you could tell how much they love each other. It radiates off them when they are in the same room. I only wish twenty-five-plus years didn't have to go by with them being apart. I was sad when she left even though it was only for a couple weeks. She wanted to give her work proper notice and tie up a few loose ends in Cedar Ridge. She flew in last night and is now a permanent resident of Phoenix. My parents officially live together and the rest of her stuff is being shipped here. I'm so excited that she's close. My grandparents are flying out in three days to spend Christmas with us. I can't wait to see them. They are going to tour a few senior communities and hopefully love it and move as well. The thought of having my whole family in the same city and never going back to Cedar Ridge feels like I've won the lottery.

We are attending the Christmas Gala tonight for HACE. Gavin surprised me, Grace, Lexi, and Olivia with a spa day that started with mani/pedis and a massage before lunch, and stylists that came to the condo to do our hair and makeup. We took over one of the guest rooms and made it into our own little studio. The girls are enjoying a glass of champagne in the living room before we change into our dresses and head out in the cars Gavin ordered. Logan, James, and Matthew are due in a few minutes. Gavin has stayed holed up in his office all afternoon, letting us girls have the run of the house. I was a little worried about having Logan and Matthew in the same room, however Gavin assured me Logan would be on his best behavior. Logan is Olivia's date tonight since Jeremy couldn't fly out with her.

Taking a moment to myself, I reflect on all that has happened in the past four months. Starting my last year of law school and internship, meeting Gavin, reconnecting with my mom and grandparents, going to LA, finding my dad. It's been a lot. And yet, I wouldn't change any of it. It's been emotionally exhausting yet so damn rewarding, and Gavin is the center of all my happiness. He is more than I ever expected or could have hoped for. Before him, I thought I was content being on my own, surviving off work, Grace, and a vibrator when I needed a release. *How wrong I was.* Now, the thought of a life without him makes me feel ill. He is my forever. I know it. I can feel it down to the marrow of my being.

"Hello, Fire." Looking over, I see Gavin leaning against the doorframe wearing a black tuxedo, his bow tie loose and laying on his crisp white shirt, arms crossed over his chest, and one ankle hooked over the other. Gavin looks good in a suit, but damn, he looks downright edible in a tux. He pushes off the wall and stalks over behind me. A man on a mission and the look in his eyes has me thanking all things holy that I don't have my dress on already.

"Hey, handsome," I say as he wraps his arms around my waist, planting kisses along my exposed neck. His cologne hits my nostrils as he leans in, making me feel dizzy from his delicious scent.

I lean my head to the side, allowing him better access. "You look beautiful, Fire, and you taste divine," his voice husky as he cascades kisses down my neck to my shoulder, his hand leaving my waist to slip the robe off my shoulder, exposing more skin to him.

Tilting my head back, resting it against his shoulder, my body presses into him, and I can feel his hardness against the fabric of my robe. Pressing back into him, I circle my hips to gain the friction my body craves.

"Ah, ah, ah, baby, I'm running this show," he whispers in my ear as he grips me tighter, preventing me from pushing back. His free hand comes around my front again, using his fingers to tease open my robe more, running his hand along my sheer lace panties. His hand moves to slide the fabric to the side...

"Guys." Both of us jump as I make sure my robe is totally closed before turning to see Grace standing in the middle of the bedroom with her hand over her eyes, Gavin's hands still pressed on my hips to hide his erection even though her eyes are closed.

Hand still shading her, she continues, "Sorry to interrupt, but we need to get dressed, Lottie. And Gavin, the boys are here, so whatever you two are doing, save it for after when there aren't ten people in the condo. You two are like horny teenagers, I swear. You have thirty seconds to be in the guest room, or I'm sending Logan in here, and we all know no one wants that." And with that, she turns around and leaves the room.

Chuckling at her nonsense, "Didn't you lock the door?"

"Didn't know I needed to in my *own* home," he says, pressing into me still hard as a rock.

Turning around and patting his chest, "Well, handsome, I guess I'll need a raincheck because I know Grace. She will send Logan in here, and I am not dealing with that."

"You're killing me, Fire," He pleads and leans in to capture my lips.

Pressing my fingers to his lips to stop him, "Hold that thought; the stylist you hired will kill me if I ruin my lipstick before we leave. I promise to make it worth it when we get back. She gave me a sample of the lipstick to reapply. I think it might look good on other things later too, don't you?" I give him my best wink and strut out of the room, leaving him there turned on and stunned.

The black limousine pulls up outside of the Phoenix Convention Center. The entire building has been closed for this event. Kristina's team has been working tirelessly on all the final details this week. I slide my hands down the ruby satin dress with a slit stopping just above my knee, the rest of the dress hugging every curve I have like a glove as I steady myself standing. The high neckline is elegant and clasps behind the nape of my neck, leaving my entire back exposed. Seeing this dress on the hanger terrified me until I put it on, feeling as though I didn't recognize the woman staring back at me. I almost fainted when Marne, the stylist, pulled out three-inch strappy gold heels to go with it. "I promise not to let you fall, babe," Grace whispered, knowing where my head was at.

"You are a fucking vision, Fire," Gavin says as he straightens his coat. Buttoning the last button and placing his hand on the small of my back, he guides me inside, the heat of his touch sending shivers up my spine.

We walk through the doors and make our way to the ballroom where the event is being held. The others head to the bar for a drink as Gavin and I walk toward where his parents are greeting people. At his side, with my arm wrapped in his, mostly so I don't trip in my heels, I take in and admire how Kristina and her team have changed this ballroom into a winter wonderland in the middle of downtown Phoenix.

White trees line the walls, covered with blue and gold ornaments and ribbon. The ceiling has fabric strung with fairy lights intertwined along them with glass snowflakes hanging down. The way the lighting is done, it looks as if actual snowflakes are falling from the sky. The tables are covered in gold cloth, crystal plates, glasses, and white and blue napkins. The centerpieces are ornate crystal vases filled with white poinsettias and roses, making the tables shine. Uplighting creates a feeling as if you are walking through a tree farm without the boots and mud involved. A band is set up on stage playing soft music, and the tables are placed around an open dancefloor. It is gorgeous.

"Charlotte, dear, you look stunning." Kristina hugs me, kissing me on the cheek as Gavin shakes his dad's hand. Kristina's navy blue one-shoulder dress that is fitted to her hips, and flowing naturally to the floor, looks absolutely stunning.

"Thank you, Kristina, you look beautiful, and this," I say, motioning to everything around me, "this is amazing."

"Thank you, dear. I am so grateful for the team I have who brought my vision to life."

Gavin moves in to hug his mom as Daniel comes up to hug me as well.

"You look beautiful, Charlotte. So glad you could be here tonight," he says as he leans back. I've learned Daniel is a man of few words, but he never says something he doesn't mean.

Olivia and Logan walk up next to us as Olivia embraces her mom in a hug, and Logan shakes Daniel's hand as well. As I spin to see where Grace and Matthew walked off to, I see my mom and dad approaching. She's wearing a black dress with three-quarter-length sleeves that flows from her waist to make it seem as though she's floating. Her hair is in a loose updo, something I've never seen on my mom, and the smile that lights up her face makes my heart swell with happiness.

"Hello, my darling girl," my mom says as she wraps me in her arms, "This dress is, wow, you look amazing."

"Thanks, mom, you look beautiful too. Isn't this place magical?"

"It truly is." My mom, dad, Kristina, and Daniel exchange hellos and make small talk. Olivia and Logan walk toward the bar where James, Lexi, Grace, and Matthew are mingling.

"Shall we get a drink, Fire, or shall I find a place we can hide so I can finish what we started earlier?" His voice is full of mischief.

"Drink, you deviant. Mischief later."

He chuckles, "Alright, just know the longer you make me wait, the more ideas I'm coming up with."

"Can't wait, handsome," I whisper as we walk toward the bar, my mind filling with all kinds of dirty thoughts for later.

"If Gavin could undress you with his eyes, you'd be naked," Grace whispers as the last course plates are cleared. James, Lexi, Logan, Olivia, Grace, Matthew, Gavin, and I were all seated together, making dinner full of the boys swapping jabs providing endless entertainment. Gavin's mother has made a speech, and there is a silent auction in the hall. Already tonight, they have raised over half a million dollars in donations and sponsorships, which will help so many people.

"I could say that same thing about Logan looking at you." I shoot back. Grace is a vision in her forest green dress covered in sequins. One sleeve goes to her wrist, while the other shoulder is completely bare. Her brunette locks are tied in a loose chignon at the base of her neck, teardrop diamond earrings dangling down. The dress makes her eyes shine even brighter green, and Logan has been looking at her all night like he wants to devour her. Matthew has been oblivious or at least acting so.

"He can fuck right off. It's all a game to him, always is, always will be, and I'm done playing games." Her tone is defensive as she glares back at him. His eyes look almost sad. I can tell there is something she isn't telling me. However, now is not the time to get into it, stashing that info for later. Switching gears completely, she says to the table, "Matthew and I are going to Colorado for New Year's."

"You are?" I ask, happy for her and sad, realizing this will be the first New Year's we spend apart since we met.

"Why would you do that?" Logan chimes from across the table. As he says it, Gavin subtly jabs him in the ribs in an effort to shut him up.

"Matthew wants me to meet his family and friends." Grace shoots back.

"You don't need new friends. You have plenty here," Logan retorts. Gavin is now actively glaring at him.

"There's a party that they throw every year at the ski lodge," Matthew chimes in, still seemingly unaware of the tension between Grace and Logan, "It's a tradition that we all fly in from wherever we live and meet up, and I want Grace to be part of that tradition." He grabs Grace's hand on the table, and she blatantly intertwines their fingers.

Looking at him with an overexaggerated smile, she says, "I can't wait, babe."

When Olivia steps in, Logan is about to say something, "Logan, think you can still twirl me around the dancefloor like last year?"

Shaking off his thoughts, he stands, taking her hand, "You bet your ass I can." Giving one more glance towards Grace, he leads Olivia toward the dance floor where couples have gathered as the band plays an instrumental version of *I'll be Home for Christmas*.

"Dance with me, Fire." Gavin holds my hand as he scoots his chair back, helping me up.

"Are you sure? I have a feeling I'm going to trip over myself in these heels."

"I won't let you fall." His words echo in my ears.

"Okay." I let him pull me up, straighten my dress, and head toward the dancefloor.

Pulling me to him after spinning me; *surprisingly, I didn't fall*. Our fingers are intertwined at his chest while he holds my other hand, guiding me slowly around the dancefloor. This moment, with him, is pure heaven.

"Thank you for bringing me tonight, Gavin. Thank you for helping me find my home, my family, myself."

"There is no one else I would ever want by my side, Fire, today and all my tomorrows." His words hit me, and I couldn't stop the smile on my face. "You are everything I never knew I always needed, Charlotte. These past four months have shown me that it was never going to work with anyone else because my soul was waiting for you. And now that it's found you, it will never let you go."

My eyes are shimmery with tears of happiness. I have no words, so I snuggle in closer, soaking up this moment. It isn't long before Olivia steps in, asking her brother to dance with her. Logan offers to take me for a twirl. However, I'm not sure my feet will hold up, so I excuse myself to go to the bathroom.

"Do you want me to go with you?" Gavin offers.

"I'll be fine, Gavin. Dance with your sister, and I'll be back in a minute." Waving off Grace as she dances with Matthew, I stop at our table to grab my clutch before heading to the ballroom doors on my way to the bathrooms.

As I clear the door and step into the hallway, something

grabs my arm with a force that instantly feels like a bruise, a body pressing against my back, and a voice that changes my feelings of euphoria to terror instantly.

"Hello, Charlotte. Miss me?" The hair on the back of my neck stands up as my heart pounds so hard I feel it might come out of my chest. "If you don't want me to make a scene, walk with me without making a fucking sound."

His grip on my arm feels like a vice as he pulls me toward a set of doors into a dimly lit room down the hall, away from people. As the door closes, my senses are heightened by the low lighting. He releases my arm, pushing me backward, my head hitting the steel door as I trip over my heels. Steading myself, trying not to sound scared, I find my voice, albeit shaky. I get out, "What...are you doing here, Gregory?" He stands in a black suit, his eyes dark as he stares at me as if I'm ridiculous for not knowing why he's here.

"You, my dear Charlotte, are what I'm doing here. Did you think I wouldn't find you? Did you really think you could leave me without a single word and you'd be free? I told you long ago I would never let you go. I meant it." His voice is sinister, and his hair is disheveled as if he has been pulling on it with his hands.

"How did you get in here?" I try to sound stronger, anxiety running ramped through my body.

"Oh, Charlotte, you're so naïve," He shakes his head at me, "It's amazing what money can get you." He starts pacing the room, "You've been busy lately, haven't you, flying to LA, lunch downtown, fucking other men when you belong to me." His voice raised with each syllable.

The realization hits me like a sledgehammer. All the times I felt someone watching, it was him. Bile rises in my throat as I push it back down, "You need to leave. Now."

"I don't think you understand, Charlotte." He says, annunciating the T. "You belong to me, damnit. Did you think it would be that easy? That you could leave, and I wouldn't come for you when you know I own you? Always have and always will. I admit, it took me longer than expected, but I knew, yes, yes, there would be a way, and lo and behold, I was sitting in a coffee shop minding my own business when who do I hear but Kelly Swanson talking on the phone about you flying to LA with Gavin Davis. Fate, Charlotte, fate brought you back to me."

"I don't belong to anyone. You're insane," I spit back.

The sting of the slap is sharp and comes before I can even react as tears instantly come to my eyes, the heat from the slap consuming my face. "You have always belonged to me. Do you honestly think I'd let you live a life with someone else? That I'd let someone else keep what is mine? The fact that you've impurified yourself with other men requires punishment, debt that will be paid as I see fit."

Holding my hand to my face, I cry, "Please, Gregory."

"Now you say, please, Fire, is it?" *How the fuck has he heard our conversations.*

"Ahh, now you are getting it. I had so many ways of getting to you. Money can pay for anyone to tap into emails, intercoms, and video surveillance. You hid well for a while, but it was never forever." His eyes are wild, unhinged. "Now here is how it's going to go, you will come with me, and after punishing you for your sins, we will finally be together, as it's meant to be." He stands over me, trapping me against the door, showing dominance in his size alone.

My head is spinning, "I'm not going anywhere with you." I turn to run, get help, something. He grabs my wrist so hard that with one twist, it would snap as his next words crash my world apart.

"Unless you want him dead, you will. Unless you want all of them dead, you will." His voice spits evil as he crushes down on my wrist.

Crying out in pain, I turn to look at the man who has single-handedly ruined my life twice as he pulls a gun from his waistband, waving it in the air before pointing it at me. His eyes are full of hate and something I can't describe, terrifying me to my core. I have never seen him like this as if someone else is possessing his body.

Tears run down my face as my heart splinters into a million pieces. The look in his eyes tells me everything I need to know. He will kill them. Everyone I love. Unless I go with him. Their lives for mine. My decision impossible, yet made for me. The people in the other room are my everything, and I won't let this monster hurt any of them, even if it means giving up my life.

"I will go with you if you promise that if I go, you won't hurt any of them," I beg, whimpering from the pain in my wrist.

"I knew you would see it my way." He says as he pulls me toward the other side of the room through another set of doors leading into the kitchen. He's a man on a mission as staff members look on, only no one offers to help, despite my pleading eyes.

Getting to the back of the building, he pushes through a set of metal doors where a black corvette is waiting. Pushing me away from him toward the passenger side of the car, I trip in my heels, my knees stinging as they hit the concrete, and my phone flying from my clutch a few inches in front of me.

Gregory laughs a crazy psychopathic chuckle, "Can't even fucking walk, Lottie, pathetic."

That moment on the ground, while I fake attempting to collect myself, I pull my phone toward me and type a message that I pray he'll understand. I hit send as my heart breaks, sending a prayer into the world that this nightmare at least will save the ones I love. I shove my phone down my dress just as my hair feels like it's being pulled out of my scalp, and I scramble to not have my knees drag on the ground. "I said, get up," Gregory yells as he flings the door open and as I trip on my dress, hearing it rip as my heel hits the fabric trying to stand, he pushes me into the car, slams the door, and goes around to the driver side, pulling out into the blackness of night, away from my happiness, fear filling every pore of my body. I should have known it was all too good to be true.

31

Gavin

*A*fter dancing with Olivia and then my mother, I make it back to the table where Grace and Matthew are sitting.

"Have you seen Charlotte?" I didn't see her return from the bathroom, figuring I missed her while walking my mom back to their table.

"No, I thought she was with you," Grace says, her eyebrows furrowed in confusion.

"She was. She went to the bathroom when Olivia cut in. I haven't seen her come back."

"I was just in the bathroom, and she wasn't in there."

My gut twists. *Something feels off.* "I'll be right back." Turning and walking toward the bar where Logan and James are standing, "Hey, have either of you seen Charlotte?"

"Nah, man, not since she turned me down on the dancefloor. Maybe she got wise to you too." Logan jokes.

"Fuck off," I say as I turn, looking around the room,

searching for the one girl I need. Pulling out my phone to call her, I see a message. Opening it, I stop dead in my tracks, and my next breath freezes in my lungs.

FIRE:

I'm sorry. Tell Grace she is my sunshine.

She's gone. No. Something's wrong. I can feel it. She wouldn't leave. She was fine just ten minutes ago. We were fine just ten minutes ago. Rushing back to the table, not caring that I look like a lunatic.

"What's wrong?" Grace must see the worry on my face as I shove my phone into her face.

"I don't know, Grace, you tell me." Her face morphs from concern to pure fear as she reads the message a few times before throwing it back at me and frantically searching through her purse until she finds her phone.

"Grace, what the hell is going on?" The word that comes out of her mouth is the last thing I thought she would say.

"Gregory."

"What do you mean, Gregory? For Christ's sake, Grace." My voice harsh, filled with irritation. "What does that piece of shit have to do with Charlotte?"

Not looking up at me, still tapping on her phone, "Sunshine, Gavin, she's in trouble. We made a code word when we were in college. If we ever were in danger to use that word without drawing attention. We have a tracking app on each other's phones in case of an emergency. She has never used it, and the fact that she sent it to you means it's him. He has her; I can feel it." Her voice raises as she speaks, scrambling out of her chair. "Look," she snaps, shoving her phone in my face.

On the screen, I see a dot moving away from the convention center.

"We need to go now." She yells, turning several heads in our direction. Not that I give a damn. My girl is missing.

Two seconds later, Logan and James are at my side. Matthew is holding Grace, her shoulders shaking.

"What the hell is going on?" James asks, brows furrowed.

"Charlotte's missing. She went to the bathroom and never came back. She sent me this text. Grace says it's their S.O.S., and the only time she'd use it was in an emergency. Grace thinks it's her ex, Gregory. Either way, she's tracking her phone, and it's heading away from downtown. I'm going after her. I need a car. Fuck, if he touched her..." I can feel my anger rising by the second.

"Take mine," John says, coming up behind me, handing me the keys and his parking ticket. I have no idea where he came from or what he heard. It was obviously enough, as Kelly is by his side with tears in her eyes. "I'll call the police." He wraps his arms around a crying Kelly, having just discovered her daughter is missing.

"I'm going with you." Grace cries.

"No, you need to stay here. Give John the best description you can, look this fucker up, I don't know, and be here in case she shows up. James, fill my parents in and start asking staff if they've seen anything. No one leaves without being cleared. Grace, I need your phone, so I can track her."

Grace hands me her phone, "Find her, Gavin, please," she begs.

"I'll go with you, brother. You aren't going alone." Logan grabs my shoulder.

I nod, and we head out toward the front handing the

keys to the valet. I will tear this city apart to find her if that's what it takes.

"Fuck." I scream, bending over and grabbing fistfuls of my hair in frustration.

Logan tries to reassure me, grabbing my shoulder, "We'll get her back. They couldn't have gotten far. And if Grace is right, he doesn't know that's their code word." The black Mercedes SUV pulls up, and we both jump in.

Logan hooks up the phone to the GPS system to tell us where to go as we peel down the road, turning right on 7th street. The GPS has them on I-10 heading south. I speed down the road swerving around cars cutting a hard left onto Buckeye Road, the fastest way to the Interstate.

"Slow down, man. Killing us won't help her."

Logan watches the red dot on the tracking app as we pull onto the on-ramp for the Interstate.

"The dot has stopped."

"What the fuck? Where?"

"Seems like they are still on I-10. Maybe they are stuck in traffic?"

"It's almost ten at night. Traffic is never bad at this time."

"I don't know, Gav, it's not moving."

"How far away is it?"

"Says about five miles." I press on the gas, speeding up.

Coming to a slow crawl on the interstate, I can see flashing lights ahead. We don't have time for this.

"Damnit." I slam my fists against the steering wheel. "Has the dot moved?"

"No, it's still flashing in the same spot. It looks like we're getting closer."

The interstate is closed down to one lane, and as we come upon the flashing lights, I see the cause. A sports car is flipped over against the median, and another car has been spun around from the collision. My stomach drops, and I feel bile in my throat. "Where's the dot, Logan?" I think I know the answer, but I'm praying I'm wrong.

"Here, Gav, right here." His face tells confirms the very thing I was dreading most.

Pulling over to the shoulder, I throw the car in park and jump out as Logan tries to stop me, holding my hand up to allow a car to stop as a dash across the lane. A police officer comes up, stopping me in my tracks.

"Sir, you can't be here. You need to get back in your vehicle."

Gasping for air as fear starts to take over, "The cars, was there a woman in any of them? Blonde hair, red dress? My girlfriend went missing tonight. Please." I don't even know why I'm saying please. For him to tell me it's her, for him to tell me it's not.

I don't know if he takes pity on me because tears are rolling down my face, but he gives me as much as he can, thankfully. "A woman was pulled from one of the vehicles. She was wearing a dress, which might have been red. They were transported to Maricopa Medical Center. That's all I can tell you. I'm sorry."

"Thank you." I manage to get out before halting another car running back to the SUV.

"Anything?" Logan asks.

"He said a woman was pulled from the car, wearing a dress. Took her to Maricopa Medical Center. It has to be her, right? She's okay, right?" I am grasping for any sort of confirmation from anyone.

"The tracking dot stops here. I'm sorry, Gav, I don't know."

My shoulders shaking from adrenaline, I put my blinker on, signaling to get back in the line, desperate to get to her. Throwing him my phone, I say, "Call John and have them meet us there." Those are the last words I speak as I focus every ounce of my attention on getting to Charlotte.

Charlotte

I can hear beeping, but when I try to open my eyes, they feel like I have twenty-pound weights on them. I attempt to move my arms, only the task seems as difficult as lifting a car. Muffled sounds surround me, only I can't make out what any of them are saying as I drift back into blackness.

Everything hurts, and I fight to open my eyes, which is a struggle. When my lids finally open, I blink a few times before anything comes into focus as fear takes over, not knowing where I am or what is going on.

"Charlotte, baby, can you hear me?" Gavin's voice fills my ears as a grip tightens on my hand. When I turn my head to the side where the sound came from, pain sears through my spine, feeling like I'm trying to stretch a rubber band at its limit. When I finally shift far enough, he's there, still in a tux, hair a mess. His eyes are bloodshot and have sunken bags underneath them, worry etching every inch of his beautifully exhausted face.

"Where am I?" My voice is raspy, my throat dry, and feeling like it's on fire.

"You're in the hospital, Fire. You were in an accident. You've been sleeping for the past eighteen hours."

Hospital. Accident. Like a tsunami, memories flood my

mind as my eyes fill with tears. Gregory. Gregory was going to hurt them if I didn't go with him. He was driving recklessly, swearing, and talking to himself. He was out of his mind. Swerving through traffic going so fast. The car, the sound of metal scraping, and then we were flying. That's the last thing I remember.

"Breathe, baby. You need to breathe." Gavin tells me as he presses a button, monitors making loud noises around me. "Your heart rate is too high. Fire, look at me." He commands, and I lift my eyes to find his.

Sobs, I can hear sobs in the background. *Who's crying?*

I try to take a breath, but my lungs feel like they have cages around them, and it hurts. Everything hurts. I can't catch my breath.

"She woke up, and fuck, I told her where she was, and then she started panicking." I hear him telling someone behind him. I didn't hear anyone ask a question. Within seconds, something warm flows through my veins, slowing everything down as I fade away. I fight to keep my eyes open, which proves to be useless.

As my eyes open, I can see sunlight flooding into the room. Turning my head again, which still hurts like hell, I see Gavin slumped in the chair beside the bed. He's in a black t-shirt and athletic pants. *How long have I been sleeping?* I squeeze his hand gently, and he immediately jumps up. His eyes are sleepy yet wide with concern.

"Hi," I whisper.

"Hi, beautiful. Don't move. Let me get the nurse." Gavin jumps out of his chair before I can say another word. A minute later, he walks back in with a nurse trailing him.

"Glad to see you awake, Charlotte. My name is Rhonda, and I'm your nurse. You gave everyone quite the scare. I've paged the doctor so he can come assess you." Her calm voice soothes me as she stands in dark blue scrubs, her brown hair tied in a messy knot on top of her head. She comes around and checks the monitor. "You have a pain pump," handing me a small tube with a red button on top, she says, "Press it if you are hurting. It's on a timer, so if you press it before it's time, nothing will happen. You also have a catheter in, so you don't need to get out of bed to use the bathroom right now."

I nod my head in understanding and embarrassment at her as I look down at my body, my left wrist is in a cast, and my legs hurt when I try to move them. My lungs feel like fire when I take a breath, all my muscles hurt, and my head feels like someone is pressing an ice pick into the back of my skull.

"What happened?" I'm afraid to ask, but I need to know.

Gavin looks at me, holding my hand, his eyes full of concern. "You were in a car accident, Charlotte. Gregory was driving, and the car flipped. You were unconscious when they pulled you out of the car. You've been sleeping for the past thirty-four hours. You have bruised ribs, a broken wrist, and a bad concussion. You're going to be bruised and sore for several weeks, but the doctor said your seatbelt saved you. It could have been a lot worse." He squeezes my hand in support. "I sent your parents and everyone home last night to get rest after you woke up. I told them I'd call when you woke up again."

"Have you been here the whole time?"

"Yes, I wasn't leaving you. Olivia brought me a change of

clothes last night after they got you settled again." He looks so tired.

"Gregory?"

Gavin is silent for a few seconds. "He didn't make it, Charlotte. His injuries were too severe."

"Oh," is all I can think of to say. I don't know how to describe what I'm feeling, sadness mixed with relief. Feeling like I need to explain myself, "I'm sorry, I didn't know what to do, he was there, and he said he would hurt you if I didn't go with him...." I start to cough, my throat raw.

"Shh...stop," he coos, running his hand down my cheek ever so gently, "we don't have to talk about this now, baby. You need to rest. I'm just so fucking thankful you gave us the clues to get to you."

"Can I have some water? I'm so thirsty." Gavin looks up at Rhonda, who nods and walks out. After taking a few sips of the water, I suddenly feel exhausted again.

"Lay with me?"

"I don't want to hurt you."

"Please, I need to feel you next to me; I need you to hold me," tears welling up in my eyes.

"Okay, baby, I'm here. You're safe." He helps me gently scoot over a bit before crawling on my good side and helping me lay my head on his chest. The simple act of moving has me pushing the pain button and closing my eyes.

"Shhh, sleep now, Fire. I'll be right here when you wake up." Gavin says as I lose the battle to keep my eyes open.

When I open my eyes again, Gavin is still holding me in his arms, and several other people are in the room. Attempting to lift my head alerts Gavin, "Careful, baby, let me help you."

He maneuvers the pillows to prop me up, being ever so

careful of my torso and head. My mom and Grace are sitting on the couch, Logan is seated next to the couch in a chair, holding Grace's hand, and my dad is pacing in front of the window. As soon as I'm settled, Gavin slips out of the bed, sitting in the chair right beside it. My mom, eyes red and puffy, comes to the other side, bending down to gently hug me, "Thank God, Charlotte, we were so worried."

"I'm okay, mom. I'm here." I reach my good arm to rub her back, which sends shooting pain through my ribs. She pulls back as I wince, squeezing my hand before going back and tucking herself into my dad's side.

"Hey, kiddo," my dad says from the end of my bed. He started calling me that a week or so ago out of nowhere. It was really weird hearing him say it, especially since I'm twenty-five, but I have to admit, I don't hate it.

"Hi, dad." I look over at Grace, who looks like she hasn't slept either, her cheeks are sunken in, and her eyes are bloodshot. "Grace," I say, lifting my arms the best I can.

"Lottie," she sobs as she sits on the side of my bed and lays her head on my chest, which hurts like hell, but I focus on my breathing, knowing she needs this. I run my hand down her hair to calm her.

"Good to see you awake, Charlotte." Looking up, a man in dark blue scrubs and a surgical cap on his head enters the room.

"I'm Dr. Hanniman. I was on call when you were brought in." Looking around the room, "Can you all give me a few minutes so I can examine her?"

Grace pulls back and stands, "We'll be in the waiting room. The others wanted to come, but we didn't want to overwhelm you. I'll call them, and if you're up for it, they would love to see you." I nod my head at her.

Gavin goes to stand up, and I reach for his hand to stop him, "I'd like Gavin to stay, please."

"I'm not going anywhere, baby. I'm just going to give the doctor a little room."

After my mom, dad, Grace, and Logan leave, Dr. Hanniman closes the curtain and examines me fully, documenting my bruises and checking my pain as he goes. I tell him what I remember of the accident, which honestly isn't much, and he says when I feel up to it, the police want to talk to me as well.

Wanting to get it over with, I let him call them. Soon after, two police officers come to my room to ask me questions about the night of the gala. I tell them everything I can remember, from him sneaking up behind me in the hall, pulling me into the room, paying off a staff member for entry, the threats he made about Gavin and my family, to his erratic driving before the crash. Gavin's body is rigid still the entire time I talk with them, his fists clenching and unclenching in his lap as he sits, he doesn't say a word, but his anger is palpable.

The police informed me that Gregory was lost in the accident and that they had found guns, rope, tape, and a briefcase with vials full of Rohypnol in it. I am unable to hold in my nausea as they tell me everything. I turn to my side and vomit, thankful for the trashcan right next to my bed. For the record, throwing up with bruised ribs and a concussion is the worst. The nurse made the police leave and gave me something to help calm me down. Gavin crawled back in bed with me, holding me until the medicine kicked in, emotionally and physically exhausted.

Today is Christmas Eve, three days after the accident, and although he was reluctant at first because of how long it took me to wake up fully, the doctor just came in and is signing off on me being discharged as long as I promise to go home and rest. I'm desperate to sleep in a real bed. My mom called my grandparents the night of the gala, and they are postponing their trip. She didn't think it would be good for me to have the extra excitement, and as sad as it made me, I agreed.

"Are you ready to go home, Fire?" Gavin asks as he helps me put my legs into sweatpants Grace brought for me. Grace has been here almost as much as Gavin, only going home when Gavin makes her. Everyone else came back yesterday after I took a nap. There were a lot of gentle hugs, and Logan joked, telling me if I ever scared him like that again, he was sending me the bill for the hair plugs he'll need, claiming he lost half his hair that night.

"Yes, I am. Thank you for being here, for helping me, for not giving up on me." Tears well up in my eyes. He kneels down, holding my face in his hands, being careful of my left side, where I have a nasty bruise on my cheek.

"I will never give up on you. Ever. You are my everything. I'm sorry, Charlotte, so sorry I left you alone. I should've gone with you instead of dancing with Olivia. That psycho should have never even had the opportunity to get that close to you. My father found the staff member Gregory paid off and gave their name to the police."

"Stop blaming yourself. He would've found a way. You heard the police yesterday. He was planning this, he would've gotten to me one way or the other, and it could've been a lot worse. I don't want to talk or think about him anymore. I know it's probably wrong, but I feel a little relieved that I know for sure he can't ever hurt me again. I can finally put that part of my past to rest."

Kissing my tears, "He can't hurt you ever again. And I will help you heal or get you the best help possible. Whatever you need, baby. I'm here, and I'm never letting you out of my sight."

I chuckle at that, even though he looks dead serious. "I love you, Gavin."

"I love you, Fire. Don't ever scare me like that again. You hear me?"

"Yes, sir."

Shaking his head as he helps me to stand, "Are you trying to kill me? Hearing the doctor tell you no strenuous activities, sexual and otherwise, for the next four weeks was punishment enough. Now you call me sir?"

"We can find other ways." I do my best to waggle my eyebrows without my face killing me as he helps me into the wheelchair.

"Behave, Fire." He warns as he wheels me out of the room.

I thank the nurses as we head toward the elevator. My parents had food catered for the whole staff on this floor as a thank you for taking such good care of me. We make it down to the lobby, and there is a black SUV at the turnaround. My dad steps out and helps Gavin get me into the back seat before getting in beside me and grabbing my good hand.

"Grace brought some of your stuff over this morning, Kiddo, so you'll have everything you need," my dad says from the front.

I turn my chin gently so I look Gavin in the eyes, "You are staying with me. Indefinitely. Grace agrees. She said if you have a problem, she'll stay with us until you are ready. I told you before I am not letting you out of my sight. The doctor said you need to rest, and that means not doing anything. I already talked to your dad and my dad, I'll be working from home for the next four weeks, and if I have to go into the office for some reason, your mom, Lexi, Grace, or my mom can come to be with you." His words are final, not demanding but definite, with no room for negotiation. It seems as though they all have talked about this already, and fighting it would be a lost cause. Not that I want to fight it anyways. I want to be with Gavin. I know I do. I just don't want to be a burden on anyone.

"Stop that train of thought, Fire." *Did I say that out loud?* "You are not a burden, we don't need to take care of you; we want to."

I nod at him, unable to say what I want. We pull up to Gavin's condo, and they help me out of the car. Dad hugs me and kisses my head before nodding to Gavin and letting him take me under his shoulder to help me in. It's crazy how exhausting walking to an elevator can be.

Gavin opens the door and helps me to the bedroom. Sitting on the edge of the bed, I feel like I just ran a marathon. He slips off my shoes and helps me lay down, tucking the navy comforter around me and making sure my hand, neck, and ribs are in good positions, as getting comfortable has been an effort. They sent me home with pain medicine, but it makes me feel out of it, so I don't want to take it unless I have to.

Kissing the top of my head, Gavin whispers, "Sleep now, baby. You're home. Safe and loved. Rest. I'll be here when you wake up."

The last thing I think before I fade into sleep is home. *I am home.*

32

Charlotte

*I*t's been four weeks since the accident. I slept the rest of Christmas Eve, and when I woke on Christmas Day, Gavin held me as the emotions of the last few days crashed down. I sobbed into his chest until I thought I had run out of tears. Gavin wanted to give me the gift he bought, and I broke down in even more tears. I can't believe I had more. I felt so terrible I hadn't gone to pick up the gift I ordered for him. I was planning on going after the gala, but that never happened.

I told him I couldn't accept any gifts from him until I could go get it. I know anyone would've gone and gotten it for me, but I wanted to be there, to make sure it was perfect. After feeding me a breakfast in bed that included croissants, bacon, fruit, and coffee, he helped me shower and change into comfortable clothes. Who knew showering with a cast could be so difficult? Exhausted from getting dressed, I laid back down and fell asleep.

When I woke up, Gavin helped me into the living room where our family and friends were waiting to surprise me. Even Joe and Maria came. It was the perfect way to spend Christmas Day. I told James and Lexi they should be with their family, only to be told this is where they needed to be. Kristina and my mom had all the food catered and, to my surprise, everyone wore comfy clothes so I didn't feel out of place. We all sat on the couches and watched movies and talked. No expectations, no pomp and circumstance, it was exactly what I needed after everything that happened. I couldn't have been more grateful for the love that surrounded me.

Grace sat next to me on the couch, and as I rested my head on her shoulder, the others scattered in the kitchen or engrossed in other conversations, I took the opportunity to ask her, "Where's Matthew? I haven't seen him since the gala. I thought he was staying for Christmas with you?"

"He went home to be with his family," she said, her voice a little detached.

"Is everything okay?"

"Yeah, babe, it is. I told him I wasn't going to come for New Years and before you say anything, don't. I told him to go home and be with his friends and family. We'll talk when he gets back and that's that. I'm not leaving you. Not right now. We could've lost you. I should've listened, Lottie. I should've listened to you after LA. You told me you felt something and I brushed it off. I should've told Gavin." A tear slides down her cheek, hitting the side of my face.

"It's not your fault, Grace. He would've done something either way. I just knew you would understand if I sent that text."

"I love you, Lottie. You are my sister, blood or not. I can't imagine losing you. You slept for so long and...I just..."

I stop her, "I love you too, Grace, and you won't, I promise."

Lifting my head up and looking at me, then nods towards where Gavin is standing, eyes watching me. "He's your person, Lottie. You two were made to find each other. The way he looks at you, finds you when he walks in a room, it's magic. You should have seen him that night, he was ready to tear the city down to find you. He never left your side the entire time you slept."

"He is, Grace, he really really is." I look around the room and lock eyes with him in the kitchen, a silent exchange with just one look tells me how lucky I am to have him.

Soon after, Gavin made everyone leave, as he could tell I was exhausted. He cradled me in his arms, being ever so gentle with my ribs. He carried me to the bedroom, helped me change, and got me into bed. He kissed the top of my head, climbed in beside me, and helped me get comfortable on his chest.

"Stay here, with me."

Sleepily, I replied, "I am staying here with you."

"Forever. Move in with me."

As my eyes flutter shut, I get out, "Okay," before they close completely.

The next day, I found out Gavin had already told Grace about me moving in, sneaky bastard, and hired movers to pack up my things and bring them to the condo. I was too tired to argue about the movers, so Grace took charge, overseeing the whole thing. She even came and put my stuff away while I told her where I wanted it.

New Year's Eve was low key as well. My head was still

fuzzy at times, with noise still triggering headaches, and my stamina, although improving, was nowhere near ready to be out and about for hours at a time. James, Lexi, Grace, and Logan came to the condo. Olivia was back in LA already, which made me sad, but she had a life to get back to.

We ordered Chinese food, the boys watched football, and the girls and I hung out. We rang in New York's New Year's—ten o'clock our time—with champagne and party hats. James and Lexi were ready to celebrate by themselves, and Logan and Grace were exchanging jabs, as they had been doing all night long.

After trying to get Gavin to engage in some extracurricular activities without success, I resolved to cuddle on his chest and bask in his comfort. One week in, I was already sick of the doctor's rules of no physical activity, and Gavin would not bend. *"Not happening, Fire. The doctor said four weeks rest for you and that means me too. You need to behave."* How he can abstain is beyond me. I am aching for my man. *What has happened to me?* I went six years without having sex and now I'm losing my mind after only a week.

"Fire, are you ready? Your mom is going to be here in five minutes. Are you sure you don't want me to go to the doctor with you?" Gavin says walking into our room, as I struggle with my hair. *Our room.* I thought moving in would freak me out. It hasn't. I think I see Grace more now than I did when we were living together, and getting to go to bed with Gavin every night and wake in his arms every day, it's the best feeling in the entire world.

"Yes, and I'm sure. I want to surprise you with both my hands. Go to the office, you've been working from home, taking care of me, for weeks," I huff, as he comes to help me get my hair in a ponytail. He's been a freaking Godsend these past four weeks, not letting anyone else help out. He has helped me shower, dress, put my hair up, even cut my food. Never again will I take for granted having the use of both of my hands.

"Okay, Fire. I'll only be gone for a couple hours. I'll be home before you get back." He pulls me into him, bending down and capturing my lips in a soul searing kiss. Not being able to do other things has made us get creative with our make out sessions, and I swear, I've almost come a few times just from the way he kisses me with so much passion, I feel it in my bones.

"Don't rush, we're going to go to lunch and do a little shopping," I say, after giving his lips a final nibble. I haven't left the house except for short walks. This will be the first time I'm going out for a few hours. I asked my mom to take me, needing to make a specific stop that Gavin isn't aware of.

Giving me one last kiss, he says, "Okay, text me when you are done."

This is the first time we'll be away from each other for more than an hour since I woke up in the hospital. He wasn't lying when he said he wouldn't let me out of his sight. If the boys want to watch a game, they come here. If I want to go for a walk, he goes with me. He's been extremely overprotective, and it's not that I don't love him for it, I'm just ready to be cleared by the doctor and be able to do things for myself again.

"I will. I love you," I say, sliding on my shoes and grabbing my purse.

"I love you too."

The appointment went well. Having the cast cut off felt like a breath of fresh air—well after they let me wash my arm —only, seeing the difference from one arm to the other made me sad. I start occupational therapy next week to regain some of my motion and strength. I also made sure to record the doctor saying I could return to full activity so Gavin couldn't question me on it. He keeps telling me we have all the time in the world, and we need to wait until the doctor says I'm ready. Let me tell you, I'm ready to climb that man like a tree.

After leaving the doctor, my mom and I had a late lunch at a cafe close to the hospital, and then made our special stop before she took me back to the condo.

"You don't have to walk me up, Mom. You heard the doctor, he said I can do anything I feel comfortable doing."

"I know he did. I guess I'm not fully over what happened, and making sure you're safe at home makes me feel better." Her eyes are full of emotion as she wraps me in a tight hug while we wait for the elevator. I'm thanking God my ribs feel better or this hug would kill me.

The gala took a toll on all of us. I have been seeing a counselor for the past three weeks, and it's helped a lot. A few days after I left the hospital, I started having night terrors—reliving the accident and Gregory waving the gun around—waking up in a sweat and shaking. Gavin suggested maybe talking to someone would help, so I did. We do virtual sessions, which has worked perfectly for me since going out was exhausting. It's definitely getting better, I've only had one nightmare this week. However, after starting therapy, I realized there is a lot to work through from the gala and all the things I've been pushing down since high school, so I plan on continuing so I can fully let go and heal.

I give my mom one more hug, "Thank you for taking me and making sure I got home safe. I'll see you tomorrow?" My grandparents are finally flying in and we are all having dinner tomorrow night.

"You sure will. I love you, Lottie," my mom says before hitting the down button for the elevator.

I open the door and walk in, and my feet instantly rooted to their spot. The entire foyer and living area are lit with candles, and vases full of allium are on every open surface. "Gavin?" I call out, then force myself to move, putting my purse down and taking off my shoes. Then I look up, and there he is. Standing there in charcoal gray dress pants and a white button up shirt, the sleeves rolled up to his elbows, showing off his forearms that I love so much.

"Fire," he says as I take a step toward him.

"How...when...why?" I don't even know what I'm asking him, too stunned by everything he has set up.

He grabs my hands and walks me a few more steps into the open living space. The entire room looks ethereal, with all the candles glowing as the sun sets on the Phoenix skyline.

"You said I needed to wait to give you your Christmas present until you were better, and since I know the doctor was going to give you the all clear, well I didn't know but I wasn't waiting any longer, I am giving it to you today."

He drops to one knee and my hands go to my mouth, my eyes wide with surprise, tears filling them. "Charlotte May Swanson, I knew you were special the first time I saw you at that club, and I knew I had to know you more when I walked up and heard you talking to yourself."

I chuckle, remembering the night we met and how I was jealous when I thought Grace was dancing with him. "When you left, I went home and couldn't get you out of my head, and you've taken up permanent residence there ever since.

You are the last thing I think of before I go to bed, and the first thing I think of when I wake up. You are strong, smart, brave, and so damn beautiful, and I thank my lucky stars every single day you decided to take a leap of faith with me. I want to be your rock, your pillar. I want to support you, lift you up, love you, and worship you in every way possible. I want to kiss you goodnight and good morning for the rest of our lives. When you are ready, I want to have a family with you. You told me you were lost before me, but damn, Charlotte, I was lost before you too. You are my home, my haven, my sanctuary. I never knew happiness and love like this existed before you, and I wouldn't survive spending my life without you. Will you do me the honor of marrying me? Be my wife, my partner, my other half, forever?"

Kneeling down to be at his level, I give him my answer. "Yes, a million times yes." I shout, as he grabs my face and pulls me into his arms, pressing his lips to mine in a kiss that blows every other kiss we have had, right out of the water.

"Can I put the ring on your finger, Fire?" he asks between kisses, his lips still pressed to mine.

"Oh, God, yes, sorry, I got carried away," I laugh as I wipe tears of happiness off my cheek.

He opens the box he was holding and places the most beautiful ring I have ever seen on my finger. The band is platinum with diamonds, holding a round cut diamond in the center. It fits on my hand perfectly and my heart explodes with happiness. Cheers and applause assault my ears and I look up to see our friends and family around us. Kristina, Daniel, Olivia, my mom, Dad, James, Lexi, Joe, Maria, Logan, and Grace are all here, and I let out a sob when I see my grandparents standing next to my mom. *They're here. My whole family is here. He did this.*

Looking back at Gavin, it's as if he reads my mind. "I wanted to make sure your whole family was here for this, and your grandparents didn't want to miss it. I had it planned for Christmas but when plans changed, I thought, what better way to celebrate getting your cast off than this."

Grabbing his face with both hands, not caring we are still on the floor, I tell him, "I love you, today and all of my tomorrows. You are my home, my family, and I cannot wait to start a life with you. I never thought I'd be here until I met you, and now, I can't imagine a minute of my life without you in it. Thank you for not giving up on me."

"I love you, Fire. Today and all my tomorrows."

He kisses me again, a kiss promising a future I can't wait to start, before we're enveloped by our family and friends, passing around flutes of champagne.

"Ahh, right there. Oh, God, Gavin, I'm going to come." I scream his name as one hand holds my hip, the other pinching my nerve bundle as he pushes in deep, hitting the spot inside me that makes me see stars.

One, two, three thrusts. "You, are perfect, Fire...shit," Gavin groans as his orgasms takes hold, his body stiffening, filling me up in the most delicious way.

After catching his breath, Gavin leans over me, brushing a sweaty piece of hair out of my face. He tucks it behind my ear before kissing me reverently, holding my face in his hand, his other arm supporting his body weight. "You, baby, are my undoing."

"You aren't so bad yourself, stud," I tease back before my eyes fill with emotion from the day. Looking into his ocean blue eyes, I tell him, "Today was perfect, it was the last thing I was expecting, and that made it that much better. Thank you."

"I would do anything for you, baby, always."

"I know, oh...I forgot." Pushing him up a little and rolling to my side, I grab the box off my nightstand.

"With all of the excitement, I didn't get to give you your present tonight."

Gavin pushes himself back, leaning against the fabric headboard, propping pillows behind him before pulling me closer into his side, with the box in my hand.

"I hope you like it." Nervousness is flowing through me. When I ordered it, I thought it was a good idea, but now, I'm not so sure.

Opening the box, he looks at me with warm eyes. A Hublot Classic Chronograph Black watch sits on a case alongside a black bracelet with a small silver square in the middle. I never spend money—mostly because I've never had money—but I may have dipped into the money that my mom had put aside for me from my dad to buy this for him. Gavin always wears a watch, and this one has a special addition to it.

"Baby, I love it," he says, pulling the watch carefully from its case. "What is this?" He eyes the black bracelet carefully.

"It's kind of for both of us. I ordered this watch specifically because it has a compass in it, a special magnet that will find where it's meant to be. Only it doesn't work as a true compass."

He eyes me suspiciously as I continue, "This bracelet has a special magnet in it too. One that only connects with the magnet in this watch." Lifting up the bracelet, I point to the arrow on his watch. "See, the arrow will always point to the bracelet." I place the bracelet on my wrist. I chose this one because the simple black design with the small silver charm in the middle is sleek and something I can wear with anything.

"Now, as long as I have the bracelet on and you are wearing your watch, you will always be able to find your way home."

He stares at me for a minute, making me a little nervous I made the wrong choice. Then he wraps his arms around me, pulling me to straddle him, before cradling my face in his hands and bringing me in close. "You are the best gift I could ever get, and this, Fire, is amazing. You, baby, are my home, and now I'll always know how to get to you. I love you," he says before taking my lips with his, his tongue sliding against my lips, gaining access, possessing me, protecting me, claiming me.

As I lift to line him up at my entrance and slide down onto him, he slides in deep, filling me perfectly, the way only he can do. This, right here, this moment, is the perfect way to celebrate the start to our forever.

EPILOGUE

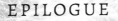

Gavin
12 Months Later

*W*alking out onto our balcony that overlooks the ocean, I see Charlotte leaning up against the railing with her back to me. Her hair is curled in beachy waves with a white flower pinned to the side. The curls are gently blowing in the breeze while her spaghetti strap silk dress that hits the floor, hugs every curve perfectly. I slowly walk up behind her, encasing her in my arms, and rest my chin on her shoulder as she lets out the most contented sigh.

"Hello, wife," I whisper softly in her ear before kissing her temple.

Placing her hands over mine, she turns her head to look back at me, "Hello, husband. Isn't this magical? I'm so glad we decided to do this here. It gives us an excuse to go somewhere tropical every year for our anniversary."

After we got engaged a year ago, we decided to take a

trip to celebrate our engagement, Charlotte's recovery, and the start of our new life. Working for family has some perks when it comes to needing time off. And after Charlotte's accident, we realized that life is short, and spending it all at work makes you miss so many opportunities. Charlotte's semester was all case studies, so she didn't have to be on campus more than a couple times, giving us the flexibility to go. We flew to St. Lucia and fell in love with the Caribbean: blue waters, the white sand beaches that felt like you were walking on a cloud, and the peaceful lifestyle. We stayed at Sugar Beach Resort, and after the first day there, we decided this is where we wanted to get married.

It was Charlotte's idea to get married on the anniversary of our engagement, and the wedding planner here was amazing, helping her pick out everything for our intimate ceremony on the beach. She was worried it would be stressful planning a wedding while finishing school.

Charlotte's grandparents found a senior condo community just outside of Phoenix that they loved and moved to Arizona in the spring. After Charlotte graduated in May, she spent the summer studying for the bar, stopping only for James and Lexi's wedding weekend. I knew she would pass with flying colors, but she was still nervous.

My dad and John decided to start a family division at the firm when Charlotte mentioned looking for jobs at other firms that had more of a family law focus. They both are protective of her and wanted her to be able to do what she loved without leaving. Her passion lies in working with people and families, trying to get out of abusive situations, using her own past as a motivator for others to not have to leave their lives to be happy. I am so damn proud of her and how she is changing other's lives. Her dedication to helping others shines in everything she does.

Kelly and John got married in their backyard in September. They kept it to just immediate family and had BBQ catered while we all shared a meal on the patio. The smile on Charlotte's face as she stood as their witness, watching her parents, who spent far too many years apart, vow to love each other is something burned into my memory forever.

That, though, doesn't hold a candle to the smile she had when her dad walked her down the sandy beach aisle toward me. She chose a simple, white satin dress with spaghetti straps that left her entire back open, the fabric scooping down just above her perfect ass. Grace, Olivia, and Lexi, who all were bridesmaids, wore the palest blue dresses that stopped below their knees, while Logan, James, and I wore khaki pants and white button up shirts. Charlotte wanted us all to be comfortable and not sweat through our shirts before the ceremony even started. It might be January, but it's still eighty-three degrees here. We joined hands under a wooden arch covered in tropical flowers, promising forever. In that moment, my heart felt like it could never be more full of love.

We took pictures on the beach and while our friends and family headed down to have cocktails, and then we returned to our room to freshen up, taking a minute to ourselves. Charlotte swatted my chest when I scooped her up to carry her over the threshold for the first time, worried I would rip her dress.

"You make it magical, Fire." Kissing her neck, she turns fully in my arms, wrapping her hands around my neck and tilting her head to give me better access. A moan leaves her lips as I dust kisses down her neck over the sweetheart neckline, cresting the top swell of her perfect breasts.

"We...should...get down there," she moans out between breaths.

"Your body is telling me otherwise, and I want to have my wife before dinner." Picking her up under her ass and carrying her away from the publicness of the balcony, I gently slide her down to her feet in front of the white vanity.

"Hold on, baby," I say as I work her dress up her body, finding her bare to me underneath. A low growl of appreciation comes from my throat at the sight before me.

Hiking one of her legs over my shoulder I dip my head to her wet core, swiping my tongue from slit to clit as her arms grasp the dresser behind me, her head falling back on a moan.

"You taste even sweeter as my wife. Eyes on me, Fire," I demand as she tilts her head, our eyes connecting. Hers are filled with lust and desire as I slide two fingers inside her, curling them up to hit that spot I know drives her wild. Her moans spur me on until she's writhing on my hand, arching her back, chasing her own release. I lean forward, nipping at her clit as my fingers hit her G-spot, sending her over the edge, my name a prayer on her lips.

Standing up and undoing my khakis, I slide them down just enough as I pick her up and slide her onto me. I will take my time tonight, worshiping every inch of my wife. For now, though, I don't think I'll make it through dinner without having her.

"Ahh, Gav," Charlotte moans as I thrust into her, her hands wrapped around my neck as I use my one hand to hold her up, the other on the dresser to keep me balanced.

"I. Love. You." I growl out as I thrust into her. "My beautiful, sexy wife; I'll never tire of saying that."

"I'll never tire of hearing it," she says breathlessly. "Oh, God, I'm almost there again."

That spurs me on, thrusting hard and fast as she comes again, clenching around me, sending me over the edge as I fill her with my release. Pulling her gently down to kiss her, we both catch our breath before I carry her, still wrapped around me, into the bathroom so we can clean up before returning to our party. "Today, and all my tomorrows, Fire," I whisper in her ear as she fixes herself in the mirror.

"Forever, Gav."

Charlotte

Hand in hand, we walk down the candle lit pathway to the small tent where our reception is taking place. I wanted us all together so the tables are set up in a rectangle, allowing us all to see each other. Gavin pulls out my chair as I slide in next to Grace.

"Have fun in your room?" She bumps my shoulder, waggling her eyes as she lifts her wine glass to her lips.

I feign indifference, although the flush of my cheeks and my hair—which I tried to fix the best I could—are dead giveaways. "I have no idea what you're talking about. I could ask the same thing of you. He hasn't taken his eyes off you all day."

"Please, you are a walking billboard that screams, *I've just had crazy sex with my husband.* Did you tell him?" she asks, effectively dismissing my question.

Shushing her with my eyes, I hiss, "Okay, it was amazing, and no I didn't. I wanted to wait until after the reception."

"Makes sense..." She's cut off by my delicious husband who stands next to me.

He raises his glass. "Before we eat, I just wanted to take a minute to thank you all for taking time to fly down here and celebrate with us. It has been the perfect day, and you all being here is a big part of that." Looking down at me, his eyes glassy, he says, "To my wife, you look beautiful every day, yet today, if possible, you look even more radiant. Meeting you was like someone turning the light on in a dark room. For the first time, I could clearly see what I wanted and needed, and that, baby, was you. I am so grateful for our love, for the life we are starting, and for our future." He looks down at the watch he wears every day, glancing at the bracelet on my wrist. My mom asked if I wanted to take it off today, and I told her not in a million years. "With you, I will always know where home is." He raises his glass. "I love you completely, with everything I am, and today is just the beginning of our happy ever after. To you, Fire."

Everyone cheers, grabbing their glasses to take a sip. I pick up my glass, looking over at Grace. She leans in and whispers, "Don't worry, I took care of it."

We all eat and have cheesecake, my absolute favorite, and as the plates are being cleared, Gavin stands, holding his hand out to me. Taking my hand in his, he gently pulls me up, leading me to the small dancefloor they laid down for us, as the speakers play Chris Stapleton's *Joy of My Life*. He wraps me in his arms, my head laying perfectly on his chest, as we sway to the music, letting the lyrics sink into my soul. Gavin is my joy, my everything, and my heart is so full of love for what our lives have in store.

After dancing with our family and friends, and the surprise firework show Gavin arranged, Gavin and I are ready to be alone. We politely excuse ourselves, but not before letting everyone know we'll meet them for the brunch we set up for tomorrow.

I asked Gavin if we could talk on the beach before heading back to our room. Holding my sandals in one hand, my other intertwined with Gavin's, I stop in the sand to take it all in.

My husband, *I love saying that,* turns toward me. "Is everything okay?" he asks, wondering why we've stopped.

"Everything is perfect, today was more than I ever could have imagined. There is just one more thing I wanted to give you. You gave me the most beautiful diamond earrings for a wedding gift, and I haven't given you mine."

Placing his hand on my cheek, rubbing his thumb across my lips, he says, "You are my gift, there is nothing more I could want."

"Are you sure about that?" I ask, taking his hand from my face and placing it on top of mine, over my stomach.

He looks at me in confusion until it hits him. "Fire, are you..." He can't even get the words out as tears fill his eyes.

"I am. I found out last week, so I decided to surprise you. I hope you're not mad."

"Mad, never...holy shit, babe, we're going to have a baby. But wait, you were drinking. Are you okay? How are you feeling?" His protective instincts kick in.

"Breathe, Gav. Relax. I am fine, I feel fine. Great actually, at least so far. And I wasn't drinking. I made Grace come with me to buy the test, so she knew and made sure my champagne and wine was replaced with non-alcoholic so no one would know. I wanted to surprise you."

Letting out a deep sigh, Gavin drops to his knees, laying his head on my flat stomach. "Hello, little one, I'm your daddy. You have the best mommy in the entire world, and I can't wait to meet you. Stay safe in there, we love you." Looking up at me, he says, "In an instant you have filled me with even more love than I thought possible. Thank you, Fire. I love you."

I run my hands through his hair, tears glistening in my eyes with my love for this man. "I love you too. Now take me back and make love to me, husband."

"Is it safe?" His eyes are full of concern as he stands and holds me.

"I called the doctor, and she said, based on my last period, I am about six weeks, and that it is perfectly fine. I made an appointment for when we get back. I didn't want to go without you."

His eyes turning dark, he jumps up, scooping me in his arms and spinning me around, his entire face lighting up with a smile that I want to bottle and keep forever. "You have made me the happiest man in the world. Our forever is just beginning. I'm going to take you back to our room and worship every inch of your body. I love you, today and all my tomorrows."

"I love you, Gav. Today, and all my tomorrows." As he carries me back to our room, I feel the greatest sense of peace. I once was lost, but that was before *him*.

THE END

ACKNOWLEDGMENTS

First, to my incredible husband, for your faith in me and your endless encouragement. For listening to all the little details constantly, and for reading romance novels purely on the basis of supporting me. You are my forever and always. To my girls, who teach me new things every day and are my biggest fans. To my mom, for being the best role model I could ever ask for. I love you all.

To the amazing T L Swan for her unending encouragement to follow your dreams. You are truly an inspiration to so many to not let something you are afraid of stop you, but to open your mind to the possibilities that it may bring you. Thank you for supporting so many of us to take the first step.

Thank you to my fellow Cygnet Inkers for your support, motivation, and wisdom. As a first-time writer, you all have helped me find my way to make this a reality and my gratitude for that is endless. To all of you who have published already, congratulations on amazing work.

To Sara, the best PA in the universe. Thank you for or taking a chance on a newbie writer and being a beta, organizer, promotor, and cheerleader. For your patience with timelines, and for providing me with all the support and feedback to make this book what it is, thank you will ever be enough.

To Jade Dollston, for your never-ending help when I was floundering to your amazing beta edits and developmental suggestions. Your belief and support for me in all things goes beyond this book and the words thank you will never be enough. I am blessed to have found such an amazing author and friend.

To JR Gale, for your guidance, motivation, and willingness to help me through every step of this entire process. I definitely would still be scratching my head wondering what I do next if it wasn't for you. I am incredibly grateful for you taking me under your wing and supporting me as a new author and friend. You're truly the best.

To Mariah Dietz, for your words and motivating me to take the leap of faith and for being a role model for me. For believing in me and not letting my insecurities get in my way. Thank you for answering my million questions and always being a sounding board. You are amazing.

To VH Nicolson, for pushing me to be my best and making me a better writer. For holding my hand and being the ultimate how to girl for everything book related and lifting me up from across an entire ocean. For making this beautiful cover and formatting for me, and for becoming so much more than a mentor, a lifelong friend and a true inspiration. Thank you, I love you.

To Chrisandra's Corrections, for talking me off the ledge when my mind was getting the better of me and for making my story pop with your intricate edits and suggestions. I am so grateful to have found you and for making my first experience with the editing process so positive.

To my ARC readers, for taking a chance on an author you've never heard of before. For helping my first book be seen and for all your support. Books would never get off the ground without you. Thank you all.

And last but never least, to you, the romance reader. Thank you for taking a leap of faith on a new writer, and making my daydream into a reality. I will never be able to fully express what that means to me, but in short, I am eternally grateful. Thank you from the bottom of my heart.

FOUND WITH YOU

CHAPTER 1

(Unedited and Subject to Change)
Logan

10…9…8…7…6…5…4…3…2…1

"Happy New Year," everyone chimes as we raise our glasses of champagne. It's only ten o'clock in Phoenix, but Lottie, my best friend's girlfriend, is exhausted, and we all agreed an early night would be better, well Gavin told us that is what was happening and no one even attempted to disagree. He's been a hawk, not letting her out of his sight since she woke up in the hospital after the accident. Lottie's crazy obsessed ex-boyfriend that she ran away from six years ago was stalking her. He paid off employees to get into the gala for the Foundation Gavin's mom runs, hit her, threatened her, threw her in a car, and while swerving through traffic flipped his car on the interstate. She ended up with a broken wrist and ribs, a concussion, a ton of bruising, and it took her over a day to wake up.

The doctors said she's lucky to be alive from the state of the car and from what the police found in the trunk when they searched it. Gregory, Lottie's ex, had Rohypnol, weapons, and a bunch of other shit in there. As much as I hate that she was in the accident, I'm also glad because who knows what he could have done if he didn't flip that car and kept going. My stomach churns at the thought. The one positive out of this whole thing was that Gregory didn't survive the crash, which probably makes me a bad person, but so be it. He tried to hurt my best friend's girlfriend, and the look on Gavin's face that night is one I will never get out of my head. So, knowing she's safe and he can't come anywhere near her again, hell yeah, I'm happy about that.

I lean back against the island taking a slow drink of my champagne. Gavin has Lottie wrapped up in his arms, and my other best friend, James, is whispering something in his fiancé, Lexi's ear. The only other person in this condo, is standing next to me with her arms wrapped around her stomach, while she stares out the floor to ceiling windows Gavin has in his penthouse condo, lost in thought.

Her chestnut brown hair is loosely tied over one shoulder, giving me the perfect view of the curvature of her neck. Her purple V-neck top shows her ample cleavage and she decided to wear fitted black jeans tonight, the ones that fit perfectly to her apple ass, making me salivate every time I see her backside.

"Stop staring at me asshole," Grace, Lottie's best friend, and the woman who hates me, spits, as she turns her head, instinctively covering her chest, effectively blocking my perfect view of her tits.

"I wasn't staring, just thinking we should probably kiss, Jade, as friends, since we're the only two people here not kissing." I shouldn't poke the bear but I can't help myself when it comes to her.

"I wouldn't kiss you even if I'd win the lottery for doing it. Wouldn't be worth it. And for the last fucking time, stop calling me Jade," her tone is clipped, as she turns her head back to look out at the skyline.

"That's not what you said a couple months ago, Jade." I shouldn't go there, I know I shouldn't. Except, poking at her is the only way I can get her to talk to me since she shut me out on Christmas.

I thought for a minute we had a breakthrough at the hospital, she softened as we all sat in the waiting room, praying for Lottie to wake up. She even laid her head on my shoulder and let me stroke her hair. I thought we were making ground, could be friends, even. *It's a place to start.* I was wrong. Christmas Day, we spent at Gavin's condo and she was cordial to me when we first got there. A few hours later, I was standing in the kitchen with Gav, Grace and Lottie were on the couch, her head resting on Lottie's shoulder. I have no clue what they talked about but after that, Gavin kicked everyone out so Lottie could rest, and as we left, I asked her if she wanted to go get some coffee. Her response was a hard, *Hell no, not now, not ever.*

That was a week ago, and she's ignored every text I've sent to her this week checking in and has been ice cold all evening, throwing jabs at me and shutting down any conversation I try to have with her. Lottie's accident was hard on Grace, she blamed herself for not seeing the signs that Gregory was going to do something. I told her in the hospital that he would have found a way and it wasn't her fault but I know she's still struggling with it. I told her I'd be there to listen, trying to gain some semblance of trust with her, but she's shut me out and it's fucking maddening. If making her mad is the only way I can get her to talk to me, so be it.

"Fuck you Logan," she turns and spits at me, before pushing off the island walking toward Lottie and Gavin. *Would love to darlin'.*

Grace and I didn't exactly start off on the right foot and it only got more fucked up from there. I screwed up, but in my defense, I am a lawyer after all, when it comes to Grace Hastings, she messes with my mind making me do stupid shit. Well, according to my friends, I do stupid shit a lot of the time, but for some reason she causes me to go above and beyond my usual stupid shit-ness.

James and Lexi say their goodbyes, wanting to continue their celebration privately, at least someone's getting laid, and Grace hugs Lottie before grabbing her purse as well. Party's over. I shake hands with Gavin and James, kiss Lottie and Lexi on the cheek, promising to see Gavin and Lottie tomorrow to watch the game, and hurry toward Grace before she grabs the elevator without me. Lexi mentioned using the bathroom before head out, so if I hurry I can talk to Grace alone.

"Bye guys, thanks for everything I call over my shoulder. Grace, wait up."

"The only thing I want to do for you is watch the elevator doors crush your fingers," she jabs back, already out the door. At least she hasn't gone radio silent on me, not that I don't believe she'd try to get the elevator to crush my fingers.

The doors are just opening as I walk into the foyer area giving me plenty of time to get in before she closes the door.

"Have you talked to Matt?" I ask, trying another tactic, as

she hits the ground level button. He's the guy Grace has been seeing since Thanksgiving and the thought of that annoys the fuck out of me for reasons I won't allow myself to go into.

"His name is Matthew, and why do you care?" She's standing right next to me staring straight forward, and I can smell her shampoo, lavender, and its intoxicating.

"Just wondering why he didn't stay back with you, you know, being your boyfriend and all." The word boyfriend sounds sour on my tongue. Grace was supposed to go with Matthew to Colorado for New Years, only after the accident, Lottie said Grace wouldn't go.

As the doors open, letting us know we've hit the ground floor, Grace takes a step out before turning toward me spewing straight venom, "What Matthew and I do or don't do is none of your God damn business. Why don't you go find some girl to have fun with, your favorite thing to do."

Her words stun me briefly, and before I can even reply, she's out the front, climbing into the back of her ride, and I'm stuck here staring after her like an asshole.

"You need a ride?" Lexi asks tapping me on my shoulder as they pass, snapping me out of my stupor.

Shaking my head as my James tells me with his glare, *I'm about to get laid do not even think about cockblocking me eyes,* "Naw, thanks, I'm good. Happy New Year, Lex, enjoy your night," waggling my eyebrows at her.

"Oh, we intend to. Happy New Year Logan, wrap it up tonight okay," she jests as James tucks her petite five-foot-two frame under his shoulder.

So now everyone needs to point out I'm a man-whore?

Fuck it, I need a drink as I pull up a ride app since I didn't drive tonight.

Two minutes later the black Audi pulls up to the curb and I climb in.

"Where to?"

"A bar...any bar."

***

Fuck, why did I come here? It's packed. *Well duh, dumb shit, it's New Years.* The place is crawling with couples practically having sex on the dancefloor and single people looking for someone to ring in the New Year with.

Four months ago, I would have been all over any one or multiple of the beautiful women who have thrown themselves at me since I got here, now, my dick could care less. Could be anyone and he's decided he's not interested. *Well, except one person, and she hates you.* Annoyed by how the night has unraveled, I throw back the rest of my scotch, put two hundred-dollar bills on the bar, more than enough to cover my two drinks and a sizeable tip. Grabbing my sport coat, I pull up the ride app on my phone and walk out the door as I hear people screaming in the background Happy New Year. Running my hand through my sandy blonde hair in frustration, I wait for the car I ordered. Right now, I want to go the fuck home, jerk off to the green eyes that haunt me at night, and get some sleep, which really means replay our last conversation where everything went to shit.

***

Late October

"Get that sexy ass back in this bed before I come over

there and spank you for disobeying." Laying on my side resting my head on my palm as the sheets barely cover my ass, I watch her sashay her naked hips as she grabs the bottle of water we left on her dresser.

"Maybe I should disobey more often if you're giving out spankings." She coos at me, glancing over her shoulder before taking a purposefully slow drink letting a few drops of water slide out of her sinful mouth dripping down her bare shoulder. Sexy minx.

"Jade, I'll spank you anytime you want." My dick is now at full attention making a tent out the sheet covering it.

"You know I hate that nickname." Grace turns and saunters towards me with a smirk on her face, giving me a full frontal of her glorious naked body. Her breasts are pure perfection, with a slim waist that lead to hips that I swear were made for my hands. She says she hates that nickname but the way her body responds says otherwise. I lift my eyebrow calling her on her bullshit answer.

This is just fun. My head screams at me. Even though the, this is just fun, has been happening since the week after I showed up at Blue, the best mexican restaurant in Phoenix, with Gavin bombarding Grace and Lottie's girls' night. She may have gotten her revenge that night for me being a shithead the first time we met but thankfully she forgave me a few days later and we met up again. We've been keeping it to ourselves, fucking every chance we get. Her place, mine, her office since mine if off limits working with Gavin, James, and now Lottie, pretty much anywhere we can and let me tell you, the sex has been off the charts. Grace is confident and sexy, knowing what she wants, and willing to try new things and damn if I'm not the lucky recipient of that adventure.

Grace leans her glorious chest in my face as she pushes my shoulder, turning me flat on my back before climbing over me, straddling my stomach and swiveling those perfect as fuck hips in a motion that has my dick aching to be inside of her.

"If you hate that nickname so much, why are your nipples so hard they could cut glass while you rub that perfect pussy on me? My stomach is already soaked in your juices." She is sharp as a tac and our back and forth jabs are such a turn on.

"My need to get off has nothing to do with your body, you're purely a vessel for my orgasms." She says, rotating her hips the other direction as precum seeps from my tip at her movements.

"Really, then why were you screaming my name when I bit your clit last night Jade?" Reaching for the nightstand to grab a condom, I rip it open and slide it on as she lifts her glorious hips while I line up and bottoms out in one quick motion, pulling a growl from my throat.

"Simple biology, nothing to do with you," her smile lights her whole face before she moans as her breath hitches, her head falling backward and her eyes closing involuntarily when I hit that spot she can't resist. Pressing my heels into the mattress for more leverage as she lifts herself up and down, I move one hand from her hip to pinch her clit, something else that drives her wild and with three more thrusts she's falling.

"Fuck, Logan, right there...yeeess." She screams as she rides out her orgasm, her muscles spasming tightening on my cock drawing my balls up and shooting off my own release. Her hands are on my chest as her breathing slows, and once she's come down from her Logan induced high, she brings her head back and slowly opens her eyes.

"Okay, maybe I don't hate the nickname." Her smile reaches her eyes and it is a sight to behold, her cheeks flushed from our activity and a gleam of sweat glistens around her hairline. This is round three, taking a break only for much needed water. She climbs off of me and heads into the bathroom to clean up. Once she's done she crawls back into bed as I take my turn disposing of the condoms we used and come back out looking for my boxers.

"Lottie is probably staying at Gavin's tonight." Grace mentions when I walk back in, she's propped up against the headboard with the sheet pulled up covering her tits that I can't get enough of. We haven't stayed the night with each other, we've fooled around, had sex, and been done. It's what I always do. No commitment, no promises. I like Grace, more than I've liked any woman ever. She's smart, sarcastic, calls me on my shit, funny as hell, and beyond gorgeous, but I can't give her what she needs beyond sex.

"I..uhh, got some work I need to get done, I should get home." I give some lame excuse sliding my leg into my boxers and grabbing my jeans. While I'm talking, my phone dings on the opposite nightstand. When I look up, Grace is sitting up with my phone in her hands and her face has morphed from one of post-orgasmic bliss to pissed off.

"Work to do, or someone to do?" She snips at me as she tosses my phone at me. A total one-eighty from the woman who just screamed my name. Looking down I see a message from Veronica, a woman I hook up when I don't feel like finding someone new, that is, until I started sleeping with Grace.

VERONICA:

My place 9pm. I can't wait to get you
inside me.

I get that her message seems suspicious. Veronica and I
never asked, just told each other when we needed a release,
met up, fucked, and moved on. No strings, never any
expectations. And definitely no feelings on either end.

"It's not what you're thinking. Veronica is someone I
hook up with on occasion, well, used to hook up with. I
haven't talked to her in over a month."

Grace's rigid posture tells me she doesn't believe my
answer. What I wasn't expecting is her next question. "What
is this? What are we?"

Not sure what to say I tell her only thing I can, "We're
having fun."

She flinches at my words stilling for a few seconds, "Fun,
gotcha. Well, I don't think we should have fun anymore."

Confused by her immediate change in attitude from one
text message, "I thought you knew what this was, and I
thought you wanted that too. Fun and a lot of hot sex I can
guarantee, but beyond that..." Before I can even finish that
sentence, her face turns hard as stone, lips set tight.

"Besides sex, what do you want with me?"

My chest tight, I give the only safe answer, "Nothing."
Although the words feel like acid on my tongue and my
stomach drops saying it. *It's for the best.*

Her eyes well with tears and she looks away, attempting
to hide her emotion to seem unaffected. When she turns
back to me her eyes are like a storm, ready to wreak havoc on,
"Fuck you, Logan. Leave. Don't look at me. Don't talk to me.
Don't even breathe near me. You are exactly who I thought

you were. God," she says raising her eyes to the ceiling holding the sheet tighter around her to cover herself up, "I knew I never should have let you touch me again after the first night, I'm such a fucking idiot."

Something inside me tells me to fix this, to get her to understand, "Grace, you're amazing, but...I can't be that guy for you, for anyone. I...fuck," I run my fingers through my hair.

"You can't...no, Logan, you won't. You want to use women and throw then away when you're done. Well I'm not going to be that girl. I'm not going to let you decide when I'm no longer enough fun for you."

If glares could kill, I'd be done by the way her angry eyes bore into mine.

I want to tell her different, I want to tell her she's the sexiest, wittiest, most intriguing woman I have ever met, but I can't, I won't do that to her. I care and respect her too much to do it. "Grace."

"Get out...Now," she screams, she's shut down.

Leaning down to grab my shirt, I look at her eyes, the anger turned to sadness, and no matter how much I want to take her pain away, I simply say, "I'm sorry," before turning and leaving her room. I walk down the hallway and open the door, and before I walk through the door, I hear cries coming from her room. *Shit.*

ABOUT THE AUTHOR

EA Joy lives in the Midwest with her husband and daughters. As a child she loved writing stories but didn't find her love of reading and returning to her childhood hobby of letting the stories in her head come to life until her thirties. She loves spending time with her family, reading everything romance, sunshine, and diet coke.

STAY CONNECTED WITH EA JOY

Facebook.com/AuthorEAJoy
Linktr.ee/eajoyauthor
Amazon.com/author/ea-joy
Instagram.com/eajoy.author

EMLYN HOOSON

Essays and Reminiscences

EMLYN HOOSON
Essays and Reminiscences

EDITED BY
DEREC LLWYD MORGAN

Gomer

Published by Gomer Press,
Llandysul, Ceredigion, SA44 4JL

ISBN 978-1-848518698

A CIP record for this title is available from
the British Library.

© Copyright: Derec Llwyd Morgan, 2014

Setting and design: Dylan Williams

Printed and bound in Wales at
Gomer Press, Llandysul, Ceredigion.

CONTENTS

PREFACE

Emlyn Hooson spent his life doing myriad things – at the Bar, in the Houses of Parliament, in international affairs, in cultural circles, in agriculture, in business – and doing them brilliantly. Few men in the second half of the twentieth century succeeded in being first-class in so many posts and professions. During the years when he was the only Liberal MP for a Welsh constituency he was of necessity the personification of Lloyd-Georgian radicalism, but he was always his own man looking to the future, eager to try new things. At the end of the lecture he gave to Clwb y Gader in Tywyn in 1996, when he had just passed what the Psalmist calls his allotted span of three score years and ten, he stated that the next new thing he'd like to do was to write his memoirs. The lecture itself, an amalgam of recollections, was obviously autobiographic. Periodically during the next few years, in London and in Llanidloes, he dictated notes about his upbringing and later life to friends and secretaries, wrote letters about aspects of his career to various colleagues, and commissioned others to prepare notes for him on specific subjects. These were exercises towards an autobiography. Then things became more difficult – he suffered memory loss and later was diagnosed with Alzheimer's disease – and the planned memoir never materialised.

Although this book is no substitute for that unwritten autobiography, perhaps in a small way it makes up for the

7

loss. For it too is a memorial, a collection of essays and reminiscences about the man and his tremendously rich contribution to the civil life of Wales, the United Kingdom and the wider world.

My chief connection with Emlyn Hooson was academic, in the best sense. In 1942 he went to study at the University College of Wales, Aberystwyth (as it was then called), and throughout his life he loved the place rapturously, as a successful man should love his *alma mater*. Half a century later I was appointed Vice-Chancellor there, and wisely – and sometimes shamelessly – took advantage of Emlyn's attachment to it. Of course, our paths had crossed several times before then, on Eisteddfod fields, in broadcasting studios, and, most memorably for me, when his wife Shirley and I served together on the Broadcasting Council for Wales and got ourselves into an altercation with the Home Office. I always found him charming, witty, cultured, enchanting company, who enjoyed talking about poetry and scholarship. I did not experience, as did a few of my friends in the politics of protest of the early 1970s, the robed and bewigged Emlyn Hooson QC cross-examining them in court with the disciplined steel that cut to the quick. The only examination he set me was to find a name for the new bridge over the Severn that was being built in the 1990s by the company of which he was Chairman. 'Why don't you call it Sabrina?' I suggested, thinking that the river's Latin name would serve in English just as well as in Welsh. I can't say whether he coupled it with the J. Arthur Rank starlet of that name or with one of the more boisterous characters of the Welsh soap opera *Pobol y Cwm*, but he never mentioned the matter again – and the bridge remains unnamed.

It was Lady Hooson who invited me to edit this volume, and did so initially through our mutual friend Dr Glyn Tegai Hughes. I didn't need much persuading, for the simple fact that I believe a sort of *festschrift* is a wonderful way of celebrating Emlyn Hooson's life and work. In his second letter to me about the book, Dr Hughes said that in the army he had once attended a court-martial as 'the prisoner's friend'. A fellow-officer had been accused of severing his little finger with a revolver to avoid being sent to France, and the rules of court allowed him to have some-one to sit in his corner, as it were; Glyn Tegai Hughes went with him. 'In very different circumstances,' Dr Hughes said, 'it's a similar role I have in this matter.' As the chief adviser in the planning and the developing of this book he has been so much more than the prisoner's friend, and I am extremely grateful to him for all his help, and for enter-taining me with stories of experiences he shared with Emlyn over the years. I am, of course, also grateful to Lady Hooson for all that she has done to ease my work: collecting and classifying papers, putting things at my disposal, finding photographs, corresponding with people on my behalf, *&c. &c.* In a way, this is as much her book as it is Emlyn's. I also wish to acknowledge the splendid support Lord and Lady Hooson's daughters, Sioned Darlington and Lowri Khan, have given to their mother and me. Calan McCreery, who worked with Emlyn in the Commons for many years, also gave me very valuable assistance.

Most of the prospective authors I approached responded positively to my requests. A few were sad and aggrieved that for various reasons they could not do so. They include Lord Howe of Aberavon, who telephoned me half a dozen times to say how sorry he was that because of ill-health he couldn't contribute; and Lady Williams of Crosby, who asked me to note 'what a lovely man Emlyn was (and what a sweet and loyal wife he had)'. Lord Steel wrote about Emlyn in his autobiography *Against Goliath* (1989), and told me in emails that he regarded him as 'a most valued colleague' and 'a huge asset' for the Liberal Party. Lord Mackie of Benshie gave me permission to print the verse he wrote on Emlyn's parliamentary golden jubilee. I thank them all, and Lady Mackie, for their correspondence.

I was delighted that so many of Emlyn's friends, colleagues and admirers were able and willing to contribute to the book, and I wish to thank them all for their contributions. For assistance with various matters I also wish to thank Beti George, Lady Geraint, Sarah Hall, Gaenor Howells, Lowri-Haf Morgan, Adrian Roberts, Buddug Roberts, Dafydd Rhys (S4C), Helen Smeed, Mair Sturrock, Jenny Thomas, Professor John Williams (Aberystwyth), the editors of the *Cambrian Law Review*, the BBC, and last, but not least, my wife Jane for her patience and support. Dylan Williams designed and prepared the book for the press with his usual professionalism and panache; and Jonathan Lewis and his staff at Gwasg Gomer adopted it as their own.

D. Ll. M.

CHRONOLOGY

26th of March 1925	— Born in Colomendy, just outside Denbigh
1936–42	— Educated at Denbigh Grammar School
1942	— Became a student at the University College of Wales, Aberystwyth
1943	— Joined the Royal Navy
1948	— Graduated Ll.B. (University of Wales)
1949	— Called to the Bar at Gray's Inn
1950	— Married Shirley Margaret Wynne Hamer; began practice at the Bar; contested Conway as Liberal candidate, and again in 1951
1960	— Queen's Counsel
1960–71	— Deputy Chairman, Flintshire Quarter Sessions
1960–71	— Deputy Chairman, then (1967) Chairman, Merioneth Quarter Sessions
1962	— Member of Parliament: won the Montgomeryshire by-election. Thereafter won the seat in 1964, 1966, 1970 and the two elections of 1974
1965	— Day President, Royal National Eisteddfod of Wales, Newtown
1966–79	— Leader of the Welsh Liberal Party
1966	— Honorary Bard of the White Robe, Gorsedd of the Royal National Eisteddfod of Wales

1968	— Bencher, Gray's Inn
1971–74	— Leader, Wales and Chester Circuit
1971	— Recorder of Merthyr Tudful
1971	— Honorary Professorial Fellow in the Department of Law, University of Wales, Aberystwyth
1971–72	— Recorder of Swansea
1975–79	— Vice-Chairman, Political Committee, North Atlantic Assembly
1979	— Lost the Montgomeryshire seat; made Life Peer, taking the title Baron Hooson of Montgomery in the County of Powys and Colomendy in the County of Clwyd
1980	— Chairman, Hafren/Severn Television (a company that made an unsuccessful bid for the ITV franchise for Wales and the West for 1982–90)
1983–86	— President of the Welsh Liberal Party
1985–97	— Non-executive Director of Laura Ashley plc; Chairman, 1995–96
1986	— Treasurer of Gray's Inn
1987	— Honorary Fellow, University of Wales, Aberystwyth
1987–93	— President of the Llangollen International Musical Eisteddfod
1991–99	— Chairman of Severn River Crossing plc
1995–98	— President of Wales International
2001	— Day President, Royal National Eisteddfod of Wales, Denbigh

2003	— Honorary Ll.D., University of Wales
2008	— Honorary Burgess of the Town of Denbigh
21st of February 2012	— Emlyn Hooson died

Emlyn Hooson
Essays and Reminiscences

A SNATCH AT AN AUTOBIOGRAPHY

E. H.

'Reminiscences make one feel so deliciously aged and sad.'
So wrote George Bernard Shaw. Here I am, getting on for
my seventy-fifth birthday, seriously trying to reminisce and
apply pen to paper. Unlike Shaw, I do not often feel sad,
although I sometimes wish I could live my life all over again
– provided I had the power to amend it here and there. I do
sometimes feel deliciously aged – generally, fantastically
so. The delicious feeling comes from reflecting on the fact
that the blood is no longer stirred as in younger days and
that I am free of the traumas that accompany passion,
ambition, responsibility and effort. The striving has been
handed over to others, and I now look back on events with
a different perspective to the one I had when experiencing
things as they occurred.

Having been brought up by a devoted Calvinistic
mother, whose theological views I never shared, even in
childhood, I must confess that her fatalism rubbed off on
me. I don't believe in Providence – rather, that history is
mainly decided by accidents – but, looking back on life, I
find it impossible not to try and justify the things that have
happened in a way I never thought about them at the time.

I must reflect at the outset on my great luck in childhood. I was brought up in a very happy family (with a great
extended family behind it) at Colomendy, a hundred-acre

farm in the Vale of Clwyd, a most beautiful part of Wales, fertile, green, redolent of history. The couplet

Ni fydd Cymru'n Gymru lwyd
Tra Dyffryn Clwyd yn glasu

[Wales will never be a drab Wales
As long as the Vale of Clwyd is green]

appeared over the counter of our local milk bar in Denbigh. In former times Colomendy was part of the Plas Clough estate, Plas Clough being a splendid house built by the famous sixteenth-century merchant Sir Richard Clough. The Plas stood about four fields away from Colomendy farm, and its most prominent buildings were its tithe barn, where my father kept some of his machines, and the *colomendy*, the dovecot – finely built, like the Plas, of bricks from the Netherlands, to house three thousand doves. In Tudor times, in winter, a family like the Cloughs would depend on pigeon for their fresh meat. When I was a barrister practising on the Wales and Chester Circuit, I remember hearing in Chester that bulldozers were about to raze the farmhouse and its buildings to the ground. I telephoned an old friend who was Town Clerk of Denbigh to try and persuade the council to save the old dovecote at least. I even offered to pay for its conveyance to San Ffagan, but to no avail. At the time, the main concern was attracting industry, and thus jobs, to Denbigh and district. Nowadays the authorities wouldn't allow such vandalism.

From the window of my bedroom, which was a large room built especially for my two brothers and me, I would gaze at the remains of Denbigh's high castle (and the old remains of what could have been in the fourteenth century a cathedral), and in my mind's eye I would fight the great battles between the Welsh princes, and the greater battles between Owain Glyndŵr and the English; then the skirmishes between the Royalists and the Roundheads. Of the subtler battles on the cultural and social fronts, which were the consequences of Denbigh's geographical position, I was then blissfully unaware – or, perhaps, to put it in a fairer way, I was only marginally aware.

The railway line connecting Denbigh and Chester ran in front of our house – the breadth of Cae Bach (as we called it) away – and the lane from the farm that led to the main road crossed the railway. Half the farm lay on the other side of the railway, in the parish of the White Church, one of the most beautiful churches in Wales, the resting place of the poet and playwright Thomas Edwards (Twm o'r Nant) and other famous men.

My memory of these childhood days is almost universally happy, sunny even in the rain and the snow. I and my two brothers, one younger, one older, enjoyed a carefree life. Although farming was going through a difficult period in the 1920s and 1930s and my parents felt the pinch, the whole rural community shared that difficulty and we wanted for nothing except luxuries. Some of my fellow school children were not so lucky, and some of the families who were fellow members of Fron Chapel lived on the poverty line, as did other families in the town. When pigs or lambs were slaughtered on the farm for home consumption, my parents would see to it that we as children would take choice pieces of meat not only to friends but also to needier families. In myriad ways the close-knit societies of rural Wales helped each other through difficult times.

Our farm, Colomendy, lay a mile or so from the town. My parents always allowed my brothers and me to bring home each week a gang of boys to play football, rugby and cricket on one of our fields. From playing sport, eventually we graduated to animated argument at the tea table about religion, politics, the development of science, and the future of the world, and in the late 1930s we discussed the threat of war. My mother, who had lost her parents when she was still in her teens, had three brothers (one of whom had been killed in the First World War) and was terribly good at handling boys; but in no way did she encourage girls to come to the farm. An annual visitor for tea at Colomendy was T. Gwynn Jones, one of the greatest Welsh poets of the twentieth century, and the biographer of Thomas Gee the political activist and publisher who so massively influenced the political and religious life of nineteenth-century Wales. Such men as Gee have been scarce in our country: too many ministers of religion (at one time), too many lawyers, teachers and Members of Parliament, and too few men of business sharing the same beliefs! Gwynn Jones was always accompanied by John Hooson of London, one of two uncles of mine who were university educated. The two would walk together for miles renewing knowledge of old haunts in the Vale of Clwyd. Although born in Betws-yn-rhos, Gwynn Jones spent much of his boyhood at Plas-yn-Green farm, whose land in part ran adjacent to some Colomendy land. I gleaned a good deal of local historical knowledge from the teatime conversations of those occasions.

It was on the eve of the Second World War that I heard David Lloyd George for the one and only time in my life. On the Thursday of the National Eisteddfod of Wales held in Denbigh in 1939 he mesmerised his huge audience with his presidential address. He spoke about the certainty of war, emphasising that the tyranny of Nazism must be overcome, and that afterwards there would be a great chance to rebuild Europe. I remember his vivid imagery, his comparing the destructive impact of war with the destructive impact of massive storms on forests; and remember how, in an extended simile, he went on to say that after the storm abated the outdated rotten trees would give people the opportunity to garner kindling to warm their hearths, and that the people also would see signs of fresh green growth between the trees which had survived.

I was then fourteen years old. My companion in the audience was my best friend Hesketh Lloyd Roberts, aged just fifteen. His father was chairman of one of the Eisteddfod's committees, and he arranged for Hesketh and me to meet the grand old man. Back stage we were introduced to him. He patted both of us on the head and wished us well.

Hesketh's father was also Chairman of the Denbigh Grammar School Governors, but that didn't stop him from suffering the lashings the headmaster, W. A. Evans, gave to most of the boys with his knotted ash stick. Mrs Roberts was once so concerned about the weals Hesketh had that she asked my mother's advice on approaching the Boss. My mother asked me if I'd been lashed, and I said, 'Yes, but don't want to make a fuss', because all the boys received that treatment. In 1944 when I was serving in the Navy I received a hastily written letter from my mother informing me that Hesketh had died during Allied action in France. I was a lucky survivor; Hesketh perished. Similar experiences must govern the recollections of tens of thousands of my generation in different countries, and might explain why so many of us were all for a much reformed society in our own countries, and why we supported a united Europe in which aggressive nationalism was a thing of the past. Another Denbigh boy I remember well is Cecil Pearce, who was drowned in the Cherwell at Oxford. He had gone to the University to read theology at St Edmund's Hall after taking a First at Bangor. I had just joined the Navy before the tragedy happened, and had received a post-card from Cecil reminding me that sailors got duty-free tobacco and that I shouldn't forget to send him some. He was a brilliant orator and preacher who would often come down to Colomendy with my brother Gwilym, and I'd sometimes go and listen to him on Sunday evenings at the White Church.

I remember the 1939 Eisteddfod for other reasons as well. As a fourteen-year-old boy I was in the chorus of *Llywelyn ein Llyw Olaf*. It wasn't much of a play, but the famous producer, Dr Stefan Hock, a Jewish refugee from the Nazis in Vienna, had learned enough Welsh to direct it. At the time he was also producing plays in Birmingham and Liverpool, and for that reason he was wont not to arrive for rehearsals in Denbigh until after nine o'clock in the evening. You can imagine the great fun my friends and I had, and everybody else as far as I am aware, with nobody to keep us in order. During those late evening waits I learned very little about our Last Prince but learned a great deal about human nature. I remember Kate Roberts's production of an interlude by Twm o'r Nant on the castle lawn. I also sold milk shakes on the Eisteddfod Field, in a large portable milk bar my Uncle George from Caerfallen in Rhuthun had erected specifically for the purpose.

After taking Matric I left school to help my father on the farm. His four farmhands were members of the Territorial Army Volunteer Reserves and had joined up. However, soon afterwards I was awarded a scholarship to the Henry Ford Institute of Agricultural Engineering in Essex, where I soon learned that I wasn't much good with my hands. Moreover, to the great surprise of the headmaster, W. A. Evans, and my favourite teacher, Stanley Rees, the English master, I then decided to go back to school to take my Higher Certificate, so that I could study Law in Aberystwyth to ease my way into politics. The old Boss told me, 'You're a fool but perhaps you'll succeed if you work hard.' I did, and after studying for two terms gained my A-levels in English, history and geography.

I loved my days at Aberystwyth, both as a seventeen-year-old when I first went there and as a twenty-one-year-old when I returned from the Navy. Professor D. J. Llewelfryn Davies and his predecessor, Emeritus Professor Thomas Levi, had created a marvellous Department of Law, and both were influential figures in my life. They were very different men, but the one essential difference between them was that Tommy Levi was his own advocate whereas Llewelfryn was, by his very nature, everybody else's advocate. Shepherding was second nature to him. He had an intense personal interest in each of his students, his courtesy was legendary and his patience infinite. He appreciated the different interests and qualities of his students and never sought to mould them into a standard type. On the contrary, he encouraged them to pursue their own interests and to follow their bent. And the distinguished Professor never patronised the seventeen-year-old student. Indeed, I always think that Llewelfryn gave to some of his students more confidence than he had ever possessed himself. He was not soft, nor familiar, and had a great sense of humour. There was a Pickwickian quality about him, and when he talked he had a twinkle in his eye, a twinkle that varied according to the quality of the conversation. I was already very active in politics at Aber, and Llewelfryn was very amused when I was invited – at twenty-two – to go on the short list for the selection of the prospective Liberal parliamentary candidate for Lloyd George's old seat, Caernarvon Boroughs, which had been held for a short time by Professor Seaborne Davies, the Professor of Law at Liverpool University who lost the seat in 1945. Llewelfryn told me that it would do me no harm but that I wouldn't get it. In the event I turned up and spoke in front of a selection panel of about a hundred and fifty people, all old enough to be my parents or grandparents. Mercifully I was the last in, and managed to rouse the audience from drowsiness. To my astonishment I was selected. When I got back to college Llewelfryn's only comment was that he hoped it wouldn't mean my cutting any more lectures!

As students we formed a flourishing Liberal Club which slackened the overwhelming grip that the Labour students from the south Welsh valleys had had for years. Levi and Llewelfryn were our Presidents, and my chief aide was Elwyn Thomas, a born organizer, and a great boon for someone like me who had few talents in that direction. Together with others Elwyn and I eventually produced a new magazine called *The New Radical*, and I suppose it was this publication that brought me first to public notice. For it was then that I began to be invited to address public meetings, meetings which were often reported upon in the *Liverpool Daily Post* and in the *Western Mail* and in more local papers.

I spoke at a never-to-be-forgotten meeting at Capel Curig in Snowdonia, where my fellow speaker was a chap of whom I had never heard before, called Jeremy Thorpe. He was staying with Megan Lloyd George, then MP for Anglesey, who had been at finishing school with his mother towards the end of the First World War. I spoke in Welsh and he spoke in English, and he promised that one day we would speak together again, with him that time speaking in Welsh and I in English.

During the middle years of the Second World War, along with two other Law students from the department in Aberystwyth, I joined the Navy. The next three years saw us being tossed about on the lower deck of a corvette that sometimes crossed the Atlantic in convoys and that at other times sailed along the coasts of Belgium and Holland trying to stop German raids.

Law, politics, war. But I still loved farming, and when I could helped a lot on the farm, with my father, and then after my father's death in 1948 with John. In the mid-1950s after I had made some money as a barrister I bought Plas Iolyn, Pentrefoelas with my cousin John. By the way, the Hoosons had few Christian names – John, Tom, David and Huw – and therefore we knew everyone by the name of his farm, John Colomendy, John Caerfallen, David Segrwyd, David Caerfallen. I was lucky to be called Emlyn. But the next cousin to be born was baptised John Emlyn! Farming keeps you close to the land. And it pays to remember Mark Twain's advice, 'Buy land, young man, they don't make it any more.'

It was at the Bar that I was most successful, and I must say I enjoyed it greatly, especially in the early days. But I wouldn't say that the Bar was the most satisfying aspect of my life. I often felt that I was fighting other people's fights instead of my own. Because I took part in a number of murder trials, the fact that I did more civil and planning cases is easily forgotten. People often refer to this case and that – the Moors murder case most often – and ask, 'How could you do it?' The simple answer is that a professional barrister, if he is wise, takes care not to be sucked in emotionally to any case. One of the worst briefs I ever took, at the behest of his family, was to defend a fellow barrister who later became a judge. It is never prudent to ask one of your friends to appear on your behalf, in case judgement is undermined by friendship. One of the best definitions of a barrister's duty is found in Boswell's *Life of Johnson*. When his biographer asked Dr Johnson how he could justify defending a man who was obviously guilty, the old Doctor said that if a barrister judged his own client he would be taking the place of the proper judge and jury. The barrister's opinion could be wrong, and society depends upon the judicial system to reach as fair a verdict as civil humanity can.

I believe strongly in the jury system. There is a story about a jury in Denbighshire years and years ago that had been prompted by a London judge after a four-day hearing to bring in a guilty verdict against a man accused of rape. After half-an-hour's deliberation the jury returned, and declared the accused 'Not guilty.' The judge was very surprised. 'Well,' said the jury foreman, 'we know the man. He's a very respectable chap. And we know the woman, and we'll say no more about her. But all of us have come to the conclusion that he wasn't obliged to use any more force than necessary to the situation.' Some cases give one professional satisfaction, others personal satisfaction. The important thing in the end is that justice is done.

During my career I went abroad for a number of cases. To the United States, for instance, and to Singapore, where I defended Ben Jeyaretnam, the leader of the opposition, a very nice man. I went several times to Hong Kong, where I enjoyed the company of members of the Welsh Society.

To Sri Lanka for the trial of the President of the country's Bar Council, and to South Africa for the trial of Moses Mayekiso, a trade-union leader who was prominent in the ANC.

I believe that the standard of practitioners at the Bar all in all is higher than that of politicians. On the other hand the Bar is more blinkered than politics. In his biography of Benjamin Disraeli André Maurois notes that a friend of the Prime Minister once asked him, 'Mr Disraeli, you were called to the Bar. Why didn't you practise and become a great lawyer?' Disraeli answered: 'I gave up the chance of being a great lawyer in order to preserve the chance of being a great man.' A barrister learns to be cautious and careful, whilst the great politician has a wide wingspan. Yes, there are more men of stature in politics than at the Bar, but I still contend that the standard at the Bar is much higher than in politics.

When I was fourteen years old and doing well in mathematical exercises involving stocks and shares, for a while I was tempted to aim for the Stock Exchange. It's a good job I didn't because later on I had no interest in them, although it could be said that stockbroking would have given me a more solid material base for a political career than the Bar. I gave up thinking about business quite early, but I want to tell this short story about Gwasg Gee in Denbigh. When I was well-established at the Bar, one day in chambers in Chester I received a telephone call from Gwilym R. Jones, the editor of *Y Faner*, asking me if I'd loan the publishing house £500 to cover that week's wages. He said that he had been advised to contact me by one or two of the staff who had been in school with me. I refused to give him the money, but telephoned my bank manager to arrange for the wages to be met that week. Then I put in some serious work to establish a little company that included Talog Davies and William Jones, Rhuthun, my father-in-law Sir George Hamer, Huw T. Edwards, David Tudor, Trawsfynydd, and persuaded them all to contribute, and we managed to save Gwasg Gee from bankruptcy. I should say that Talog dutifully told me that if we'd wait a while we could buy the company debt-free, but I felt it our duty to help the old firm. We gave the great Welsh novelist and short-story writer Kate Roberts a small pension, we cleared Gee's debts, and the company made some headway. Later David Tudor took it over. I never got a word of thanks from Kate Roberts or from Gwilym R. Jones, but much thanks from Mathonwy Hughes, *Y Faner*'s deputy editor. Reading about that episode in *Annwyl Kate, Annwyl Saunders* it's pretty obvious that Kate couldn't bear to contemplate the fact that I came in and saved them!

The acquisition of Gwasg Gee stimulated my cousin Tom – who in 1979 became Conservative MP for Brecon and Radnor – to write a long letter from New York, where he lived in the early 1960s, chock-full of ideas about how to develop it, from setting up a mail-order business to reach the scattered Welsh readership – 'Siop Gymreig y Post' (*A Postal Welsh Shop*) – to printing Christmas cards designed by star Welsh artists, calendars, &c. His enthusiasm for all sorts of new projects was such that he was adamant that Gee should also take over the back-list and any new publishing work previously done by firms that were now nearly defunct, Hughes a'i Fab and Hugh Evans. Madison Avenue had obviously entered his blood stream. As our friend Glyn Tegai Hughes once said, 'timidity in enterprise' would be swept aside by Tom's 'total conviction of success' in nearly everything.

But because I was and am essentially a political animal, I didn't have enough interest in the publishing business to direct it anew. The political animal in me nevertheless believes that in one narrow sense the United Kingdom is too party-political. During my life I've seen many politicians become members of the Cabinet for one reason only – that they belong to a certain party: they'd never be chosen for their merits. In a way, the system is rooted in the British Empire and depends on a tradition of an opposition attacking everything the government does, and *vice versa*. Today's world demands more than such attrition. Having said that, I confess that I've greatly enjoyed politics, in the Commons and in the Lords. They are very different places. There is more excitement in the one and greater sense in the other. But I wouldn't reform either until we see how Europe develops. To ensure that things are not over-centralised I believe we need a federal Europe.

The best speakers in the House of Commons during my time there were Enoch Powell and Michael Foot, the Powell and Foot of the backbenches. Both were eloquently destructive. Great as their merits were Powell should not have taken ministerial office nor Foot his party's leadership because they were not cut out for such posts. History will put them in their appropriate places. When Herbert Morrison suggested that history would put Winston Churchill in his appropriate place, the grand old man said, 'I entirely agree, ... particularly as I will write that history.'

The two best questioners in the House, in my opinion, were Ian Macleod and Jo Grimond, both exceptionally talented, both excellent at getting to the crux of the matter. Macleod was a better speaker on the floor of the House than Grimond, but Grimond was better on a public platform. (I must add that Grimond had something of an anti-Welsh attitude. He was a patrician, in the mould of his grandfather-in-law, Asquith, and I fear that to an extent he had inherited the attitude of the Asquiths and the Bonham-Carters to Lloyd George and everything Welsh.) At the Dispatch Box the best performers were Harold Wilson and Margaret Thatcher. If you ask me who the nicest prime ministers were, I'd say Alec Douglas-Home and Jim Callaghan. There's a story about the playwright William Douglas-Home, Alec's brother, coming to the House to visit him when he was Prime Minister. Like every other visitor he had to fill in a green card, giving the name of the member he wished to see, his own name, and the purpose of his visit. On the first line William wrote 'The Prime Minister, Alec Douglas-Home' and under Purpose of Visit wrote 'Assassination'.

One of the best things I did during my political career was to represent the United Kingdom in what was called the Atlantic Assembly, previously NATO Parliamentarians. There I became great friends with John Lindsay, later Mayor of New York, and with Donald Rumsfeld, later Defense Secretary of the United States. I also cherish my connections with Arthur Ross, a very successful business-man in America, with Senator Jack Javits, and with Arthur Schlesinger. On this side of the Atlantic I got to know Helmut Schmidt, who became Chancellor of the Federal Republic of Germany. And in the company of these friends I travelled much in Europe and in the United States.

This precis of an autobiography shows that I am some-thing of a liquorice allsorts who has greatly enjoyed life, who has been blessed with a very happy home and with an intelligent supportive wife and children with whom I am firm friends – a fortunate man now looking for a new career. If I could discipline myself I think from now on I'd like to write.

THE LAW

EMLYN IN THE LAW

Eifion Roberts

It was in the Law Department of the University College of Wales, Aberystwyth, in the Autumn Term of 1946 that I met Emlyn for the first time. He was then returning to Aber from the Royal Navy, whereas I had gone there the previous year straight from school. Thus it was that we began our second year at the same time. His impact was striking – all the more so as he was nearly three years my senior and had seen the world. Even after sixty-seven years I still remember his natural self-confidence, his high intelligence and his youthful exuberance, not to mention his friendliness and charm. Over the ensuing years I came to know his parents and two brothers when I stayed at Colomendy. Gwilym, the eldest, was a successful and popular general practitioner at Holywell all his working life, and John, the youngest, like his father before him, was a dedicated farmer. Both predeceased Emlyn by some years. It became evident to me that Emlyn had inherited his more dynamic qualities from his mother, his charm and gentleness from his father, and his generous spirit from both parents alike.

He knew from the start that he was cut out for the Bar. Early on at Aber he told me that someone of note had said that he was the best Bar candidate that Aber had seen for a long time. No wonder he felt able to warn youngsters like me that it was a mistake for any aspiring advocate to devote all his time to the study of Law as an academic subject. Some of the great advocates of the past (whose biographies he may well have read) had spent their student years honing their debating skills in readiness for the cut and thrust of the Bar, and, if they were so inclined, in laying the foundations of a political career to run in harness with it. Admittedly, the Bar Final lay in wait as a necessary evil after leaving University, but it was easily taken care of by early enlistment on a six-month cram course in Chancery Lane with Gibson and Weldon of blessed memory. I need hardly say that, as a son of the manse brought up on Calvinistic principles of struggle and strife, I listened with amazement to the prescription for what seemed to me a somewhat effortless passage to the Bar.

However, I have to say that by 1949, only three years after he had left the Navy, it had all come to pass virtually as he had mapped it out. He had made the most of his opportunities at Aber, becoming President of the Debating Society in his last year, and, what is more, immersing himself in Welsh politics. I always felt that, even in his early twenties, he was looking for a leading role. He saw his chance in what many regarded, after the Labour landslide of 1945, as the dying embers of Liberal Radicalism in Wales. This was the brand of Liberalism that David Lloyd George had championed. On the one and only occasion when my father met Emlyn at our home in Anglesey, they were discussing a Liberal revival with some passion when my father remarked, as if he had seen a vision, 'And, do you know, you look like Lloyd George when he was a young man.' Emlyn did not demur but looked my father in the eye and took it very seriously. What I learnt much later on was that Emlyn had listened to Lloyd George deliver a highly charged political speech from the platform of the National Eisteddfod at Denbigh in August 1939, only a month or so before war was declared against Germany. According to Emlyn, the thrust of the speech was how naïve Chamberlain had been to accept Hitler's word at Munich in 1938 and then to proclaim the achievement of 'peace in our time'. My feeling is that the example of Lloyd George remained with Emlyn as a constant reminder that there are broader horizons than the Law although no lawyer can ignore the old adage that the Law is a jealous mistress.

There can be no doubt that Emlyn did see the return of Welsh Radicalism as his political mission. He launched his own magazine at Aber under the title *The New Radical*, and tried to rekindle Undeb Cymru Fydd (The Union of Future Wales) in the hope of giving the new Radicalism a really Welsh flavour. Of course, these activities became known outside the University and led to his adoption in 1949 as the parliamentary Liberal candidate for the Caernarvon Boroughs, Lloyd George's old constituency. Thanks to Gibson and Weldon and Emlyn's focused studies with them, he passed the Bar Final and thereby paved the way for his Call to the Bar at Gray's Inn in June 1949. Professionally the next step was to seek pupillage with an experienced practitioner in a recognized set of chambers. Normally he would have looked to London, but two pressing reasons propelled him to Chester: one was the need to keep an eye on Colomendy after his father had passed away following an accident on the farm and after John had taken over, and the other was the need to be near the Caernarvon Boroughs for the campaign for the General Election in 1950.

Chester then had a small Bar concentrated in one set of chambers in Hunter Street. By arrangement, he approached one of the joint heads, Sir Francis Williams, Bart., QC (as he later became). In Emlyn's words, Francis, a kindly man, gave him 'the brush off', no doubt with what he thought were Emlyn's best interests in mind. There was hardly enough work for those already there let alone a mere novice who would not know what the Chief Justice looked like. Francis then suggested the Colonies, where the prospects were much better. As Emlyn had no wish to spend the rest of his days in darkest Africa, he cast his eyes towards Liverpool and obtained a helpful introduction to a set of chambers with an illustrious pedigree which included Sir David Maxwell Fyfe QC (later Lord Kilmuir, Lord Chancellor) and Sir Hartley Shawcross QC (the Attorney General in the immediate post-war Labour government). He secured a pupillage there with Robertson Crichton, a delightful man who had a lucrative practice and who later became a High Court judge. It was understood between them that Emlyn intended to practise from Chester on the Wales and

Chester Circuit. This meant that he was unlikely to pick up any crumbs during his pupillage, as they would be reserved for pupils in Crichton's chambers who intended to practice in Liverpool.

Through frequent attendance at trials in St George's Hall and elsewhere, Emlyn learnt a great deal about the art of advocacy for which he had a natural flair. He spoke of Henry Burton QC as the greatest advocate he had ever heard. Sadly, Burton died in a railway accident before his huge judicial potential could be realized. Another who commanded his admiration was Daniel Brabin QC, a flamboyant advocate of immense ability who was elevated to the High Court. Emlyn, himself no stranger to the swashbuckling style, was quick to emulate these forensic heroes.

As his time in Liverpool drew to a close, he decided to reinvestigate the prospects at Chester, after hearing rumours that an elderly practitioner, John Pascoe Elsden, had left the chambers in Hunter Street, taken a talented Clerk with him, and was now practising from his home at 12 Curzon Park. The situation was not without promise. No doubt the occasional brief might be going spare, Elsden might relish the help and companionship of an able young man, and no doubt the Clerk, as Elsden was getting on, would be thinking ahead to the succession. An interview with Elsden was arranged. When Emlyn knocked on the door of 12 Curzon Park it was the Clerk who opened it. Emlyn told him he had an appointment with Mr Elsden. 'I'm sorry to disappoint you, sir,' replied the Clerk, 'Mr Elsden passed away yesterday.' This was the first time these kindred spirits ever met, the young Emlyn and the older but ever youthful Bill Jones who would shape his career for the next ten years and beyond.

It must have occurred to Emlyn that as Elsden had died Bill had been left in the lurch, and a mutual need must have stared both of them in the face – Emlyn's need of a good clerk to set him up and Bill's need of a promising barrister to serve. Having once been rejected in Hunter Street, Emlyn, if he were to practise in Chester, had to set up on his own. For a twenty-four-year-old barely out of pupillage such a course was unheard of. It was a gamble. In order to prove his worth Emlyn had to overcome the prejudice in a conservative profession against youth and inexperience. Equally it was a gamble for Bill, who had to sell him to discerning solicitors. Suffice to say, a deal was struck. Bill, who was very much a man about town, found suitable premises at 39 White Friars, a professional street within walking distance of the courts in the Castle. By then Emlyn had met Shirley, the only child of George, later Sir George, Hamer, Lord Lieutenant of Montgomeryshire, who came all the way from Llanidloes to scrub the floors and put two rooms in reasonable order, one for Emlyn and one for Bill. (Shirley was and is an unusually capable woman, confident, practical, kind and hospitable, and in terms of sheer wit and intelligence a match for Emlyn himself. They were both engaging personalities and the success of 39 White Friars was due in no small part to the broad range of Shirley's constructive endeavours over the years.)

Given the right people, the spirit of enterprise, once in action, often attracts a run of luck. That certainly was Emlyn's experience after he embarked on his practice in Chester as a one-man band. He had received his first brief in Liverpool shortly before the end of his pupillage. A matrimonial application had been listed for hearing at 4 p.m. The Clerk in chambers had to give it to Emlyn because no one else was available. Although he knew nothing about family law and only had an hour to read the papers, he managed to obtain the order that he sought, and that against some opposition. The opposing solicitor was so impressed with him that on learning that Emlyn intended to practise on the Wales and Chester Circuit (to which Birkenhead then belonged) he recommended him to the well-known firm of solicitors in that town, Messrs Berkson and Berkson. A stream of criminal defence work began to flow from one of the senior partners, Barney Berkson, a gifted and amiable man, whose tactics appealed greatly to Emlyn. By eliciting a series of good answers in the magistrates' courts, he would establish the groundwork of the defence at Quarter Sessions or Assizes, and Emlyn always looked forward to building on Barney's groundwork.

One of the first cases that Barney Berkson sent him was the defence of an incest case. The defendant had been expected to plead guilty, but, in the event, he chose to contest the charge and take his chance before judge and jury. The visiting criminal judge at Chester Assizes was no less a person than the Lord Chief Justice himself, Lord Goddard, who had a formidable reputation. Who can forget the mesmeric experience of being the unfortunate victim of a prolonged Goddard stare as he pondered deeply over a legal problem? He could be mischievous, especially if he saw the chance to bring the mighty down a peg or two. On one occasion in Chester Assizes Edmund Davies QC and Elwyn Jones QC were faced with what both thought was an unprecedented procedural situation. From on high Lord Goddard stepped into the argument. The words that he uttered were 'Pray a tales' but deliberately slid over them so rapidly that no one could make them out, and both Edmund and Elwyn stood there as if made mute by the visitation of God. Goddard took great delight in their discomfiture, and, after a suitable pause, explained to them in the simplest terms, as if they were schoolchildren, what the antiquated practice to which he had alluded meant, namely that twelve good men and true gathered from the precincts of the court might be empanelled there and then to determine the matter on a formal direction from the judge. On the other hand, Goddard could be kindness itself, as I well remember when I appeared in the Court of Appeal in a complex bankruptcy case: he helped me wade through a huge pile of papers as I made my submissions. He had little sympathy for criminals, and strongly supported the retention of the death penalty, as did many religious people up and down the country. Even Emlyn must have been intimidated by the prospect of conducting his first contested criminal case before him. As the defendant was now pleading not guilty, and because incest was amongst the gravest offences in the criminal calendar, Barney

Berkson instructed Emlyn to apply for an adjournment of the trial in order to bring in a QC to lead him for the defence. Lord Goddard well knew that Emlyn was a beginner: the previous evening he had been the principal guest at a Bar Mess dinner at which Emlyn had been sworn in as a member of the Circuit. When the youngster made his application at 10.30, Goddard rejected it out of hand and ordered him to be ready to commence the trial at 2.15 that day without fail.

In the event it was as well for Emlyn as for his client that Goddard had taken this robust view. At the outset of his summing up to the jury he paid Emlyn the most handsome compliment imaginable. 'This is,' he said, 'a very serious case and it is not an easy case. It is, therefore, a great satisfaction to me, and, I have no doubt, to you, that [the accused] has been defended by a counsel who has put a proper, an able and a courageous defence. I can say of Mr Hooson that, in similar difficult cases, I have never heard a counsel put a case for his client better than he has done. Therefore, we can approach the case confident that everything proper to the case for the defence has been laid before you.' Those of us who remember the judges of old might be disposed to interpret such lavish praise as a soft prelude to a thunderous crescendo of criticism, but the judge's remarks were totally sincere, and seasoned observers of the Bar, solicitors, court officials and journalists, took them literally. What is more, their effect was quite dramatic. The publicity that followed the end of this case virtually overnight established Emlyn as a very promising member of the Circuit he had just joined. To crown everything, the jury disagreed, causing Lord Goddard to order a retrial before Mr Justice Oliver and another jury. Oliver had as formidable a reputation as Goddard, but this time, after Emlyn's spirited defence, the jury acquitted the defendant. So, at the end of this case, Emlyn achieved what might be called in today's language a double whammy, a precious tribute from Lord Goddard and an acquittal at the hands of the second jury.

Emlyn became such a dedicated member of the Wales and Chester Circuit, and it had such a profound influence on his career, and, indeed, on his whole outlook, that some account needs to be given of its history, traditions, life and people. At first it had consisted of two circuits, namely the South Wales Circuit and the North Wales and Chester Circuit. To the understandable annoyance of the Northern Circuit, at some time in the past Chester had been appended to North Wales in order to create a viable circuit in a sparsely populated area. Although North and South Wales were separated, silks were allowed to practise on both circuits. In 1943 the two circuits were amalgamated into the Wales and Chester Circuit. Recently, with the advent of devolution and the need to conform to national boundaries, Cheshire has seceded to the Northern Circuit, but the local Bar remains centred on Chester. In 1950 Chester as a legal centre was something of a backwater, but, to the discerning eye, it had potential. Although the volume of work was low when I joined in 1953, there were only eight of us to share it. Even in 1971 when I took silk and moved up to London the number had only gone up to seventeen. Of course, we faced competition from Liverpool and from members of our own circuit who were based in London. With Emlyn's arrival on the scene there were two sets of chambers, and that tended to enhance public confidence in the local Bar. The other chambers were ably led by Robin David (later His Honour Judge Sir Robin David QC). Robin and Emlyn had different styles which ensured that they matched each other very well as practitioners in court. Rules had been introduced a long time ago to help maintain the viability of each circuit and thereby ensure that the services of advocates were spread as evenly as possible throughout the country. For example, if solicitors wished to instruct counsel 'off circuit' to conduct a case on circuit they had to send a 'kite brief' to a member of that circuit. In time such rules were seen to be restrictive practices and abolished.

Legal aid was still in its infancy in the early 1950s. The rewards for criminal defence work were abysmal. Nevertheless, it was only by doing such work that one became known and obtained prosecution briefs and civil work. At both Quarter Sessions and Assizes the old system of 'dock briefs' was available to enable prisoners to obtain the services of an advocate. When advocates became aware that an application for a dock brief was to be made all the advocates within the precincts of the court, except the silks, would be expected to sit bewigged with their backs to the dock. The prisoner was then allowed to pick any one of them (usually – on the advice of a prison warder – the one wearing the oldest-looking wig) and to be represented by him on payment of the princely sum of £2/4/6, of which

2/6 was for the Clerk. Sometimes, if one was unlucky, one could be held up for days or weeks on a dock brief, but often enough a kindly judge would relieve the situation and exercise his discretion by granting legal aid. The fact remains that a dock brief was not to be scoffed at by a youngster, for it was an opportunity for him to find his feet in court. My recollection is that it was after Lord Gardiner became Lord Chancellor at the end of the 1950s that legal aid came into its own and the old dock brief simply vanished quietly into oblivion.

Against that background it will be seen that crime (except, of course, when privately paid, which was comparatively rare, and unknown among beginners) was the Cinderella in the professional estimation of things. The be-all and end-all for a young barrister was to build up a substantial civil practice which would ensure that one's name appeared on as many pleadings as possible when the visiting civil judge would be studying a whole pile of papers before the hearings began at the Assizes. In time, such a success would justify an application for silk, and, if granted, a move up to London. That was certainly the pattern in Emlyn's career and in mine. Later on crime acquired a sophistication of its own and shed its Cinderella status.

The Circuit was very active socially. The High Sheriff of each county gave a splendid lunch at each Assize. Members of the Bar were always invited and the youngest was privileged to propose the vote of thanks. The Assizes ended up at Chester Castle, where the criminal judge sat in Court 1 and the civil judge in Court 2. Bar Mess was held at the Grosvenor Hotel. The speechifying after dinner afforded the opportunity to settle old scores in the nicest possible way. In one of the Assize towns of North Wales an argument had arisen in court between the Judge of Assize, Mr Justice Hallett (notorious as a 'much talking judge'), and Elwyn Jones QC (the erudite and polished Labour MP born and bred in Llanelli) about the admissibility of a piece of evidence. 'But, my Lord, I have now practised at the Bar for upwards of twenty years.' 'Yes, Mr Elwyn Jones,' came the judicial retort, 'but with some distractions, I understand.' It so happened that Elwyn presided over the Bar Mess dinner at the end of that Assize and got his own back when welcoming Hallett as the chief guest. 'It gives us all great pleasure,' he said, 'to welcome to the Mess tonight Mr Justice Hallett who has just returned from a Teutonic tour of Germany where he has been lecturing the Germans on the benefit of free speech.'

Whenever a member of a circuit was elevated to the High Court Bench, a celebratory dinner was held at the Inn of Court to which that member belonged. These were fabulous occasions. We all made our way there, as did the judges of the Circuit. After the speeches the Southerners would burst forth into Welsh hymn-singing of the more raucous kind, usually led with great gusto by such endearing characters as Sir Alun Talfan Davies QC, interspersed with the occasional Rugby song, notably 'Sosban Fach', led with much feigned solemnity by Lord Justice Tasker Watkins VC, not to mention 'Lloyd George knew my father, Father knew Lloyd George', led in a characteristic gargantuan style by Tommy Rhys Roberts, the son of the Rhys Roberts who had set up the firm of London solicitors known as Rhys Roberts & Co. in partnership with Lloyd George himself. Each of these dinners was a truly Welsh invasion of legal London, and, when Emlyn served his term as Leader of the Circuit, he presided impressively over several of them.

Beyond its more organized life the Circuit was blessed with a wealth of character among judges, barristers and solicitors whose formative influence on us youngsters was considerable, as Emlyn acknowledged. The most dist-inguished of the judges who figured in the North was Lord Morris of Borth-y-gest. He was not a member of our Circuit. As a Liverpool Welshman he had joined the Northern Circuit as a young man, taken silk, been elevated to the High Court, and finished up at the very top of the judicial ladder as a Lord of Appeal in Ordinary. He ranks among the greatest judges of the twentieth century. One of his lesser roles was being Chairman of the Caernarfon Quarter Sessions, a welcome escape four times a year from the higher echelons of the Law. If ever a man personified the image of justice in court, it was Lord Morris. Not only was he by far the most handsome man on the Bench – tall, elegant and majestic – he was also a model of courtesy, patience and tolerance. As Emlyn used to say, he was such a modest man that when you spoke to him you were made to feel that you were Lord Morris. His qualities were reflected in his dealings with everybody in court, including the prisoners. Local magistrates would turn up in good numbers on the opening day of the Quarter Sessions and enjoy the privilege of sitting with him on the Bench. He would politely take their opinion on every issue and instruct them meticulously on matters of evidence and procedure. As a result, whilst little work was done on the first day, public relations were on a high. On one of these days, as he took lunch at a local hostelry, someone asked Captain Livingstone Learmouth, one of the magistrates, how they were getting on at the Quarter Sessions, and he jokingly replied, 'Oh, we haven't finished bowing to the prisoners yet!'

Incidentally, I once led a small deputation from the Bar to ask the Lord Lieutenant of Caernarfonshire, Brigadier Wynne Finch, if he would be good enough to change the opening day of the Quarter Sessions from Thursday to some other day because it clashed with the opening day somewhere else. The request was rejected with a mild outburst of staunch local conservatism: 'Oh, no, we can't have that. It's been Thursday at Caernarfon since the Middle Ages, and it would be disrespectful to our ancestors to change it.' Little did he or we think then that the Courts Act of 1971 would abolish both Quarter Sessions and Assizes and bring them under the same roof in what became known as the Crown Court.

Mr Justice Austin Jones was the Chairman of the Flintshire Quarter Sessions. He had fought in the Great War, and my impression was that having seen such carnage he looked upon criminals as traitors of the dead. In his younger days in the 1920s and 1930s he had practised on the old North Wales and Chester Circuit, and, much to everyone's surprise, then accepted a county court judgeship in the South of England. It so happened that he had been Clement Attlee's fag at Haileybury. During Attlee's time as Deputy Prime Minister the need arose to appoint a suitable lawyer to undertake the difficult task of co-ordinating the differing procedures of the various countries in the persecution of the Nazi leaders at the Nuremberg Tribunals. It seems that Attlee had no hesitation in nominating Austin. In fact, it was an inspired choice. One always felt that he was in some ways more fitted for a top administrative job than for a judicial role. So efficiently did he perform his task that the Lord Chancellor's Permanent Secretary was despatched to Nuremberg to offer him a High Court judgeship, which he accepted. On the Bench he was a stickler for form and compliance, and, as Emlyn and I knew from altercations with him in different cases, could be very abrupt. I remember standing at the back of the Court in Mold when Austin was presiding, and who should come to stand beside me but Kerfoot Roberts, the police court king of North East Wales: 'I've been a Tory all my life,' he said, 'but, as for that b----- up there, he's an eighteenth-century Tory.' For all that, he was a kind and generous host at the Lodgings, to which he would invite us for dinner when he came on Assize. He always wanted to know what we were reading, and, as it happened, some of us, like him, were P. G. Wodehouse fans. He would also give us helpful and friendly lecturettes based on his long experience. In one of them he said that he always asked himself in every case, 'What is the right thing to do?' No doubt the public thinks that that is such an obvious question that it hardly needs to be asked, but in practice it is not so simple: often one is circumscribed by statute or legal precedent and has to be careful to keep one's own personal views and idiosyncrasies well in check, and there is much to be said for reminding oneself of Austin's question. I had a sneaking admiration for him which I know Emlyn did not share, and we simply agreed to differ.

The doyen of the Bar in North Wales was John Jones Roberts who belonged to a London chambers, but who, to all intents, practised from his home in Rhiw, Blaenau Ffestiniog. As he did not drive he travelled everywhere by train. He was touching seventy when I first met him in 1953. We all adored him. He was a kind, helpful and considerate man. It was said that when young men returned to the Bar from the Second World War he distributed briefs among them to get them started again. In 1927 when he himself was waiting for work to come in he published one of the first books in Welsh on political theory under the title *Elfennau Gwleidyddiaeth* ('The Elements of Politics') and in 1929 stood unsuccessfully as the first Parliamentary Labour Candidate in Meirionnydd. Above all, J. R. was our link with the past. He told me once that he and his wife, the scholarly and highly articulate Kate Winnie, on a fine summer's afternoon in the 1920s stood in the Temple Gardens in London, when, unbeknown to them, the famous Welsh advocate Sir Ellis Jones Griffith KC approached them from behind and blessed them with the words, 'Teyrnas Nefoedd, o'ch mewn chwi y mae' ('The Kingdom of Heaven is within you'). The last time Emlyn and I saw him was at the bar of the Lion Royal during a luncheon break from the Dolgellau Assizes. A petite little lady walked in wearing a black costume as she always did. 'The bar,' said she, Kate Winnie, playfully, 'has a pernicious influence on John!' Then, after a longish pause, she said, 'The car is waiting outside.' Thus it was that J. R. vanished from our scene to the relative solitude of Blaenau Ffestiniog.

Among the solicitors who practised in the North were Dr William George, Lloyd George's brother, who was still active at the age of a hundred and one; his son Dr W. R. P. George, a crowned National bard; Milwyn Jenkins, the mid-Wales champion of Welsh soccer; Marshall Meredith, the standard bearer of old Meirionnydd; Dafydd Cwyfan Hughes, a keen observer of the legal scene and one of Emlyn's closest friends; and Dennis Diamond, the colourful ambassador of Walker Smith and Way, who, at Emlyn's behest, carried the Liberal torch in Flintshire in two general elections. Perhaps the most original, the most eccentric, and certainly the most rebellious of them was Rowland Jones, whose bardic name was Rolant o Fôn, twice chaired in the National Eisteddfod and an acknowledged authority on *cynghanedd*. Having served his articles for ten years after leaving school, he passed the solicitors' Finals and set up on his own in Market Square, Llangefni. He treated the Law only as a means of livelihood and had a healthy scepticism of its institutions. In Rolant's time, because he cited the Bard so often in mitigating for his errant clients, the magistrates of Anglesey knew more Shakespeare than their predecessors ever did or their successors ever would. If he lost a case before them, it was not unknown for Rolant to get on his feet and proclaim, 'There is no justice in this court. My client will have to seek it elsewhere.' The elusive 'elsewhere' was never identified! He once pleaded for mercy for an old lag before a bench of magistrates presided over by Sir William Hughes Hunter, who thundered, 'How can you expect us to show mercy to your client when he has a list of previous convictions as long as my arm?' 'Well, your Worship,' replied Rolant, 'what you can say without fear of contradiction is that he's been a good customer of the court.' Rolant's name survives on two dimensions – legal anecdotes and splendid poetry of a high quality.

Emlyn and I and others of our generation knew them all. Their presence and influence enriched our professional lives as we travelled from one court to another. We were privileged to practise in such a congenial part of the country and to participate in the camaraderie that we found there.

Emlyn and Shirley then built a house on the City Walls in Chester overlooking the Dee. Their hospitality was proverbial and Shirley was the perfect hostess. During the Assizes some of the leading QCs of the Circuit would drop in on them at their new home. Three of these luminaries stand out.

The first was Edmund Davies QC, a native of Mountain Ash, who had distinguished himself at both London and Oxford Universities. Although he could easily have become a leading academic, he had chosen to practise at the Bar and had brilliantly adapted his talents to the needs of advocacy. In cross-examination he had a knack of asking important questions in a puritanical tone, prefacing them with a phrase which always drew the right answers – as when, for instance, he would begin his first question to a senior prison medical doctor with the words, 'Realizing, doctor, that you and I are here to serve the same ends . . .' Through such questioning he seemed to impress his own personality on the witness. Once Edmund became a High Court judge there was no stopping him. The more he advanced, the more his academic prowess helped him. Like Lord Morris of Borth-y-gest he finished up as a Lord of Appeal whose classic judgments will adorn the annals of the Law for many years. At one of his elevation dinners at Gray's Inn, an apology for absence was received from the parliamentary wit and raconteur, Roderic Bowen QC, then on political business in Canada: 'Roddy Bowen from the Canadian Rockies saluting Mountain Ash!' In Edmund's time, Mountain Ash was a hallowed place.

Another of the visitors to the City Walls was Vincent Lloyd-Jones QC, brother of the Reverend Dr Martyn Lloyd-Jones, the cardiologist turned evangelist and minister of Westminster Chapel for many years. Vincent, a former President of the Oxford Union, was a tolerant, broad-minded and cultured man. I once heard him say that he would gladly leave the Bar if he could spend the rest of his life conducting an orchestra. His son, David, realized that very ambition with great distinction. Vincent became a High Court judge in the Family Division where his humanity was much in evidence.

The third famed visitor was Elwyn Jones QC. Very much the lawyer-politician, Elwyn had been a junior member of the British prosecuting team in Nuremberg. After spending years in the political wilderness as a backbencher he became successively Attorney General and Lord Chancellor in the governments of Harold Wilson and James Callaghan. He was an able and urbane advocate.

Emlyn was still only in his early twenties at the time, but held his own with these brilliant men who were twice his age. Belonging to a somewhat later generation was Bill Mars Jones, who dominated the North Wales scene as a Junior, and, after taking silk in 1957, became an impressive leader until his elevation to the High Court in 1969. They all shared the same Welsh background and got on well. Looking back, it seems that the fifties were the beginning of a new era in the history of advocacy and of the judiciary on the Circuit. Advocates of our generation could not have had better role models.

As the general election of 1950 approached Emlyn had a stroke of luck. A substantial case of medical negligence against the Liverpool Regional Hospital Board was listed for hearing at Chester Assizes. A number of QCs had been retained for the various parties and the trial was scheduled to last for several weeks. Leading for the Board was Daniel Brabin QC, who seemed to have taken a shine to Emlyn in Liverpool. He was instrumental in persuading the Board's solicitors to instruct him as one of his juniors out of courtesy to the Circuit on which the case was being heard. Emlyn accepted the brief in the hope that he would be able to leave Chester no later than 5 p.m. every evening in order to address meetings in his constituency. I remember it well, for I had taken two weeks' leave from my National Service in the RAF in order to hold the fort night after night at every meeting until Emlyn arrived. I thoroughly enjoyed the experience, in part because the Liberal manifesto was so vague that I had *carte blanche* to say whatever I wished. The case was an ideal opportunity to enable Emlyn to get to know some of the leading lights on the Circuit, most of whom admired him for his courage and initiative in setting up on his own in Chester. Naturally, there was some criticism that 39 White Friars lacked the guidance and direction of a senior practitioner. But that was to underestimate Emlyn, for it soon became evident that his qualities far exceeded some of his seniors. Moreover, he did invite some of them to join him, but they had no wish to move.

Once Emlyn had established himself in No. 39, other newly called practitioners joined him, Roy Woolley in 1951 and David Trevor Lloyd Jones in 1953. It was understood between us that I would join him after completing my two years in the RAF, another two at Oxford, and a further period in London passing the Bar Final and doing a six months' pupillage. Even in our Aber days Emlyn used to pull my leg saying that by the time I had completed that programme he would have three or four years' experience under his belt, and would be able to take me on as his pupil. In fact, that is precisely what happened, as I still had six months to serve as a pupil when I moved to Chester in 1953. Some years later, while Emlyn was still there, two other young men joined us, Allen Phillips and Christopher (Kit) Bedingfield. Kit, who served his pupillage first with Emlyn and then with me, took silk in the 1970s, moved up to London and became a Bencher of Gray's Inn. His death as the age of sixty in 1996 was a great shock to us all. By his will he bequeathed to Gray's a substantial legacy to fund a number of valuable scholarships which bear his name. Emlyn delivered a moving tribute to Kit at his memorial at Gray's.

The life and soul of No. 39 was the Clerk, Bill Jones. He always spoke of chambers as 'the happy home' and it was a happy place. The Clerk will normally address you as 'Sir', but with the occasional lapse into familiarity. He will be your severest critic. In court he will stand somewhere in the wings watching you perform. He will know many solicitors who are never slow to praise or criticize as the case may be. He will have friends among the court staff and in the Press. Having formed his own impressions he will not hesitate to pass them on to you. We all benefited from Bill's comments.

I first met him in December 1950, at Emlyn and Shirley's wedding in Llanidloes. He was then a young man of about thirty-two – a perfect blend of Irish charm on his father's side and Welsh emotion on his mother's, with a strong underlay of Cestrian wisdom. He had a superb rapport with people. If he met the Archbishop of Canterbury the Archbishop would be 'my old son' in no time, and would not be offended. I have never known anyone who could project the warmth of his personality over the telephone as Bill did. None of us will ever forget the wealth of goodwill at the end of a telephone conversation: 'Bless your cotton socks, old lad. Look after yourself; and thanks a million.'

During the Second World War he served in the Middle East with the Cheshire Yeomanry, the noted regiment of cavalry. Much of his rich vocabulary, not to mention his practical psychology, was derived from his equestrian experience in the Yeomanry. If we should be waiting in court a long time for our case to come on, we would be 'champing on the bit'. If we lost a case he would console us by saying, 'Well, lad, you can't come without the horse.' Again, if a recalcitrant client refused to take advice, 'Well, lad, you can take a horse to water but . . .' His love of horses extended to the Chester Races where he was once mistaken for a dashing bookmaker from the Irish Republic.

If he thought any of us were showing signs of fatigue or irritation, he would prescribe either of two remedies, a 'new charabanc' or 'a new whistle'. And he practised what he preached. He ran the cutest little 'charabanc' – an open-top MG two-seater known to us all as 'The Red Devil'. He had a fabulous wardrobe of suits, shirts and ties for every occasion, and wore a red carnation in his lapel. Emlyn used to say that, when Bill accompanied him to Ede and Ravenscroft to be fitted for a silk gown, a full bottomed wig and all the other regalia, the tailor who greeted them was so impressed with Bill's sartorial elegance that he took it for granted that he was the future QC, and directed to him the time-honoured inquiry, 'May I be of service, Sir?'

The one thing that Bill loathed was the drudgery of sending out fee notes for work done. In the genteel world of his imagination fee notes should not be required, for, as in medieval times, a barrister should be entitled to rely on an honorarium freely given by a grateful client without any demand. Not everyone in Chambers went along with this quaint view of professional relationships in the second half of the twentieth century. Inevitably, the occasional friendly rebellion broke out, usually led by the redoubtable David Trevor Lloyd Jones. David, by far the most senior member in years in Chambers, was a kindly man at heart but outwardly an authoritarian figure known to us all as 'the Admiral' because he had been a Lieutenant Commander in the Royal Navy during the War, and, in the words of the Apocrypha, was a man 'imbued with the holy spirit of discipline'. For him life in the Law was inconceivable without a proper and efficient system of fee notes, and it did not help that he had, before the War, begun life in the bank. 'What's the Admiral trying to do?' cried Bill on one occasion, 'convert a civilized set of chambers into a debt collecting agency? I'd sooner go and sweep the streets of Chester than stoop to that.'

The esteem in which Emlyn held him is demonstrated by the efforts he made to persuade Bill to move up to his London chambers when he took silk in 1960, but because he was well entrenched in the life of Chester he refused. Right up to his death in 2005 at the age of 87 Emlyn and Shirley telephoned him every Sunday afternoon. I last saw him at the Countess Hospital in Chester a week or so before he died. He was weak and frail and kept lapsing into sleep. The tea lady came along. She approached the bed and in the sweetest of tones said, 'Hello, Bill, cup of tea, dear.' With that he sprang into life and for a couple of seconds it was all 'poppet' and 'darling' just like the Bill we used to know. As Emlyn was born to be an advocate, so Bill was born to be a star among clerks – incomparable, a man of his own time and place.

Advocacy, which is often defined as the art of persuasion, varies with age and experience, and sometimes with status and reputation. Never was Emlyn's advocacy the product of laborious preparation. That is not to say that he did not mull things over in his mind – he certainly did precisely that, and with some thoroughness – but he always left ample room for inspiration, spontaneity and flexibility. Indeed, it was in those vital qualities that he excelled. He was a gifted cross-examiner. Mr Justice Austin Jones once reproached a senior counsel in the middle of a tedious cross-examination. 'You're floundering, Mr So-and So,' he said, 'Haven't you yet learnt that you need a plan in cross-examination?' If Emlyn had a plan, which he probably did, it was only in the mind. His notes in a trial were unbelievably sparse. One good reason is that he was a painfully slow writer. It puzzled me that his hand did not begin to match his phenomenally quick mind. I can only speculate that a vague awareness of this incompatibility taught him to think everything through in his mind and to cultivate a retentive memory, invaluable assets for a successful advocate. Shortly after moving to Chester in 1953 I attended at the Assizes the hearing of a civil claim for damages for nuisance in the form of industrial contamination over a wide area. Emlyn was retained for the claimants and Daniel Brabin QC for the defendants. Brabin called an expert witness who was supposed to be a top-notcher in his field. Emlyn's cross-examination of him was so devastating that, when he sat down, Brabin asked the judge for a short adjournment. The judge passed down to Emlyn a confidential note with the one word 'splendid' written on it. Then Brabin, for the first time in the long history of this litigation, made an acceptable offer in settlement of the claim. That happy result was wholly due to Emlyn's cross-examination.

In a civil action a number of issues will often arise. In addressing the judge at the end, one possible course – the safe course – is to exhaust each and every one of them. In many cases what the judge is more likely to welcome is a focus in the closing submission on 'the bull point' in the case. What is vital, however, is that an advocate identifies the same 'bull point' as the judge himself has been groping towards for several days, if not weeks, in his own thinking. In this Emlyn was uncannily good. He was always alert to every word, reaction and gesture that might betray the judge's thinking, and, once he was sure of 'the bull point', he would focus on it for all he was worth.

It is one thing to appear in a civil case before a judge alone; it is another thing to appear in a criminal case before judge and jury. In his younger days at Chester Emlyn was adept at deploying his charm and good looks to the best advantage with the jury, and unquestionably his smile did have a magnetic quality. Closing speeches at the Bar are rarely specimens of classical oratory – if only because there is little time to prepare a speech that has to be delivered in the light of evidence which has only just been concluded. Emlyn had always been highly relevant and concise in his submissions in civil trials, and this had endeared him to judges. As he advanced in the Bar, these twin features became increasingly evident in his speeches to the jury in criminal trials. It is only after years of practice that one begins to realize that constant repetition in a long speech is usually less effective than a lucid presentation of key points in a short speech.

After about ten years the pressure of work on Emlyn at Chester became relentless. The only way to relieve it was to apply for silk. In the event, it was granted to him on his first application at the exceptionally early age of thirty-five. This meant that he would be able to rid himself of most of the paper work and concentrate on fewer but more substantial cases. Under the conventions that then applied, if one took silk in the provinces one was expected to move up to London. Thus it was that the whole family had to be uprooted, and the two young daughters, Sioned and Lowri, were both placed in the Welsh School, of which Emlyn became an enthusiastic supporter.

From the outset he flourished in silk. That is no mean achievement, especially considering that in silk a barrister is only entitled to appear in court with a junior whose fees are fixed as a proportion of one's own. Among the many criminal trials in which Emlyn appeared in silk was the Moors murder trial at Chester Assizes in which he represented Ian Brady. Although I met him frequently in the 1960s I cannot recall him ever discussing the case with me. The actor Emlyn Williams sat in the public gallery for three whole weeks listening to the case unfold and then wrote a book about it, a book called *Beyond Belief*. Perhaps these two words convey everything about the case. It was important in a case such as this one that the two accused were represented by the best counsel so that at the end of the day it would rightly be said not only that justice had been done but that it was manifestly seen to have been done by everyone concerned, including the accused themselves.

On the civil side Emlyn was often involved in heavy claims for damages for personal injuries. In order to encourage settlements the system permits defendants (and in practice this often means their insurers) to pay into court a sum of money in satisfaction of the claim, and, if the claimant recovers a lesser sum in damages, he will have to pay the cost of the defendants as well as his own from the date of the payment into court. The claimant's counsel has a daunting task in these situations. In some of them only a quantum of damages will be in dispute, but in others both liability and quantum. Sometimes there will be further negotiations in the robing room and in the corridors of the court before the hearing begins, but in some instances defendants will refuse to budge and simply rely on their payments into court. As it could be disastrous for a claimant to recover less than the amount paid in, nerves of steel are needed. Emlyn, to all appearances, never betrayed tension, doubt or weakness in such cases. What he used to do was to stipulate a settlement figure to his opponent with utter self-assurance and complete composure and then refuse to entertain any lesser figure. In nine cases out of ten, just as he was about to get up in court to open the case for the claimant, that settlement figure or a very close approximation to it would be offered. Part of the secret is to keep cool, but that is easier said than done!

Only two years after Emlyn took silk, Clement Davies QC, who had been Liberal MP for Montgomeryshire since 1929, died. Having married a Llanidloes girl and having shared a platform with Clement Davies many times, Emlyn by then was well-known in the county. Naturally, therefore, he was chosen as the prospective candidate in the parliamentary by-election, in which he doubled the majority gained in the previous general election. Shortly afterwards I attended a public inquiry at Porthmadog where one of my opponents was a Conservative MP who was also a planning silk. Over lunch one day he told me how thrilled he was to have been present in the House of Commons when Emlyn was introduced. 'It was wonderful,' he said, 'to see the youngest silk in the country walk in and take his place in the House, a spring in his step and a sparkle in his eye, like a breath of fresh air to waken us all up.'

As an MP he had the opportunity of seeking to reform the criminal law in which he had practised. One issue of great moment was capital punishment. The Homicide Act of 1957 had abolished it for some forms of murder but had retained it for others, namely, murder by poisoning, murder in pursuance or in furtherance of burglary or theft, and murder of a police officer or a prison warder. It was as a result of a private member's bill brought in 1965 by Sidney Silverman, a Labour MP and a prominent Liverpool solicitor, that capital punishment was abolished for murder generally. It so happened that back in 1954 Emlyn and I had been involved in a murder case which, as he told me many times, had convinced him that the threat of capital punishment did not deter some people from committing murder, but did cause them untold agony and torment for weeks or months as they awaited their fate in the solitude of the condemned cell. It was a case in which an essentially decent hard-working man had been caught up in the storm of the world. Foolishly, he had brought with him from his place of work a marlinspike, as he maintained, only to frighten his girlfriend. As happens so often, a rousing temper caused him to bring down the spike, but, as the girl's mother stepped in to shield her, it was she, not the girl, who received the fatal blow. In panic he ran out of the house, and as he was about to throw himself into the Mersey a passing police officer saved him. It was plain that the death penalty had not deterred him from taking the marlinspike home, or, in the event, from using it. But when the realization of what he had done dawned on him in prison he suffered the most alarming spasms, as we witnessed when we saw him in conference in the cells at Chester Castle. He was convicted, sentenced to death, and in due course executed. I had to take his two sisters to see him in his cell after he had been sentenced. They were both sobbing. 'What are you crying for?' he asked, 'I'm the one who has to hang, not you.' That was the last I saw of him. It came as no surprise to me that Emlyn supported Silverman's bill and much later opposed another bill brought by Duncan Sandys to restore capital punishment.

We were concerned for the defence in another murder case which had an indirect bearing on the effect of capital punishment as a deterrent. The accused, a woman in her early thirties, had arranged a rendezvous with the wife of the man with whom she had been carrying on a clandestine relationship for four years. The wife turned up in her Mini car. As she walked up some steps near the accused's home, the accused struck her a series of violent blows with a sledgehammer, and she died from her injuries. The accused put her in the boot of the Mini and drove it a distance of twelve miles in snow and ice. Then she abandoned the car with its headlights on and walked back the whole of that distance wearing her fur coat. As the heavy falls of snow that night had obliterated the forensic evidence, a week elapsed before the police were able to arrest her. They held her under interrogation all night. At 5.45 a.m. she asked the interrogating officer, 'If I confess to murder will I hang?' He replied, 'As an Englishman to an Englishwoman I assure you that you will not hang.' He was right. It was 1963, and the Homicide Act of 1957 was still in force, and the kind of murder she had committed was not one of those for which the death penalty had been retained. She then made a full confession of murder and was sentenced to life imprisonment. This was yet another case where the death penalty had been no deterrent before the murder but where it clearly operated on the accused's mind afterwards, as her question plainly showed.

After his death Emlyn was called a legal conservative. Save for his supporting the abolition of the death penalty, that description is strictly correct. But in fairness to him one needs to look at things in context, for he was no reactionary, as that term is usually understood in legal and penal terms. Following the abolition of the death penalty several measures were introduced to facilitate convictions in serious cases. One was to allow verdicts by a majority of ten where juries were unable to return unanimous verdicts. Another was the abolition of a defendant's right to challenge up to three members of the jury without giving a reason. Yet another was to permit a judge in certain circumstances to comment on a defendant's failure to give evidence. Emlyn opposed these on the grounds that they deprived the subject of historic rights and took us down a slippery slope. It was not his conservatism which lay behind his opposition to these measures but rather his Liberal Radicalism.

The loss of Montgomeryshire in the Thatcher avalanche of 1979 was a devastating blow after seventeen years in the Commons. But he was not a man to stay in the doldrums for long. In retrospect, one of the best things that happened to him was his elevation to the House of Lords. Sometimes people ask why he did not then become a High Court judge, for, in terms of ability, experience and personal qualities he was well fitted for that role. Moreover, he had a good springboard for it, in that he had held the prestigious Recorderships of Merthyr Tudful and Swansea. He was highly respected in the Law: he had served on the Bar Council and presided over Gray's Inn for a term in the revered office of Treasurer – an office that meant a great deal to him as so many Welshmen had received their legal education at Gray's over the centuries. There are many able men who find complete fulfilment on the Bench, where they discharge one of the highest, if not the highest, duties in the land, and where they have the opportunity of contributing to the organic growth of the Law. But there is a world of difference between holding part-time judicial posts, no matter how august, and committing oneself to a full-time permanent post in which one has to forsake many other interests, including, as I need hardly state, politics. Throughout the years that I knew him Emlyn never disclosed to me an ambition to go on the Bench. I suspect that he would not have relished what he might well have regarded as the daily tedium of deciding one case after another for maybe fifteen or twenty years. Emlyn had a broad compass. He was forever looking for something new. Even in his busy days as a junior barrister in Chester he was fascinated by the sheer challenge of trying to rescue Gwasg Gee, a printing and publishing house that was a bastion of Welsh literature then unable to pay its way. Although he knew nothing about publishing he succeeded for a time. The campaign for a Welsh Parliament in the 1950s was another diversion to which he devoted much of his time. In the Commons, and later in the Lords, the scope for new pastures multiplied. He found them irresistible, and in each gave a good account of himself. Although they were only remotely connected with the Law, I believe that his legal instinct and experience, not to mention his understanding of people from the practice of advocacy, played a significant part in the success of all the things he undertook.

And so, in Emlyn's case, as in the case of other lawyer politicians, at the end of a long and illustrious career, it is tempting to ask which came first, the Law or politics. Young people are sometimes drawn to the Law because they see it as an avenue into politics. Emlyn began with a firm political conviction which stayed with him all his life. Equally he was blessed from the start with great forensic gifts. What one can say is that he led a full and happy life moving freely from one sphere to the other, exploring them all in a spirit of true enterprise. He was his own man, and none of us can forget him.

NOTES

I. ON BUYING 39 WHITE FRIARS *by D. Ll. M.*

On the 8th of June 2000 E. H. wrote to Robin Spencer QC of Upton, Chester, who had written to him some time before asking him to set down his recollections of opening the chambers at 39 White Friars, which subsequently became Spencer's Sedan House. The main point E. H. made in that letter was that he financed 'the start' of chambers 'by using my advocacy on the bank manager of Barclays Bank, Denbigh'. That was a time 'when local bank managers had much more authority and discretion than they have now and he was well disposed towards me and was a friend of my old schoolmaster and of my father ... when I put to him that I wanted to put £1,000 on overdraft to open a chambers to start at the Bar, he had little concept of what it was all about and the risks he was taking. However, he told me that not one of the Hoosons had ever let him down so far and naïvely thought I would succeed.' By the end of that financial year E. H. 'had a large outstanding fee from the first big negligence case in the country under the National Health Service' [to which Eifion Roberts refers above], a 'large outstanding fee' which enabled him to pay off all his debts and move into 'the very nice house on City Walls' where the family lived for the rest of their time in Chester.

2. ON TAKING SILK *by E. H.*

I had never hidden the fact that my main aim was a political career, and I thought I might have an important part in re-establishing the Liberal Party in the United Kingdom. Although always attracted to the Bar, it was largely as a way for a man with no private means to earn an income that would finance a political career. My political aspirations had a fair part to play in my decision to turn down offers of chambers in London and Liverpool to go to Chester. After fighting an election during my pupillage in 1950 and then another after only one year in practice in 1951, I gave my Clerk Bill Jones a solemn promise that I would not seek to fight another election until after I'd taken silk. This was a great spur to me to concentrate on my practice although for most of the years between 1953 and 1960 I was the Chairman of the Liberal Party in Wales.

However, I did concentrate on my legal practice, and it grew greatly. According to the clerks' gossip, my earnings in my first year of practice were a record for the Bar, and certainly for any circuit practitioner. The year ending the 30th of September 1959 I realized that I had a large enough practice to justify an application for silk. The actual initiative or push to apply (which I barely needed) came from an unexpected quarter. Mr Justice Edmund Davies, as he then was, was sitting as a civil judge in Chester, and Mr Justice Pearson who was sitting in charge of the criminal list there accompanied him. Edmund was a supporter and confidant of mine, and I had appeared once or twice before

Pearson in civil cases off Circuit. That autumn I appeared before him in several difficult cases, including defending a woman for murder. She was acquitted, and I obviously made an impression on him. He asked Edmund to invite me to dinner at the Judges' Lodgings along with Elwyn Jones QC who was a great friend of mine. After dinner Pearson took me for a walk and asked me whether I'd considered putting in for silk. He didn't think my youth – I was only thirty-four – was an impediment. He also told me that he'd discussed the matter with Edmund, and then offered to be one of my sponsors, with Edmund, if I did put in for it. Later on, I think by telephone, Edmund suggested that as I was young and had only nine years' experience in practice it might be as well if I had somebody from the Court of Appeal and possibly the House of Lords to support me. He mentioned John Willie (as we called him), Lord Morris of Borth-y-gest, before whom I'd regularly appeared at the Quarter Sessions at Caernarfon and once or twice in the Lords where he was a Law Lord. I'd also done a fair amount of work before Lord Justice Sellers. I immediately got in touch with both. So, my array of backers were very substantial people, and this no doubt helped.

The Lord Chancellor of the day was Viscount Kilmuir, formerly Sir David Maxwell Fyfe QC, an old Northern Circuiteer and in the distant past a member of the chambers in Liverpool in which I had spent my pupillage. Although I had never met him, *circa* 1958 I had defended an old friend of his from student days, at a police court in Corwen, where he had been involved in a collision with a local railway delivery lorry. An Edinburgh solicitor and his agent in Liverpool (an English solicitor) accompanied the client in a chauffeur-driven Bentley and picked me up at Chester to conduct the case. It had snowed for a week or more and snowploughs had dug a route through. My recollection is that the client had been charged with dangerous or careless driving, and the chief witness was the very comical driver of the railway lorry. When I managed to get on the right side of him he conceded that he and not my client in his Bentley might well be the one to blame for the accident. That, of course, was the end of the case.

On the way back to Chester we stopped at a number of hostelries to celebrate – my client was the chairman of a big brewery or distilling company in Scotland – and it was over a drink or two that he told me it was Maxwell Fyfe who had suggested that he should get a Welsh barrister to defend him, and, if possible, that he should seek to brief me. I presume Maxwell Fyfe had received this recommendation through the old chambers in Liverpool. As young men my client and he had shared lodgings in Liverpool. There, Maxwell Fyfe had married Rex Harrison's sister and my client had married the daughter of the owner of a Liverpool brewery, also (I believe) related to Rex Harrison.

I mention these matters because sometimes I wonder if they had anything to do with my being preferred to other applicants for silk who were all substantially senior to me and who had been in practice for very much longer. On the other hand, I know I had the highest earnings on the Circuit and that the Lord Chancellor's Department discreetly used to enquire about them. The great day came and I saw mine as the last name in a list of twenty silks published a few days after my thirty-fifth birthday.

3. ON THE NATURE OF EVIL: The Moors Case *by E. H.*

The firm that retained me to lead for the defence of Ian Brady in the Moors murder case was the well-regarded firm of Bostock, Yates and Chronnell of Hyde which, when I was a Junior, had briefed me in a variety of civil as well as criminal cases. It so happened that at the time I was in the midst of a general election campaign to try and retain my seat in Montgomeryshire, and knew nothing about the case until my wife one evening told me that Charlie, my Chief Clerk in London, had telephoned to say that I'd been retained on Brady's behalf. Although I vaguely knew that there was a gruesome case coming up, I'm afraid the news meant little to me, for, quite like a number of others in my profession, I never did read newspaper reports of crime or of trials after my first couple of years at the Bar. Election day was the 31st of March 1966, and until that day I had thoughts for nothing but the campaign.

However, late in the evening of the day it had been announced that I had been retained, David T. Lloyd Jones, my appointed Junior, telephoned me in a state of some excitement. David was a very capable and experienced counsel but was rather prone to dramatize events. After telling me a little about the nature of the case he implored me to drop everything and ask the solicitor to arrange an immediate consultation for us with Brady at Strangeways Prison, Manchester. I very coolly said that there was no reason for that at all at this stage, for we had not even received a Brief, and that we should treat this case like every other. He rejoined by telling me that I had been briefed to defend in 'The Case of the Century'. Needless to say, we did not have the consultation until well after the election, and we had plenty of time to read and digest the thoroughly prepared brief sent to us by Mr Fitzpatrick the solicitor. We had time also to discuss matters with the barristers retained to defend Myra Hindley, Brady's accomplice: they were Godfrey Heilpern QC and his Junior, Philip Curtess.

In the meantime I'd asked Mr Fitzpatrick to arrange for Brady to be examined as to his mental condition. The examination was carried out by a very distinguished pathologist, Professor W. L. Neustatter. I had also discussed with Godfrey Heilpern the possibility of raising a defence of *folie à deux* – that Hindley, completely besotted by Brady, was the victim of a referred madness. To our knowledge this defence had never been raised in this country, but had been raised successfully in France and unsuccessfully in the United States. In order to establish such a defence it would be necessary for my team to produce cogent evidence that Brady was insane and for Hindley's barristers to produce evidence that she, because of her uncritical adoration of him, had absorbed his approach but did not have the necessary criminal intent to murder. This would have been a novel point in the history of criminal law in this country, but of course it was never raised because the basic evidence was never available.

When Brady was finally introduced to David Lloyd Jones and me, my immediate mental response was to think how ordinary a person he was. He was polite, quietly spoken, and had a rather staccato, precise turn of phrase; and he looked one straight in the eye. There was no indication that he was a man who had committed inhuman crimes on children. Whilst he did not initiate any conversation himself, he listened intently to what I had to say to him and in response made three matters absolutely plain. First, that although he appreciated the weight and the strength of the evidence against him and the defence's difficulty in not having answers to the most vital questions, he would not contemplate pleading guilty to any of the charges. Second, that on no account was I to raise directly or indirectly the possibility of a verdict with regard to him of 'Guilty but insane'. Third, that, subject to the above, his instructions to us were simply to do everything we could to assist the defence of Hindley and try to get her acquittal. In contrast to the virile, totally aggressive and frightening side of his personality which he demonstrated at one stage in the trial (in the absence of the jury), when discussing with us the points raised by the evidence amassed by the prosecution he showed no animation whatsoever.

Even at that first meeting I concluded that here was a totally amoral person, seemingly unmoved when reminded of normal human concerns about his allegedly brutal and horrific behaviour. He gave the impression not just of his indifference to any moral considerations but also of a lack of understanding what these were and how they could be of relevance to him.

In the course of my professional life I have been involved in a fairly large number of murder cases, sometimes for the prosecution, sometimes for the defence. In the former case, one's contact with the accused is confined to cross-examining them and occasionally catching their eye when they are in the dock. In the latter case, one sees much more of them, through consultations, examining them, discussing notes of instruction, and representing them. I can think of no case, except for a couple of undoubted insanities, where I have not established a wavelength of communication with the accused, except in Brady's case where all my efforts to penetrate his indifferent, cold exterior failed.

Because of the alarming and horrific nature of the case and the enormous public interest which it aroused, the then Attorney-General Sir Elwyn Jones QC rightly decided to lead for the prosecution himself. William Mars Jones QC and Ronald Waterhouse assisted him. It so happened that they were all members of the Wales and Chester Circuit, as David Lloyd Jones and I were, and we were all very good friends. And I think it is fair to say that there was complete candour between all the counsel in the case. Elwyn Jones invited the defence teams to look at any documents they wished and ensured that every facility was available to us. Indeed, he showed me various reports on Brady which never saw the light of day, reports that showed him to have plumbed all the depths of depravity but that he too had had horrific experiences as a Borstal boy.

A number of authors have commented on the case and the trial. I particularly remember Pamela Hansford Johnson and Emlyn Williams following the trial avidly from the press box at Chester Assizes. The latter had always had a great interest in the morbid and darker side of human nature as one of his early plays, *Night Must Fall*, demonstrates. Now he was writing a book called *Beyond Belief*, based on much research on Brady's boyhood. When it was published he sent me a copy inscribed with these words, 'I un Emlyn oddi wrth un arall' ('To one Emlyn from another'). I didn't read it, but out of politeness glanced at it quickly before writing to thank him for it.

There is no doubt about Brady's intellectual pretensions. He had read, or at least scanned, a considerable number of books on Fascism and Nazism, biographies of the more brutal political leaders of the twentieth century, and other books on sex and violence. The work that seemed to have influenced him most, and the only work in his library I felt that I ought to read in order to try and understand him better, was one of Marquis de Sade's – the confessions of a wealthy, corrupt, cruel aristocrat who indulged in sadistic practices because they brought him pleasure and rewarding sensations. The crazy thing about Brady is that he took this very seriously, and, in one of his few volunteered observations to me, said with great conviction that de Sade was a great philosopher whom few understood.

The judge who tried the case was Mr Justice Fenton Atkinson, a fine man, a devout Christian of high intellectual calibre, and very civilized. He was always polite and courteous to everyone, including Brady and Hindley, but he only allowed matters which were really relevant to the case to be canvassed, and relied on counsel not to protract proceedings with matters which might be of interest to the lurid press but which had no relevance in establishing the guilt or innocence of the accused. However there was one awful occasion when I received a note from my instructing solicitor informing me that Brady would not admit that the shrouded body found on the Moors was as described in the evidence, and insisted on its production. We asked the judge for an adjournment and went to see Brady, who, totally pigheadedly, insisted that it was his right to have this shroud produced. I told him that I could not accept his instruction, and that I might have to leave the case. He simply grunted. When I went to see Mr Justice Fenton Atkinson and explained the situation to him, he very quietly said, 'I perfectly well know how you feel, Emlyn, but for heaven's sake don't leave this case. If he wants it produced, let it be produced.' As it happened, it was passed out of court in about half a minute. But Brady's irrational insistence on seeking the production of that exhibit illustrates the strange personality with whom we were dealing.

POLITICS

THE LAST BASTION: The Liberal Tradition in Montgomeryshire, 1880–1979

David M. Roberts

The 1880 general election in Montgomeryshire began innocently enough. Charles Wynn expected to retain the seat for the Tories. After all, he had been unopposed in 1868 and 1874, and the Wynns had secured unbroken parliamentary representation in the county since 1799. They were the most dominant of all the Tory landowning dynasties in Wales. And for most of the nineteenth century, Montgomeryshire had presented an outward appearance of calm and contented deference. There were cultural and socioeconomic crosscurrents in the county – between the western, more sparsely populated Welsh-speaking areas and those nearest the border with England, and between Anglicans and Nonconformists – but conflict rarely surfaced. Industrialisation, which together with the growth of Nonconformity had prompted upheaval in other parts of Wales, barely touched Montgomeryshire. Unrest had broken out only sporadically: riots in Newtown and Abermule in 1819 and a few Chartist disturbances in 1839. Agriculture was the main source of employment. Times may not have been easy, but the majority of tenant farmers and agricultural workers impassively accepted their lot.

In fact, a remarkable break with the past was about to occur, though it took a curious Liberal standard-bearer to break the Conservative stranglehold on the county. Stuart Rendel was a forty-six-year-old English businessman: wealthy, Anglican, a resident of Kensington, a product of Eton and Oxford and a partner in an armaments firm, he did not seem a natural champion of the Welsh tenant farmer. Indeed, Rendel, who accepted an invitation to stand as the Liberal candidate in 1878, considered himself an unusual candidate. He decided to present himself as a 'mysterious stranger', a 'liberator', 'a *deus ex machina*', a friend of the oppressed farmers, within Gladstone's broad 'Peace, Retrenchment & Reform' platform.

The contest was a stormy one. Towards the end of March 1880 Rendel struggled to address a large group in Llanfair Caereinion above shrill barracking. On the 27th of March Wynn's meeting in Llanidloes was persistently interrupted. In early April tempers reached boiling point. A Liberal meeting in the Tory stronghold of Welshpool had to resort to admission by ticket to avert the threat of disturbance. The tactic did not forestall trouble. A large crowd jostled David Davies of Llandinam as he left the hall, while Denbighshire's MP, George Osborne Morgan, was mobbed, though he escaped with nothing worse that the loss of his hat.

There is little doubt that the Tories sensed a real challenge to their authority for the first time, though they still expected to win. Rendel put his heart and soul (and some finance) into the fight, travelling the length and breadth of this large constituency to speak to tenant farmers, tradesmen and freeholders. After a tumultuous campaign, Rendel and the Liberals carried the day by 191 votes out of a total of 4,273 cast. The reign of the great Wynn family was over, and Rendel captured – in Gladstone's words – a 'virgin fortress'. It was unquestionably an historic victory, and it lived long in political folklore in the county. Fifty years later local people could recall the torch-lit processions, the victor's carriage hauled with long ropes by hundreds of willing hands. *The Cambrian News* surmised, with some prescience, that the result 'seals the doom of Toryism in the county for many a long year to come'. The seat was to remain in Liberal hands for the next ninety-nine years.

It is tempting to conclude that this was the beginning of a great Liberal tradition in Montgomeryshire, the sweeping away of one political establishment, to be replaced by another. Montgomeryshire was to be the only seat in England and Wales that remained constantly Liberal as the strange death of Liberal Wales and England took place after 1918. After the Second World War the decline became acute. In general elections between 1945 and 1974, the Liberal Party never won more than twelve seats in the whole of the UK. In the late 1960s and early 1970s Montgomeryshire was the only Liberal-held seat in Wales. Yet the true picture of Montgomeryshire's Liberal politics in the twentieth century is more complex, and to understand it fully it is necessary to examine the careers and electoral fortunes of the Liberal representatives in Parliament from 1880 to 1979.

Notwithstanding the Liberal Party's dominance in Wales after 1880, the flame, which Stuart Rendel lit in Montgomeryshire that year, was constantly flickering. He was to have a distinguished career, and he became the acknowledged 'leader' of the 'Welsh Party' in Parliament. He championed the cause of both the University College of Wales in Aberystwyth and of the National Library of Wales, giving land for its construction. He was personally close to Gladstone – his daughter married Gladstone's third son – and he was to be a pallbearer at the great statesman's funeral. High office eluded him, but he was held by almost everyone in the highest regard. Yet he was to fight three more elections in Montgomeryshire before he retired to the House of Lords in 1894, and in none was his position secure.

Of course, the Tories hoped and planned to regain the seat. Moreover, it should be recalled that until 1918 a second seat – Montgomery Boroughs – existed, and that it was more often in the Tory hands than Liberal. In 1885, the Newtown entrepreneur Pryce Pryce-Jones won Montgomery Boroughs back for the Conservatives, and although Rendel increased his majority in Montgomeryshire he clearly felt his hold on the seat was precarious. In the 1886 election, when Gladstone's conversion to Irish Home Rule pitchforked the British people into the polling booths again, Rendel pinned his faith on an electoral pact which would see him unopposed in the county seat if the Tories were given a free run in Montgomery Boroughs. He had expended much energy (120 meetings across the county) and considerable finance in consolidating his position, but he feared defeat. Rendel was crestfallen when the proposed electoral arrangement collapsed, and was close to standing down: 'I hold the seat only by extraordinary exertions . . .' he grumbled privately.

As it happened, Rendel held on with a reduced majority, and in 1892 increased it to over 800, but when he retired two years later his successor only narrowly (by 225 votes) held off a Wynn challenge in the by-election. Arthur Humphreys-Owen was one of Montgomeryshire's few Liberal landowners. A barrister, educated at Harrow and Cambridge, he had inherited the Glansevern estate at Berriew, and had been a strong supporter of Rendel, and Chairman of Montgomeryshire County Council. Like Rendel, he was deeply concerned with Welsh education, and higher education in particular. However, he did not have Rendel's charisma or crusading zeal; he rather had the air of a well-to-do intellectual. Just over a year after the by-election, when Rosebury's government fell and a general election was called in July 1895, the Tory campaign in Montgomeryshire, spearheaded by Robert Wynn, stormed through the county. They put considerable resource into the contest (they had far more carriages than the Liberals), and held between forty and fifty meetings. It should be recognized too that the Wynn family was certainly not hated in the county, and the land question was now not quite the flashpoint it once had been. A Land Commission report in 1896 showed a notable lack of disgruntlement amongst tenant farmers in Montgomeryshire. In the country as a whole the Liberals were unceremoniously ejected from office in 1895, but in Montgomeryshire Humphreys-Owen somehow clung on by just twenty-seven votes. 'What a debacle!' was his despairing verdict.

Humphreys-Owen was a respected and reliable Liberal loyalist: he supported Irish Home Rule, he opposed Balfour's Education Act, and was passionately pro-Boer in 1900 – when he was opposed again in Montgomeryshire in the Khaki election by Robert Wynn, even though the latter was on active service in South Africa. Wynn received letters of support during the election from both Balfour and Joseph Chamberlain. *The Times* thought 'a close contest' possible: in the event Humphreys-Owen increased his majority, but only to 264. He had ploughed a hard furrow in the county for just over ten years, and sadly he died just before the great Liberal election victory of 1906.

Yet again the Liberals turned to a prominent, wealthy family in the county. David Davies – grandson of 'Top Sawyer', the first Welsh industrial tycoon who had built a fortune in railway construction and coal mining – was twenty-six years old and had been educated at Merchiston Castle, Edinburgh, and Cambridge. His father had died when David was eighteen, propelling the young David Davies at an early age into business and public service. He was adopted in 1906 as the Liberal candidate in Montgomeryshire (his grandfather had been a Liberal MP), but the key feature of Davies's political views was that they were not necessarily tied to the party line. He had maverick tendencies from a party point of view, and was never afraid to speak his mind. Given his background and the mood of the times, it was perhaps not surprising that David Davies was elected unopposed in Montgomeryshire in 1906, and although he was to hold the seat for twenty-three years – covering seven general elections – it was contested on only two occasions.

David Davies's political career was decidedly erratic. He was a close associate of Lloyd George, and became his parliamentary private secretary in June 1916. When Lloyd George became Prime Minister in December 1916 (and Davies had played some part in the moves to replace Asquith), David Davies at the age of thirty-six was rewarded with a position in Lloyd George's secretariat (the 'garden suburb', as it was known). But this was not to be a springboard for a dazzling political career. Davies was never reticent about entering a quarrel with anyone, and he took his self-appointed role as the Prime Minister's 'candid friend' too far, advising him in June 1917 that his stock was 'tumbling down'. Lloyd George promptly dispensed with David Davies's services and their relationship never recovered. Davies was issued with the Coalition 'coupon' in 1918, but he rejected it and was returned unopposed again in Montgomeryshire.

In any event, Davies always felt he had wider concerns. After the First World War he campaigned relentlessly for a more internationalist policy, and was instrumental in establishing in Wales a League of Nations Union with many active branches. He was a generous supporter of the University College of Wales, Aberystwyth, and in 1919 he endowed a Chair in International Politics in Aberystwyth – the first of its kind anywhere in the world. He was to serve as President of the University from 1929 to 1944 – though this relationship had its ups and downs. He also provided scholarships for Montgomeryshire school children, founded hospitals, launched the Welsh National Memorial Association, and was involved in the creation of the National Library of Wales. He was the most conspicuous Welsh philanthropist of the age, and his personal position in Montgomeryshire and in Wales generally was unassailable. However, his strictly political achievements were limited, and whether he played any role in consolidating the Liberal hold on the seat is somewhat doubtful. In 1927, David Davies, dismayed at Lloyd George's leadership of the Liberal Party, announced that he would not seek re-election.

The 1929 general election was to mark the most potent challenge for thirty years to the Liberal Party in Montgomeryshire. It was the first contested election there since 1910, and the first since the 'Boroughs' became part of the constituency in 1918. Moreover, the Conservatives selected a strong and popular local candidate, Murray Naylor. In 1928 the Liberals finally chose their representative. Clement Davies, a forty-five-year-old Cambridge-educated lawyer from Llanfyllin, was a reluctant politician. The Law was his first love, and he had spurned the opportunity to stand for Parliament in Montgomery Boroughs and in Oswestry before he eventually succumbed to political persuasions and ambition. Added to this, the Liberal Party organization in the country – lulled into a state of torpor because of the lack of electoral contests – gave cause for concern. There were many who felt that the Liberals held the seat only because of David Davies's good public works. Nor was it clear that David Davies approved of the choice of his successor. He actually would have preferred another candidate, W. A. Jehu, but the county's Liberals unanimously selected Clement Davies. Although he had dithered over standing, once selected he threw himself into the fray with spirit. He was helped by the Conservative government's unimpressive record on agriculture. 1927 had been one of the wettest years on record in Wales, resulting in a poor harvest, and Davies (a Welsh-speaker) received much support from farmers, particularly in the Welsh-speaking areas of the county. Nevertheless, the result was uncertain right up to polling day in May 1929. When it was declared, Clement Davies had triumphed over the Conservative Naylor by just over 2,000 votes.

Clement Davies was to hold Montgomeryshire for the next thirty-three years, was to become leader of his party and was to play a much more significant role in British political life than has been generally appreciated. Yet he also led a chequered political career, and the notion of a strengthening Liberal tradition in the county from 1930 to 1960 remained a fragile one.

Clement Davies entered Parliament with hope as one of a small band of fifty-nine Liberals, but he quickly became disillusioned. Tensions with Lloyd George surfaced, Unilever offered him a position of managing director of the company and in September 1930 Davies told his local Liberal Association that he would not stand again at the next general election. They duly selected a new candidate, C. P. Williams, and Clement Davies's brief flirtation with politics appeared to be at an end. No one had bargained, however, for the great political and economic crisis of 1931. As it deepened, and Ramsay MacDonald formed a National Government (which Clement Davies supported) and a general election was called, the political landscape became utterly transformed. In a flurry of activity, Unilever released Davies from his commitment with them, C. P. Williams gracefully stood down, and Clement Davies was returned to Parliament unchallenged in October 1931 – as a Liberal National, rather than a Liberal, MP.

Clement Davies attracted considerable hostility over the events of 1931 and in subsequent years, but he remained a steadfast 'Liberal National' – supporting the governments of MacDonald, Baldwin and Chamberlain – for most of the decade, even after the Liberal Party had crossed the floor of the House and joined the opposition. The Liberal Association in Montgomeryshire was affiliated neither to the Liberal National nor the Liberal Party organizations, and in fact the local party machinery again fell into decline. There were ideological tensions too within the Montgomeryshire Liberal community, particularly over Clement Davies's support for rearmament. At one point in 1935, after a bout of ill health, Davies again considered retirement from politics and local support seemed in doubt. The counsel of senior colleagues prevailed, however: 'he is too good a colleague to lose' wrote Sir John Simon. In the event, in the 1935 general election he was again returned unopposed.

But rearmament remained a bone of contention. In late 1938, while Davies was out of the country, a partial revolt was staged in Montgomeryshire. In December, a meeting of the local party declared its wish to be affiliated to the independent Liberal Party, even though its MP was a Liberal National. David Davies, now Lord Davies of Llandinam, and still a force in the county, was at the heart of the mutiny. In the same month, he wrote to his successor as Montgomeryshire's MP – who was in Africa – attempting to persuade him to resign as a Liberal National supporter of the government. On the same day, the *Western Mail* reported rumours that Lord Davies's son intended to stand against Clement Davies at the next election. Not surprisingly, this all drew an angry response from the sitting MP ('Call your caucus. Do as you like' he wrote back to Lord Davies – although the letter was never actually sent). And after a tense meeting of the local party at Lord Davies's house in January 1939, which Clement Davies's wife attended, the storm blew over.

As it happened, the international situation was becoming worryingly grave. Having voted in favour of the Munich Agreement in 1938, Davies became convinced of the inevitability of war, and of the total unfitness of the government to wage war successfully when it was finally declared in September 1939. In December 1939, pleasing the Montgomeryshire Liberals at last, he resigned as a Liberal National, became one of Neville Chamberlain's mordant critics, and in May 1940 he was to play a critical role in the events which led to the removal of Chamberlain and his replacement by Churchill. From an early stage, however, he was also disappointed with Churchill's government, and became a strong but measured critic (or 'candid friend' as Harold Macmillan labelled him). In August 1942 Davies rejoined the Liberal Party, began associating with a 'Radical Action' group within the Party and astutely stood in 1945 as a 'Liberal & Radical' candidate.

Clement Davies's political journey to 1945 was in many ways symptomatic of the decline of the old Liberal Party. He was, without question, an independently minded MP. As he said when he became a candidate in 1927, referring to his support for Lloyd George whom he much admired: 'I am not an out and out supporter of anyone, I will test them by their measures'. What no one could deny, however, was Clement Davies's dedication to his const-ituents and to Wales. He understood the issues affecting people's lives in mid-Wales, and particularly the acute problem of rural depopulation. In the first three decades of the twentieth century, the population of Montgomery-shire declined by 11.6% – a much greater decrease than in Meirionnydd or Ceredigion. He drew attention to this time and again in Parliament. 'He always used to talk about "my people, my county",' recalled Labour's James Griffiths many years later. In 1937 Davies was invited by the government to chair a committee of enquiry into tuber-culosis in Wales, and his report in 1939 was a shocking revelation of wretched social and economic conditions in

Wales, and a powerful indictment of local government. It had a major impact. Not everyone appreciated the criticisms in the report, but its appearance greatly enhanced Clement Davies's reputation.

For the first time since entering Parliament sixteen years earlier, Davies faced an electoral contest in Montgomeryshire in 1945. Labour decided not to oppose the Liberal & Radical candidate, and Davies won reasonably comfortably by over 3,000 votes. But the Liberal Party nationally was decimated, returning just twelve members. Moreover, they were a somewhat motley crew, and with the party leader, Sinclair, defeated it was little surprise that the eldest of the group – Clement Davies – was elected Leader of the Party (or Chairman of the Parliamentary Liberal Party, as he was initially described). For the next ten years, Davies led a national party fighting for survival. The Liberal Party's fundamental challenge – determining where they stood in the political spectrum – was brought into sharp focus by the emergence of a reforming, majority Labour government, and Davies faced constant reproaches from both the left and right of the party. In the 1950 general election Clement Davies privately feared that he would lose Montgomeryshire, though in the event he increased his majority to over 6,000. 'I am frankly surprised at my return,' he wrote privately. In fact, he remained safe in the county as the number of Liberal MPs declined even further, though he was assisted by Conservative support in the elections of 1951 and 1955. It was a testing period nationally, but Davies refused to align the Liberals with any other party (even declining the offer of office in Churchill's 1951 government) and steadfastly maintained the Liberals as an independent party. Throughout his career he had also battled personal and health problems. In 1956, in a surprise move, Davies relinquished the leadership at the Party Conference. 'The Liberal Party owes you an immense debt of gratitude for your unselfish work,' wrote Clement Attlee privately. In the 1959 general election, facing a Tory opponent, and with the Liberal Party plumbing new depths in Wales, his majority in Montgomeryshire slumped to 2,970 – the smallest since his election in 1929. In fact, it was to be Clement Davies's last campaign. In May 1960, at the age of seventy-five he decided not to stand again for Parliament, and just under two years later he died in a London clinic.

There were interesting nominations to succeed Clement Davies which hinted at dynastic tendencies within the Party in Montgomeryshire. Two sons of Lord Davies, and Clement Davies's son, Stanley, were among the names put forward. In fact, no one had more appropriate credentials to succeed Clement Davies and represent the Liberals in Montgomeryshire than Emlyn Hooson. A farmer's son from Denbighshire, he had studied Law at Aberystwyth, been called to the Bar in 1949, and had stood (unsuccessfully) for the Liberals in Conway (as it was then called) in 1950 and 1951. Moreover, in 1950 he married Shirley Hamer, daughter of Sir George and Lady Hamer of Llanidloes, the staunchest of the county's prominent Liberals. For the next seventeen years, he was to be a lawyer by profession, a politician by occupation, and a farmer by inclination.

What Hooson experienced in Montgomeryshire, how-ever, was a situation which none of his Liberal predecessors had faced. At every election from April 1962 until May 1979 (seven in total) he faced three opponents. In the by-lection following Davies's death in 1962, Hooson polled exceptionally strongly and secured a majority of 7,549 over his Conservative challenger and 51.3% of the vote. It was to be his largest majority, but by no means had he felt certain of victory. In succeeding elections he won with lesser majorities – with slightly greater reductions in general elections in which the Conservatives did well. Few could match his success or effectiveness as a Liberal member, however. For a period, in the late 1960s and early 1970s, he was the sole parliamentary representative of Welsh Liberalism.

Although sometimes depicted by English colleagues as a conservative-minded Liberal, Emlyn Hooson's politics had a strong radical hue, particularly in social and economic policy. As a youngster he had heard Lloyd George at the 1939 National Eisteddfod in Denbigh, and he greatly admired Lloyd George's 'New Deal' economic analysis in the 1930s. He was concerned, as his predecessor had been, about rural depopulation and poverty, and was one of the authors in 1965 of *The Heartland*, a Liberal plan to revitalise rural mid-Wales. He felt also that the Liberal Party needed a sharper Welsh focus, and he worked to develop the Welsh Liberal Party as a loyal but distinct body. In terms of age, politics and temperament, he was effectively a bridge between older Welsh Liberals – such as Clement Davies,

Roderic Bowen and Rhys Hopkin Morris – and a younger generation including Martin Thomas and Alex Carlile (both of whom worked in Hooson's London chambers). He believed in the resurgence of the Liberal Party as a focal point for the fundamental strands of Welsh radicalism that he felt were nestling in the Liberal Party, the Labour Party and in Plaid Cymru. This led him to a less tribal, more co-operative approach to politics, and it was not surprising that he was to play an important role in the Lib-Lab pact of the late 1970s. These positions and predilections probably did Emlyn Hooson's political career little good. He had come close to becoming Liberal leader in 1967 (Jeremy Thorpe was eventually victorious) and it did not help that some colleagues felt able to portray him as the 'Welsh' Liberal leader. Moreover, the Liberal Party and Hooson's support for James Callaghan's Labour government and for Welsh devolution in the Referendum of March 1979 did not play well with voters in Montgomeryshire. In May 1979, as Margaret Thatcher swept to power, and as Montgomery-shire Liberals prepared to celebrate their 'century' in terms of parliamentary representation, Emlyn Hooson lost his seat by 1,593 votes to the Conservative, Delwyn Williams.

Montgomeryshire had seemed like the last great bastion of Liberalism in Wales, possibly in Britain. It was the one constituency that the Liberals had not at any time surrendered in sixty years of decline. Is there a Liberal 'tradition' in Montgomeryshire? There are certainly many who genuinely and firmly hold Liberal principles, and who can point to Liberal allegiances in successive generations of their family. Yet the notion of an entrenched Liberal orthodoxy, of an automatic political behaviour pattern in the county, is largely fanciful. There have been no mighty majorities in Montgomeryshire, and Liberal victories were often far too close for there to be any confident assumption that it was a safe seat. In the 1970s it remained the most agricultural county in Wales, perhaps inducing a natural rural conservatism and reserve. It had distinctly fewer radical strains than Ceredigion, Meirionnydd, Caernarfon or Anglesey – all of which had Labour MPs at some point after 1945. Despite areas of acute deprivation and notable Welsh-speaking regions, Labour and Plaid Cymru rarely polled strongly in the county. The survival of Montgomeryshire as a Liberal outpost in the years from 1880 to 1979 was due principally to the qualities and industry of the county's MPs. All were held in the highest regard in their constituency; all worked unflaggingly on behalf of the people they represented; all were unafraid to take an independent line when they thought it right to do so. Such strands continued into the twenty-first century. The Liberal Democrats regained the seat in 1983, until 2010 when the Conservatives overturned what had become a sizeable Liberal Democrat majority. Different circumstances now prevail: the extent of the influence of coalition politics, and the future political trends are impossible to gauge. What is certain, however, is that the narrative of Montgomeryshire's political development will continue to fascinate – and to make its mark.

EMLYN HOOSON AS A POLITICIAN

J. Graham Jones

Emlyn Hooson first made a contribution of note to politics when he gave ready support during the general election of July 1945 to E. Garner Evans, the Liberal candidate for the Denbighshire West division. He was then twenty years of age and on leave from the Royal Navy. Two years later he was adopted as the Liberal candidate for Lloyd George's old seat, the Caernarvon Boroughs (which was then abolished by the Boundary Commissioners of 1950). He contested Conway unsuccessfully in the general elections of 1950, which was won by the Labour candidate, and 1951, which was won by the Conservative. On both occasions he came third. Ten years later he was adopted the Liberal candidate for Montgomeryshire, and in the by-election held in May 1962 easily retained the seat held since 1929 by Clement Davies.

National interest in the by-election was avid, and a substantial number of MPs of all political parties poured into the large rural constituency. For the first time ever there was a Plaid Cymru candidate, the distinguished Welsh novelist and former Nonconformist minister Islwyn Ffowc Elis, who waged a worthy campaign but forfeited his election deposit. There was still something haphazard about the organization of the Montgomeryshire Liberal Association, and the money in its bank account was relatively small, but their veteran county organizer Mrs Mary Garbett Edwards had been reluctantly cajoled out of retirement to co-ordinate the campaign with her customary efficiency and persuasiveness.

The portrait of Emlyn Hooson published in the *Montgomery County Times* on the 9th of April 1960 when he was awarded silk suggests that he had, over many years, been groomed by Clement Davies as a rising star in the Liberal Party. In his first speech as candidate at the Welshpool rally on the 5th of May, in the presence of Jo Grimond, Emlyn Hooson paid a generous tribute to Davies using scriptural language. He described him as 'the Moses who brought the Liberal Party to the edge of the wilderness and in sight of the promised land, and then handed over the leadership to a younger man, Jo Grimond, whose destiny is to lead the Party across the Jordan to the promised land.'

Following his dramatic victory at the polls three weeks later, local farmers proudly carried their new Liberal MP shoulder-high through Welshpool. His majority was surprisingly large, 7,549 votes (compared with Davies's majority of 2,794 in 1959), a most comfortable margin which augured well for his future success. Trebling the Liberals' majority, at a stroke he dispelled the view held by all parties in the constituency that Clement Davies for years had been the beneficiary of a substantial personal vote. Emlyn Hooson went to Westminster as the fifth representative of a Liberal succession which extended – as was noted above in David Roberts's essay – back to the general election of 1880 when Stuart Rendel captured the 'virgin fortress' of

Montgomeryshire. In victory Hooson was convinced that Welsh Liberalism had the capacity to return to its nineteenth-century hegemony. He regarded the dominance of Labour through much of the twentieth century in Wales as an anomaly which would disintegrate as the Liberal Party emerged triumphant once more. And he once claimed that Plaid Cymru's role was simply to demonstrate Labour's vulnerability in the valleys of south Wales.

In the early 1960s the Liberal Party experienced something of a minor national revival, encapsulated above all in Eric Lubbock's sensational victory in the Orpington by-election held on the 14th of March 1962, where a swing of 22% from the Tories surprised most analysts. Although an eleventh-hour candidate, Lubbock won a 7,855-vote majority, and held the seat until 1970. This wholly unexpected success gave the Liberals a boost in the opinion polls, a new lease of life in many constituency associations, and further success in the local government elections of May 1962. That year saw the appointment of a chief Liberal organizer for Wales, a novel position, and much increased party activity in the south. But it all led – perhaps inevitably – to severe financial problems for the Party. Indeed, many Welsh constituencies proved reluctant to pay the annual quota of £100 to the Party's central organization.

Emlyn Hooson's policies included agricultural development and new road-building to reverse the escalating depopulation of rural Wales. He demanded that the Liberal Party should become a 'wholly modern, radical and classless party'. In 1964 he was elected to the party's National Executive.

Although he still continued his professional activities at the Bar (a preoccupation which invited sharp criticism from some sections of the Party), he was at once at the centre of things Liberal in the UK and much involved with the revival and reorganization of his party in Wales. In striking contrast to Jo Grimond, the Party Leader, he was determined that the Liberals should reach no formal agreement with Harold Wilson's Labour government elected in October 1964, and imaginatively depicted a distinct future for the Liberal Party as 'a radical, non-Socialist party in Britain'. When in March 1965 Grimond elaborated on his proposals for a possible working agreement with the Wilson Administration which for five months had tried to govern with a tiny majority, proposals which had previously been discussed with some enthusiasm, Emlyn Hooson was one of only two Liberal MPs who openly deprecated this seemingly public offer to Labour. Three months later he told his party executive that there is 'only one course open to the Liberal Party', and that is 'to soldier on in complete independence of any arrangement with the Conservatives or Labour and press for politics in which we believe'. These words succinctly represent the nub of his political convictions. He stated in his Welsh Political Archive Lecture of 1993 that it was the parliamentary debate on the nationalization of the steel industry in 1965, which he totally opposed, which marked the end of any notion of an agreement with Wilson.

Hooson was keenly interested in international affairs, and served as an eager parliamentary delegate to NATO. An admirer of President Lyndon Johnson's Appalachia Bill in the United States, he devoted much time and energy in the late 1960s preparing a similar Liberal economic plan for Wales. Adopting an internationalist Atlanticist attitude towards economic and social problems, he found himself sharing ideas and ideals with the former Congressman John Lindsay, who, between 1966 and 1973, served with great distinction as Mayor of New York. As Vice-Chairman of the North Atlantic Assembly's political committee, Hooson worked constructively with Lindsay on one of the early reports recommending détente with Eastern Europe.

As the leader of the Liberals through the agonizingly difficult years between 1945 and 1956, Clement Davies had been compelled to concentrate on the survival of the party nationally, and therefore had done little to encourage Welsh party devolution. Once elected in his place, Emlyn Hooson, together with other prominent Welsh Liberals such as Lord Ogmore, Martin Thomas, G. W. Madoc-Jones and Geraint Howells, was determined to pursue a far greater degree of devolution for the party in Wales. He was much involved in the negotiations which led in September 1966 to the establishment of the quasi-independent Welsh Liberal Party (based on the Scottish Liberal Party model, with federated links to the Liberal Party organization in London), and then served devotedly as its Leader until 1979. Some of Hooson's supporters in the Montgomeryshire Liberal Association expressed great unease concerning the establishment of the new group, and as late as 1969 Martin Thomas reported to the party's executive committee that many Montgomeryshire Liberals 'had not really participated in the scheme'. But others rejoiced that, with the creation of a Welsh Liberal Party, Lloyd George's cherished dream for Cymru Fydd in the 1890s at long last had become a reality.

Was Hooson himself that naïve? Although he occupied a distinctive niche in Welsh and in British politics, he was in many ways a one-man band. In the *Liverpool Daily Post* of the 15th of April 1967 Norman Cook described him as 'a kind of one-man parliamentary party like Mr Gwynfor Evans, the solitary Welsh Nationalist at Westminster . . . There Mr Hooson sits, the solitary pride and joy of all that is left of the glorious Welsh Liberalism of years gone by.' His personal standing was certainly considerable, not only in politics but also at the Bar. In May 1968 he was made a Bencher of Gray's Inn, at forty-three years of age the youngest there, joining a number of eminent Welshmen who were his friends, Sir Elwyn Jones the Attorney General, Lord Justice Edmund Davies, and Mr Mars Jones, then Recorder of Cardiff. Yet there were some Liberals who still resented his pursuing his professional career as an advocate, echoing Margaret Lawson's earlier concern that 'he ought to spend more time on his job as Member of Parliament, or else we shall have another Roderic Bowen [MP for Cardiganshire], but one who does not spend so much time in his constituency.'

At the second annual conference of the Welsh Liberal Party held at Llandrindod Wells in 1968, Hooson claimed that 'all internal criticism' of the once contentious decision to establish an autonomous Welsh party had been stilled. He asserted with gusto that it had become in its very short life 'the thinking party of Wales . . . the think tank of Welsh politics'. 'Liberalism,' he added, is now 'more thrustful, it is attracting more people . . . We must avoid the deadening hand of consensus politics if we are to have thrust and determination.'

As the 1960s ran their course, Hooson was very conscious of the seemingly ever more menacing Plaid Cymru challenge. In an address to Undeb Cymru Fydd at the National Eisteddfod in Llandudno in August 1963, he proposed than the Advisory Council for Wales and Monmouthshire reluctantly set up by the Attlee government in 1948 as a nominated body with no elected representatives should be transformed into an elected Welsh Council with much increased powers and responsibilities. He hoped that the three major political parties in Wales would support this proposal, but it was merely a damp squib. He subsequently keenly supported other devolutionary initiatives, and was the major force behind the 'Take Wales ahead with the Liberals' campaign. Nearer home, his constant concern for his constituency was displayed in the new Liberal *Plan for Mid-Wales*, published in March 1964, proposing the establishment of a new town in the area, a substantial increase in the population of key towns like Welshpool and Newtown, and the establishment of new factories with government support to give employment to their inhabitants.

At the same time there was much discussion about the establishment of a rural development council. The newly convened Welsh Radical Group charged Emlyn Hooson and the distinguished anthropologist J. Geraint Jenkins, a member of staff at the Welsh Folk Museum at San Ffagan, to prepare a volume entitled *Brave New World* crystallizing radical Liberal policies for the Wales of the future. They also collaborated in 1965 on a scheme for the development of mid-Wales specifically, published as *The Heartland*, which evoked memories of Lloyd George's 'Yellow Book', *Britain's Industrial Future*, published in 1928. This scheme proposed that the population of Aberystwyth, under the provisions of the New Towns Act, might well increase to some sixty thousand by the end of the century by attracting migrants from both north and south Wales (it was feared that a new town established near the border with England would attract substantial numbers of people from the Midlands anxious for a better life). Other proposals included the establishment of a Rural Development Corporation to develop the towns of rural Wales, and a radical overhaul of rural transport facilities to include the building of trunk roads to link north and south Wales and Aberystwyth and Shrewsbury. Hooson came to believe that these ideas were later cherry-picked by later Labour governments.

On the 1st of March 1967 in the House of Commons he introduced a Government of Wales Bill which proposed an 'all-Wales Senate' of eighty-eight members to take responsibility for industry, trade, agriculture, education, health and transport. Westminster would retain control of matters of defence, Commonwealth and foreign affairs, and the administration of common law. And Wales would continue to elect its complement of thirty-six MPs to Westminster. As anticipated, the bill was simply given a nominal first reading. There were twenty-nine members present in the House – including six Liberal MPs, most wearing daffodils – but it made no progress. At least the Liberal Party's commitment to the cause of Welsh devolution had been underlined. Hooson also introduced a succession of measures with a view to tackle rural depopulation, and various bills in support of the Welsh language. But he resolutely refused to countenance any agreement or electoral pact with Plaid Cymru.

Meanwhile, following Jo Grimond's retirement, he had stood unsuccessfully against Jeremy Thorpe and Eric Lubbock for the Liberal Party leadership in January 1967. At forty-one Hooson was the oldest of the three candidates. A year or two earlier he had been widely tipped as Grimond's successor, but Grimond let it be known that Thorpe was his chosen successor, and when the election came the anti-Thorpe vote was simply split between the other two. Defeated in the first ballot, Hooson then gave his support to Thorpe, but subsequently he was never a strong supporter of his. It was widely felt, then and later, that if Hooson had been less brilliant and busy as a barrister he might well have become leader of his party. Moreover, there were unpleasant undertones surrounding this contest. Almost forty years later Hooson claimed that Laura, Jo Grimond's wife, had urged one Scottish colleague not to support 'that

Welshman'. Had he succeeded, he would certainly have been a more right-wing leader, and would have been more willing than Thorpe to fight the Labour governments of the 1960s and 1970s. Being initially Eurosceptic he would also have wanted the Liberals to take a less pro-European line. He was the only Liberal MP to vote against joining the European Community. At the same time, he was more anti-imperialist than his colleagues: he fiercely opposed the Vietnam War in the 1960s and also the British pursuit of the Falklands War in 1982.

Hooson had early suspicions about Jeremy Thorpe, which he reckoned were justified when the former male model Norman Scott arrived at Westminster to claim to him, David Steel MP and Lord Byers, the Liberal leader in the Lords, that Thorpe had had a homosexual relationship with him. Thorpe denied the allegation, but Hooson conducted an internal investigation that triggered a party inquiry. Although that inquiry cleared Thorpe, Hooson told him that he should consider resigning both the party leadership and his North Devon seat, and asked another Liberal MP, Peter Bessell, if he would back him should Thorpe quit. Thorpe got to hear of this, and accused Hooson or 'running around trying to stir up something'. Thorpe was eventually forced out of the party leadership in 1976 after news of the affair became public and was subsequently tried in court for incitement and conspiracy to murder Scott. Bessell testified that Hooson, who was not called as a witness, knew of 'retainer payments' of up to £700 made to Scott, and feared that he might be accused of a cover-up. The court also heard a tape-recording in which David Holmes, one of Thorpe's co-defendants, told Bessell that Hooson had been 'firmly sat on' for trying to force Thorpe out. Thorpe was cleared.

Hooson retained Montgomeryshire in five successive general elections, winning a handsome, substantially increased majority of 4,651 votes in February 1974, an election that witnessed something of a national Liberal revival. The following October, Hooson's majority over W. R. C. Williams-Wynn, an Eton educated chartered surveyor of squirearchical pedigree, was still a highly creditable 3,859 vote, a margin of 17.3%. From 1966, when Elystan Morgan defeated Roderic Bowen in Cardiganshire, until February 1974, when Geraint Howells recaptured Cardiganshire, Hooson had been the only parliamentary representative of Welsh Liberalism. Following the near decimation of the Liberal Party in the general election of June 1970 he had returned to Westminster with a heavy heart. In the new House of Commons there were only six Liberal MPs, Hooson, Grimond, Russell Johnston, John Pardoe, David Steel and Thorpe, and it seemed to many that the party's days as a leading political player were numbered. Of the six, only Hooson and Grimond had anything resembling comfortable majorities. The very small number of Liberal MPs in the new House inevitably led to bitter recriminations within the fractious party. In the September edition of *New Outlook* Hooson stated his opinion that the former leader Jo Grimond had sown the seeds of disaster by courting Labour during his leadership years.

By the early 1970s Hooson was widely viewed as '*the establishment figure*' within the Parliamentary Liberal Party, sometimes accused of harbouring right-wing views. As already noted, he was the only Liberal MP to vote against British entry into the EEC in the historic 'free vote' of the 28th of October 1971. And he remained one of the very few Liberals who were critical of the European Community, fearing that British membership could harm Welsh hill farmers. He was also concerned about the ensuing loss of British sovereignty. In *Rebirth or Death?*, his Welsh Political Archive Lecture, reflecting on these matters twenty years later, he wrote: 'Whereas almost without exception the Liberals of Wales were for it, I had developed doubts about that particular route to a United Europe and voted against entry. In retrospect I think I should have voted for it, although I believe my reasons for delaying our entry, as I explained them then, largely proved to be correct.'

Most of his more radical MP colleagues perched firmly on the left wing of the Liberal Party, rightly or wrongly tended to view Hooson as a conservative-minded Liberal whose role was confined mainly to the Welsh political stage, and consequently believed he was somewhat remote from the Westminster vortex. He attracted abuse from some party activists, particularly some Young Liberals who at one party conference waved sticks of rhubarb at him when he opposed sanctions on South Africa. Yet they were allies in opposing the Vietnam War, and the Young Liberals' leader, Peter Hain, relied on Hooson's advice when forced to apologize to Edward Short, Leader of the Commons, for suggesting he was implicated in the Poulson affair.

But he often adopted a forward, progressive stand on domestic matters, and there is no doubt that he was the Parliamentary Liberal Party's most fervent critic of the centralizing measures of Edward Heath's government. In Wales, Hooson, the warm admirer of Lloyd George, encapsulated the progressive Welsh Liberalism of the 1960s and 1970s, seeing the 'second coming' of the party as a worthy successor to the somewhat declining Labour Party. After the heavy Liberal losses of 1970 he told the Liberal Assembly that the public wanted a middle-of-the-road party, and blamed Grimond and Thorpe for trying to take it leftward. During this difficult period, Hooson played an important role in recruiting into the Welsh party a younger generation of activists, men like Martin Thomas, and, later, Alex Carlile.

The traditional sociocultural divide in Montgomery-shire politics was still very apparent. Hooson was clearly most secure in the areas well removed from the English border, the Welsh-speaking parts of the county, the rural uplands and the market towns of Machynlleth, Llanfyllin and Llanidloes. At Newtown there was a delicate balance in the support for the two main political parties, while Welshpool contained significant pockets of Conservative support. The farming communities generally continued to rally to the Liberal banner, encouraged by their MP's on-going part-time role as a practising farmer and by his ready understanding of their problems. The county, with a population of around 45,000, remained one of the most intensely agricultural constituencies in the whole of the United Kingdom, containing over 7,000 individual holdings, some as tiny as one acre. As late as 1974 some 40% of school-leavers went to work on farms or found employment in rural trades associated with agriculture.

But there were significant changes afoot. The introduction of light industries had meant that by 1974 there were some two thousand new voters in the Newtown wards alone, and there was further suburban growth around Welshpool, particularly in the Guilsfield area. To survive, it was imperative for Montgomeryshire Liberalism to adapt to the new social admixture within the county. Many of the immigrants into the county had absolutely no tradition of voting Liberal or any interest in Liberal politics.

Surprisingly, Emlyn Hooson was an – admittedly, notably cautious – advocate of the Lib-Lab pact concluded between the Prime Minister, James Callaghan, and the Liberal Party leader, David Steel, in March 1977, a step which he grudgingly tolerated as a necessary evil. Indeed, in his opening speech at the Liberal Party Assembly in September 1976, he paved the way for David Steel's declaration on this matter by making an outspoken statement of support for the Liberals joining a coalition. He even played an active role on the Liberal-Government Consultative Committee, which, he believed, gave the Liberal Party a much-needed opportunity to destroy the deeply embedded image of it as a party in the wilderness. But many prominent Welsh Liberals were extremely sceptical of the arrangement, and the support for it given by the Welsh Liberal Party at its conference in April 1977 was most guarded. Hooson told them that such an unprecedented pact, initially at least, was bound to be unpopular. But many Liberals, including many innately conservative members of the party in Montgomeryshire, were highly critical of their leaders' apparent preparedness to keep in office a Labour government which was so clearly on the brink of ejection. In January 1978 the Welsh Liberals clamoured for the pact to be brought to an end – long before a general election was likely to be called. Hooson himself tended to favour bringing the pact to an end in the autumn of 1978. There was further indignation in Liberal circles in Montgomeryshire because of the warm, amicable working relationship which had developed between their MP, the Liberals' home affairs spokesman, and Merlyn Rees, the Labour Home Secretary.

Hooson later described the Lib-Lab pact of 1977–78 as 'a genuine attempt . . . to put the interests of the country first'. But he was keen for the Liberals to extract themselves from it, and 'get at arm's length' from the government as the general election neared. He knew full well that his support network in Montgomeryshire included a substantial conservative element which was aghast that the Liberal Party was sustaining in office a Labour administration on the brink of defeat. As the pact was nearing its end, Hooson remained of the view that the experience had been beneficial to both his party and the country, but in his speech to the Welsh Liberals at their annual conference on the 15th of April 1978 he said that he now anticipated 'a return to that position of complete independence and freedom of manoeuvre which we so rightly value.' During the period of the pact he had been a very active member of the House, delivering more than forty major speeches in the Commons and asking forty-two questions to government ministers on a very wide range of issues.

It was sometimes difficult to see what Hooson had in common with his party's radical mainstream. The Lib-Lab pact notwithstanding, he saw the Labour Party as the main enemy, and after Enoch Powell's 'Rivers of Blood' speech he upset David Steel by telling constituents that he could see nothing wrong with assisting immigrants who sought repatriation. Yet he had no truck with Margaret Thatcher's right-wing brand of Conservatism. In 1978 he said, 'People are superficially attracted by her violent swing to the Right, but she cannot even work with Conservatives like Mr Heath and Peter Walker.'

His colleague Geraint Howells, by then MP for Ceredigion, was perhaps more obviously a Welsh devolutionist, in that he saw devolution from a nationalist perspective. Emlyn Hooson was also a warm advocate of a Welsh Assembly during the devolution campaign of 1978–79, but did not reap personal benefit from that advocacy. In the fateful Referendum of the 1st of March 1979, Powys, by now an Anglicized county, recorded the highest 'No' vote (53.8%) of all the counties of Wales. A severely dejected Emlyn Hooson could only comment that Welsh devolution was 'a dead duck for a decade'.

A long-anticipated general election was also on the horizon. Since October 1974 their MP had written over 5,500 letters on behalf of the people of Montgomeryshire. In his election address of May 1979 his proud boast was that '*Everyone* knows *someone* who had been helped by Emlyn Hooson'. But during that period, too, far-reaching social changes had taken place, the electorate had increased by 2,200, and the constituency had become much more Anglicized. It was calculated that, of the 888 new families living in housing estates built by the local Newtown corporation, 435 had moved there from England. Many of these newcomers had disapproved strongly of their MP's hands-on support of devolution and of his commitment to the Lib-Lab pact. And local Conservative canvassers were not slow to remind the electors of the scandals, ranging from homosexuality to attempted murder, which had beset the Liberals' former leader Jeremy Thorpe.

In the general election of May 1979 the Liberal vote in the country slumped badly, and even the seemingly impregnable 'man for Montgomeryshire' unexpectedly lost his seat to the Conservative candidate Delwyn Williams, like Hooson a local lawyer and farmer and a graduate of the Law Department of the University College of Wales, Aberystwyth. The ninety-nine year Liberal tenure of the seat thus came to a dramatic end – to the intense chagrin of the party faithful in Wales. It appeared to many that the last great bastion of Welsh Liberalism had gone, the most secure Liberal seat in the whole of the United Kingdom, defended since 1880 by MPs of great quality. Many commentators ventured that Liberalism would survive in Montgomeryshire only as a historic, backward-looking remnant. But in the general election of June 1983 the division was re-captured by the Liberal Alex Carlile. Apart from the four years following Emlyn Hooson's defeat, and the years following Lembit Opik's defeat by the Conservative Glyn Davies in 2010, Montgomeryshire has had Liberal or Liberal-affiliated MPs since 1880. A few months after his defeat Hooson entered the House of Lords as a life peer, and at once became prominent in the affairs of the Upper House, active in improving the Mental Health Act, urging police reforms, and speaking on law reforms and drug trafficking.

He remained a prominent Liberal Democrat and public figure in Welsh life until his death. At various times he was his party's spokesman in the Lords on Welsh affairs, legal affairs, agriculture and European affairs. Between 1983 and 1986 he served as President of the Welsh Liberal Party. When the Liberals merged with the SDP in 1988 he backed Alan Beith for the leadership against the less cautious Paddy Ashdown. Predictably, Lord Hooson gave his full support to the 'Yes' campaign in the 1997 devolution debate and subsequently to the development of the Welsh Assembly established in 1999. But he constantly criticized 'aggressive and self-glorifying nationalism' as 'one of the great curses' of the twentieth century. As a lawyer and as a politician he was enthusiastic in his pursuit of civil liberties, arguing for a Freedom of Information Act from 1985. During his later years, his position on Europe changed, and he was anxious to overcome 'the baleful influence of the Euro-sceptics' among the Tories. In a lifetime in politics Hooson made few real enemies. He saw himself principally as a radical politician, and yet he was very much at the heart of a certain kind of Welsh establishment.

WORKING WITH EMLYN

Helen Hughes

It was in the summer of 1968 that I started working as private secretary to Emlyn Hooson. I was already working in London, at Guy's Hospital, when he telephoned me to say that his secretary was leaving and to ask if I might be interested in the position. With my roots firmly in Montgomeryshire this was an ideal opportunity for me, and after a short and informal interview on the Terrace of the House of Commons it was agreed that I would start work at the beginning of the summer recess.

Because Emlyn and his family left for a holiday abroad just as I started my new job this proved to be something of a baptism of fire. He had left me a tape of instructions that was an introduction to both the range and method of his work. Leading a very full life as a barrister and an MP he used his travelling time on trains to dictate tapes for me. This could mean that some of his dictation was inaudible, for it had been done as the train whistled through a long tunnel or during an over-amplified station announcement. With regards to the first tape, he had simply disregarded the fact that I knew none of the people mentioned or where I could contact them!

In those days – and this may still be the case in certain circumstances – House of Commons secretaries and researchers were required to share rooms with colleagues who worked for other political parties, My desk was in a small, windowless room on the Upper Committee Corridor North which had been built on the roof of the Houses of Parliament and which is now visible from the London Eye. Two of my colleagues were Conservative and one worked for Labour members, including Tom Ellis, the MP for Wrexham, and, later, John Smith, the future Labour Leader. We had an unwritten code of practice whereby no one would divulge any information overheard during our work. Therefore, the colleagues in my room knew nothing of matters concerning Emlyn's work. And because my predecessor, who had no Montgomeryshire links, was on the verge of emigrating to Australia, there was no hand-over as such.

After an initial panic I built up a network of useful contacts for Emlyn's areas of interest. Primarily these were Mrs Wyatt-Jones, his constituency organizer, the Clerk in his chambers, the Secretary of the Welsh Liberals, who lived in Bala, and, of course, other Liberal secretaries in the House of Commons, particularly those in the Whips' Office. At that time Emlyn was the only Welsh Liberal MP in the House, so I had no Welsh colleagues there.

As it was the beginning of the summer recess when I started, the House was like the *Mary Celeste*. There were very few people around who could teach me the practicalities of working there. The other rooms on our corridor were the offices of MPs who had either gone on holiday or decamped to their constituencies. The man who gave me most help was a very left-wing member of the Labour Party who pointed me in the direction of essential equipment such as the photocopier.

When the Hoosons returned from holiday I went back to the constituency with the family for the duration of the summer recess. This was to be my pattern of work for the eleven years that I was employed by Emlyn, and it suited me extremely well. Although my parents lived in Hampshire at that time, I had lived in Montgomeryshire as a small child and had spent all my school holidays with grandparents in the county, in Welshpool where my paternal grandparents were head teachers, and in Llanidloes where my maternal grandfather lived. He had died four years before I started work for Emlyn, but I still felt part of the community and knew many people in the town and the surrounding countryside. These connections proved to be a great help in my work.

The work during parliamentary recesses involved what would now be called multi-tasking. There were surgeries to be arranged in the main constituency towns and in many villages. Also meetings with interest groups, the farming unions for instance. Emlyn was always accessible to the people of Montgomeryshire and could be contacted through the constituency office or directly at home. In both places Shirley Hooson's intimate knowledge of Montgomeryshire and Welsh Liberal politics – like her knowledge of the people – was of huge advantage to him. It must also be remembered that, despite his incisive mind and intellectual interests, Emlyn was an extremely kind and affable man whom people could easily approach.

And because he came from a farming background and had great interest in agriculture throughout his life he was highly respected and sought after by the farmers of the county, some of whom were of course of different political persuasions. A pleasurable and important activity during every summer recess was attending the many agricultural shows in Montgomeryshire, from the County Show held in the grounds of Powis Castle to the smaller shows held in rural villages.

I inevitably became involved in some of these farming activities, and, like his wife and daughters, I had some pedigree Welsh Black cows named after me. He was immensely proud of the herd that he had reared, and to lend one's name to one of them was considered to be an honour! I dealt with some of the farm paperwork at my desk at the House of Commons. After a weekend at home Emlyn would return to London with bundles of invoices and delivery notes from Pen-y-banc, his farm near Llanidloes. Some of these had been in his farm bailiff's pocket for several days, sometimes weeks, and had attracted every kind of muck found on a Welsh hill farm. Moreover, in preparation for a reduction sale of some cattle, I'd spend many hours researching the genealogy of the animals involved, the results of which would be printed in the sale catalogue. My job was certainly interesting and certainly varied!

A great deal of Emlyn's time and energy was dedicated to the leadership of the Welsh Liberal Party. This involved organizing meetings, maintaining contact with officers and prospective candidates, and liaising with personnel at the party headquarters in Aberystwyth and, later, Cardiff. When Geraint Howells won Ceredigion for the Liberals in 1974 it was of enormous assistance to Emlyn to have a colleague with whom he could share the work of the Party in Wales. They had a close working and personal relationship, and happily shared a Members' room with an interesting group of Scottish Nationalist MPs with whom they became great friends.

By that time things had improved vastly from the late 1960s when the small number of Liberal MPs in the House each held briefs for three or four Parliamentary portfolios. In those days there were no House of Commons research assistants, and Emlyn had to rely on a network of highly competent experts and friends to supply him with background information for his contributions to Parliamentary debates.

Back in Montgomeryshire, the hub of the constituency organization was the Liberal Office at 3 Park Street, Newtown, a typical Montgomeryshire half-timbered building opposite The Park. Here the county organizer worked under the general direction of the County Liberal Association, maintaining links with local committees, managing meetings, organizing surgeries and dealing with the many enquiries that came into the office. The county chairman and treasurer were frequent visitors. Constituents who wanted advice from Emlyn were encouraged to see him at the first available surgery or to write to him. If a matter were urgent, the organizer would contact Emlyn or me at the House.

In the late 1960s and 1970s there was a well-established network of Liberal Associations in most of the towns and villages. Each one had officers and members, many of whom were County, District or Parish Councillors. Where there was no Association we had individual contacts. These good people would inform Emlyn about local problems and other issues of concern. And the communication system worked well, especially when migration into the county was negligible. But in Newtown, where the population had increased dramatically after the developments instigated by the Mid-Wales Development Board and the Development Board for Rural Wales, it was more difficult to establish networks of communication, especially in the large new estates which housed newcomers to the county.

As soon as an election was called the Liberal machine in Montgomeryshire went into overdrive. One of the first events to be organized was the adoption meeting, which was always held in the large School Room at the rear of the imposing Baptist Church in Newtown. It would be packed with supporters from all over the county who would listen to tributes and eulogies in praise of Emlyn before his formal adoption as the Liberal candidate for the forthcoming election. It must be remembered that the Montgomeryshire 'establishment' at that time was mainly Liberal, and the great and the good would add their praises in commending the candidate. Pledges of financial support – by Liberal Associations and individuals – would then be made, and everyone would leave the highly-charged meeting full of optimism and fighting spirit!

Elections were always exciting but extremely hard work for all concerned, particularly for the election agent and, of course, for Emlyn and his wife Shirley. Meetings would be arranged for every town and village and for many hamlets, where Emlyn addressed the people of that area, listen to their concerns, and field questions from supporters and from members of other political parties. Each meeting had to have a chairman who would speak to the audience pending Emlyn's arrival, performing something akin to what we today would call 'a warm-up act'. Nearly eighty of these meetings would be held during an election campaign, and it was necessary to plan tours of the constituency so that its different parts could be covered in a day and/or an evening.

Campaign offices set up in the main towns became the nerve-centres of their respective districts. There, plans were made for the distribution of election leaflets, door-to-door canvassing, and for collating the information attained. To ensure that Liberal voters got to the polling stations on election day no stone was left unturned, and postal votes were arranged for students away at college and for others working away from home.

A more 'cloak-and-dagger' activity during an election campaign was the preparation of posters on display boards for after-dark forays into the countryside. Overnight an area would be peppered with Liberal posters whilst those belonging to other parties would mysteriously disappear. This was always great fun, but the exercise was often counter-productive due to retaliation by another party the following night. These unofficial activities were usually carried out by Young Liberals – and some not so young!

In addition to fighting a strenuous campaign in his own constituency, as leader of the Welsh Liberal Party Emlyn often had to travel to Cardiff to take part in a television debate. Naturally, this extra task meant taking time out of his schedule in Montgomeryshire, but it also meant that his message reached a wider audience.

At the very end of a campaign, when all was over bar the shouting, the traditional eve-of-poll meeting of all the candidates was held in Welshpool Town Hall, which was always packed with supporters from each of the parties. The order in which the candidates spoke was decided by the drawing of lots. Although they and many of their followers were exhausted from their campaign endeavours this meeting certainly helped to keep the adrenal levels high for polling day, and for the day after, when the count took place. It rarely – if at all – had much influence on the election vote, but it was a good test of each candidate's calibre and debating skills. Naturally, Emlyn's training and experience at the Bar stood him in very good stead at these somewhat knock-about events.

Because Liberalism in Montgomeryshire was long established and closely bound to its social history and religious Nonconformity, adherence to the party was akin to something spiritual. When Emlyn won the by-election in 1962 and toured the constituency to thank his voters, a loyal and devoted Liberal from Llanfihangel-yng-Ngwynfa, Councillor Dai Ellis, led the local people on their knees in prayer of thanks for his return at the polls. Equally moving for me were the tears running down the faces of the people lining the streets of Llanfyllin when we lost the election in 1979.

When I look back on the years between 1968 and 1979 when I worked for Emlyn Hooson, I wonder at the commitment and the energy that enabled him to maintain a highly successful career at the Bar whilst at the same time representing Montgomeryshire as a hard-working MP and leading the Welsh Liberal Party. His happy family life and his farm allowed him to relax and provided opportunities for him to re-charge his batteries. He also got nourishment from books – he was an avid reader – and from his love of music, particularly opera. Undoubtedly, his quick and incisive mind made a huge contribution to his ability to achieve so much. Added to this was his amazing propensity for hard work and application to the task at hand. I well remember an eve-of-poll meeting in Welshpool where a member of the audience thought he would catch Emlyn out. 'How can you manage to do two jobs properly?' he shouted from the back of the hall. 'By working twice as hard' came Emlyn's reply, to huge cheers from his supporters.

These were interesting years which I was fortunate to experience. Because it is covered elsewhere in this book I have not touched on the close involvement with Laura Ashley, but I do remember helping out on Saturdays at the first London shop in South Kensington. There would be three or four of us, including Bernard Ashley, selling frilly dresses in the shop, and Laura would telephone from

Carno every two or three hours to ask how many had been sold! I had never thought of Emlyn as material for heading a fashion empire – or for building a huge bridge over the Severn for that matter – but it was a measure of the man and his agile and brilliant mind that he ended up being responsible for both of those things.

A MONTGOMERYSHIRE VALLEY UNDER THREAT

Gareth Morgan

[In one of the notes he compiled about his political career Emlyn Hooson states that the threat to drown one of the valleys of Montgomeryshire was by far the gravest problem with which he had to grapple during his first years as MP. This essay is a brief history of that affair, written by one who experienced it first hand. Mr Gareth Morgan was the solicitor for the Dulas Valley Defence Committee.]

No sooner had Emlyn Hooson been elected MP for Montgomeryshire than he was faced with a serious issue that had already reared its head before 1962, but not publicly, I believe. The Severn River Authority (as it then was) had identified twenty-four sites within the constituency as potential reservoir sites for the supply of water to southeast England. Put in context, this scheme within a few years followed the highly unpopular drowning of the village of Capel Celyn as part of the Llyn Tryweryn project in Meirionnydd providing a water supply for Liverpool. A long sustained campaign had been fought against that project led by Plaid Cymru, whose President, Gwynfor Evans, had stood as parliamentary candidate in Meirionnydd several times. Tryweryn was also the subject of sabotage by young nationalists impatient with Plaid

Cymru's diplomatic protests. This was a time when Plaid was rising as a political force, a time that also saw the establishment of Cymdeithas yr Iaith Gymraeg, a society formed specifically to campaign for greater recognition and official use of the Welsh language.

To make matters worse for Hooson, an announcement was made in 1966 that no fewer than twenty-nine sites in Montgomeryshire were being examined as potential reservoir sites. This was a period when much industrial growth and a significant increase in population was expected in south-east England – and Montgomeryshire, with its topography, low population and high rainfall, was considered a suitable area to conserve water for future developments there. At the same time, the Central Electricity Generating Board was responsible for the invest-igation and selection of sites in England and Wales for large sources of water for the purposes of generating electricity and cooling purposes at existing power stations. It was said, for example, that there was a need to double the flow of water over the measuring gauge on the Severn at Bewdley in Worcestershire: future demand required 300 million gallons a day of an 'unfailing supply' of cold water.

As soon as these threats were in the public domain Montgomeryshire set up a countywide Defence Committee. Its secretary was Mr R. P. Davies, county secretary of the Farmers Union of Wales. The chairman was Mr Leslie Morgan, an ironmonger and the owner of an agricultural engineering business in Llanfair Caereinion. It was a very large committee with representatives from all affected areas. With regards to the Dulas Valley, one of the most vulnerable on the list, it should be noted that it was partly in Montgomeryshire and partly in the parliamentary constituency of Brecon and Radnor, then represented by Mr Tudor Watkins, a man well-known for his diligence and the care and attention he gave to constituency matters.

In the House of Commons Emlyn Hooson secured an adjournment debate on the issue on the 27th of May 1966. Presenting the case for his constituents he expressed the fact that Montgomeryshire was expected to undertake more than its share of responsibility for supplying water to the growing population over the border. He received cross-party support. In his winding-up speech, Cledwyn Hughes, then Secretary of State for Wales, gave assurances upon which the Dulas Valley Defence Committee was able to build its own case in years to come. For example, he said: 'I do not propose to consent to the drowning of any villages in mid-Wales. I am satisfied that if regulating reservoirs are required then the two or three which I mentioned can be built without disrupting whole communities. I can assure the hon. and learned gentleman [Mr Hooson] and the hon. gentleman the Member for Denbigh [Mr Geraint Morgan] that communities count as far as I am concerned.'

When Tryweryn was drowned Wales did not have a seat in cabinet. In 1964 Harold Wilson appointed James Griffiths as the first Secretary of State for Wales, and he set up a Welsh Water Committee to advise him. This, no doubt, was one of the lessons learnt following the turmoil throughout Wales resulting from the Tryweryn débâcle.

Following the adjournment debate, in September 1966 Cledwyn Hughes announced that no less than nineteen sites were to be eliminated. This still left ten in the melting pot. Further investigations by Binnie and Partners reduced the number to six, one of which was the Dulas Valley. Dulas was presented as two different projects according to size, both within the same valley.

After much deliberation by the promoting authorities, led by the Severn River Authority and supported by the Water Resources Board, the decision was made under Section 67 of the Water Resources Act of 1963 to publish an application for consent for compulsory powers to carry out trial borings at Tylwch near Llanidloes in connection with the proposed Dulas Regulating Reservoir.

A very strong Defence Committee had been set up in the Dulas Valley, which included the parishes of Llandinam, Llangurig and St Harmon. Most of the land affected was in Radnorshire and the remainder in Montgomeryshire, which included the site of the dam or buttress itself. Under the proposed scheme seventeen farmhouses and their outbuildings were to be inundated as well as six other residences, and a further twenty farms were to be affected by land acquisition. There was also mention of building some aqueducts, which would affect fourteen other holdings. The Severn River Authority went on record admitting that 'disturbance would be relatively high and disruption is appreciable' – an understatement if ever there was one. In fact 50% of a valley with a total population of 380 was to be affected.

In due course it was announced that a public enquiry would be held to consider the application. It was set to open on the 3rd of December 1969 in the Community Centre in Llanidloes. The Dulas Valley Defence Committee had only modest funds and no legal representation. Plaid Cymru tried to persuade the Defence Committee to let it handle its defence. But the Committee resisted all the overtures, both public and private, that it received. It wished to disassociate itself from any political party because it felt that a show of political allegiance might prejudice the outcome of the enquiry. Furthermore, press reports from that time refer to the Defence Committee asking political demonstrators to keep away from the public enquiry. Its chairman Mr Iorwerth Evans and its secretary Mr Gordon Pugh are quoted as saying 'that they are totally opposed to any demonstration taking place at or during the public enquiry'.

Because my firm's file of papers on the subject, including the brief to Counsel, was thrown away by my successor when I retired from practice, I cannot now say exactly when I was instructed to act for the Defence Committee. It was certainly at the eleventh hour – probably towards the end of October or the beginning of November 1969. I was invited to attend a public meeting in Pant-y-dŵr, which was very well attended and which comprised all the affected members of the community. I was then aged 34 and it was undoubtedly one of the most challenging cases I had undertaken. Due to deaths there was no one older or more experienced than I in the practice. I had the advantage of friendship with Emlyn Hooson, as distinguished a Queen's Counsel as one could find, and he was always available to discuss problems and to give advice. In my address to that first public meeting I first referred to the limited time factor available to prepare the case. As I've already noted, the enquiry was listed to commence on the 3rd of December, some four weeks away, and I asked the residents of the Dulas Valley for their consent to seek an adjournment of three months to prepare. I knew, and they knew, that this was a tall order, for they had known the date for quite a time. I then suggested that rather than make the application myself, and risk refusal, the obvious step was to ask Emlyn Hooson MP to make the request directly to the Secretary of State for Wales, George Thomas. I also suggested that in the light of the remarks made by the previous Secretary of State we needed a professionally researched sociological report on the valley community, a report illustrating the impact that the development would have if it went ahead; and advised them that we should approach the Department of Geography at the University College of Wales, Aberystwyth. I told them too of the need to collate much further evidence; I sought authority to brief Counsel for the hearing, and referred to the cost involved, etc. Finally I stated that I was fully committed to their cause, that Emlyn Hooson was committed to support their endeavours, and how this was the beginning of what would be a historical case of its kind in Wales.

It was for me, a solicitor who had been in practice a mere nine years, a moving experience. The emotion generated by the community, its sincerity, and the belief they had in their cause, was overwhelming. I knew that no amount of monetary compensation in the future was likely to divert them from their cause. When I sat down elderly farmers had tears running down their cheeks, fearing that their homes and farms, which had been in their families for generations, could be taken away from them.

Given their unqualified support to proceed as I suggested, my first move the next morning was to seek the adjournment of the enquiry. By coincidence my secretary at that time was the daughter of the chairman of the Defence Committee. I made the application to Emlyn Hooson, who immediately made formal application to George Thomas. Very soon he replied in the affirmative. But there was a sting in the tail when he added, 'I doubt whether the extra time will help you in the long run', or words to that effect.

Then I made an appointment to see Harold Carter, Gregynog Professor of Geography at Aberystwyth. This was before I had the adjournment. His response was that in the time available he could do nothing to help. However, when the adjournment was granted I went back to him and received a positive response. This was without doubt the vital turning point in the fortunes of the Defence Committee. Professor Carter said he would undertake the social study on one condition, namely that my firm should be responsible for interviewing the entire valley population to seek their response to a comprehensive questionnaire the University would prepare: the time factor dictated that a team effort was totally necessary.

Colomendy, near Denbigh, a hundred-acre farm in the Vale of Clwyd.
Tomos and Marged Hooson; E. H.'s grandparents.
E. H. at the crease.
Taid Hooson with grandchildren. E. H. is first left in the back row.

Brothers Gwilym, Emlyn and John.

Last day at school 1942. From the left: Dennis Glyn Jones, E. H., Gordon Thomas and 'Jug' – John Gwyn Hughes.

Boreham House, home of the Henry Ford Institute of Agricultural Engineering where E. H. enrolled and pondered farming as a living.

The Department of Law, University College of Wales, Aberystwyth 1947–48. Fourth from the left in the front row sits Eifion Roberts, next to him is E. H.. Eighth from the left is Professor Llewelfryn Davies, next to him sits J. A. G. Griffith, who later became Professor of Law at the London School of Economics. Tenth from the left sits J. D. B. Mitchell, who later became Professor of Law at Edinburgh.

Hugh Hooson of Colomendy, E. H.'s father.

Elsie Hooson, E. H.'s mother.

Hugh Hooson in later life.

E. H. at war 1944: sweeping the decks of one of the Royal Navy's ships.

Emlyn, friend and walking stick.

Royal Navy colleagues. For three years E. H. was 'tossed about on the lower deck of a corvette . . .'

Young Liberals at play and in good voice: Eifion Roberts, E. H., Glyn Tegai Hughes, Elwyn R. Thomas and Harri Evans Jones.

The New Radical/Y Rhyddfrydwr Newydd was published by the Liberal Society of the University College of Wales, Aberystwyth, and co-edited by H. Emlyn Hooson, Dewi C. Jones and Elwyn R. Thomas.

An early foray into Montgomeryshire politics for the prospective candidate for Conway. E. H.'s future father-in-law was in the chair. It was at this public meeting that Shirley Hamer first met E. H.

THE NEW
RADICAL

SPRING 1948

1/-

VOLUME 1. No.2

Y RHYDDFRYDWR
NEWYDD

DON'T MISS
THE
PUBLIC MEETING
TO BE HELD IN
CHINA STREET SCHOOLROOM,
ON
Friday, November 12th, 1948,
COMMENCING AT 7-45 P.M.

SPEAKERS:
THE RIGHT HON.
CLEMENT DAVIES, K.C., M.P.
AND
MR. EMLYN HOOSON
(Prospective Liberal Candidate for Conway Division of Caernarvonshire).

Chairman - - Ald. G. F. HAMER.

ALL ARE CORDIALLY INVITED.   NO COLLECTION.

J. Ellis, Printer, &c., Llanidloes.   'Phone 203.

Wedding day, the 2nd of December 1950.

Robin Day, E. H. and Ronald Waterhouse abroad on holiday.

The one-day school at Newton on Saturday, May 5th, 1951.
'Seated: Mrs Emlyn Hooson and the guest speaker – Mr Emlyn Hooson,
Prospective Liberal Candidate for the Conway Division.'

The youngest QC for a generation.
E. H. in silk.

The poster boy for the 1962
by-election in Montgomeryshire.

The last train leaving for Tylwch, 3pm, December 30th, 1962.

Lowri's christening at the Crypt of St Stephen's Chapel in the Houses of Parliament, the 11th of November 1964. Sioned is with her parents. The Reverend Richard Jones can be seen on the stairs. And five years later.

The counsel for the Moors murder trial. From left to right:
D. T. Lloyd Jones. G. Heilpurn, Philip Curtess, E. H., W. Mars Jones,
Ronald Waterhouse, Elwyn Jones.

Admission ticket for the Moors murder
trial at Cheshire Assize, April 1966.

The view the Hoosons had from their
house on the City walls in Chester.

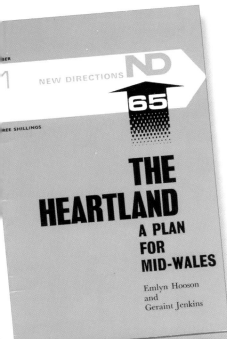

The Heartland [:] A Plan for Mid-Wales (1965) focused on the 'problems of the five counties of Mid-Wales' which had 'not shared in the ... prosperity that has come to Britain since the end of the war.'

'The Montgomeryshire seat is still ours.' Liberal supporters celebrating E. H.'s victory in the 1966 general election.

Fundraising for the Welsh School, London. The Speaker of the House of Commons, George Thomas (left) hosted the meeting. The others seen are Geraint Howells, MP for Ceredigion, Helen Roberts (later Hughes, E. H.'s secretary) and Shirley Hooson.

A cartoon by Peter Clarke. The first sentence of the accompanying text reads: 'If you can't make a silk purse out of a sow's ear you can, apparently[,] make one of the youngest Silks in legal history out of an agriculturalist.'

Opening the new Royal International Pavilion at Llangollen in 1992.

E. H. the committed 'agriculturalist'. On the farm with cousins David Hooson (left) and John Hooson.

16th May, 2002

For Lord Emlyn Hooson QC, on the occasion of the anniversary of his 40 years service to Parliament, a ditty by Lord Mackie of Benshie.

Forty years ago today
You took a step which didn't pay.
To be an MP and a Lord
Is something one cannot afford.
If you had kept the legal pitch
You would by now be stinking rich.

Still politics ain't all that bad
And all your friends are bloody glad
That after that you didn't budge
And become a pompous judge!

— *George*

Shirley Hooson, E. H., Laura Ashley and cars.

E. H., Chairman of Severn River Crossing plc at the second Severn Crossing, three weeks before the official opening in June 1996.

E. H. and Bill Jones, Clerk of his Chambers at Chester between 1950 and 1960.

Llanidloes with Summerfield Park, the home of the Hamers and later the Hoosons, on the bank behind. *Photograph: Adrian Roberts*

My next step was to instruct Martin Thomas, a young and able barrister from Emlyn Hooson's former chambers in Chester, to accept the brief for the Defence Committee. I had briefed him in many other matters over the previous few years and so he was already well-known to me. I was confident that he was more than competent to undertake the presentation of our case at the enquiry.

By now the whole issue had caught the attention of the national press. Simon Hoggart, the distinguished correspondent for *The Guardian*, visited the community and the proposed site of the reservoir, and wrote an expansive piece which was published on the 20th of December 1969.

Many weeks went by while the defence case was prepared. Statements of evidence from the officers of the Defence Committee defined the cultural richness of the community they represented, the importance of sustained agriculture for their society, and the impact the development would have on the population as a whole. I also obtained from a Ceredigion sheep farmer with a wealth of experience of hill-farming comments on the Dulas Valley's farming stock and the viability of the farms themselves: he was by then an MP himself, the late Geraint Howells. The report from the University came in good time. A key piece of its objective evidence was an argument which the Defence Committee had used time after time and which had been extracted from the Secretary of State by Emlyn Hooson in the adjournment debate in the Commons four years previously, namely the magic words that reservoirs should be built only if they did not disrupt living communities.

Before finalising the brief for Martin Thomas I had another general discussion with Emlyn Hooson, reporting on progress, etc. He came up with a wonderful idea. 'Why not get the local community to give a concert in the Community Centre, the venue for the enquiry, the night before it commences? Invite the Inspector to come to it so that he can see for himself what a talented and cultured community is under threat. You can charge the public admission, and that will add a little to the fighting fund.' What a challenge! I asked the local organizations in the Valley if they were agreeable, and of course they were.

Further discussions took place between Emlyn Hooson and me just a few days before the enquiry opened. Quite out of the blue he asked, 'What would you think if I should offer to lead for the Defence Committee with Martin Thomas as junior counsel, and that I should give my services free?' As the saying goes, I snatched his hand off. Morale surged within the entire community. I still had to ensure the success of the concert. I arrived tense, concerned about the morrow's enquiry and that an adequate audience would turn up. I need not have worried. The hall built to accommodate 450 seated was full to the rafters. The press reported that a thousand people attended.

On day one of the enquiry there was one further hurdle to negotiate. The application before it was simply to seek an Order for access to undertake trial borings. The Defence Committee needed to widen the argument to include sociological and other implications. Emlyn Hooson put forward this point to the Inspector, Mr Brough, in the early stages of his first speech. What was the point of granting permission for trial borings, he asked, if the whole application would finally fall on sociological grounds as outlined in the adjournment debate? Emlyn Hooson's sound advocacy persuaded Mr Brough to agree, and he said that he was willing to receive objections on the widest basis and report to the Secretary of State on the full evidence. This was yet another milestone on our journey.

For nine tense days the scheme's promoters were challenged on every point by the Defence Committee's legal team. Finally, winding up for the defence, both Counsel gave moving speeches. At the end of the enquiry one felt that no stone had been left unturned to assist them. But it was impossible to predict the outcome. Wales had a very poor track record in preventing developments of this sort taking place.

The outcome of the enquiry was long awaited. Following delivery of the Inspector's report no doubt there was much political debate between government departments. Moreover, in 1970 there had been a change of government in Westminster: the Conservatives were now in power and the new Secretary of State for Wales was Peter Thomas, a solicitor's son from Llanrwst. The decision was finally made public on the 2nd of December 1970, when the Secretary of State announced that he had accepted Mr B. I. Brough's recommendation that the application be refused. In the report Mr Brough stated that 'A reservoir would put an end to the present way of life . . . of the valley' and concluded that 'because of the consequences for agriculture and particularly for the community, the use of the Dulas Valley for the next regulating reservoir in the Severn would not be authorised.' As Geraint Talfan Davies reported in the *Western Mail*, the victory 'over the reservoir planners [was] hailed as a triumph for the democratic way of opposing reservoir plans.'

Soon afterwards the community, well versed in its religious tradition, held a thanksgiving service in Nantgwyn Baptist Chapel, Pant-y-dŵr, a service in the form of a prayer meeting which was a moving experience not only for myself but also for Martin Thomas who also attended.

CHAMPION OF DEVOLUTION

Elystan Morgan

I feel deeply privileged to have been invited to subscribe a few comments concerning Emlyn Hooson's parliamentary career, and in particular in relation to his attitudes towards the devolution of parliamentary powers to Wales.

We saw much of each other during the last fifty years. Differing political allegiances often made us opponents but we were never enemies, and I always held him in the highest regard and respect. He was a charming gentleman of wide-ranging talents, a parliamentarian who so effortlessly adapted his scintillating advocative courtroom skills to inspired public leadership and political campaigning.

A Welsh speaker, he was steeped in the culture of Wales as well as being an international statesman whose comprehensive vision conceived of a Welsh Parliament as a significant part of the architecture of a federal Britain and a united Europe on the one hand, with reformed local government providing a balanced subsidiarity on the other. Few other political leaders in the last hundred years have woven such apparently diverse strands into a credible tapestry of government for their native land.

In his first foray into parliamentary policies as an unsuccessful Liberal candidate in Conway in 1950 (a constituency that included substantial parts of Lloyd George's old seat of Caernarvon Boroughs) Emlyn always placed dominant emphasis upon the attainment of a Welsh home rule parliament. The same factor characterised his by-election campaign in Montgomeryshire in May 1962.

He was a devolutionist to the backbone, but two things must be said about his attitude to devolution. The first is that his commitment lay not with the geometric niceties of balancing government between the centre and the periphery by outward transfer of legislative and executive authority, but rather with securing for an ancient nation-community a meaningful and authoritative voice in its own affairs. His commitment to home rule sprang in the first instance from his Welsh patriotism. For him it was the irrefutable fact of nationhood that established the incontrovertible case for a Welsh parliament, and his commitment to that cause was more a visceral instinct than an intellectual conclusion. The second and equally pertinent comment I wish to make is that as much as anyone else in public life over the last half century he had the classically correct concept of what devolution essentially was and is. It is the deliberate transfer of authority and responsibility from central government outwards to the periphery. The creation of the Welsh Office in 1964 was such an act of administrative and executive devolution. The transfer thereafter of decision-making powers from the Welsh Office to the Welsh Assembly was *not* devolution as such, although of course it placed powers in the hands of the Welsh people through their elective representatives. Emlyn with his razor-sharp legal mind saw this reality with greater clarity than almost anyone. Seldom in the House of Commons or the House of Lords did he fail to submit any plan for the reform of government in Wales to the litmus test of the crucial question, 'Does this particular measure involve a direct transfer of power from Westminster to Wales?' If the answer was in the negative it was *not* devolution to Wales. In 1967 Emlyn founded and became president of a new organization called The Welsh Liberal Party. Not everyone amongst his constituency supporters approved of this. On St David's Day that year Emlyn sought leave to introduce in the Commons a Bill 'to provide a scheme for the domestic self-government of Wales and for connected purposes'. The measure provided for a senate of 88 members with powers to make and enforce laws on all matters appertaining to the domestic life of Wales, her industry, trade, agriculture, education, health, transport, etc. Of his Welsh nationhood he said:

> I am happy to say that, in many facets of our national life, we are still conscious of that harmony of spirit which unites us a nation. We inherit a small but distinct culture whose origins are lost in antiquity. Our language is an expressive language of lyrical and emotive beauty. But we are bound by something beyond language, beyond culture only, by that curious blend of romanticism and radicalism which in one way or another finds expression in every son of Wales. This is the peculiar fervour which for well over 1,000 years has enabled us to preserve our individuality and enabled us to make contributions to life outside Wales as well as within Wales in a distinctive way.

In seeking today to introduce a Bill for a domestic Parliament for Wales, I do not come to the House of Commons looking to the past, although I am conscious of it. I do not come here nursing grievances or imagining injustices. I do not subscribe to the myth that the English are bent malevolently on the destruction of Wales. (There are exceptions of course.) If that were so we could easily deal with them and far more effectively. What I fear far more is their sympathetic but inactive benevolence. There is in this House a great measure of sympathy and kindly feeling towards Wales, but there is not here the time, the committed interest, the single-mindedness, the overwhelming concern to ensure that the economic, social and cultural life of the Welsh nation is properly safeguarded.

Emlyn, the distinguished internationalist that he was – he was chairman of an all-party group on World Government and a Parliamentary Delegate to NATO – always conceived of Wales constitutional development in an international setting:

It is in that context that I would like the House to consider the Bill that I seek leave to introduce. I am not a Universalist; I am an internationalist. I believe that people will come under the same law only when they consent to do so. Their consent will be obtained only when is recognized that their vital interests, culture, social heritage and rights must properly be safeguarded.

He ended his address with these ringing and challenging words:

> I ask leave to bring in the Bill, and I hope that the House will take courage to ensure that this time next year, this time in a hundred years and so on into the 22nd century, not only will the daffodils still bloom but the Welsh nation will survive and grow and make its own distinctive contribution to a greater whole in Britain, Europe and the world.

In the context of Welsh devolution Emlyn was always eager to co-operate with others who genuinely held such views. In that he echoed the policy of his hero Lloyd George who said famously, 'I will accompany any man provided he is going my way.' But he always opposed those deviations that could dangerously distract effective constitutional progress. He despised sham devolution. Nowhere is this more clearly expressed than in a speech he made in the Commons on the 25th of July 1967 on the proposal of the government to set up a Nominated Council for Wales. To him such would be 'the fool's gold' (my description, not his) of devolution, as aberrant as it was irrelevant and unreal. Emlyn referred to an earlier proposal by government in 1948 to create a nominated body for Wales. He quoted the flabby words used by Herbert Morrison in introducing that plan:

> I think this scheme will prove to be acceptable to the gener-al body of Welsh Members, but the fact is we cannot think

of anything better. We think this is the best expedient open to us and we should be most regretful if honourable members took such an opposite view that we did not go on with this. We are unable, as have been governments before us, to think of anything better than this, we think this is good.

Emlyn concentrated on the relevant post-1948 developments which included the creation of the Welsh Office, and argued that a nominated council in 1967 was an even more grotesque monstrosity than it would have been in 1948. He contemptuously described the proposal as being 'of a kind normally reserved for backward colonies who cannot elect their own representatives.' He went on to expose mercilessly the supreme uselessness of the government's proposals:

> It is suggested in the White Paper that the Welsh Council should have among its responsibilities: 'To provide a forum for the interchange of views and information on developments in the economic and cultural fields, and to advise on the implications for Wales of national policies.' Why on earth do we need nominated people to do this? Wales has elected Members in this House. Other areas do not need nominated bodies to advise the Minister how people think, and on developments in the economic and cultural fields.
>
> The next power suggested is: 'To assist in the formulation of the plans for Wales, having regard to the best use of its resources and to advise the Secretary of State for Wales on major land use and economic planning matters.'

Why is it necessary to have a nominated council for a purpose of this kind?

Emlyn's plea during the next few years up to and including the Referendum in 1979 was for the swift transfer to an elected Welsh Assembly of substantial administrative functions as well as meaningful law-making powers which included but which also exceeded those powers already vested in the Secretary of State for Wales. In the mid 1970s Emlyn's advocacy on behalf of Wales increasingly linked the devolution of executive and legislative powers to the reform of local government. He saw with total clarity that unless the two developments were to proceed in tandem, Wales would soon find itself with an additional, but unnecessary, tier of government. I well recall that it was during this period and in the context of this issue that he indulged in the immortal parody of Mark Antony's tribute to the murdered Caesar: 'If you have tears (tiers) to shed prepare to shed them now.' He put the matter most succinctly in his speech on devolution in the Commons on the 4th of February 1975. It was an exhibition of both political foresight and of courage, since he well knew that in advocating the most urgently required amalgamation of county and district councils he would earn the instant enmity of members of both bodies. The dominant passages of that speech read as follows:

> We have no fewer than three main tiers of government. The first is the Westminster tier – and I regard the Welsh Office, which takes executive decisions, and all bodies

associated with it, as part of that tier. The second tier is
the county councils, which are excessively remote, highly-
centralized and were thrust upon an unwilling people by
the Conservative government. Below that, as the third tier,
we have the district councils. It may also be the case with
others parts of the country, but I know that in mine I hear
... complaints of the excessive government from which we
are suffering ... I do not believe that the ordinary people
of Wales are prepared to accept an additional tier. I think
that the real issue is that of balance. Either we abolish the
county councils – and there is a good case for that – and
have multi-purpose authorities close to the ground in the
form of district councils, and above them a Welsh domestic
Parliament or Assembly dealing with the matters that are
devolved to it from Westminster – and possibly one or two
matters which could come out of the county councils –
and have that as a second tier; or the real alternative is that
the devolved powers proposed by the government should
go to the existing large county councils. I do not think
the people of Wales will stand for the present proposals
super-added, as it were, to the county councils.

On very many public occasions Emlyn also emphasized
the false move achieved by the Conservative government of
1970–1974 in prejudicing the debate on devolution by their
doctrinal determination to rush through the 'reform' of
local government – their so-called reform of health services
and the reorganization of water supplies. It would have
been wiser to deal with all those matters as part of a wider

and comprehensive devolution plan. The government had rushed on blindly as if the Kilbrandon/Crowther Commission had never existed.

Emlyn's intellect and vision as a constitutional lawyer came very much to the fore in the debates which formed the backcloth to the devolution legislation which led ultimately to the Wales Act of 1978 and the ill-fated referendum of the 1st of March 1979. In a debate on the White Paper on Scottish and Welsh devolution on the 15th of January 1976 Emlyn stressed five elements. First – and consistent with his constant test in the context of devolution – that transfers of existing powers from such Welsh institutions as the Welsh Office to a Welsh Assembly (actually called in the statute a 'senate') was *not* devolution from Westminster to Wales. Secondly, that the model proposed for the Assembly was essentially that of a local government council as opposed to a parliamentary model, in that the decisions would be made by committees. In his opinion, that would be a massively retrograde step. Thirdly and fundamentally, that the Assembly would have no real legislative powers and would thus lack the status of a parliament. He reminded the House that each of the states of the USA had legislative powers, so too had each of the states of the Länder Parliaments of Germany, and that was also the case in Northern Ireland. He reminded the House that 'Wales is not having any legislative powers. It is an absolute sham.' Fourthly, he submitted that such changes could only operate successfully within the structure of a Bill of Rights. In that context Emlyn was anticipating a reality which only became totally apparent in the debates concerning the reform of the House of Lords many years later, when it became obvious to many constitutional experts that fundamental changes to the machinery of parliamentary government can only be effectively made within the structure of a Bill of Rights. Fifthly and lastly, he returned to his favourite plea for proportional representation, reminding everyone that this was the sole recommendation in regard to which the Crowther/ Kilbrandon Commission had achieved unanimity.

When the Second Reading of the Scotland and Wales Bill came before the Commons in December 1976 Emlyn again made a contribution of great wisdom and authority. He appealed to the government to concentrate its effort more upon seeking to meet the real doubts of its friends rather than defending itself from the wholly negative attacks of the Conservatives. In that speech he also showed that his far-sighted intellectual reach in relation to Welsh constitutional development exceeded his immediate tactical grasp. He defined his views on federalism thus:

> I am basically a federalist, and I think that that is the arrangement we shall eventually be driven to in any event. If we want to keep the unity of the whole country and yet give meaningful devolution to its constituent parts, logic and the need to preserve that unity will drive us to a federal system.

He identified two strong tendencies currently prevalent in Western Europe. The first was the need for people to get together to gain greater security against attack. The second was a feeling prevalent in Wales, Scotland and in some of the English regions that government was too remote and that communities should be able to express their own identity through local organs. These two trends far from being in conflict with each other were essentially complementary. This is how he ended his speech:

> I have said on many occasions that it is more important for Wales to get devolution right than to get it in a hurry. I am sure that is so. It is vital that we take the people with us. In Committee we shall be watching to see how willing the government are to accept changes in their Bill. I am sure that there will be increasing pressure within the country and from Europe for greater unity within Europe. That is a dimension that will have to be considered. I have said on a number of occasions that although I have always been interested in devolution – this is a matter that my party has argued for for many years – the debate is still in its infancy for many people. We regard the Bill as possibly a *pro tem* measure, but in the end we shall have to find a system of government that ensures that we are not over-governed, a system that gives us vastly more control over local affairs and regional matters and yet enables us to keep the unity of the United Kingdom with a view to even greater unity by the end of the century.

The third reading of the Wales Bill of the 9th May 1978 was a bitter affair. Emlyn however saw the historic significance of the legislation despite its obvious structural defects. He said:

The Bill has one merit which transcends all its other merits and demerits. It provides the people of Wales with a great opportunity that they have not had for centuries, if ever, and which over the years they have wanted – to have an elected body to speak in their name.

He ended his speech on a justifiably sombre note:

All in all, the progress of the Bill through the House has been an example of the House at its worst in many respects. The whole matter has been used as a propaganda exercise to try to defeat the Bill and misrepresent its content. I think that in the end the people of Wales will have a vote on the matter, and that they will not lightly reject the opportunity, which they have never had, of establishing an Assembly that can speak for them. No Right Hon. or Hon. Member in any part of the House should underestimate the eventual realization of the power of the Welsh people when it comes to the referendum to decide not to miss this opportunity.

In the Referendum campaign that preceded the vote on the 1st of March 1979 Emlyn played a leading and gallant role. As I have already noted, for him the case for an elected Welsh Assembly was founded upon the fact of Welsh nationhood. That nationhood could not ultimately survive – and certainly could not flourish – without the protective carapace of an Assembly. Emlyn tirelessly put the 'Yes' campaign case in speeches, broadcasts and statements to the press. His nationalism was linked to his Europeanism. In an article in the *Liverpool Daily Post* in late February 1979 he wrote: 'If we are going to have a United States of Europe we must have Welsh devolution, for we would only be tolerant of the former if we had the later.'

The electors of Montgomeryshire rejected the prospect of an Assembly in a more crushingly determined fashion than almost any other part of Wales. Emlyn, who could read the political runes as well as any man, appreciated the risk he was taking as one of the leaders of the 'Yes' campaign. He could well have played a more anonymous role but he chose the courageous alternative. Two months after the referendum he lost the seat that he had held for seventeen years and thus had to leave the House of Commons in which he had so distinguished himself and where clearly he had so much more to contribute. His defeat at the hands of the Conservative candidate Delwyn Williams, with the benefit of hindsight, can be seen in its historical context. Kenneth O. Morgan, in his book *Modern Wales* (1995), analyses in some detail the processes which led to Emlyn's defeat, and they included his leadership role in the Referendum debate.

In 1979 Emlyn became a life peer and for many years graced the Upper House with his youthful enthusiasm and effervescent wit. He worked assiduously in the Lords with regular contributions to radical politics on a British and European and world plane but with his customary intimate concentration on Welsh and rural affairs. He made his maiden speech there on the 20th of February 1980 in a debate entitled 'Wales: Social and Economic Policy'. This speech, which was well received by the House, above all shows how much Emlyn, the country dweller and farmer that he was, knew about the intricate and historic problems of industrial Wales and the decline in heavy industries which so threatened our national economy. He saw with great realism that the Welsh steel industry was in jeopardy, although, together with the declining coal industry, it still employed some fifteen per cent of the Welsh male working population. He probed the government about its specific plans to combat these structural problems and also questioned closely the specific finances they were prepared to invest to alleviate them. He ended with a humane and original suggestion that the pensions of coal miners and steel workers should to be paid at the earlier age of sixty.

Emlyn was in his element in his speech on the Second Reading of the Welsh Language Bill, 1993. He opened by repeating the comment of a friend of his. Upon being told by Emlyn that the purpose of the Bill was to give the Welsh language equal status in Wales with the English, the friend said, 'Good heavens! Have you had to wait until 1993 for that?' He supported the Bill with enthusiasm and saw it as a natural progression from the work of the Welsh Language Board which had been created by Peter Walker in 1998. As a lawyer well versed in the constitutional history of Wales, Emlyn was thrilled by the fact that the Bill repealed the remnants of the Act of Union of 1536 and its complementary legislation of 1543. After many centuries, at long last a grave national injustice and dishonour had been expunged. But in addition to this *tour d'horizon* of Welsh history he stressed the failure of the Bill to apply its provisions to governmental departments and to public utilities. Furthermore, he showed imaginative foresight in pleading the case for every child in Wales to be taught the language. He rightly regarded this as crucial to the future of Welsh. His words parallel those of Cardinal Newman on the religious education of the young ('give me the children of England under the age of five and in a generation I will give you a Catholic Country').

Emlyn's contribution to the Local Government (Wales) Bill [HL] on the 14th of December 1993 again illustrates local government as a crucial part of the seamless web of governmental structure. The simile he adopted to describe his wife's experience in local government with his own more strategic role in Parliament is typical of the warmth and colour with which he could illustrate a point:

> Although I have no direct participatory experience of local government, my wife has a good deal. When we compare notes I sometimes feel that she is very much the worker at the coal face while I am looking at the same problems from the remoteness of the coal board area manager's office.

On the 10th of December 1997, in a debate on BSE, Emlyn spoke as a hill farmer and country dweller who had no illusions concerning the grave jeopardy in which British agriculture stood at that juncture. He exposed with his characteristic advocative skills the hollowness of the government's case in seeking to justify the panic measures they had taken:

Scientists estimated that no more than three out of the 2.2 million cattle slaughtered for consumption next year might carry infection . . . They said there was a 5 per cent chance that one person in the entire population may be infected with BSE by eating beef from these animals. So the chance that anyone eating beef on the bone would contract BSE is roughly one in one billion! How does that justify the reaction of the Minister of Agriculture? What right has Big Brother to prevent British customers from exercising their traditional right to buy beef on the bone?

On the 17th of June 1997 Emlyn showed how vital he regarded the necessity of winning the forthcoming referendum on the Welsh Assembly. He quoted the words of Peter Hain in the Commons: 'If Wales votes No to devolution for the second time in a generation Wales can kiss goodbye to devolution.' He scorned the pathetic negativity of the Conservative Party's doctrinaire obstruction to the Bill as unjustified in the light of the sweeping mandate the Labour Government had received in the general election of that year. He quoted from the *Rubaiyat of Omar Khayyam*:

> The moving finger writes; and, having writ
> Moves on: Not all thy Piety nor Wit
> Shall lure it back to cancel half a line,
> Nor all thy Tears wash out a Word of it.

In a detailed speech on the Government of Wales Bill on the 21st of April 1998, Emlyn stressed the central deficiency of the Bill in that the government had failed to incorporate this legislation in a constitutional settlement involving the whole of Britain. This was undoubtedly a wise and penetrative comment although absolute adherence to this view might have postponed the establishment of a Welsh Assembly for very many years. In that debate Emlyn again spelt out his Welsh political nationalism in the concentric structure of a federal Britain and a United Europe. In a moving and poetic passage he said:

> In the end we have to think of Wales as part of Britain. I have always thought of myself as a Welsh, British, European and world citizen too, [although] these are different spheres. Years ago I became a convinced European and federalist when I heard a marvellous address by the ex-Secretary General of the League of Nations, Salvador de Madariaga. In 1947 I heard him talk at the University about the end of the nation state being in sight, not necessarily in this century. I think that he was right. He pointed out that Europe is a really great river, with enormous contributions to make to the great civilization of the world. There were [he said] various contributories and Britain was probably one of the main, if not the main, contributory. I have thought of Wales in that context ever since. Wales is a little mountain stream – Nant y Mynydd – contributing, but no river can flow without its tributaries, and no tributaries can contribute without mountain streams. It is in that context that we want to see Wales. It is for us to make sure that we provide Wales with the means of maximising its contribution. We shall not do so through fighting the old battles of the past but by appreciating the world in which we live.

Then on the 21st of February 2000 Emlyn spoke in another House of Lords debate relating to Wales. He stressed as before the failure to transfer to Wales powers of primary legislation, and that the devolutionary effect of the Assembly was not to transfer fresh authority to Wales from Westminster but to indulge in a secondary devolution within Wales, namely the transfer of authority from the Welsh Office to the Assembly. He summed up his concern in one sentence: 'because it is an elected assembly it can have far more influence than a mere administrative office.' Emlyn as much as anybody appreciated the massive significance of creating a body elected by the people of Wales meeting on the soil of Wales and possessing the moral authority to speak for the Welsh nation.

Two years later he contributed substantially to yet another debate in on Welsh Devolution. He expressed deep regret of the fact that no statutory powers had been transferred to Wales with regard to any control of the media, particularly in the case of television. He spoke also of the need to look at each and every quango operating in Wales. In regard to these matters his incisive and mature analysis anticipated the struggles of the last few years in relation both to the quasi-autonomous bodies and the future of S4C, in respect of which the present government has gratuitously placed itself in such impossible difficulty. His ardent hope for the future of the Assembly is contained in this passage. They are the wise and prophetic words of a distinguished statesman who held his Welsh nationhood in such high esteem:

The success of the Assembly depends upon the ability, knowledge, dedication and application of its members. It is up to each political party to ensure that its candidates for the Assembly want to make it work and that they are people who have a good deal to contribute to its success. It is not a training ground for Westminster. It would be a poor one in which to train for Westminster and it would not be a good one for the Assembly if it attracted that kind of person.

The Assembly should not try to mirror the party battles of Westminster. I believe that it should form its own agenda for Wales. So far as concerns the Cabinet in Wales, it would not worry me if it were formed of a coalition of members of all parties. The members could evolve the idea of filling the post of Minister with the best person for the job. After all, they are discharging administrative functions. Their other powers are very limited.

In the years immediately preceding his death we met on many occasions in the precincts of Parliament and often exchanged reminiscences of distant days. Although the memory of more recent matters may have been fading, his countenance would suddenly light up as the recall of a certain event became total. Once again his elegant wit would flow and his puckish charm and humour was all dominant. Emlyn was a splendid man, whose brilliance radiated in so many directions, none more so than in the two Houses of Parliament whose historic environment he so adorned.

POLITICIAN AND LAWYER

Alex Carlile and Russell Deacon

[Lord Hooson's life in politics and Law was anything but dull. Across his lifespan he became involved in some of the most famous legal and political events of the age. By the mid 1960s he was nationally recognized by the media, the public and his fellow professionals. He was widely seen as being at the top of both his political and legal profession from this period onwards. This essay explores the advances of his legal and political careers with specific reference to his leadership qualities, his legal progression, and his views on Europe and the former Liberal leader Jeremy Thorpe.]

HOOSON THE QC

When Emlyn Hooson died on the 21st February 2012, aged 86, there passed with him a great era of Welsh advocates who had learned and practised their craft in the days of a strong Wales and Chester Circuit and in the Assize Courts and Quarter Sessions; and of Liberal politicians whose memories of Lloyd George and his radical, rural legacy were actual and powerful.

Emlyn had been called to the Bar in 1949 by Gray's Inn, where he was Treasurer in 1986. After pupillage with Daniel Brabin (later Mr Justice Brabin) in Liverpool, as noted in Eifion Roberts's essay, he formed his own chambers in

Chester in 1950, and acquired as his Clerk Bill Jones, one of the great characters of the Wales and Chester Circuit and a confidant of many distinguished lawyers. As a team they flourished quickly. That Emlyn took silk in 1960 (becoming a Queen's Counsel), at just 35 years old, speaks for itself. He had developed a formidable mixed practice, combining crime, personal injury law, substantial family law cases, and planning. One of his great qualities as an advocate was his ability and willingness to turn his hand to anything, especially if the issues interested him. Emlyn could conduct cases with equal comfort in English and Welsh.

His meteoric Bar career included the chairmanship of Flint Quarter Sessions from 1960, and Merioneth Quarter Sessions from 1962. Emlyn presided over the last ever hearing in Merioneth Quarter Sessions, at Dolgellau in December 1971. Appropriately, it was a sheep-stealing case, full of the drama and tension that he so enjoyed in court. It even included a young witness collapsing after a flash of lightning and a clap of thunder when he gave some evidence favouring the accused.

In his professional life he was at his very best in criminal defence, dangerously charming to unsuspecting witnesses before hitting his point. Among his best-known cases were the defence of Ian Brady in the Moors murder trial, and the defence of a young airman in the Cyprus spy trial of 1985. Of Brady he spoke very little in the years that followed. Emlyn had seen it as his duty to defend him, once asked, and did so with skill and realism. However, he never spoke about it to colleagues save when he thought that his experience in that case might serve to instruct others. His many juniors always appreciated his instruction and advice, and his willingness to entrust real responsibility to them in difficult cases. In politics as in Law, Emlyn saw the key points at a glance, sometimes uncannily so. This was an extraordinary talent, a talent you cannot bottle.

HOOSON THE POLITICIAN

Despite criticism throughout his period in the Commons that Emlyn was dedicated to his legal rather than to a parliamentary career, the opposite was in fact the case. He refused the Bench (the office of judge) because this other professional life – politics – was his real passion. He was born into Liberalism. His was true Welsh Liberalism: he believed in significant autonomy for Wales, and was delighted when devolution occurred. Emlyn was a social Liberal, convinced that a quality education system and an excellent National Health Service were important rights. In legal policy, he was a strong campaigner against capital punishment, and had appeared in some notable capital cases. In economic policy he was far from the left leanings of many modern Liberal Democrats. He had a firm conviction that wealth had to be created by ideas and effort, so that the State could collect the fruits in fair taxation. His years as a non-executive director of Laura Ashley plc, including a period as chairman, and a tenure as chairman of the company owning the second Severn Crossing, were testament to his acumen, knowledge and support of quality private enterprise.

Emlyn was a much-loved MP who had won Montgomeryshire in a by-election in 1962 upon the death of the former Liberal leader Clement Davies, who was also a QC from Gray's Inn. Losing the seat in 1979 was a shock, a political event which, if anticipated, would never have occurred. We will see later in the essay some of the political factors that Emlyn felt were central to the loss of his seat. This aside, he was delighted when the Montgomeryshire seat was regained for the Liberals at the next election in 1983 by Alex Carlile QC (later Lord Carlile). He remained involved in Montgomeryshire and national politics for the rest of his life.

In 1979, after a short gap, Emlyn, newly ennobled, returned to Westminster where he worked closely again with Geraint Howells MP, who would himself join Emlyn in the Lords after losing his Cardiganshire seat in 1992. In the House of Lords Emlyn spoke well and often, and was a great champion for Wales. He had made a study and speciality of international defence on which he spoke with authority. Emlyn also became an active member of the NATO Council with many contacts around the world with specialists in defence and related matters, who included the former US Secretary of State for Defense, Donald Rumsfeld.

His wife Shirley was the perfect partner for Emlyn, a distinguished and tireless public servant herself, and a determined councillor. She came from a deeply imbued

Liberal family and her instinctive understanding of mid-Wales politics always kept Emlyn grounded in his constituency.

HOOSON THE WELSH LIBERAL LEADER

On the 17th of January 1967 Jo Grimond announced that he would step down as Liberal leader. Grimond had been responsible for a Liberal revival in Scotland. When Emlyn became an MP in 1962 there was also a widespread hope within the party that he would revive Liberal fortunes in Wales. This was something which Emlyn had every hope of doing and he had already helped set up the Welsh party as a devolved part of Liberals' federal structure. Even before he became the MP for Montgomeryshire Emlyn had been on a mission to revitalize the Welsh Liberal Party.

Seeking to do in Wales what Jo Grimond had managed in Scotland meant Emlyn was the driving force to re-radicalize the party in Wales. As part of this process at the Welsh party's August 1965 Conference Emlyn outlined the Welsh Radical Group's plans for revitalizing the Welsh economy in a pamphlet entitled *The Heartland*. Despite the optimistic note made there about the Welsh Liberals' opportunity of becoming an alternative to Labour in Wales, there was little evidence of any real Liberal growth. Roderic Bowen's loss of Cardiganshire in the 1964 general election and the failure to gain Denbigh or regain Carmarthen or Meirionnydd (both possibilities) left the Welsh Liberals in a disappointed and weakened state. The Welsh party during Emlyn's first decade at Westminster remained one of near misses and a party unable to stand up to Labour's gradual encroachment into its traditional Liberal heartland. After the loss of Cardiganshire in 1964 Emlyn for the whole of the next decade remained the sole Welsh Liberal banner-holder in the House of Commons. Although he revitalized the party in Wales by giving it a strong structure, and in 1966 created the Welsh Liberal Party as a separate entity, under his leadership it never had a widespread revival electorally. But he did inspire many younger colleagues to work with him.

Whilst seeking to develop the party in Wales Emlyn also maintained a strong desire to revive the British Liberal Party. Since Clement Davies had stepped down as leader in 1956, there had been little Welsh influence on the Liberal Federal Party. Therefore when in January 1967 Jo Grimond declared that he no longer wished to be its leader, the contest for a new leader opened a door of opportunity for Emlyn. Was this now the time to bring back a Welsh leader? Emlyn thought so. After all, Welsh Liberalism had for over a century been the backbone of Liberalism in Great Britain, and in the 1940s and 1950s was one of the reasons it survived as a national party.

The Liberal leadership contest was opened and held the day after Grimond's resignation with an electorate of just twelve MPs. Despite the fact that the Liberal constituencies wanted a direct voice in choosing the leader, in 1967 this was denied them. Of the party's twelve MPs, Jeremy Thorpe was the most well-known nationally. He had spent much of the previous decade touring the country and establishing a name for himself. Whereas Grimond was related to the Asquiths, Thorpe's family was strongly connected to the Lloyd Georges, a relationship that went back generations; of later significance is the fact that Lady Megan Lloyd George was his godmother. The Lloyd Georges, however, had, for almost a generation, aside from Olwen, not influenced Welsh Liberal politics. Therefore as the election was only open to MPs, and Emlyn being the sole remaining Welsh Liberal MP, having a Lloyd George pedigree would be irrelevant in the leadership contest.

Aside from Thorpe, two other MPs threw their political hats into the ring. One was Eric Lubbock (then Chief Whip), the victor of the Orpington by-election in 1962, who was based in London and had never played a part in Welsh affairs. The Welsh party leader, Emlyn, had tried to persuade Richard Wainwright, MP for Colne Valley, to stand for the leadership, but he had been a conscientious objector in the Second World War and felt this would be a burden when leading the party. Failing to get Wainwright to stand, Emlyn was left in a dilemma. He did not trust Thorpe to lead the party, thinking of him as a 'Jekyll and Hyde character', and concluded that he must stand against him. Would Montgomeryshire now produce another federal party leader to follow in the footsteps of Clement Davies? Emlyn had laid out his own manifesto for the leadership a year before, a manifesto entitled 'The three conditions for Liberal growth', which were:

First, the Liberal Party must maintain absolute independence of the Labour and Conservatives parties.

Secondly, we Liberals must never allow our policies and
our attitudes to change in the hope of small, short-
term gains.

Thirdly, we Liberals must reaffirm strongly our beliefs
that human progress comes largely through individual
efforts.

Through this brief manifesto and his public determination in the general election of 1964 to place the Liberals
as a 'radical non-socialist party' with no formal agreement
with the Labour government, Emlyn was seen to be to
the political right of the party. Thorpe and Lubbock were
further to the left. When the votes were cast on the 18th of
January 1967 Emlyn got three votes, Eric Lubbock three and
Thorpe six. Having lost, the two failed candidates and their
supporters then publicly got behind Thorpe as their leader.

Alan Watkins, the political columnist, commented at the
time that many in the party believed that 'Mr Hooson is in
some quarters thought to be too mild mannered, and too
immersed in his legal practice, to make a wholly successful
party leader.' It was not, however, the party members
that rejected him but his fellow MPs. Emlyn would now
concentrate on building both his legal and parliamentary
career, whilst it would be up to Thorpe to lead the party
into the next general election. Emlyn's attempt at the party
leadership was to be the last bid for the party's federal
leadership by a Welsh Liberal MP. For the rest of the

century, the British Liberal Party would be led by MPs from the West Country and Scotland, with only the occasional Welsh federal president showing that the Welsh too were an active part of the wider Liberal Party.

HOOSON AND EUROPE

Emlyn had illustrated his pro-European credentials for the first time publicly in articles for *The New Radical*, a journal produced by Liberal students in Aberystwyth in 1947. It was here that he strongly advocated the Free Trade and the United Europe movement.

International matters were always close to Liberals' hearts, and in 1973 many Welsh Liberals were delighted that Edward Heath was able to complete, after long drawn-out negotiations, Britain's entry into the European Community. Although this was at the core of the internationalist beliefs of generations of Welsh Liberals, and initially beneficial for Welsh farmers, it did not have total support within the Welsh party. In the European Community debates, Emlyn had been the sole Liberal Parliamentarian against joining the Community. He thought both agriculture and industry would take a 'hammering if we go in'. In 1971 he declared at the party's Scarborough conference that although he did not challenge the party's deep commitment to Europe, he did not share the romantic view of Europe which believed that the Common Market was the answer to all ills. Hooson's views on Europe were to put him on the right of the party during both this and the next two Parliaments and thus at odds with many other Welsh Liberals.

When it came to the 1975 European referendum, however, both Geraint Howells and Emlyn campaigned for a Yes vote, in part because of their own internationalist convictions and in part because the farmers in their constituencies were heavily in favour of it. At the time Emlyn felt that the Common Agricultural Policy, CAP, provided a good deal for Welsh farmers. The Welsh result saw 64.8% of the Welsh population vote Yes. In Emlyn's own county of Powys, with some 74.3% voting Yes, the result was the highest in Wales. Both Geraint Howells and Emlyn welcomed the result of the referendum as they believed it enhanced Wales' European connections. They called for better links with the Common Market with roll-on, roll-off terminal ports for Cardiff and Newport, and called for the Welsh Secretary to attend European Council meetings. Ironically for the Welsh Liberals, from now on they would consistently remain one of the most pro-European parties in Wales but would never get an elected member of the European Parliament in which to demonstrate this enthusiasm.

In 1979, for a time, Emlyn became the Liberals' Lords spokesman on Europe and would further endorse both his own and his party's commitment to the European ideal. As Andrew Roth's obituary of him in *The Guardian* noted, in his later years his position on Europe softened. He was anxious to overcome 'the baleful influence of the Eurosceptics' among the Tories. Speaking 'as one who represents a minority culture', he said 'it seems to me that aggressive and self-glorifying nationalism is still one of the great curses of our century.' As a Royal Navy sailor who served in the Second World War Emlyn was only too aware of where 'aggressive nationalism' could lead.

THORPE AND HOOSON

Thorpe had spoken on behalf of Emlyn during his 1962 by-election campaign and the two had frequently campaigned together in Wales. As colleagues they could not avoid close contact at Westminster and in party events. In the 1964 general election campaign Emlyn had campaigned in the south of Wales with Jo Grimond, leaving Roderic Bowen to campaign in the north with Thorpe. In later elections, as the sole Welsh Liberal MP, he campaigned with Thorpe across Wales. As leader it was Thorpe, in November 1973, who provided Emlyn with his large portfolio, asking him to speak for the parliamentary party on Agriculture, Wales and the Law. Emlyn, however, was on occasions at odds with Thorpe's leadership and direction of the party. This became more noticeable towards the end of Thorpe's period as leader. In February 1975 Emlyn sent Thorpe a despairing letter which stated:

> The low profile which the party has adopted since the last election is a mistake. Although there is tremendous

enthusiasm among Liberals in the country, there is a general sense of the party drifting and lacking a sense of direction . . . Both Tories and Labour are going for the middle ground which is the only fruitful ground in politics for the Liberals.

Emlyn and some Welsh Liberals believed that the only solution to this problem was to raise the Welsh Liberal Party's profile. Other Welsh Liberals believed that the party's problems had come about not because of a low profile but because of its obsession with proportional representation in elections, at the expense of other issues. The Liberal Party had spent nearly the whole of 1975 campaigning on both devolution and what it described as 'The Great Vote Robbery', that is, the way it had lost out electorally in the 1974 general elections. Despite Emlyn's protests, proportional representation would be central to Liberal Party policy for the next two decades. But Thorpe, as events turned out, would not be.

HOOSON AND THE THORPE AFFAIR

There has been extensive coverage of the Thorpe Affair both at the time and in the decades that followed. Much of this has now developed into myth. What is certain is that Emlyn together with the then Liberal Chief Whip David Steel were central to the initial development of the affair. In May 1971, Mrs Parry-Jones, an active Liberal in Tal-y-bont,

Ceredigion, had contacted Emlyn, her nearest Liberal MP, noting her concern about what she saw as the 'ruining of a young man's life by a leading member of your party'. Initially Emlyn thought that the 'leading member' was Peter Bessell, a former Liberal MP of some disrepute, but it was not. Over the next five years the issue involving Thorpe developed into a substantial sexual scandal which would culminate in his resignation. The Thorpe Affair reached its height when a man called Norman Scott, who alleged that he had had a homosexual affair with Thorpe in the 1960s, was taken to court for defrauding the benefit system. He there asserted that Thorpe had tried to have him killed the year before. Although these allegations were never proved either at Scott's trial or at Thorpe's own trial in 1979, it was enough to make Thorpe resign as leader in 1976.

Emlyn had already privately described Thorpe to his face as a 'combination of Horatio Bottomley [an MP jailed for fraud] and Oscar Wilde [the well-known nineteenth-century homosexual writer]'. When Thorpe eventually resigned on the 9th of May 1976 his resignation was soundly welcomed by the public. Emlyn had advised him to go at a much earlier stage, and Emlyn later regretted that this resignation, the circumstances of which damaged the Party, had not been forced much earlier. He also came to believe that the loss of the Montgomeryshire seat in 1979 was in some way connected to the Thorpe Affair.

In the subsequent leadership election, Emlyn Hooson thought about standing for the leadership once more. In

March 1976 he stated publicly that he would do so, but in the end, because of the lack of party support outside Wales, he did not stand. This was despite a supportive campaign led by Martin Thomas to reassure Liberals within the wider party and to reassure the media that, notwithstanding Emlyn's right-of-centre reputation, he was a sound candidate. With Emlyn out of the running, at a special Welsh party meeting in Westminster on the 11th of May 1977, both Welsh MPs and John Roberts, chairman of the Welsh party, declared their support for Jo Grimond to take over as a caretaker leader. Then in the final leadership contest between David Steel and John Pardoe both Emlyn and Geraint Howells backed David Steel.

The whole business of Thorpe's resignation was damaging to the Liberals electorally across Britain. It brought their own morale to a low ebb as their disgraced leader and, later on, former leader, was dragged through the law courts. As much as the Welsh Liberals deplored the continued references to the 'Thorpe scandal' in the daily press and the impact it had on their own fortunes, there was little they could do to stop it and its political fallout. When he lost his seat in 1979 Emlyn would put the Thorpe Affair combined with the failed devolution referendum as the central reasons for losing his Montgomeryshire seat.

Unlike many Liberals, he tended to see Labour as the real enemy. Radical in Welsh matters, he was really a centrist, as he showed when he supported Alan Beith against Paddy Ashdown in the 1988 leadership contest. Neverthe less he came to admire Ashdown's dynamism, personality, commitment and conceptual approach to Liberal politics.

HIS TWO PROFESSIONS

Emlyn Hooson was one of the last of the QC/MPs who managed a fine career in both parts of their professional lives. It is nigh impossible today to work as he did, conducting complex cases 200 miles from London whilst representing a constituency that respected him enormously, and knew him personally. The huge number of people attending his funeral in Llanidloes and his memorial service in London provided compelling evidence of his personal popularity and esteem. Some believe that politics and Parliament are ill served by 'part-timers' with heavy professional commitments. Others argue that the breadth and experience of such people is good for the country's polity. Emlyn provided sound evidence for the latter view.

THE WEEK IN WESTMINSTER

E. H.

[There was a time when the BBC broadcast quarter-hour talks entitled *The Week in Westminster* on the Home Service, transmitted on Saturday evenings between 6.45 and 7 o'clock. Emlyn Hooson was invited several times to script and broadcast these talks. Published here is his talk of the 12th of December 1964, two months after Harold Wilson had gained office with a four-seat majority. In speeches before the election Wilson had emphasized – rhetorically – how he would harness 'the white heat of technology' and had emphasized the importance of his 'first hundred days in government'. This script testifies to Emlyn Hooson's love of the Commons and his acute and critical understanding of its work and workmen.]

The House of Commons is now really settling down. Half the hundred days promised us by Mr Wilson have now gone. The drama of the early debates has given way to the normal measured pace of Parliamentary life. Not that MPs have any less work to do; in fact they have a great deal more.

On Monday this week the House sat through until almost three in the morning; on Tuesday until after one; on Wednesday night it sat again until after three. Sitting in the House from lunchtime until the small hours can be very, very tiring. After all, a Member has also to attend to many constituency matters, to dozens of letters and to a great deal of Parliamentary work that goes on outside the Chamber itself. Early on Wednesday weary Opposition Members were treated to Mr Mikardo's description on them as 'Weary Willies and Tired Tims'. But this did not stop a younger group of Labour Members, fresh from their battles with the Party Executive over pensions and over regular meetings for the Parliamentary Party, feeling unhappy about this unaccustomed business of going home at four o'clock in the morning. Indeed, many people think that one of the most urgent reforms necessary in Parliament is of Parliament itself and the way it does its work.

The House of Commons without the Prime Minister, whoever he is, is almost like *Hamlet* without the Prince. This week Mr Wilson was in Washington. His absence meant the leading role for one of the supporting cast. The Prime Minister's place at Question Time on Tuesday was amply filled by the First Secretary of State. Mr George Brown stood at the Dispatch Box in the Prime Minister's place for the first time to the cheers of all sides of the House. It was as if he had at last come into his birthright; and the House, with its usual humour on these occasions, appreciated what the less charitable might call the irony of the situation. Mr Brown was at it again on Thursday in the Prime Minister's place, acquitting himself with the aplomb that we have come to expect of him, against the banter of the Opposition Members. Indeed, Mr Brown looked as if he had been in the job for months as he confidently dealt with the barbs and flippancies of his opponents.

Much of the week has been spent considering The Machinery of Government Bill. It is, after all, the government's most urgent piece of legislation, for until it's passed none of the newly created Ministries can pay their Ministers. The rather grandiose title of the Bill conceals not, as one might expect, a thorough-going revision of the whole structure of the government machine, but a few minor changes in the existing law to give legal standing to several Ministers. For the Prime Minister, returning from Buckingham Palace seven weeks ago with that hair-breadth majority in his mind, found that under various Acts he had to draw a certain number of his Ministers from the Lords rather than from the Commons. This unforeseen obstacle made Cabinet-making a little difficult, so Mr Wilson decided to change the law. The government claims the law is of Queen Anne vintage, anyway, and is out of date. Indeed, the restrictions were first introduced in the reign of Queen Anne to prevent the Crown, and nowadays the Prime Minister, from packing the House of Commons with loyal Ministers by handing out jobs for the boys. The Opposition claims, however, that the Act to be amended is actually an Act of 1957 which largely confirmed this piece of 18th-century legislation. They claim that there is no need for the new Ministries, and that Mr Wilson is doing exactly what the Act set out to prevent him doing.

So discussions on Wednesday centred on the need for these Ministries. First under fire came the Ministry of Land and Natural Resources, and the chief marksman was Mr Grimond. He recalled that the government had already been asked to justify the extension of patronage, but had failed to do so. He questioned the efficiency of an administration so full of Ministries, and feared clashes of interest and overlap of functions. Some new Ministries, he declared, might just as well have been mere divisions of existing ones. Mr Douglas Houghton had been given the task of answering these criticisms, and dwelt for some time on the problems of land and the need for some new Ministry to come to grips with it. The House was still in doubt, however, as Mr Boyd-Carpenter made clear, as to whether this was a Ministry with real functions or a mere estate agency for other departments. In the end, the government got a majority of 20, although the Liberals voted against them.

Soon afterwards we saw Mr Quintin Hogg in action again. It is no insult to him to say that he is considerably more assured in exposing the defects of his enemies than in covering up the skeletons in his own Party's cupboard. This was one of his days. Lancing into the new Ministry of Technology, he asked what its tasks would be, and how they would be separated from government departments that use technology, as indeed all of them do. He was in favour of a Research Council independent of politics, which would do the same work without having a *Minister* over it. Mr Houghton rose again. Psychologically, he said, the Ministry of Technology was most important. It symbolised the attitude of the government towards scientific progress. It was essential to sell technology to industry, and this, he said, was the best way to do it. It was headed not, as Mr Hogg had said, by the heavenly but slightly incongruous twins (meaning Mr Cousins and Lord Snow), but by men of ability whom everyone respected. The government obtained their majority on that amendment, too, and the clock ticked on long past the usual closing time of ten-thirty.

There have, of course, been skirmishes this week. There was the Member for Stroud, Mr Kershaw, tackling Colonel Wigg, who, under the title of Paymaster-General, is responsible for security. He asked him to disclose his duties and his place or places of work – a request which met with stony resistance until the Speaker firmly closed what was becoming an ill-mannered general debate. Not for the first time there was a brief exchange of angry phrases by two of the most mutually incompatible Members in the House: Mr Manuel from the collieries of Ayrshire, and Sir Walter Bromley-Davenport from his rolling acres in the Cheshire Plains.

Happily there are occasions when the House actually agrees about something, and when the deep and very real divisions of Party background are at least temporarily forgotten. Such an occasion was Mr John Tilney's Motion on Monday, drawing attention to the faults and successes of the United Nations, and calling for the institution of a permanent peace force. Mr Tilney, one of the Conservatives to escape their general massacre in Liverpool in October, received support from all sides of the House. Member after Member rose to express his concern at the difficulties under which the United Nations has to work to be able to keep the peace. The only dissident, apart from one or two

Members seeking clarification on certain points, came from the inveterate right-winger, survivor of the Suez Group of 1957, Mr Anthony Fell, the Member for Yarmouth, who contrived to put as many spanners in the works as he could. He saw too many difficulties in the creation of a peace force for it to succeed. The debate was brought to an end by Mr George Thomson, the Minister of State for Foreign Affairs. He supported Mr Tilney and recommended the House to do so, which it did. Not even Mr Fell wanted a division on the matter. The House was agreed that it was in favour of a peace force, though until the United Nations decides to set one up the Motion by Mr Tilney will have the force of the resolution of a school debating society. One was left with the impression, too, that on both Opposition and Government benches there was a certain amount of apprehension. Certainly, after the debate, no one was committed to anything new.

It was Mr Bowden, Leader of the House, who stopped the debate on The Machinery of Government Bill, in the early hours of Thursday morning. Exasperated columnists from at least one national newspaper commented that the Conservatives were keeping the House sitting late to tire out the government. Whatever the truth of the matter, this tactic has been tried in the past, and is particularly effective. The government after all need to keep more Members in the Chamber than the Opposition, to maintain a majority if a Division is called. Very often these main props of the government are Ministers, such as the tireless Mr Houghton. It will be a tribute to the three Ministers, and to him in particular, if, after a year of this attrition, they will still wish to be in government.

Thursday afternoon saw the statement by Mr George Brown on economic planning. His plan for six regions of England, excluding a mammoth and bloated South-Eastern region, drew immediate criticism. It came from both sides. Mr Heffer, the new Member for Liverpool Walton, complained that Merseyside had not been given an area of its own. Mr Osborn from Sheffield put the claims of Sheffield to a region. Further criticism from Members mentioned the merging of the far west of England with the middle west of Dorset and Somerset. Conspicuously absent from the plans was any element of democratic control. Power, said Mr Brown, was not to be centred on Whitehall. The Members of the Boards would be drawn largely from the regions themselves. The more sceptical replied by asking who appointed these Boards, and were told that the Minister would select them. Whatever the faults of the plan, and no one can yet say what they are in a practical sense, it is a first step towards bridging the gap between the richer and the poorer regions. Drawing the boundaries of the regions had probably been a more difficult task than deciding their structure and composition; and Mr Brown's Department was firmly of the opinion that such regions as were created must be large. Room would be found, he said, with evident relief at being able to fend off particularist critics, for sub-regions within them.

On Friday there was a most interesting and informative debate which centred again on the Ministry of Technology.

The impressive Mr Michael Stewart explained the functions of the Ministry. The main new feature is that the Minister will be responsible for government purchases from the computer, machine tools, telecommunications and electronics industries. Other departments such as the Post Office will still be in charge of purchasing their own requirements, and Mr Stewart did not make it clear where exactly the dividing line would come. Mr Ernest Marples, who led for the Opposition, made a highly controversial speech. 'The trouble with scientists,' he said, 'is that too often they dribble on and never come to a decision,' and later he said, 'The constructional industry is one of the weakest points of the economy but it was not the industry's fault,' and continued, 'It is the fault of the *architects* because the builder merely builds what the architect tells him to build.'

There were two very good maiden speeches from the new Members for Doncaster and Eccles. Mr Harold Walker of Doncaster came straight to the House from the shop floor of an engineering factory and spoke loudly and wittily on the application of technology in his own industry.

Several speakers were concerned with the prestige of engineers and engineering, and pointed out that there would be a shortage of engineers in the years to come. They referred to the latest report of the Advisory Council of Scientific Policy which was published on Thursday. This said that new measures ought to be taken to popularize technology and to persuade able young people to choose engineering rather than other disciplines. Television programmes on both BBC and ITV were suggested as one means of doing this. Mr Eric Lubbock said it would be a good idea if 'Sunday Night at the London Palladium' were replaced by a programme on nuclear power stations.

And so the work of Parliament goes on. Far more words pass in the Chamber than are ever reported in the press. The House deals with what to the general public would be obscure matters as well as larger issues. For example, on Thursday evening there was an interesting short debate on transportation facilities in the Shetlands which saw considerable agreement between Mr William Ross, who has so impressed the House as Secretary of State for Scotland, and Mr Jo Grimond, who of course represents Orkney and Shetland. As Mr Grimond said, this is a matter which may affect a small number of people but it affects them very deeply. He continued, 'Many of them have given long service to their country and they are glad to think that the House of Commons gives as much attention to them in their islands as it does to the less fortunate people who are jammed up in this great wen of London.' From this great wen Members must have been glad this week to catch their trains or planes or cars back to their constituencies. Of course, when they got there I don't expect they got a rest.

OTHER ACTIVITIES

EMLYN HOOSON AND THE WELSH SCHOOL, LONDON

Elinor Talfan Delaney

The post-war period saw a proliferation of groups interested in founding new Welsh-medium primary schools, and the London Welsh community was no exception. In August 1955, following a rallying call from the actor Meredith Edwards, an unremitting enthusiast for Welsh-medium education in the capital, Saturday morning classes began at the London Welsh Centre. They soon grew in number, and following advice on the feasibility of establishing a Welsh school from Dr Haydn Williams, the progressive Director of Education for Flintshire, a committee was formed. Its members were Meredith Edwards, who was elected Chairman, Mrs D. Williams, Secretary, John Roberts (Dolgellau), and Parry Richards, Treasurer. Jenkin Alban Davies was invited to be President, an office he filled, according to John Roberts, with great energy.

At a public meeting attended by three hundred enthusiasts in which one of the speakers was Sir Ifan ab Owen Edwards, founder of Urdd Gobaith Cymru and the Welsh school at Aberystwyth, it was decided to ask the London

County Council to provide Welsh-medium education in London. After much prevarication the LCC capitulated.

On the 8th of September 1958 Welsh-medium education in London was born. The first pupils arrived at Hungerford Road School, Camden Town, to be greeted by reporters, ITA News, and Polly Elwes from the *Tonight* programme. The enormous amount of media interest in the school continues to this day.

Children were ferried to school by 'Nellie' (as the school bus was called) who plied her way around London to collect them. Beryl Jones was the driver for some time, but there were servicing and other problems with Nellie, and repair bills became a frequent headache. She became increasingly unroadworthy, and when she was decommissioned she left a large debt.

The progress of the school was followed warily by the LCC Education Committee, which put constant pressure on it to keep up the numbers. As the older pupils reached secondary school age the Committee was aware that they too would be under pressure from parents who wanted continuation of this undoubted success.

Then the parents, under the guidance of Kynric Lewis QC, started to piece together a plan to go it alone and establish a private school. In the Deed drafted by Leonine Price for the London Welsh School Trust it was stated that the purpose of the Trust was 'the advancement of education by the provision, in London and elsewhere, of education for children which includes the teaching of the Welsh language and may include the use of the Welsh language in teaching other subjects.' To keep things simple the number of Trustees was restricted to four, and they were Jenkin Alban Davies (Chairman), Thomas Ivor Jones, Kynric Lewis QC and John Robert Roberts (Joint Secretaries). R. Parry Richards remained Treasurer. The Charity – number 313651 – was registered in October 1961. Under the new regime parents were asked to contribute a recommended sum each term to defray the school's running costs, but from the beginning no child was debarred from entry on financial grounds. The resulting shortfall has had to be made up with an unrelenting programme of fundraising.

On taking silk in 1960 Emlyn Hooson and his family had to move from Chester to London. In 1963 the three-year-old Sioned was enrolled at the Welsh School, which by then, after a period at Dewi Sant, Paddington, had been relocated to Willesden Green Chapel. Sioned was followed a little later by Lowri. Their parents were soon fired with the enthusiasm experienced by all generations of the school's parents. Emlyn was recruited as a valued Trustee and Shirley involved herself with the formation of the Friends of the School.

Earlier I mentioned the debt that was left by the operation of the bus. It was hanging over the parents for years. Then, in 1963, it was decided to form an association of Friends, the main purpose of which was to recruit sympathizers to assist in fundraising. Since then every generation of parents has had to come up with innovative ideas to increase the school's income, but they all recognize that the founding of the Friends testifies to the dedication of that particular generation of the mid-sixties. The Reverend Richard Jones, minister of Charring Cross Chapel, became the first chairman, Eryl Hughes the treasurer, and Shirley Hooson and Edwenna Hughes shared the secretaryship. This hard-working team soon paid off the bus debt, and then became the source of funding for equipment. The Friends of the School are still at work today, raising money for additional equipment and salaries, and the school owes Shirley Hooson and her colleagues an enormous debt of gratitude for their foresight.

The heady enthusiasm of the 1960s was hit by inflation and by the growing financial requirements of running a school. Many early crises were overcome. But in October 1975, with inflation rising alarmingly and with a sharp increase in teachers' salaries and in parental contribution, the numbers dropped so badly that the Trustees and Governors had to meet to discuss the school's position. An item on the agenda for the meeting held at Gray's Inn on the 18th of December called for discussion on the closure of the school. In a heated debate, with much talk about belief or unbelief in miracles, John Owen Parry, Vincent Hughes and I argued for a stay of execution. The only Trustee to offer his support to us was Emlyn Hooson, and he immediately became a rallying point for the parents. We were given until the 1st of March to prove that funding was available for three years. A campaign was started immediately. We targeted Welsh schools in Wales. Emlyn lobbied the Welsh Office, whose civil servants provided mailing lists, and he joined in the many evenings of envelope stuffing and stamping. Hundreds of letters were posted, the press was mobilized, and by St David's Day 1976 we had collected £6,000 and pledges for three more years. We were in business once again.

Changes were made to the Board of Governors, and it was at this juncture that Emlyn took over the chairmanship. For the next eleven years he continued to lead, advise and encourage the parents, and to persuade, cajole and proselyte wherever and whoever possible. The parents could rely on him for procedural advice and enthusiastic encouragement. And Governors' meetings were held mostly in the House of Commons so that Emlyn could be available for the division bell.

From this point fundraising became an increasingly important subject at school meetings. The sums that had to be raised were far in excess of the jumble sale or summer fayre potential, and new ideas were desperately needed. In 1978 the Welsh School's Trust Catering was formed. Dorothy Hughes, a parent and Executive Chef for Lombard Bank at the time, approached me, and with the help of other parents and Friends we started taking bookings for dinners and receptions. Parents and Friends became cooks, waitresses, wine-waiters and dishwashers who received no payment for their work and time, and therefore every penny of profit went into the school fund. Emlyn recruited the support of Baroness White who was then in the European Office of the House of Lords. He persuaded her to hire us for numerous functions, and we became adept at coping with the long corridors and the security restrictions of the House of Lords. He later persuaded Nicholas Edwards to use us for catering at Gwydyr House, and alerted us to the fact that the Mid-Wales Development Board was about to open a showroom in Berners Street, WCI, and after introductions we catered for many events and launches there. It was Emlyn too who persuaded Mati Prichard to engage us for the party to launch the first volume written by her son-in-law, Humphrey Carpenter. We continued to cater for events both great and small – the largest a garden party for 800 guests in College Garden, Westminster Abbey. As a result of all Emlyn's advocacy of our venture 1982 and 1983 showed a profit of £4,000 directly attributed to the catering.

In 1977 in Wrecsam the parents of the Welsh School hired their first stand at the National Eisteddfod. Emlyn and Shirley, always anxious to show their support and cheer us on, were among our first visitors. The Governors under his chairmanship and the Trustees sought alternative methods of funding from the beginning. On the 28th of August 1974 the school was the subject of 'The Week's Good Cause' on Radio 4. In 1983 Emlyn persuaded John Morris, then MP for Aberavon, to launch another appeal. On the 1st of March 1988 Emlyn, then Lord Hooson, launched a second appeal with an optimistic target of £150,000. The previous November, in preparation for that appeal, he had approached the then Chairman of the PTA, Calan McCreery, to ask her and Elin McCormack, an expert on computers, to help him write and send hundreds of letters in Welsh to all Welsh MPs and all Welsh chapels and churches. All the expenses were paid by Emlyn himself. The launch was held in the school with only a few MPs present, but among them was Ken Livingstone, the local Member for Brent.

Following that appeal Calan continued to be Emlyn's Welsh language secretary until his death. She says that he was relieved to have someone who could type in Welsh. Before then he had either had to write in Welsh in long hand or dictate a letter in English and add to it a sentence in Welsh. He was courteous, charming, patient, answered every letter he received, and gave sound advice to many people, always free of charge. He was well-liked and highly respected by members of all parties in the House of Lords – a very rare accomplishment – and this helped enormously in negotiations on behalf of the school with the various Secretaries of State for Wales, be they Tory or Labour.

The aim was always to establish a Capital Fund, but over the years it has proved impossible to accumulate capital. Inflation, successive recessions, salary increases, pupil-roll fluctuations, educational and Health and Safety regulations have all made increasing demands on our funds. Throughout the years Emlyn continued to support us both practically and financially, and we asked him many times to use his diplomatic skills to ease the tensions and to placate the personality clashes that are inevitable in an institution which lives on the edge.

In 1989, in a bid to reduce the school's salary bill, Emlyn, with the support of Menai Williams from Bangor Normal College, entered into consultation with Gwilym

Humphreys, Director of Education for Gwynedd, who agreed to second a teacher from Gwynedd for a period of one year. Siân Edwards consequently joined Eleri Elliott, but luckily for the school Siân enjoyed London so much that she stayed for a further twelve years. These years were another period of turbulence and change for the school – it had to move house yet again – but Siân Edwards testifies to the unfailing encouragement and support she received from Emlyn.

Others too testify to his support. Margaret Evans, secretary to the Trustees for many years, notes how much effort he made over the years to secure government backing. Thanks to Emlyn's skilful handling of Ministers, of senior officials in the Departments of Education and Culture and of course in Gwydyr House, the Welsh Office and latterly the Welsh Government have aided the Welsh School. Alun Thomas, the school's treasurer, notes how Emlyn liaised with Laura Ashley plc and later with the Laura Ashley Foundation to secure their generous support for it, and how he continued to give his own personal financial support. A recent chairman of the school, David Parry-Jones, testifies that when he took over the chairmanship with a brief to increase numbers and improve the finances, Emlyn was particularly helpful in a notably difficult period.

The last school event which Emlyn attended was the grand celebration of its golden anniversary held at Mansion House in the City of London, hosted by Sir David Lewis, the Lord Mayor, a native of Carmarthenshire. Emlyn was very much a guest of honour, and tribute was paid to his unstinting support for most of those fifty years. No wonder that he is remembered with huge affection by all in the Welsh School, London community.

EMLYN HOOSON AND THE LLANGOLLEN INTERNATIONAL MUSICAL EISTEDDFOD

Gethin Davies

Emlyn's connection with the Llangollen International Musical Eisteddfod began in its very early days, but not as early as that of his wife, Shirley. Sir George Hamer, Shirley's father, was a friend and business associate of Sir Clayton Russon, who was one of the prime movers of the International Eisteddfod, and as a result of this friendship Sir George and Lady Hamer attended the very first Eisteddfod in 1947. Shirley accompanied them and developed a love for the Eisteddfod which still remains. When Shirley and Emlyn married in 1950 they lived in Chester, to be near Emlyn's chambers, but during Eisteddfod week they stayed with an aunt of Emlyn's who lived in Trefor, near Llangollen, and who was the widow of a brave teacher who was killed in the war while working as a fire-fighter. Emlyn's busy practice prevented him from attending the Eisteddfod during the day sessions but each evening he would accompany Shirley to the concerts and in this way he gained a great affection for it, an affection that lasted for the rest of his life.

When Emlyn took silk in 1960 he and Shirley had to move to London, so it was less easy for them to attend the International Eisteddfod, and of course following his election to Parliament in May 1962 Emlyn had even less time to be at Llangollen, but that did not detract from his interest in, and his love of, this unique festival. When he and Shirley moved to Shirley's beautiful family home at Summerfield Park, Llanidloes in April 1969 they were once more within easy reach of Llangollen and so they renewed their acquaintance with the Eisteddfod.

Even before this, however, Emlyn's great contribution to Welsh life and culture had been recognized by the Llangollen Eisteddfod. The Presidency of the Eisteddfod is double-layered: it has a President, who in the early years was usually the Foreign Secretary and later the Secretary of State for Wales, and in addition each day of the Eisteddfod has its 'President of the Day', who attends on the day of his/her presidency, meets competitors, officials and volunteers, and addresses the audience. In 1966 Emlyn was invited to be the President of the Day on Thursday the 7th of July and his name appears as such alongside two other distinguished Welsh politicians, the Rt. Hon. James Griffiths (who was also at the time the President of the Eisteddfod as Secretary of State) and the Rt. Hon. Cledwyn Hughes, who later became Secretary of State for Wales. Emlyn's address to the audience, as one would expect, charmed all who heard it, and it was very much appreciated by the supporters of the Eisteddfod that he was prepared to give time from his hectically busy life as a Queen's Counsel and a Member of Parliament to attend and to preside over the day's proceedings.

The Eisteddfod also has a number of Vice-Presidents,

who are people of distinction prepared to honour the Eisteddfod by indicating their support for its aims and ideals
by accepting a Vice-Presidency of the festival. During
the early years, Shirley's father, Sir George, was a Vice-
President, and in 1966 the Eisteddfod invited Emlyn not
only to be President of the Day but also to become a Vice-
President, an invitation that he was pleased to accept. His
name appears in the printed programme for 1966, and it
is remarkable to realize that it subsequently appeared in
the programme every year until his death. The list of Vice-
Presidents in 1966 makes for interesting reading, including
as it does such names as Sir Arthur Bliss, Sir Malcolm
Sargent, Sir Lewis Casson, Dame Edith Evans and Dame
Sybil Thorndike, together with Emlyn Williams. It is also
interesting to read in the 1966 programme the names
of such famous adjudicators as Sir Thomas Armstrong
(the Principal of the Royal Academy of Music) and the
composer Herbert Howells, and such concert artists as the
Belgian mezzo-soprano Rita Gorr, the Spanish pianist José
Iturbi and the Italian tenor Luigi Infantino, together with
the exotically titled 'Grand Orchestre d'Harmonie de la
Musique Royale des Guides' also from Belgium.

From 1966 onward Emlyn remained a Vice-President of
the Eisteddfod, taking great interest in its affairs, and attending, together with Shirley, whenever his busy schedule
allowed. It was during the 1980s that he became more deeply
involved in the Eisteddfod. In 1987, Terry Waite, then the
Special Envoy of the Archbishop of Canterbury, accepted
an invitation to be the Day President for Friday the 10th of

July. It was some time after he accepted the invitation that he was kidnapped and held as a hostage in Lebanon. There was no word as to when, or indeed, whether, he would be released, and the Eisteddfod committee decided that his name should appear in the programme in the hope that he might be suddenly released. It was a matter of two weeks or so before the festival began that the Chairman, Dudley Richards, and the Vice-Chairman, Gethin Davies, decided that alternative arrangements must be made in case Terry Waite could not attend. They both agreed that the obvious person to invite to stand in the breach was Emlyn, on the basis that it was the sort of thing one could only ask a good friend to do. Emlyn very kindly accepted the invitation, and so, for the second time, he honoured the Eisteddfod as President for the Day, although his name does not appear in the printed programme as such.

The Eisteddfod President at that time was, as had been the case for several years, Lord Chalfont. He stood down after the 1987 Eisteddfod and it was the unanimous view of the Board of Trustees of the Eisteddfod that Emlyn should be invited to become its President for the following year. Everyone in the Eisteddfod organization was delighted when he accepted this invitation, and it immediately became clear that he did not regard the post as any sort of sinecure, taking a great interest in its affairs and even taking the time to attend some meetings of the Board. It was during the six years of his presidency that the most important development in the history of the International Eisteddfod took place.

From its beginning, the Llangollen International Eisteddfod had been held in a huge tent, holding some 4,500 people. It was hired each year from a Chester firm who erected it and took it down while separate contractors installed a temporary stage together with minimal back-stage amenities. The tent had served its purpose well, and had provided what was once described as a 'canvas cathedral' in which the faithful were fed with the fruits of international music and dance. There is no doubt that the creaking canvas created a wonderful carnival-like atmos-phere which contributed greatly to the sense of informality and friendliness for which the Eisteddfod was famous. Over the Eisteddfod's history, the tent had been replaced and redesigned twice, but by the mid 1980s it became clear that it was no longer fit for an international festival. It leaked badly during rain and flapped loudly in windy conditions. Thus it was that in 1986, Lord Chalfont, as Eisteddfod President, launched a Development Appeal which had the aim of raising half a million pounds with a view to acquiring a new marquee with a stage and facilities that would be worthy of the event. The director of the Appeal, Mr R. W. (Bobby) Manners, approached industrial and commercial organizations across Wales inviting contributions to this cause. One of the companies approached was Laura Ashley plc, the famous fashion and design company, the eponymous founder of which had died the previous year, in 1985. Emlyn Hooson was a director of the company, and it was undoubtedly as a result of his enthusiasm for the Eisteddfod that the company donated generously to the Development Fund, contributing in no small measure to the achievement of its aim.

Before the Development Appeal had reached its target sum of £500,000, the Eisteddfod Committee was approached by the Chief Executive of the then Clwyd County Council who proposed a partnership between the Council and the Eisteddfod which would have the result of providing a permanent pavilion, rather than a tent, as a home for the Eisteddfod. He proposed that if the Eisteddfod granted a peppercorn lease to the Council of all its land, the Council could make an appeal to the European Economic Community (as it then was) for funding to construct a permanent structure to house the Eisteddfod and also to serve the community of Llangollen throughout the year. This was a revolutionary proposal, and the Eisteddfod was very fortunate to be able to look to Emlyn, as its President, for advice. He counselled caution, but advised that given sufficient safeguards the scheme should endure to the long-term benefit of the Eisteddfod. Thus it was that in 1991, the Eisteddfod, with the consent and encouragement of the Charity Commissioners, granted a 99-year lease to the Council and agreed to contribute the sum collected by the Development Appeal (which had by then achieved its target) toward the cost of construction. The County Council submitted a successful application to the EEC for funding, and so, on the final day of the 1991 Eisteddfod, Emlyn, as President of the Eisteddfod, together with the Chairman of the County Council and the Secretary of State for Wales, David Hunt MP, cut the first sod of the new development.

The very next day, the builders moved in and began work on the exciting new development, the capital cost for which would be over three million pounds.

Over the following twelve months the people of Llangollen watched in amazement as the huge structure of the new pavilion took shape. The brief that had been given to the architects included the requirement that the main auditorium should, as far as possible, give the impression of being in a tent, in order to retain the atmosphere of informality previously described. Hence, the roof of the building was constructed of a triple-skinned, translucent fibre which looked for all the world as if a huge tent was being constructed atop stone walls. As the 1992 Eisteddfod approached, much anxiety was felt as to whether the pavilion would be ready in time. However, it was then made known to the contractors that the building would be officially opened by Her Majesty the Queen, and suddenly a far greater despatch was to be seen in their efforts. Emlyn took a keen interest in the progress of the construction, and it was very much thanks to his efforts that the attendance by the Queen was arranged. Thus it was that Her Majesty, dressed in brilliant yellow, came to Llangollen in July 1992, and was escorted on to the brand new stage of the brand new pavilion by Emlyn, who invited her to name the new structure, which was, with her kind permission, named the Royal International Pavilion, and which has, ever since, been a worthy venue for an international festival. Following the brief ceremony, the Queen toured the Eisteddfod site, and one of Emlyn's most treasured possessions, which remained in his bedroom right up to the end of his long life, was a charming photograph of himself escorting Her Majesty around the field. This photograph is still on display in the beautiful drawing room of Summerfield Park.

After the 1992 Eisteddfod the Chairman, Dudley Richards, retired from office, and Emlyn, who had by then served as President for five years, indicated that he also would like to retire. However, the incoming Chairman, Gethin Davies, felt very much in need of Emlyn's wisdom and guidance as President, and begged him to remain for a further year. In a typical act of kindness, Emlyn agreed to serve for another year and the new Chairman profited very much from being able to turn to him for advice when this was needed. Emlyn was aware of the importance of succession planning, and during his last Eisteddfod as President in 1993 he invited another distinguished legal figure, the High Court Judge Sir Ronald Waterhouse, to attend. Acting on Emlyn's advice, the Chairman invited Sir Ronald to accept the Presidency of the Eisteddfod for 1994, and to the delight of everyone, especially Emlyn, he accepted. Thus Emlyn was able to stand down as President after the 1993 Eisteddfod, having filled the office with grace, dignity and good humour for six years, and knowing that he was leaving the Presidency in safe hands.

Shortly after his retirement, Emlyn was invited to become a Life Vice-President of the International Eisteddfod. This is the highest honour that the Eisteddfod can bestow, and it has been accorded only to a handful of people since the title was created in the 1970s. Emlyn was delighted to accept, and he maintained his close connection with the festival until ill health prevented him from attending. Until his health broke down, Emlyn and Shirley were regular, and very welcome, visitors each year, and all Eisteddfod workers and supporters were delighted that he should want to keep in such close touch. His beaming smile, his charm and his lively conversation always made him the centre of attention whenever he visited the Chairman's room in the Pavilion, and of course Shirley, who was such a tower of strength to him in the later years, was equally welcome. Following Emlyn's passing in 2012, Shirley has kindly accepted a Vice-Presidency of the Eisteddfod, so that the name Hooson continues to appear in the programme each year, and long may that continue.

The debt owed to Emlyn by the Llangollen International Eisteddfod is immense, but no doubt, being the charming, modest man he was, he would not have admitted that. He and Shirley loved coming to Llangollen and regarded their times at the Eisteddfod as being among their happiest. No one at the Eisteddfod who had any dealings with him will ever forget him.

EMLYN HOOSON AND
LAURA ASHLEY PLC

John M. James

Emlyn's business career began with Laura Ashley plc and his appointment as a non-executive director in 1985, but his interest and connection with the company went back over twenty years to a meeting with Bernard Ashley in 1962 or 1963. At the time Emlyn was the Liberal MP for Montgomeryshire, and, as a good constituency MP, was fundamentally concerned with the issue of rural de-population and how it might be slowed or arrested.

Despite the best efforts of the Development Board for Rural Wales, entrepreneurs were fairly thin on the ground in Montgomeryshire, particularly entrepreneurs who, by creating well-paid and fulfilling careers, would slow the drain of the brightest and best from the county. Emlyn recognized that Bernard and Laura Ashley had the potential to do just that. As MP Emlyn wholeheartedly supported them in their efforts to build their business, first at Machynlleth and then at Carno.

There were many crises along the way, most of them brought about by Bernard Ashley's impatience with officialdom and his inexperience in the importation of machinery and in planning matters. Mrs Helen Hughes, who was then Emlyn's secretary, recalls many frantic phone calls threatening to leave Wales if something was not done about these things. Emlyn helped in all possible ways and the result was that the company grew exponentially, in particular its production side in Wales.

After Emlyn lost the Montgomeryshire seat in 1979, his contact with Laura Ashley plc became a lot less. But he remained a strong supporter of the company, through his personal friendship with the Ashleys and the facts that he continued to live and farm at Llanidloes, and that he remained tied to the political and economic affairs of the area. However, at that time, a career as a non-executive director of a company, or, indeed, any sort of corporate career, didn't seem possible, for he was still very active in the Law and, through his membership of the House of Lords, in politics. And, of course, he continued to farm.

By 1980 the Laura Ashley Company had reached a crossroads. It had grown very rapidly through the 1970s and had relied on the forbearance of its creditors, many of whom were local businesses, and its bankers to see it through. In short, it was a classic case of over-trading. The Midland Bank, the company's bankers at the time, placed it in what they termed the Corporate Banking division, better known in the City as the 'hospital ward'. The Midland insisted that further support for the company would only be forthcoming if a review of its organization was conducted, at the company's expense, by external management consultants who would report directly to the bank. The final recommendation was that the company should seek a public listing on the London Stock Exchange within five years. The basis for this conclusion was twofold: the fact that the business opportunity available to the company was too great to be supported by bank borrowings; and the reverse – that is, the Midland was not prepared to continue to support further expansion. So the Ashleys had a stark choice, to stand still until such time as the company's cashflow would support resumed growth, or accept the Midland's terms and drive the business towards a flotation and the opportunity to raise new capital. Bernard Ashley, after initial hesitation, supported the move from private to public company. Laura did not, and thereafter had little to do with the running of the business, preferring to concentrate on her design role and exercising influence through her husband.

Detailed preparation for a public offering began in 1984, under the aegis of Kleinwort Benson, at that time a first-rate merchant bank in the City heavily involved (amongst others) with the British Telecom flotation. One of their major requirements was the appointment of a non-executive director. The Ashleys' involvement with the banks and by extension with the City had been a chequered one: they saw banks as an extension of officialdom, a drag on their ambitions rather than a necessary aid to their company's operations. This antagonistic attitude ruled out the appointment of a banker or City type, and left the Board with a dilemma.

Who to appoint? It had to be someone of national stature, who had the respect of the Ashleys, who would be able to take a firm line with Bernard Ashley as chairman when necessary, and someone who would add another dimension to the Board. Being Welsh would be a bonus.

Acceptability to both the City and the Ashleys became the prime consideration. With hindsight it can be seen that there was only one possible candidate – Emlyn Hooson. He was approached, he accepted, and he joined the Board in early 1985.

The Board members of Laura Ashley at that time had little or no experience of life in a public company, or, except for Bernard Ashley, of being businessmen in the public eye. Emlyn brought with him a wide knowledge of public and political life and a host of contacts in all areas of public life. A keen intellect allied to his legal background allowed him to assimilate Board papers with ease and bring a novel line of questioning to Board meetings. He was a serious man, but one with a keen sense of humour, at ease in all company, and on social occasions he kept the Board amused with his anecdotes of legal and political life. He was a diligent Board member. Despite a busy working life he attended all Board meetings and the Annual General Meeting, and whenever possible also attended the annual retail conferences in the USA, UK, and Europe. His assiduousness allowed him, through socializing with the company management, to informally take the pulse of the business. He also could be relied on for an off-the-cuff speech when required!

Why did Emlyn agree to join the Board? Undoubtedly his decision to join was prompted by the influence he could bring in preserving and increasing employment in rural Wales. There was also his friendship with the Ashleys. Certainly it wasn't the money: non-executive directors were not well-paid at that time, particularly when compared to his potential – or, perhaps, foregone – earnings at the Bar. He may also have been mildly flattered by the approach. From the company's viewpoint he may well have been the obvious, if not sole, candidate; from Emlyn's he would have identified a number of other well-qualified persons who could fill the role very well.

Emlyn's acceptance as a suitable director by the City was slightly compromised when the finance director told his City contacts that the new non-executive was appearing at the Old Bailey – neglecting to add that he was defending in the Cyprus Spy trial!

Through the spring and summer of 1985 the company focused on preparing for its flotation on the London Stock Exchange with Emlyn as the only non-executive director. The flotation date was set for late 1985. On the 7th of September of that year, her sixtieth birthday, Laura Ashley fell downstairs at her daughter Jane's house in the Cotswolds. She was rushed to Coventry hospital and spent the next ten days on a life-support machine. On the 17th of September 1985 she died. Naturally, Bernard Ashley and the children were distraught, but he made it clear to the Board that the flotation was to go ahead. This was a matter of some relief to the Board and company in general, for their onerous and detailed preparation work was well advanced and was being carried forward with great enthusiasm.

The City thought otherwise.

Up until this point Emlyn's career with the company had been relatively uneventful. There was a lot of reading involved with the on-going preparation for a flotation, but with his legal background it was easy for him to keep up with the development of the prospectus. But here was a full-blown crisis.

David Clementi was the banker assigned by Kleinwort Benson to oversee the flotation process. The evening after Laura's death the Board members, except for Bernard Ashley, met with him at Kleinwort Benson's City offices. He was insistent that the flotation should be pulled. It was a fraught and dramatic meeting. Emlyn was supportive of the Board's position that the flotation should go ahead, and was a calming influence in a meeting where tempers were getting short. In the end a compromise was reached, brokered in part by Emlyn, namely that the meeting should be adjourned until a week later when the evidence for continuing, or abandoning, the flotation would be considered further. The re-convened meeting, or, rather, Kleinwort Benson was presented with a fifteen-minute video of the world's press, TV and radio reports, illustrating comprehensively the wave of positive feeling and sympathy towards Laura Ashley, and, by extension, the company. Kleinwort Benson accepted that the flotation should go ahead. Laura Ashley plc was finally launched in 1986 and was a resounding success. Emlyn marked the occasion, memorably, by hosting a reception and dinner at the House of Lords, attended by people from all parts of the company, including those who had been closely involved with the flotation and very early employees of the Ashleys.

Over the next two years the company grew rapidly both in terms of production facilities and worldwide retail shops.

Board meetings were peripatetic, and Emlyn, despite his other interests, continued to attend them all, as well as the annual retail conferences on both sides of the Atlantic. His time commitment to the company was considerable and onerous, and led now and again to some confusion with his other roles. At a Board Meeting in Vienna he received a number of telephone calls both during and after the meeting, and at its end he announced that he had bought a pedigree Welsh Black bull to add to his herd of Welsh Blacks at his farm in Llanidloes. This is an excellent example of his ability to combine his various interest and make the best use of the time available!

From 1989 until his retirement in 1997 Emlyn went through many ups and downs with the company, frequent changes of chief executive (nine in all), a change of ownership, and a run of very poor results. Throughout this period he worked hard to maintain as much employment as possible in mid-Wales although he was pragmatic about the need to manufacture goods elsewhere also.

A NOTE ON THE LAURA ASHLEY STORY

E. H.

There is no doubt that the Laura Ashley story is one of the most remarkable and romantic in this country in the latter third of the twentieth century. Laura Ashley the woman and Laura Ashley the legend were two different *personae*. The latter was largely created by the combined but differing talents of the woman herself and her husband, Bernard. It is fair to say that he was the dominant personality and the driving force, but it was Laura who was the creative talent who had the taste and judgment that made their product so attractive. It was an amazing husband and wife partnership – although at times, I suspect, it was almost a partnership of conflict.

When I first met them they had had rather daunting experiences in London, Kent and elsewhere, and had decided to come to Wales to try their luck, for Laura had a great attachment and family connection to the country. They fell in love with Montgomeryshire and decided they wished to develop there. I first met Bernard at a meeting which I think was in 1962 but which he thought was early in 1963. It doesn't matter much. However, I still remember this very tall, youngish man with a shiny black raincoat – a fashion not hitherto seen in Montgomeryshire, as far as I was aware – who got up at a public meeting I was addressing to ask me a couple of questions. At the end of the meeting he came over and we had a chat. Apparently, he'd thoroughly approved of the burden of my speech, which, from recollection, was directed to the need for a united Europe and at the same time the need for a plan to strengthen local and regional prosperity. Shortly afterwards I met Laura and discovered that she and Bernard at that time directly employed, I think, two people, but had a number of out-workers, and ran a small company which produced clothes and printed fabrics of a very distinctive character which were sold wherever possible but aimed mainly at the London market. Incidentally, the name of the company then was Ashley Mountney, a combination of both their surnames.

I became very interested in the company and saw it develop. It had much help from the Mid-Wales Development Board and its indefatigable Secretary, Peter Garbett-Edwards. At a fairly early stage the Ashleys decided that they must find their own retail outlet and decided to operate not under the name Ashley Mountney but under the name Laura Ashley. It was Bernard's idea, enthusiastically taken up by Laura, for they saw it was a much more evocative and intriguing name for a fashion company than the more prosaic Ashley Mountney. In retrospect I suppose it was at that stage that the legend was born, the public assuming that Laura alone was the founding creator, the driving force, &c. Although she was a crucial contributor, Bernard's contribution was also essential. He was among other things a skilled engineer, and onlookers were always astounded that this impatient man took such care with machines, be they printing machines he had developed or adapted himself, or helicopters or jet planes or motor cars.

Between them they created a marvellously happy atmosphere in all parts of their business – in their design sections, in their factories, and in their retail shops. I suppose that part of the secret of the Ashleys' success was that they didn't regard the workforce as employees so much as fellow participants in a great enterprise.

The City of London never began to understand the reasons for the success of Laura Ashley, and I believe their advice and suggestions were almost always wrong. When Laura tragically died on the eve of its public flotation, they counselled postponement, because they assumed that she personified the firm, that she was its dominating, guiding light. That wasn't true. But they tended to regard Bernard as a highly eccentric and impractical man, whereas, essentially, he was the creator of the company, marvellously aided and abetted by Laura.

THE FARMER

A piece compiled by D. Ll. M. after a discussion with
Sir Meuric Rees, Peter Sturrock and Alwyn Phillips

It was no surprise to anyone that Emlyn Hooson the barrister-politician took up farming, for he was of farming stock on both sides of the family. Except for John Hooson, one of his father's brothers, and Elias Percival Jones, one of his mother's brothers, both of whom were university graduates who had mastered several European languages, all his nearest relatives lived on the land. At twelve years of age he could milk cows and plough fields. Until he was eighteen it was the only life he knew intimately. In 1940, after passing his Senior Certificate exams, because all four Colomendy farmhands had received their army papers, Emlyn left Denbigh Grammar School to help his father on the family farm. Soon afterwards he too went away, to take up a scholarship at the Ford Institute of Agriculture in Essex. There he learned three things: first, after failing to refit a stripped tractor, that he wasn't mechanically minded; second, to enjoy participating in sports, boxing and rugby football especially; and third, a particular interest in breeding cattle and sheep. He didn't stay long in Essex. The boy who had decided when he first heard Lloyd George speak that he too wanted to become a politician now decided that his ambition would best be served by reading Law at university. He returned to his school to study for his

Higher at speed, and then entered the famous Department of Law at the University College of Wales, Aberystwyth.

In the vacations he continued to help on the farm at Colomendy, first with his father, and, after his father's death in 1948, with his brother John. In the mid-1950s, 'after I made a bit of money at the Bar', as he notes in his lecture to Clwb y Gader in Tywyn, he helped his cousin, another John, to buy Plas Iolyn in Pentrefoelas. Plas Iolyn is famous in Welsh history as the home of Dr Elis Prys, the learned henchman of many leading Tudor politicians, and his son, the poet, adventurer and warrior Thomas Prys. Every week-end for years Emlyn and Shirley would go from Chester to the cottage they had there – to enjoy 'the mountain farming very much' and to enjoy just as much the close community of their neighbours, Welsh mountain farmers who were acutely 'aware' – as he himself noted – 'of the bright stars above them and the great thoughts within them'.

After his election to the House of Commons Emlyn bought Pen-y-banc just outside Llanidloes, and set about farming it in conjunction with Pen-rhiw, which had previously been farmed by his father-in-law. At Pen-y-banc, the former agricultural student whose interest in breeding had been nurtured in Essex by a rugby-playing lecturer called Wilcox, became, in a short time, a pioneering and proficient breeder in his own right. In 1966, following the example of Henry Rees of Escuan in Tywyn, Meirionnydd, an old friend of the Hamer family, and Gwilym Edwards, Hafod yr Esgob, Emlyn established what became a herd of about forty pedigree Welsh Black cattle bred for scale, hardiness and longevity. A few years later, having seen dehorned cattle in the United States and closer to home, although Rees and Edwards insisted that Welsh Blacks should remain horned in order to keep their character, he decided to raise his own dehorned cattle; and from the mid-1970s introduced to his own herd cows and heifers he bought from the best polled herds in Wales and Scotland. His reading informed him that the traditional black cattle of the Isles of Britain were long-horned, but as Trow-Smith in his *History of British Livestock Husbandry* notes, 'there was a polled strain running through them ... and although this hornless characteristic was very ancient it had rarely, if ever ... been bred for and its carriers deliberately multiplied.'

Mr Hooson QC, sometimes in court and sometimes as after-dinner-speaker, liked quoting Dr Johnson, and did so pretty often. Johnson's put-down of his old friend John Taylor, a country clergyman, was 'His talk is of bullocks.' Did the barrister make a note of that insult? Mr Hooson the farmer's first polled bull was the home-bred Idloes Ceiriog, fathered by Dôldowlod Addewid, as famous in the ring as his owner at the Bar. He was named after Emlyn's adopted home town and the famous Welsh poet Ceiriog, who between 1865 and 1870 became friendly with the Hamer family when he served in Llanidloes as stationmaster for the Cambrian Railway Company. Idloes Ceiriog fathered famous successors, including Idloes Tudor, the Champion Welsh Black Steer at the Christmas Fayre in Llanelwedd in 1997. Leading his great bulls in fairs and shows, Emlyn was in his element.

By then, having been engaged in the breeding of Welsh Blacks for forty years he was so concerned about their future as 'a serious breed' that he wrote a paper setting targets for his fellow farmers. They were, first, to enlarge 'the presence of the breed in Wales itself by developing a specialized meat market for Welsh Black beef' in a way that certain individuals and small associations were already doing. Second, to aim at 'producing good scale bulls for crossing on the Hailstone Dairy herds with a view to producing from them an ideal commercial suckler cow for further crossing with continental bulls'. And third, to target those areas of the world 'which might be described as less favoured' and where 'the traditional virtues of the Welsh Black, enhanced by further development, will make them ideal cattle' – that is, in parts of Canada and of the USA, the hill areas of Eastern Europe, parts of South America and Australia.

Referring to his Welsh Blacks, the internationally minded politician said more than once that, as a cattle farmer, he was a nationalist, but a European as a sheep farmer. He had flocks of Texels, sheep – so he claimed – with 'the best confirmation of all breeds' that originally came from the island called Texel off the northern coast of the Netherlands, but which – he also claimed – were crossed at some time with *defaid Llŷn* (Lleyn sheep). He first became interested in them when he had a flock of Improved Welsh that needed better confirmation and greater length. For that purpose he bought some Texel rams and gradually bred up his commercial Texel flock from the Improved Welsh foundation. By the early 1990s the sheep in his commercial flock were what he called 'virtually pure-bred Texel' – and 'every bit as good' as his pedigree flock which had 'cost a good deal more money!'

Farming obviously gave him great satisfaction. For a very busy barrister and politician, it was also therapeutic. Weekends in wellingtons were wonderful. The defining image of Hooson as farmer is a piece of film from Dai Jones's television programme *Cefn Gwlad* that captured Emlyn leisurely driving the old grey Fergie – registration number EEP 202 – to feed his animals, in the company of his faithful farmhand John.

But breeding Welsh Blacks and Texels wasn't just a professional man's rural hobby. Emlyn immersed himself in the science, discussing its details with fellow farmers, and attending agricultural seminars. And for him farming was not only about animals. It was also about the environment and rural society, the careful conservation of fields, hedges, hillsides and scrub oak, and the maintenance of a society fundamental to the welfare of Welsh life and culture. Being part of all that was to him a civil necessity.

THE COMPANY CHAIRMAN

Jon Rushton

Severn River Crossing plc (SRC) is the company set up by John Laing plc, GTM Entrepose, Bank of America and Barclays de Zoete Wedd, to bid for the contract for the Second Severn Crossing project. The contract awarded to it in April 1990 was for the design, construction, financing, operation and maintenance of the new crossing, and of the operation and maintenance of the existing crossing, until the toll revenues had paid off the accumulated debt, when both crossings would revert to government.

The project was an enormous undertaking, materially, politically and diplomatically. The overall length of the new crossing was to be 5,168 metres, the main bridge being 948 metres long; 450,000 cubic metres of concrete would be poured into it; and a thousand people would be employed. When the contract was awarded, the enabling Bill authorising the work had not received parliamentary approval, and construction work could not commence until it had. The design, construction and operation would have integrated Anglo-French teams – and, recognizing the potential for misunderstandings and disagreements, the Directors of SRC agreed that they should appoint an independent Chairman.

They also agreed that they would like to have a Chairman who was associated with Wales, who understood the parliamentary process, and who had the experience and personality to deal with the media and with the government. A number of the Directors favoured an approach to a former Secretary of State for Wales then sitting in the House of Lords. But I had no doubt who the ideal candidate was.

I had met Emlyn Hooson in 1970, when he had kindly accompanied Roger Cuss, then the Liberal parliamentary candidate for Northwich, and me to the Cheshire Agricultural Show. Although twenty years had passed I remembered his charm and easy way with people, and, after satisfying myself that he was still active and might be interested, I recommended him to my fellow Directors. Having been a Member of Parliament for seventeen years he clearly understood the parliamentary process and how government worked; he was experienced in responding to the media; he was an eminent QC; and, being so manifestly Welsh, he would be and be seen to be a genuinely independent Chairman. He was, in a word, the *ideal* candidate. My fellow Directors were impressed, contact was made, introductions followed, and in 1991 Lord Hooson became Chairman of Severn River Crossing plc.

His duties were 'to Chair formal Board Meetings', 'to represent the Company and be identified as its Chairman', 'to represent the Company in dealings with government departments, the media and other external bodies', 'to assist in the resolutions of any significant differences among the Directors where unanimity [was] required', and, at the invitation of the Directors, 'to provide assistance and advice in the resolution of disputes/differences between the

Company and outside bodies.' For a man of his character and achievement this was – I use the word again – the ideal appointment.

During the period we were considering this appointment Lord Hooson was recovering from a heart attack. On the 20th of May 1991 he wrote to me to say that he had been examined by a cardiologist the previous week 'and had had a very good report and prognosis'. He had previously made up his mind to reduce greatly his practice at the Bar, but because he didn't want anybody to believe that he was wholly retired from it he suggested that in the press release announcing his chairmanship we should state that he 'still conducts a civil and planning practice'. In order to emphasize his international links, to the paragraph in the press release referring to his political career, his Membership of Parliament for Montgomeryshire for seventeen years and his presidency of the Welsh Liberal Party, he added references to his vice-chairmanship of the Political Committee of the Atlantic Assembly and his chairmanship of the World Government Group.

His term as Chairman of SRC started on the 1st of June and he set to work immediately, reading documents for background information and planning receptions in the House for interested parties. He took a keen interest in all aspects of the project, monitoring progress and visiting the site on many occasions. He was particularly interested in the financial model, how finance could be raised privately without a substantial share issue. When the Second Severn Crossing was opened by HRH the Prince of Wales on the 5th of June 1996, Lord Hooson took great pleasure in introducing the Prince to many members of the SRC team. Three and a half years later he retired as Chairman, and I believe he thoroughly enjoyed his involvement with this exciting project.

PORTRAITS

EARLY MEMORIES OF EMLYN HOOSON

John Gwyn Hughes

Before the war Colomendy had a horse-drawn wagon which toured the town selling vegetables, eggs, etc., and on Saturdays Emlyn and his older brother, Gwilym, helped out. One day in 1935 they stopped outside my home. We then lived in the police station on Vale Street, and Emlyn found a very nice cauliflower for which my mother had asked.

'Do you live here?' he asked me.

'Yes.'

'In the police station?'

'Yes.'

'What's it like?'

'Come in. I'll show you.' I then gave him a conducted tour of Denbigh police station, and my father obliged by locking us in a cell for ten minutes. We became close friends at Denbigh Grammar School, where Emlyn used to ride about on the shoulders of an enormous boy, named D. O. Davies, like a mahout on the neck of an Indian elephant.

He was a great asset during religious instruction classes. We were bored, and so was the headmaster, W. A. Evans, who had failed to find anyone to take the period. As soon as some Biblical place-name was mentioned Emlyn would call out, 'Wasn't there a battle there in the Great War?'

'No, no, you're thinking of General Allenby's campaign in 1917,' said the head who had won the MC in that war. We spent the rest of the period enthralled by tales of battles in 1914–18.

In Form V we sat together for the French oral exam which was part of the requirements for the dreaded CWB school certificate. The examiner was an attractive lady in a floral hat and dress.

'How do you pass the time?' she asked Emlyn in French.

'*Je jouer pêl-droed,*' he answered (a mixture of French and Welsh).

'*Et quand il pleuvoir?*' (And when it rains?) she asked.

'*Je jouer pêl-droed* indoors.'

I fared no better, but we both passed. I think the lady succumbed to the fatal Hooson charm!

Soon afterwards my father thought that we both would do well as lawyers and smuggled us into Rhuthun Assizes to sit with the press. The first case on the list was simply described as 'carnal knowledge'.

'What is that?' asked Emlyn.

I didn't know. 'Perhaps it means stealing books from the public library.' We were soon disillusioned. I was fascinated, but Emlyn was bored. On that showing I should have become a QC and he a farmer.

Emlyn missed the first term in the sixth form because he had gone to the Ford Agricultural Institute in Essex. He wanted to come back to school in January but many of the staff members were opposed to his coming because he had missed a vital term in the exacting Higher certificate course. However, he persisted, and showed a talent for picking out essentials which later became his hallmark as an advocate.

In 1942 we joined the Law Department at UCW Aberystwyth and shared rather shabby digs. The landlady told us that her husband had been in the building trade but had fallen off a scaffold. 'Why was he being hanged?' asked Emlyn. Fortunately, the lady was deaf! We asked if we could have cocoa at night and were given some undrinkable stuff. Not having the courage to complain we took it in turns to flush it down the toilet. We both took an active part in the Debates Union and joined many societies which provided free refreshments!

Emlyn was very athletic and played soccer and rugby for the college. On one occasion we went to watch a boxing match between Aber and Swansea. One of our contenders was unwell, and Emlyn agreed to make a token appearance. Stepping into the ring he went to his corner and then came out and struck the other such a blow that he fell down, and his second threw in the towel. Walking home I bought Emlyn a chocolate cake which made him violently sick. He didn't box again until he went to the Navy.

Wednesdays were devoted to military training. I joined the University Air Squadron, but whenever I donned the rather smart uniform I was addressed by Emlyn as 'little boy blue'. In his Senior Training Corps khaki I likened him to a sack of potatoes.

I saw little of him during the War. But an abiding memory is of a weary sailor coming home on leave from some distant base but always – *always* – carrying a large tin of Navy Tobacco for my father, Sergeant Hughes, and gifts for family and friends.

Gwilym and Emlyn both gained university degrees, in medicine and Law respectively, and it was characteristic of Emlyn to offer to postpone his career at the Bar for three years so that younger brother John too could go to university. But John declined and dedicated his life to farming, at which he was very successful.

In December 1950 I had the honour to be an usher at Emlyn and Shirley's wedding in Llanidloes, together with Glyn Tegai Hughes, my Liberal opponent in the general election of that year, and Eifion Roberts, who became a respected circuit judge.

THE EXTENDED FAMILY MAN

John Hooson

I write as Emlyn's cousin, his uncle George's son, who farmed Caerfallen near Rhuthun, so I can say that Emlyn was a family man – a cliché, I know, but a cliché that fits the man. And his family was not just his contemporary family, but past family members as well. Some years ago he sent me a copy of *The Miners' Dictionary* edited by William Hooson, published in 1747, a discovery that gave him much pleasure. We always knew that it was a depression in Cornwall's tin-mining industry that led to the migration of the Hoosons to the Midlands and north Wales, and with this book he had found one of them.

Fast forward to the nineteenth century. A lady in a Flintshire mining family bore a baby boy and died in childbirth. Her sister carried the baby on horseback all the way to the top of the Conwy Valley so that it could be brought up by his Taid and Nain at Trefriw, who were, by today's standards, subsistence farmers. In the care of such able and God-fearing guardians, Thomas Hooson learned about basic living off the land.

From Trefriw his next move was to Denbigh to learn more about farming. He then rented a farm which was infested with rabbits. To control them he set snares daily, but unfortunately a neighbour's dog was caught in one of them. At the end of the harvest that year all his stacks of corn were set alight and destroyed, and Thomas and Margaret his wife were nearly bankrupted. When his solicitor asked him if he knew who had done the bad deed he said 'Yes', but refused to pursue the matter. The story goes that twenty-five years later Thomas was called to his neighbour's deathbed, who asked his forgiveness for setting the stacks on fire. Soon afterwards, he approached Denbigh Town Council and agreed to be responsible for the disposal of the town's waste, its rubbish and the contents of its earth closets. After several years of hard, unpleasant work, the farm once described as 'land to starve a tape worm' was turned into a highly productive one. Thomas and Margaret had been productive too: they now had seven children.

One of them was Jack, our uncle 'Jack Llundain' ('London Jack'). A very bright boy, at twelve years of age he was preparing to leave school to help on the farm when the schoolmaster told Thomas that he should be encouraged to go to university. He did. He was the first Hooson to do so, and was not followed by another for over forty years. Such was his concern about the sacrifice his parents had made to allow him to study that he came home to help at harvests, and for twenty years after graduating – he became a teacher in London – he sent home a quarter of his salary. Uncle Jack and his wife Gwen generously gave advice, gifts and encouragement to all their nephews and nieces, and invited them to stay in their house on Wandsworth Common to be led around London taking in the sights.

Another of Thomas and Margaret's children was Hugh. He too was pressed to go to university, but preferred to take part in trials for the Agriculture Department of the University College of North Wales, Bangor, farm Colomendy and sell his produce in a shop in Vale Street, Denbigh. Hugh and his wife Elsie had three boys: one became a GP, one took over the farm, and then there was Emlyn.

As far as I could see, the teenage period seemed to pass fairly easily for Emlyn. He was a good-looking lad, an above-average scholar but not a swot, who enjoyed chasing oval and round balls and chasing girls – with ease and quite some success! He pondered farming, and enrolled at Boreham House, the Henry Ford Institute of Agricultural Engineering. Much much later, when he was an MP, in an argument in the House of Commons, Fred Peart the Minister for Agriculture appeared to treat Emlyn's question rather lightly, and Emlyn challenged him to a ploughing match. Hansard did not record the result. During the War he was called up and joined the Navy. He often said that the most dangerous thing he did was to compete in the Canadian Naval Boxing Championship – he was doing his training there – and became the welterweight champion for that year.

Compared to the earlier generation of Hoosons, his was a comfortable, safe and loving childhood. His mother was formidable and energetic, and his father was thoughtful, intelligent and most civilized. He also enjoyed his brothers' company. And always acknowledged the debt he owed not only to them but to all his relatives over the generations who had left their mark on him. A few years ago, an elderly relative of ours, whom none of us had seen for half a century, died. The funeral was hundreds of miles away. I am ashamed to say that Emlyn, an MP and a QC with a host of other commitments, was the only Hooson to attend. A family man indeed.

I referred earlier to Jack Llundain. In some ways, Emlyn became 'Jack Mark 2'. His interest in younger members of the family, his help and advice to them, and his encouragement of them, testify to this. And his invitations to London included a visit to the Houses of Parliament. When Emlyn's father died prematurely Uncle Jack bought the farm, and a little later, when Emlyn was on the second step of the legal ladder, suggested to Emlyn that he should buy it back from him. He did, and gave the major share of it to his brother John.

My personal reasons for being grateful for his friendship for eighty years are legion – starting when I was about three years old. Colomendy Farm literally lay astride the railway line at Denbigh Junction. My earliest memories include being transfixed by the smell of smoke, the noise of shunting, the shrill of the whistle, and the shining caps of my heroes, the train drivers. Much later, Emlyn took me to Cardiff Arms Park for an international rugby match, and then to San Ffagan. About that time, my mother called my name whilst I was milking, and said, 'Get someone else to milk. Emlyn Colomendy has called with a very pleasant girlfriend. Come and meet her.' I did not realize at the time that it was the start of a most happy relationship for all of us, a relationship that lasted over sixty years.

Their wedding day, when it snowed heavily, ended with all the guests leaving Llanidloes, except for me. Snowed in, I spent two surreal days and nights in the Hamer family home – Summerfield – marooned with George and Sybil in glorious isolation surrounded by mountains of wedding presents. Even now when we stay at Summerfield we use that same bedroom with the fantastic view down the valley.

My experiences with Emlyn went further. In 1950 I was still farming with my father, a man sometimes described as eccentric, who was a touch overbearing but well-meaning. I was in my early twenties, and, although I had some self-doubt, several family friends suggested that I should fly the nest. Emlyn and Shirley were among them, and their confidence in my ability was in great part responsible for persuading Nesta (my future wife) and me to seek a farm of our own.

When we were staying with them at City Walls, Chester, one afternoon we walked the walls and in town took the opportunity of showing Emlyn and Shirley a sofa we had ordered from Brown's. They said it was nice but asked us why we hadn't bought another that was nicer. My answer was simple: 'Because it cost £50 more, and our budget won't stretch that far.' They then said that they would lend us the money. At first we refused, but later were persuaded to accept the loan for six months. Six months later we took them out to Sunday lunch, and at the end of the meal I pompously waved a cheque for £50 with much thanks. The conversation changed – we argued. 'I'll ask for it when I'm short,' said Emlyn. But I won the argument by replying, 'If you don't take this now, how can I ever ask for a real loan if needed?' As it turned out that was a very shrewd move.

Some months later we found a 75-acre farm near Rhuthun. Being some £1,500 short we approached Emlyn and Shirley to see if they would lend us the money at 5% interest. 'Yes,' they said. Later in the day when Emlyn phoned to say 'Good luck' he asked me why I didn't buy a larger farm 'in case you want to go into NFU politics, for instance.' I laughed. That very night Nesta's father phoned to tell us of a farm for sale in Pentrefoelas that looked cheap but challenging. When asked for help again Emlyn said, 'Yes.' In hindsight I know that I could have borrowed the money from a bank or the Agricultural Mortgage Company, but at the time I didn't have the confidence in myself. But what I got was the personal backing of a shrewd operator who put his faith in me, a precious asset indeed.

The Pentrefoelas farm was Plas Iolyn, famous (as noted already) as the home of Dr Elis Prys, the politician and scholar, and his son, the poet-adventurer Thomas Prys, renowned as much for his piracy as he was for his connections with royalty and for smoking his long new-fangled pipe in front of disbelieving friend in the Pied Bull in London. Emlyn enjoyed Plas Iolyn's history and enjoyed talking about climbing the same stairs as Tomos Prys, wondering whether Tomos made use of the gallows three yards from the back door and how he built the tithe barn dated 1604.

Nesta and I are so much richer because of Emlyn and Shirley's generosity towards us, richer too for the friendships made through them – but because there are too many to number I'll mention only two, Bill Jones the Clerk at Chester and Glyn Tegai Hughes in Montgomeryshire. Our riches are but reflections of his, the richness of a life well and usefully lived, with panache, for over sixty years with Shirley at his side. Well done, girl! Thank you, Emlyn, old friend. We miss you.

MY FAVOURITE UNCLE

Jane Ashley

At Emlyn's funeral I was inconsolable. Not only did I feel as if I had lost a favourite uncle, as many others also did, but it felt as if an era of Welsh life had ended – an era that, for me, he defined more than anyone else. His deep love of Welsh music and its literature was reflected in the service, and mourners came from all the very diverse walks of life in which he had immersed himself.

I had arrived with my family in Machynlleth in 1962, just in time to help the local Liberal Party with leafleting to elect a young lawyer as the Montgomeryshire MP. He and his wife Shirley became friendly with my parents Laura and Bernard Ashley quite soon after their arrival, when my father asked Emlyn for help in cutting through red tape to help him expand their business. From this point on he was integral to its expansion in Wales and eventually out of Wales. Particularly useful in these early Welsh years was his help in getting planning consent to develop the old railway station at Carno, and the fields around it, into a factory site. My father and Emlyn were such opposite characters that they complemented each other and understood each other. As direct and impulsive as my father was, Emlyn was patient and tactful. I got the impression at the time that he needed to be in order to get those planning permissions! Emlyn's timely interventions with matters my father termed 'bureaucratic' and 'dealing with the goons' were necessary for many, many years, and because of his contributions he came to know the business very well. He and my mother were always very fond of each other, sharing a deep understanding and shared values – values of loyalty, tradition, hard work, consistency, and of course a deep passion for rural Welsh life.

As a schoolgirl at Newtown High School I was a little in awe of him, the local MP with whom my parents were friendly. It's well known that he was a very popular MP, equally at home in the House of Commons as in the Welshpool livestock market. He took the loss of his seat in 1979 very badly, but being appointed as a peer soon afterwards suited him.

When my mother died suddenly and tragically in 1985, he was close to us, and read the eulogy at her funeral in Carno church. The point he made so well was that my parents' talents and personalities complemented each other, and that the one could not have built such a business without the other.

A year later, in 1986, the Laura Ashley Foundation came into existence, and my father appointed Emlyn as its first Chairman. Then in the late 1980s he was appointed to the board of the company, by now Laura Ashley plc. Everyone who worked with him found him insightful, thoughtful and balanced, like the excellent QC he was. Most crucially he had a unique way of persuading my father – or dissuading him – about some decision or other. Emlyn knew that my father missed my mother's judgment in business after she died, and provided some necessary restraint on many occasions. The pressures on the company now being listed on the Stock Market were building, and when they inevitably came to a head in the early 1990s Emlyn was appointed Chairman and steadied the ship during a rocky time. (Almost inevitably, in 1996, my father lost control of the company.)

In 1991 I had lunch with Emlyn in the House of Commons and he persuaded me to get more involved in Welsh politics, which I had always been very interested in because of him. Although my first career was as company fashion photographer, I was also a graduate of the London School of Economics, and thus my interests spread outside the family company. I spent an interesting year as Alex Carlile's researcher – he had become Montgomeryshire's MP in 1983 – and during that time I was almost persuaded to become a candidate. When I asked Emlyn for his advice on this matter, knowing me well, he agreed with my instinct that it wasn't the right role for me. However he did say that I would make a good politician's wife! Perhaps I was damned with faint praise.

In 1994 Emlyn suggested I take over his role as Chair of the Foundation, which was a great honour, a post I continued to hold until recently, when I stepped down to be co-director with my sister Emma. Through the years I continued to seek Emlyn's advice on the running of the charity, especially on matters Welsh.

He had an extraordinarily rare ability to excel in very different fields, an ability aided by his personal qualities of warmth and humour. These were evident right up until the end. Glyn Davies, the current MP for Montgomeryshire, came with me to say goodbye to him in the nursing home in Newtown and he was as sweet as ever. Because of his illness he could only speak in Welsh. He would probably have thought that quite fitting.

THE MAN WHO WAS ALWAYS THERE

John I. Morgans

Twenty years ago Emlyn Hooson gave me a copy of *Cyfaill Carcharorion* (Friend of Prisoners), a tribute to his close friend Merfyn Turner, founder of Norman House, one of the first half-way houses for the rehabilitation of those coming out of prison. Merfyn and his wife Shirley shared their house with ex-offenders. Emlyn told the wonderful story about Merfyn Turner receiving a phone-call from an ex-resident at Dartmoor:

'Are you there, Boss?'

'Yes,' said Merfyn, 'I'm here. What do you want?'

The answer was 'Nothing at all, Boss. Just to know that you are there.'

Emlyn often referred to that story, and recorded it in his personal tribute to Merfyn Turner. Many people who knew Emlyn Hooson could apply the same sentiment to him. They knew he was always there – and he always was, for those who knew him personally and for those who only knew him by reputation, but who needed his help. Emlyn – and Shirley – were always there for family, friends, the local community, and for circles of concern that stretched to the widest limits.

This expression of gratitude could be replicated by hundreds of people who have been touched by the life of Emlyn Hooson, a man who enjoyed the natural gifts of an incisive mind, a concern for detail and a broad catholic spirit. He cultivated these gifts by a listening ear, an observant eye and a width of reading, especially in English and in Welsh. He shared these gifts with a multitude of connections. Emlyn never forgot his formation in Colomendy, Denbigh and the enriching experience of living in Llanidloes, Montgomeryshire. The appreciation of his Welsh roots deepened a natural, common touch which was recognized and appreciated by all who knew him. Emlyn was at ease with people for the simple reason that he loved people. A legal training made him more aware than most of the foibles and frailties of our human clay, but he always combined this insight with the recognition of qualities – and the desire to encourage those qualities – which enable the human spirit to flourish. Never cynical, he saw the best in people. This seemed a very natural gift, part of his personality and background. Although he worked with some of the most powerful and influential of men, nationally and internationally, he remained a farmer's son and a Welsh upland farmer himself. Emlyn was the man who loved Welsh Blacks, whose regret was that he had not planted enough trees. Although he may have regretted that, he was always grateful that he had shared his legal skills with the defenders of the Dulas Valley in the 1960s. His life was earthed in the lives of all sorts and conditions of men and women. His position of leadership never divorced him from the lives of ordinary people, but offered him opportunities to serve. This was never contrived. It was what made him the man he was.

Our personal friendship goes back to the mid-1960s when Norah and I came with our young family to serve as minister of Congregational churches in Llanidloes and the upper Hafren valley. We were soon friends of the family. For many years Shirley was a faithful member of ecumenical discussion groups meeting in dozens of people's homes, including Summerfield. Our young children were great admirers of Lowri, the oldest child on 'Mr Bunford's bus' taking Llanidloes children to the new Welsh-speaking school in Trefeglwys. Sioned was a member of Norah's teenage discussion group, and later I enjoyed the privilege of participating in Sioned and Bob's marriage at Bethel Street Presbyterian chapel.

Emlyn combined an insight to recognize people's potential with the ability to enable that potential to come to fruition. Many years ago, three young women from Llanidloes were eager to take what was at the time the daring step of studying theology as an academic subject in one of the constituent colleges of the University of Wales. Their venture was a completely novel concept and was looked on as something not quite proper for women. Emlyn knew each one of them and respected their families, and when he was convinced of their sincerity and ability he pointed out to them the proper channels by which they were to be successful in their application for local government funding. He appreciated that they were breaking new ground; he took the risk of supporting them, and was proved right. Forty years later all three continue to exercise their considerable skills in the service of their communities.

Emlyn seemed to possess an encyclopaedic knowledge of what was going on in every corner of Wales. How? In 1986, when we moved to live and minister in the large housing estate of Pen-rhys, Rhondda, Emlyn knew all about our challenge. The fact that he had been Recorder of Merthyr made him far more alert than most to what was going on in the south Wales valleys after the destruction of the coal industry. Norah and I unfailingly recall the conversation with Emlyn and Shirley on Great Oak Street, Llanidloes: 'Your move to Pen-rhys is important. Now, what can we do to help? The United Nations has recently declared 1990 as *The Year of International Literacy.* As Chairman of the Laura Ashley Foundation I can suggest to the Foundation that they might help the community of Pen-rhys tackle its educational challenges. Let me know what we can do.'

Consequently, after consulting the head-teachers of the primary schools on Pen-rhys, it was agreed that we should apply to the Laura Ashley Foundation for a grant for an education worker who would be based in the church and who would draw connections between schools, parents and community. For three years from 1991 Laura Ashley funded a literacy worker, and one of the first homework clubs in the country was established. The work continues to flourish more than twenty years later. A seed sown through a conversation one morning on Great Oak Street germinated through the concern, connections and persuasive powers of Emlyn Hooson.

Ten tears later there was a similar conversation. This took place after a visit in the year 2000 to Madagascar, one of the poorest countries in the world. In co-operation with the leaders of Akany Avoko, a home for destitute girls in Antananarivo, a programme was initiated, and a fund established, whereby a young woman from Akany Avoko would come to Pen-rhys on a year's scholarship to participate in and contribute to the life of what was, by western standards, a materially impoverished community. Young people from Pen-rhys also went to serve as volunteers in Akany Avoko. Emlyn and Shirley were among the first to encourage this new project, which continues to the present.

Perfect hosts, Shirley and Emlyn were assiduous in their attention to their guests, and enjoyed the genius of enabling perfect strangers to become friends within minutes of being introduced. They were always able to recognize connections that would be of mutual interest to erstwhile strangers. They were always gracious, whether they were helping at breakfast in the flat at Gray's Inn, entertaining visitors to the House of Lords, or welcoming at Christmas-time the thirty or forty carol-singers from the Llidiart-y-waun Young Farmers' Club to Summerfield. This tradition began in the 1960s and continued every year, and in the process the Llidiart-y-waun YFC raised tens of thousands of pounds for numerous charities.

A great storyteller, Emlyn was not only able to paint pictures of people in all sorts of circumstances, but also had the ability to see the inside of people – and loving them for who they were. His humour was never malicious, but he was quite prepared to see balloons punctured and let down gradually, but kindly.

He loved music. He supported choirs like Côr Meibion Pen-y-bont-fawr (who sang at his funeral), he enjoyed the Gregynog Festival, and was President of the Llangollen International Eisteddfod for six years. We recollect being the guests of Emlyn and Shirley at Gregynog for a memorable concert given by Benjamin Britten, Peter Pears and Osian Ellis, an old friend of his. Perhaps even more significant was Emlyn's presence at the local Music and Arts Club (of which Shirley is the president) where he always showed his appreciation of the widest range of music, Mozart's especially.

A man of international stature, Emlyn Hooson was *there* for so many.

THE EXTRAORDINARY EMLYN HOOSON

Alan Beith

It has been noted already that Emlyn Hooson was one of the last criminal bar QCs to combine an active legal career at that level with a similarly active life in the House of Commons. As one of the handful of Liberal MPs in the late 1960s and the 1970s he was constantly in demand to speak for the party in the Commons on legal issues, defence and agriculture, at a time when he was also leading for the prosecution or for the defence in some of the most notorious criminal trials. It was not unusual, particularly during the Callaghan government, for Emlyn to address a jury in Preston or Chester, board a train for London, vote until 10.30 p.m., then get the night-sleeper back to the North to resume the case next morning. In order that his appearances in the House did not go unnoticed he would intervene in a Minister's speech to inquire precisely what the Minister had meant by 'short term', thus ensuring that his name appeared in that day's Hansard. We would tease him about this. But he knew what he was about. He had a mischievous streak, usually signalled by a smile and a twinkle in the eye, and he would throw into the discussion a controversial point which set things off in a completely different direction. His dissent could be equally visible in his expressive face, and a quiver of the chin gave warning of a vigorous challenge to the drift of the discussion.

He was the nearest thing to a Eurosceptic in the Parliamentary Liberal Party, but that is not to be confused with the Euroscepticism of the Tories of today. He was in fact a true traditional Liberal, respecting human rights, individual freedom, the rule of law and social responsibility. When Liberalism came close to being unrepresented in the House of Commons he kept the flag flying, and helped to achieve the 1970s revival which provided the foundation for the Liberal Democrats to become a party of government.

Emlyn never fully accepted the leadership of Jeremy Thorpe. He and Eric Lubbock had both stood against him for the post. More significantly, he was the first to be approached with damaging allegations about Thorpe's private conduct. But, despite his reservations about the Leader, he did not cut himself off from colleagues and remained active and committed.

For many of us Emlyn Hooson was a supportive and encouraging friend and excellent company, with a criminal lawyer's fund of courtroom tales. A Denbighshire man, with the Welsh poet I. D. Hooson in his family, deeply committed to the Welsh language and culture, he was also deeply proud of his adopted county of Montgomeryshire and served it wonderfully. But he was, perhaps, a bit slow to realize the political impact of the demographic change in the county, when many incomers from the English Midlands who were not part of its tradition became initially attracted to Thatcherism. The seat which had been Liberal for ninety-nine years now became a Lib Dem/Conservative marginal. But as Lord Hooson he remained active in

Parliament until ill health imposed increasing limitations on him. To have done what he did, in politics and in the Law, retaining individuality and operating at the top of his profession, while supporting a variety of good causes and running a farm, proves how extraordinary Emlyn was.

FRIEND OF FRIENDS

Glyn Tegai Hughes

When alone, we usually spoke in Welsh and with that degree of intimacy that comes from the use of the second person singular *ti*. Emlyn, however, had friends all over the world; I was just fortunate to be one for some sixty-five years, and, for over forty of them, to live within less than half an hour's drive from his home. Neither of us could remember when we first met, but it must have been in the late 1940s, and came about initially through our activities in the Liberal Party. Then, a few years later, when he and Shirley were living in Chester and I came to my father and aunt's there every weekend from Manchester, they were generous in their invitations to City Walls. Not infrequently there would also be some young lady present, but I pre-empted any future matchmaking attempts by getting married, and Margaret joined the circle of friends.

All this would be mere tittle-tattle except for the fact that it emphasizes a lasting feature of the Hooson household – a highly developed capacity for making friends and continuing to care for them. Friends came in all shapes, sizes, colours and trappings, and it made no difference. Emlyn had an unbelievably extensive range of friends, into which was merged an equally impressive collection of Shirley's. They would constantly be off to faraway places for a godchild's christening, to a wedding, or, alas, as time went on, increasingly to funerals. Emlyn stayed in touch with former Aber students, with those of different nationalities who had stayed at Colomendy during the War (including a South African diamond-mine owner), with Bill his chambers Clerk from Chester, with old friends from Denbigh or new ones from NATO, to legal colleagues like the Finnish judge Paavo and his wife Killike, to some who were friends of friends, and to a legion of those to whom he had been mentor, whether in Britain, Singapore, Hong Kong, or Sri Lanka. He himself remained the same, whether in the company of a Welsh hill farmer or the Lord Chancellor, earning the highest accolade that the Welsh can give to a successful compatriot: 'He's the same with everybody'. In fact, he liked on occasion to think of himself as a farmer who had strayed into various other occupations, and he did indeed have the solidity and inherent self-worth of yeoman stock, a self-confidence without self-importance, which intriguingly enabled him to identify the best hotel in any strange town and walk into it as if he were their most longstanding and valued guest. His character was formed by a notably stable family background and nourished by the two fiercely independently minded, would-be city states of Denbigh and Llanidloes (he was, incidentally, very proud to have been made a Burgess of Denbigh a few years ago). The remarkable thing was that he moved seamlessly from one to the other, fitting perfectly into the Summerfield culture of hospitality and public service. He was a product of Welsh Nonconformity, with its mental toughness, stubborn integrity and sense of obligation, but without its former harshness and occasional intolerance, and without much of its outward show of piety. He used to say that, if accused of some serious offence, he would hope not to appear before a Welsh Nonconformist judge, and was fond of telling a story, apocryphal one hopes, of a very senior Welsh judge, puzzling about a sentencing task and consulting an English colleague who rather off-handedly said, 'Oh, about nine, I suppose', only to find that the Welsh judge had interpreted this as nine years rather than the intended nine months.

His background predisposed him to a nineteenth-century radical, some might say romantic, view of politics, at least in his early years. Liberal politics, in the wilderness years of the 1950s, were a heady combination of nostalgia and imagination, with policies often worked out in implausible detail. Emlyn, in those days, was a master of policy making, often on matters he knew something about. I dimly recall an occasion when we were both speaking at a north-Wales coast event and a topic had cropped up that day on which, as far as we knew, no party pronouncement had been made. So we produced a policy in the car on our way to the meeting, and Emlyn expounded it, to everyone's satisfaction, including mine. It is perhaps worth noting that, even if instant communication with party head-quarters had been available in those days, we would probably not have bothered. We were both, in 1950, fighting ostensibly winnable seats, and London was disinclined to rock our boat.

The 1962 by-election in Montgomeryshire, at which Emlyn was first elected to Parliament, was one of the last at which public meetings really counted, and at them he was direct, well grounded in either language, and well attuned to the audience. Some visitors from London were much impressed by what they perceived as his 'fiery oratory', but it was not quite that. He was not a barnstorming spellbinder in the mould of the great princes of the pulpit; he had no desire or need to browbeat his hearers. Engagingly eloquent, shrewd and persuasive, he could charm them and reason with them, showing a sensitivity and humanity that suited time and place. He became an outstanding constituency member, careful, considerate and unfailingly anxious to help. It would be understandable if he had regarded the loss of his seat in 1979 as poor reward, but, natural disappointment aside, he knew well enough that politics is not like that and that national considerations had played their part. So his attachment to the shire and his support for successor candidates remained firm. His loyalty to the Liberal and then Liberal Democrat parties for over seventy years was manifest, and he was indeed the inspiration behind the establishment of the Liberal Party of Wales. But he was no unthinking zealot. Neither was he a cynic, but he did have a serviceable allowance of scepticism that continued to operate even within the party stockade. There were, for instance, one or two of the party's MPs who were unwelcome in his constituency. Once, when we were discussing an iconic figure in another party in Wales, Emlyn observed that he was the vainest man he had ever met; he then paused a moment and added 'except for X', naming a leading Liberal figure. Not all his political friends were obvious; one, among many exceptions, was the staunch trade-unionist, S. O. Davies, for many years Member for Merthyr, and in later life Emlyn never tired of saying how S. O. had arranged for him to have honorary membership of Merthyr's Labour Social Club. He was a good judge of character, though less good than his wife, but his tendency was to raise people up rather than to behead tall poppies. He suffered fools politely, if not gladly, but had more time for those doing what he thought was wrong but which they believed in, than for others doing the right thing for the wrong motive. And he was notably large-minded; many will have heard him say, perhaps provocatively, that some of the nicest people he had defended were murderers; of only one person did I ever hear him use the term evil.

He took an active part in Westminster politics, without haunting the precincts of Parliament. Certainly he was not one to go out of his way to ingratiate himself or to cultivate influential figures, though he had natural allies, some of whom have contributed to this volume. Others, who later also became members of the Lords, were Geraint Howells, John Bannerman, Eric Lubbock, and George Mackie. He had, I believe, few if any real enemies, but in the 1950s and 60s the Liberal Party had still not quite shaken off the sense that it had its Lloyd George and Asquith wings, and Emlyn was certainly held to be in the former camp, not least because of his participation, under Lady Megan's chairmanship, in that shambles that was the Parliament for Wales Campaign – a campaign, incidentally, during which we were both rebuked by Goronwy Roberts, probably justly, for youthful arrogance in expressing rather too forcibly our disdain for the platform bombast of one of his Labour parliamentary colleagues.

He was the Liberal Party's wise head in, for instance, the Jeremy Thorpe crisis, and in marginally different circumstances, and had he been a person who would have devoted himself to plotting for it, Emlyn might well have become leader of his party in the Commons. He would, of course, have done the job with his usual care, efficiency and decency, but I am not altogether sure that his heart would have been in it. He had one disadvantage in a day-to-day politician; he allowed himself the luxury of broad ideas, not normally an indulgence suitable for hard-pressed party leaders. In, I think it was 2003, Emlyn read and was very impressed by *The Shield of Achilles: War, Peace and the Course of History* by the American military and constitutional theorist Philip Bobbitt, and, with his usual kindness, he gave me a copy for my birthday. It has an introduction of 32 pages, followed by 922 pages of text. I never had the heart to admit to him at what page I gave up the struggle. None of this should be taken as suggesting that he had no interest in the day-to-day goings on of people in public life. He was as interested in gossip and anecdote as the next man but he did not actively seek them out, though he was gratifyingly appreciative when *clecs* came his way, relayed perhaps by some of us who subscribed to *Private Eye*, or who had picked up rumours in broadcasting circles. A particularly juicy item would be met by a surprised laugh and a long-drawn-out 'No!' It should be added that he could deploy his own ample store of anecdotes and quips, predominantly from the legal world.

Interest in large ideas and the formation of friendships were joined together in the political committee of NATO, of which he became Vice-Chairman. Among those he then came to know, in perhaps ascending order of friendship, were Donald Rumsfeld, the liberal Republican US Senator Jacob Javits, John Lindsay, sometime Mayor of New York, and Arthur Ross, the New York businessman and philanthropist. When Ross celebrated his ninetieth birthday, he flew out three guests from the UK: Mary Soames, Edward Heath and Emlyn. What Emlyn seems to have found attractive in American public figures was not a lack of preconceptions (Ross, for instance, told him that he always tried to appoint a Presbyterian as finance officer in his companies), but that their assumptions differed so markedly from those of British politicians that he was encouraged to speculate beyond the conventions and priorities of home politics. Occasionally the speculations resulted in some hare-brained scheme about which Shirley would say 'Hooson had one of his bright ideas', with Emlyn smiling benignly in the background.

An alternative climate of thought was what he also found exhilarating in his chairmanship of the Second Severn Bridge enterprise. He had, of course, had experience of business with Laura Ashley, but at a difficult stage in the company's development that perhaps allowed him little room for creativity. In the case of the bridge his ability to understand different mind-sets, added to his conciliatory

skills, enabled him to bring together bankers and engineers, French, American, and British, and was one of the
achievements he looked back on with most satisfaction.
On a considerably lesser scale, but with its own emotional
overtones, he had at an earlier period been the architect of
a rescue package, even if only a temporary one, for Gwasg
Gee of Denbigh, the immensely influential publishers of
the nineteenth century (and half a century later still stuck
there in attitude and equipment). It should be noted in this
context that for some years he bought nearly every Welsh
book published, because he thought he should, even if
the subject did not greatly interest him. Some mistakenly
thought his attitude to Wales and the language ambivalent,
but he was never a single-issue politician, however worthy
the issue. The Welsh School in London would scarcely have
survived as it did without him, and he supported countless
eisteddfodau and local activities in both languages. But he
did not feel torn when professional obligations required
him to appear in court against various Welsh activists. In
truth he had limited sympathy with direct action, other
than that located in the nineteenth century. He admired
strikingly different Welsh personalities: Saunders Lewis
and Thomas Jones (T. J.), Nye Bevan and Martyn Lloyd-
Jones.

Emlyn was quite devoid of pomposity and was happy
to indulge in gentle ribbing. I was always greeted with an
exaggerated 'Doc-tor' and had to wait for some years before
being able to respond with 'Your Lordship'. I happened to
be in hospital for a relatively short time just after the Moors

murders trial, and, no doubt to cheer me up, he sent me some unsettling photographs relating to it. I had to wait a few years until he was recovering from surgery before I was able to speed his convalescence with a Welsh pamphlet of 1832 on *cholera morbus* in Denbigh. It was customary, at least in semi-public gatherings, for us to joke about his curious reluctance to engage with anything mechanical: oddly, for an ex-naval person and one with his farming background, he was a technophobe. I remember remarking on one occasion that it was a mercy the second Severn Bridge was built by engineers under Emlyn's guidance and not by Emlyn under the engineers. He maintained a resolute ignorance of the operation of any domestic appliance more complex than a carving knife, not to mention those modern terrors, computers, mobile phones or video recorders. He could be teased with allegations that domestic incompetence was a stratagem rather than a disability, and took the implied criticism with equanimity, perhaps even mild satisfaction. He certainly had no difficulty at all in agreeing that the digital revolution had entirely passed him by. On one occasion, fifty years or so ago, calling on an old friend and his family, he saw that the small son, aged three or four, had a new book, but one that was too hard for him. 'Ask Daddy to read it for you' said Emlyn, in Welsh. 'Daddy can't read' said the small boy in all earnestness. Emlyn was much amused by this subterfuge maintained for so long, and it perhaps reinforced his claimed inability to tackle the technical. For, as I understand it, if some complex technical problem came up in a brief, he would master it.

He liked solid things and solid people, the straight-forward and unflashy, the Victorian brass fittings rather than semi-conductors. His own appearance was reassuring. There is a Welsh word *trwsiadus*, which I suppose one would have to translate 'well turned out', and that indeed he was, in appearance and in conduct, in any and all circumstances. Well, in everything except his handwriting. He valued good sense in others (in later life he was much inclined to refer to Lord Justice Sellers as a fine example), but was also intrigued by the idiosyncratic (one of his uncles was gloriously such). He valued, but was not overwhelmed by, tradition; ceremony and pageantry had their appeal, but preferably, as in Parliament, Gray's Inn, or university graduations, with some patina of age. In later years, and partially through friendship with Sir Geraint Evans, Emlyn came to appreciate theatricality mediated through opera. He and I spent a week in 1955 at the National Eisteddfod in Pwllheli at a time when Cynan, as Archdruid or as Recorder of the Gorsedd, was endeavouring to introduce some semblance of order and discipline into proceedings, by banning umbrellas in the robed processions, substituting white cricket boots for hobnails, and the like. During the chairing ceremony we were, for once, seated in the pavilion, and were treating all these novelties, but especially the Floral Dance, with some levity; unfortunately our seats were immediately behind Emlyn's mother, who berated us soundly for lack of respect.

Emlyn was a serious man, who did not take everything too seriously. He would not have subscribed to Arthur

Balfour's dictum, 'Nothing matters very much, and few things matter at all.' But there was something of that in him, some inner calm, some unwillingness to be rattled, some reluctance to take things just at their face value, to submit to the appeal of fashionable nostrums. He was well aware that he was fortunate above all in a loving family, but also in a full and rewarding life with its unusually varied range of engagement with public affairs. Some of us will remember, even overshadowing the career successes, the decades of unclouded friendship which, even in the cruel months when speech had failed, revealed itself in a characteristic smile.

Emlyn Hooson
Essays and Reminiscences

LIST OF CONTRIBUTORS

JANE ASHLEY, the elder daughter of Laura and Bernard Ashley, was educated at Newtown High School and the London School of Economics. For twelve years she worked as an in-house photographer for Laura Ashley plc. For twenty years she was Director of the renamed Ashley Family Foundation (a role now shared with her sister Emma). She works as a part-time researcher for the Liberal Democrat MPs Roger Williams and Mark Williams.

SIR ALAN BEITH after leaving Oxford became a Lecturer in Politics at the University of Newcastle upon Tyne (Hon. DCL, 1998). Since 1973 he has been the Member of Parliament for Berwick-upon-Tweed. He was Deputy Leader of the Liberal Party, 1985–88, and of the Liberal Democrats, 1992–2003. UK representative to the Council of Europe, 1976–84. Since 2003 he has been Chairman of the Historic Chapels Trust.

LORD CARLILE QC was Liberal (then Liberal Democrat) MP for Montgomeryshire, 1983–97. Chairman of the Welsh Liberal Party, 1980–82. Called to the Bar in 1970, he became a Bencher at Gray's Inn in 1992. He has been a Deputy High Court Judge since 1998, and was made a Life Peer in 1999. President of the Howard League for Penal Reform, 2006–. Hon. Fellow, King's College, London.

PROFESSOR RUSSELL DEACON was educated at Cardiff University and the University of Glamorgan. A former civil servant and sometime Head of Humanities at Cardiff Metropolitan University, he now lectures in politics and history at Coleg Gwent. He is an Hon. Research Fellow in the Department of History and Classics at Swansea. Author of books on Devolution, Liberalism and Welsh Governance, he is the Chairman of the Lloyd George Society.

ELINOR TALFAN DELANEY (née Davies) was born in Barry, educated at Swansea and Cardiff, and trained as a Staff Registered Nurse at University College Hospital, London. Before retiring in 2003 she served as Matron at St Paul's Cathedral, where she now holds office as Wandsman. She was Chairman of Governors of the Welsh School, London for thirteen years, and is a Trustee. She founded the Welsh Playgroup, London. She is Secretary of the Honourable Society of Cymmrodorion.

LORD ELYSTAN MORGAN was Labour MP for Cardiganshire from 1966 until 1974, and Under-Secretary of State in the Home Office between 1968 and 1970. Barrister-at-Law, 1971. Circuit Judge, 1987–2003. Chairman, Welsh Local Authorities Association, 1967–73. President of the Parliament for Wales Campaign, 1979. He was made a Life Peer in 1981. President of the University of Wales, Aberystwyth, 1998–2007, and Hon. Fellow.

JOHN HOOSON, a cousin of Emlyn Hooson's and a man of renowned wit, was brought up at Caerfallen near Rhuthun in the Vale of Clwyd. He was a successful farmer who farmed for much of his life in Plas Iolyn near Pentrefoelas. Now retired, he lives in Glan Conwy.

DR GLYN TEGAI HUGHES, a Cambridge graduate, taught at the Universities of Basel and Manchester before becoming the University of Wales' Warden of Gregynog, 1964–1979. He stood for the Liberals at Denbigh in three general elections in the 1950s. BBC National Governor of Wales, 1971–79. Board Member, Channel Four Television Co., 1980–87, and S4C, 1981–87. Author of works on Romantic German literature and on modern Welsh literature. Hon. Fellow of Aberystwyth and Bangor Universities.

HELEN HUGHES lived in Cemmaes in the Dyfi Valley when she a small child, but spent her formative years in Winchester, where her father practised as an architect and planner. Following training at the London College of Secretaries she worked for the Dean of Dental Studies at Guy's Hospital, and then, from 1968 to 1979, for Emlyn Hooson. Since 1988 she and her husband have lived in Whittington. She has been the Organising Secretary of the League of Friends of The Robert Jones and Agnes Hunt Orthopaedic Hospital at Gobowen for the last twenty-four years.

JOHN GWYN HUGHES was born in the police station at Bwlchgwyn, Denbighshire, where his father was the village constable. Invalided out of the Royal Air Force in 1943 he completed his Law studies at the University College of Wales,

Aberystwyth and then served as a magistrate in Southern Rhodesia. Returning to the UK he contested Denbigh (1950) and the City of Chester (1951) as parliamentary Labour candidate. He then spent forty years as a Law lecturer in London. Now lives in Llandudno.

JOHN M. JAMES, a graduate of the University of Wales (Cardiff), qualified as a Chartered Accountant in 1963. In 1967 he joined Unilever in Ghana. In 1972 he returned to the UK and worked for the Fitch Lovell Group. Two years later he joined Laura Ashley as Group Finance Director and between 1980 and 1990 was the company's Chief Executive and Deputy Chairman. Between 1989 and 2002 he was non-executive Director and then Commercial Director of Welsh Water (later Hyder plc). Treasurer of the University of Wales, Aberystwyth, 1992–2002.

DR J. GRAHAM JONES, educated at Aberdâr and Aberystwyth, until 2013 was Senior Archivist and Head of the Welsh Political Archive at the National Library of Wales. His MA thesis on 'The 1929 General Election in Wales' (awarded the Prince Llewelyn ap Gruffydd Memorial Medal) and his PhD thesis on 'Lloyd George and Welsh Liberalism' testify to his expertise in modern political history, as do his many publications. Fellow of the Royal Historical Society, 2001.

DEREC LLWYD MORGAN, a Professor of Welsh, was Vice-Chancellor of the University of Wales, Aberystwyth, 1995–2004, and Senior Vice-Chancellor of the federal University of Wales, 2001–04. He has been Chairman of the National

Eisteddfod Council and President of its Court. Member for Wales, Independent Television Commission, 1999–2003. Chairman of the Kyffin Williams Trust, 2006–. Hon. Fellow, Bangor University, Jesus College, Oxford and Trinity College, Carmarthen.

GARETH MORGAN, educated at Llandovery College and the University College of Wales, Aberystwyth, was from 1963 until 1996 Senior Partner of Milwyn Jenkins and Jenkins, Solicitors in Llanidloes, Newtown and Welshpool. Between 1990 and 2005 he was President of the Residential Property Tribunal for Wales. He has been a county councillor since 1973 and in 1999–2000 was Chairman of Powys County Council.

THE REVEREND JOHN I. MORGANS, born in Tylerstown in the Rhondda, was ordained to the ministry in 1967. He served in the United Reformed Church in Llanidloes and Manselton, and as Moderator for Wales. In 1986, with his wife Norah, he helped form the Ecumenical Church of Llanfair in Pen-rhys, and worked there until 2004. He then returned to Montgomeryshire and lives in Newchapel.

ALWYN PHILLIPS was Chairman of the North Wales Agricultural Society, 1973–75. In 1978 he was awarded the Meat and Livestock Commission's Prize for the best Lowland commercial flock in the UK. North Wales Area Director of the British Texel Sheep Society, 1991–2003. In 2000 he founded and chaired the Cofnodi Texel Cymreig Sire Reference Scheme. In 2011 he was given the Royal Welsh Agricultural

Society's John Gittins Award for outstanding contribution to Welsh Sheep farming.

SIR MEURIC REES is a farmer who was President of the Royal Welsh Agricultural Show in 1978 (Fellow, 1973). Made a JP in 1957, he was Chairman of the Bench at Tywyn, 1974–94. He has been Chairman of the Welsh Committee of the Countryside Commission, Chairman of the North Wales Police Authority, and Chairman of the Welsh Council of the National Union of Farmers. He was High Sheriff of Gwynedd in 1982–83; and served as the county's Lord Lieutenant between 1990 and 99. Knight of the Order of St John, 1997. Hon. MSc, Wales, 1999.

DR DAVID M. ROBERTS is a native of Llanymynech in Montgomeryshire. He trained as a historian in Aberystwyth, but spent his working life as a university administrator. Between 1988 and 1999 he was Academic Registrar at Bangor University, and between 1999 and his retirement in 2014 was Registrar and Secretary there. He has written many articles on Clement Davies and the history of the Liberal Party.

EIFION ROBERTS QC, educated at Aberystwyth and Oxford, was called to the Bar in 1953. A Recorder of the Crown Court, 1972–77, he then served as a Circuit Judge between 1977 and 1998. He was Member for Wales of the Crawford Committee on Broadcasting Coverage. Sometime Assistant Parliamentary Boundary Commissioner for Wales. Chairman of the Council of Bangor University, 1992–2002, and Hon. Fellow.

JON RUSHTON joined John Laing Construction as a junior Quantity Surveyor at the age of twenty-two and retired almost forty years later as Group Chief Quantity Surveyor and Director of John Laing plc. He worked initially in the Engineering Division, then transferred to the Building Division, and, although he has never lived abroad, progressed Laing interests in contracts in the Middle East, in Europe and in South America.

PETER STURROCK, a native of Liverpool whose family used to rent a summer cottage near Llanidloes when he was a boy, farms near Caernarfon. He has served as a member of the Gwynedd River Authority and of the Caernarfon Harbour Trust. In 1986–87 he was High Sheriff of Gwynedd. An NFU representative on the English branch of the Parliamentary Committee, he has also served as Vice-Chairman of the Council of the Royal Welsh Agricultural Society.